DANCING
WITH
TOMBSTONES

DANCING
WITH
TOMBSTONES

A Decade-Plus of Short Horror Stories (2009-2020)

Michael Aronovitz

CEMETERY DANCE PUBLICATIONS

Baltimore

❖ 2021 ❖

Cemetery Dance Publications
132B Industry Lane, Unit #7
Forest Hill, MD 21050
www.cemeterydance.com

First Cemetery Dance Printing

ISBN: 978-1-58767-814-1

Cover Artwork and Design © 2021 by Lynne Hansen
Interior Design © 2021 by Desert Isle Design, LLC

CONTENTS

Foreword

I have been involved in the reading and study of weird fiction for nearly fifty years. I've read a great deal of the stuff—good, bad, and mediocre. One of the disadvantages of specializing in this (or any other) field is that you tend to get jaded: very little writing, old or new, has the capacity to move you, shock you, affect you beyond an academic awareness of whether the work is well done or poorly done.

But when I first read the tales of Michael Aronovitz, around 2007, they provided the *frisson* that I had been so desperately seeking.

I almost jumped out of my skin when I read the conclusion of "How Bria Died," an early triumph of Michael's. And yet, as I read these tales I quickly became aware that there was a lot more going on than merely the attempt to send a shiver up one's spine. Long ago the poet Winfield Townley Scott wrote, "To scare is a slim purpose in poetry"—and that applies to prose fiction as well. No matter how skillfully a writer can make your flesh creep, such work is aesthetically and intellectually empty unless it addresses broader issues relating to human beings and their relations to one another, to their society, and to the universe.

Michael has the enviable gift of writing stories that are eminently readable and accessible to a wide audience, but that also provoke deep reflection about the fragility of our psyches and the tenuousness of our place on this earth. As a teacher at both the high school and college levels (and as a devoted husband and father), Michael is keenly aware of the wonders and traumas of adolescence—and many of his stories (to say nothing of his already classic ghost novel, *Alice Walks*) are focused on teenagers as they tread the confusing borderline between childhood and adulthood.

As a writer, Michael himself treads a different borderline—the one separating supernatural fiction from the fiction of psychological terror. "The Sculptor" is one of the grimmest tales of a serial killer you're likely to find; it bears similarities to his chilling novel *Phantom Effect*. "Puddles" is a profound display of aberrant psychology. We can all empathize with the protagonist's obsessive-compulsive disorder: perhaps we are aware of how close we ourselves are to descending into similar terrors and phobias originating in our own minds.

And Michael exhibits an enviable range of theme and subject-matter. "Soul Text" is a gripping tale fusing the weird with science fiction; "Quest for Sadness" could almost be considered a philosophical horror story; "The Girl Between the Slats" is metafiction at its best.

In many ways, the expansive novella "Toll Booth" sums up Michael's achievement. Here crime, adolescence, and weirdness all fuse into an exquisite amalgam, horrifying and poignant at the same time. It is the tale of a thoughtless act that leads to unexpected tragedy, and the wasted lives that act engenders. This work has all the concentrated terror of a short story, along with the rich character development of a novel.

I have been privileged to have shepherded several of Michael Aronovitz's books through the press—but in no sense do I regard him as my protégé. He doesn't need me or anyone else to be his mentor: he has, from the beginning, been a writer fully aware of what he wants to say and how best to say it. *Dancing with Tombstones* may be a culling of his best short stories, but there is in fact very little in his output that isn't among his best: his level of achievement, in work after work, is consistently high. So if you like the tales in this book, you should seek out his other books—collections and novels alike—so that you can fully grasp why Michael Aronovitz is one of the shining lights of contemporary weird fiction.

—S. T. Joshi

GIRLS

How Bria Died

Bria jumped rope all alone
And now her eyes are made of stone
She calls for Mommy from the grave
And crawls out of the drain
She drags her jump rope on cement
And calls you from the heating vent
Turn a promise to a lie
And you will be the next to die

Ben Marcus didn't like it messy, but it was that time of the year. His feet hurt. A ninth-grade boy in the lunchroom had not liked the fact that the volunteer serving girl with the hairnet had given him only one taco off the cart, so he had chucked it on the floor. Ben had walked over, retrieved the plate, and stuck it back on the kid's portion of the long brown table. After a stare-down, the young man had taken it, a bit too slowly, to a trash receptacle in the middle of the room by a white pillar with a picture of Frederick Douglass on it. Ben had followed. When the kid tossed in the garbage there was some up-splash that got on Ben's sleeve. He hated lunch duty.

It was wrap-around Thursday and Ben had his homeroom for the second time that day. His legs were crossed. He was sucking on one of the temple-tip earpieces of his wire-framed glasses, and he had one shoe

11

off at the back heel. He was sort of dangling it on the end of his toe. It was the time of the year when the kids started jumping into their summer vacations a month early. Right around May 5th, the boys started untucking their dress shirts and removing their ties before the first bell. The girls somehow found ways to roll their blue skirts far above the knee and show off a bit of bra strap up top, even though the uniform requirement clearly stated that they were limited to bulky, formless, long-sleeved white blouses. Suddenly, they all wanted to follow each other consecutively to the bathrooms like a parade and trick you into thinking you had the due dates wrong for their final papers. You had to keep up the game face all the way through June or they walked all over you.

Marcus knew the deal, and his reputation as the most popular teacher at The People First Charter School in downtown Philadelphia usually carried him through these tough final weeks. All year, he was strict when he had to be and bitingly sarcastic. He was known for pushing the envelope and talking about controversial things in class, like sex and death. He made kids laugh and he cursed frequently. He was an expert at finding a student's one vulnerable moment and filling that moment with insight. The girls liked him because he could out-dance the boys in verbal confrontation, and the boys liked him because he was so popular with the girls. The school was set up first grade through twelfth, and given that Ben was the head of tenth grade and the sole English teacher at that level, most kids at People First looked forward to high school. He always found a way to make it interesting, often taking rude interruptions and turning them into stories. Then he'd wrap it all back into the given lesson.

Last week Rahim Bethea had activated a talking SpongeBob key chain in the middle of a lecture about totalitarianism in *Animal Farm*. Ben had stopped, rode the laughter, and gone into a rant about how SpongeBob's friend Patrick, the pink starfish, was really a symbol for the penis. The class had roared, and many defended the character. Marcus walked the room, one side to the other. He started the kids chanting, "Patrick is a penis!" so loudly that Rollins, the security guard for the second floor, poked his head in. Ben immediately mouthed, *"Johnson?"* the name of the school's Chief Administrative Officer. Rollins gave a quick shake of the head, *"No, she ain't coming down the hall,"* and gave the thumbs up sign. Ben turned back to the kids and said that the human cock was the symbolic foundation of every story ever made, including *Animal Farm.* A conversation started, hands in the air. Half the class claimed that the story was clearly about money, and the other half argued that the story did, in fact, leave females to the side like a void. It became a discussion about which lens the story was better to build from, economics and exchange or feministic absence. Marcus wrote those headings on the board, and as a class they filled it in. Yes, he was that good.

His wife Kim was a paralegal and kept a nice garden behind their comfy twin in Havertown. She had long red hair with a streak of gray in it, and slight age parentheses at the corners of her mouth. She had crinkles at the edges of her eyes that Ben still liked to kiss softly. He knew she adored him, but it had become clear that she thought his style was far too risky and inappropriate for an educational system so quick to slap teachers with harsh consequences delivered by stern lawyers and passionate advocates. It wasn't an issue. Ben had stopped discussing his methods with her years ago.

He put his glasses back on and rolled up his sleeve. It had come undone down to the last fold at the cuff, and the taco stain was showing. Behind him were some compare-and-contrast papers pinned to the cork board, their edges curling. His desk had been moved to the side almost to the end of the whiteboard by the hall door, and he was trapped behind some desks that had been pushed all the way to the wooden cubbies, those overflowing with hoodies, sweaters, old papers, binders, and ratty textbooks that looked as if they had been run over by an army of sixteen wheelers.

The parts of speech and number tables competition was tomorrow. It was Mrs. Johnson's baby. People First was a back-to-basics school, and while the elementary grades were required to chant the parts of speech in English class every day, Mrs. Johnson had the upper school kids unveil complex dance routines based on those drills to showcase her philosophical "Method" for guests at the end of the year. At the last staff meeting she had handed out an official memo that instructed teachers to set a week of class time aside for rehearsals. The mayor was there for the performance last May, along with a representative from the N.A.A.C.P. It was no joke, and neither was Mrs. Johnson.

The woman ran a tight ship and everyone was terrified of her. She was six foot three inches tall. She wore her hair back in a tight bun and had eyes that always looked wide and wrathful. She was handsome in the way statues were handsome, and walked the halls like a general. She believed in old-school discipline. So did Ben. His vision of how to administer that discipline, however, was a bit off-color at times, and he was thankful that what went on behind closed doors mostly stayed between himself and the kids.

Ben put up his hands and waved them.

"No!" he said. "Yo. Yo! Turn the music off for a minute."

The kids stopped their routine and shut off the boom box. Monique Hudson rolled her eyes. A few boys sat on desks off to the side and Joy Smith popped her gum. Ben worked his face to a mask of gentle concern. Actually, he had the beginnings of a headache coming on and he looked forward to his prep coming up in thirteen minutes. On Thursdays he had two free periods in a row to end the day, and he planned on putting his head down in the lounge.

"Guys," he said, "this is the last day you have to practice before the competition, and you're bringing in new dance steps all of a sudden. It's asinine. First off, the girls coming down in rows and doing the shoulder shake thing was great. You trashed that for this puppet-puppeteer pop-lock thing, and it throws off the group. Everyone is just standing and watching Steve and Jerome. It's like a big donut with a hole in it. I also have to tell you that my 'B' class is doing the same kind of puppet thing and they have Rob and Tiny."

"They ain't shit," Steve said. His tie was off and his shirt was dirty. Marcus hoped Ms. Johnson didn't do a pop-in right now. Most of the kids were out of uniform code at the moment.

"The hell they're not," Ben said. "They've been doing that routine longer than you, and you know it. Also, Rob is so tall that Tiny really does look like a puppet when he stands in front and they mirror each other."

Jerome made his eyes go to half-mast and curdled up an angry grin.

"That don't matter. They gay."

"If I wanted shit from you, Jerome, I would have squeezed your head," Ben answered.

Everyone laughed. Marcus looked over toward Malik Redson. He was in the far corner of the room listening to his iPod, juking his head a bit, shirt untucked, hiking boots up on the desk in front of him. Ben made the sign to take out the ear buds. Malik did so reluctantly.

"What?" he said.

"You're the show," Ben said. "Your routine comes in after the girls hop down in their rows. Once they are in-position they make perfect backing for you with that cheerleader thing they do with the hand-claps. You have to dance."

Malik yawned, then licked his lips. The peach fuzz moustache he had going was an illusion. He was as grown as any man out on Broad Street. He had two kids already, and he worked nights at the BP gas station on Market Street. His solo routine was also the best in the school.

"The music sucks," he said. "And I also don't give a Goddamn."

"Fuck the music!" Ben snapped. All the little side whispers stopped. He stood up. He did not like losing. Not even a trivial moment like this one. "I am aware that you think this contest is retarded, I'm not fucking stupid. But when the whole upper school is watching and the other homerooms have a better show than you, it's going to matter."

"The fuck it is."

"The fuck it ain't!"

They stared at each other. Malik stood up. He paused. He took off the gold around his neck.

"All right, Mr. M. For you."

Laquanna Watford, a two-hundred-and-fifty-pound girl with the face of an angel and a reputation for street fighting, walked to the middle of the room. She smiled and her big caramel cheeks bunched up. There were huge sweat stains on her white blouse, under her arms, and at the love handles.

"Ready?" she said. "OK. Now make the square and let me see you bitches gallop."

The door opened. It was Mr. Rollins. Ben got himself out from behind the maze of chairs and approached. Rollins winked.

"Y'all got to sub next period," he said.

Ben sighed. Don't shoot the messenger.

"Where?"

"Sixth-grade science. First floor by the Cherry Street entrance, one room-in."

Ben cursed softly. He hated middle school. They were too young to really understand his humor, and too old for intimidating with the drill sergeant stuff. He thanked Rollins and went over to his black bag. He looked in the emergency pocket and got out a piece of paper that was a bit yellowed, almost falling apart at the fold lines. Writing prompts, slightly edgy. Usually kept kids in their seats for at least a half hour.

The bell rang and he hurried out to the hallway. The worst thing he could do was show up late. Impression was everything, and a teacher waiting behind a desk with an angry scowl on his face usually filled the chairs rather quickly. A harried guy with a soft leather briefcase coming in after the fact and pleading for order usually led to kids spouting off irrelevant questions, fighting over seats, sneaking out to the hall, chucking rolled up pieces of paper at the trash can, and pleading for constant trips to the bathroom, guidance, or the nurse's office.

He got down to sixth-grade science with about two minutes to spare. About half the students were standing by their seats in gossip circles. Other kids were still commuting through the space, shoving a bit, snaking through to get to the rear door leading to the social studies room. Three boys were back by the lab tables toying with dead frogs in jars. There were larger containers with what looked like pig fetuses on the shelves, and a skeleton hanging in front of an anatomy chart. Ben walked over to the boys. The tall one with the little crud rings at the edges of his nostrils started to exclaim that it was the other boys who had been messing with the frogs.

"I don't care about that," Ben said. "Look, I need a favor."

All three looked skeptical, but they were listening. Ben bent his head in and whispered, therefore making them lean in and make a huddle.

"See, I know some are going to try to cut because I'm a sub. I don't want you guys to snitch or anything, but I need for you to get all the kids in their chairs for me."

He looked from one boy to the next.

"Of you three, who was the last one to get in trouble? And don't lie, 'cause I'll know it."

They snickered and pointed to the tall kid. Ben raised his eyebrows.

"Look," he said. "I'm meeting with Ms. Johnson after school. I run the tenth grade up there and she listens to me. A good word to her and a nice phone call home wouldn't hurt, now would it?"

The tall one blinked, then glanced to the other two.

"Well, go on," he said. "You heard the man." He gave both a shove and the three immediately split up to tell their classmates to sit the hell down. Within about a minute, Ben had nineteen middle schoolers in their chairs with their hands folded, and that was the way that he liked it. He got out his prompt sheet and introduced himself. He told the kids that they were going to play a game of write for a minute and listen for a minute as other kids read back their answers. The first prompt was "When is it all right to lie?"

The writing part went well, and during the answer phase he was pleased to get a fair response. Hands in the air led to discussions and little anecdotal stories. Most kids were OK with his rule of not calling out and only two kids broke the atmosphere to go to the bathroom. There were a couple of instances where he had to goad a light-skinned boy with a bushy afro set in two large puff balls not to lean back in his chair, but altogether it wasn't so bad.

Half the period was gone when it happened.

Ben was on the third prompt, "What is your favorite violent movie and why?" and the kids were drifting a bit. Most were writing, but the illusion of order had eroded at the edges. A boy with close-set eyes was struggling with the girl who sat next to him over a red see-through ruler. A girl wearing too much makeup for her age was texting on a cell phone she thought was well hidden in her lap, and the boy one seat up and across from her was crossing his eyes and making bubbles with his spit. About five kids had suddenly gotten up to sharpen their pencils and Ben was getting aggravated. Suddenly he shouted at the top of his lungs,

"For God's sake, close that book!"

He was pointing at a girl in the front row who had slipped her English textbook up to the desk and was looking at pictures of the *Titanic*. Ben walked a step closer.

"Shut it now! You've unlocked the door! Now the spirit can get in! Do you want to freakin' die tonight?"

She clapped the book shut and put her hands up to her mouth. No one was fighting over rulers now, and all the chair legs were on the floor.

"Sit down," Ben said. "Now." Those waiting at the sharpener scurried to their desks. Ben was in control again. In the back of his mind a warning flare went up. Were these kids too young for this? Too late. A lead-in this good couldn't go to waste.

"Don't you guys know the story of Bria Patterson, the third-grade girl who died right here in this school?"

Kids shook their heads. Eyes were wide. Ben's body and voice reflected a controlled patience, the elder who bestowed cautious forgiveness for a catastrophic blunder just this one last time.

"Don't you know about second-to-last period and how you never, ever open a book that's not the subject being taught? That opens the archway from hell and lets her in through every opening, every heating vent, every window, and every door."

A boy raised his hand. He had a smirk on his face.

"Put your hand down," Ben said.

The hand went down, the kid's expression now flat. No one giggled. Once more, Ben considered what he was about to do. He had told this story up in the high school many times; it was tradition. Once, at the climax, Leah Bannister had been leaning against the wall by the door and someone in the hallway had bumped right into that spot. She had burst across the room laughing and screaming.

Well, risk none win none, right? He walked back to the center of the room. He had never started the Bria Patterson story with the idea of an open book being a doorway. That part was improvised. Quickly, he tried to think of how he could tie it back in, but he came up blank. Would the kids notice the foreshadowing he left dangling in the wind? Too late now.

"Bria was a third grader," he started. "She lived up in Kensington, by L and Erie. She had a single mom, and went to school here the year it opened back in 1999. Bria was a white girl, and she always wore her blonde hair in two pigtails on the sides, like the little Swiss Miss character on the hot chocolate can. Now, Bria was known for two things. First, you know the little cross-ties you girls wear? You know how Mrs. Johnson yells and screams when you leave them unsnapped and casual? Well, Bria started that tradition. Ms. Johnson used to fight with her about it all the time; just ask your older brothers and sisters."

A girl sitting in the second row with expressive eyes, corn rows, and braids to one side said,

"What's the second thing she was known for, Mr. Marcus?"

He stepped forward, almost touching the desk of the boy sitting up front. The kid was so short that his feet didn't hit the floor. He had been slouching way down in his seat the whole period, but he was not slouching now. His hands were folded and his mouth was open. Ben folded his arms.

"Close your mouth, son. Flies are going to get in there." The kid snapped it shut and there was some nervous laughter. Ben stepped back to his power position in front of the white board.

"The other thing Bria was known for was her jump rope," he said. "You know how every morning in front of the Korean hoagie shop on the corner the girl's play Double Dutch until the first homeroom bell?"

Heads nodded.

"That was not Bria's thing. She didn't have many friends here, and the girls out on Cherry Street never invited her to jump with them. Bria jumped alone. She had a single girl's jump rope that she had probably owned since she was six. It had red painted handles, but they were rubbed down to the wood grains where her thumbs always went. Its cord was a dirty blue and white checkerboard pattern that was worn down to a thread where it always hit the street on each rotation. And Bria was never without her jump rope. It was like that kid with a blanket in that cartoon."

"Yes!" a heavy girl with big golden earrings exclaimed from the back row. "Like Linus from the Charlie Brown stories!"

"Right," Ben said. "But think about our skinny hallways. If Bria dragged that jump rope behind her, everywhere she went, what do you think happened?"

The short boy in the front row dropped open his mouth once again. Then his hand shot into the air.

"Ooooh!" he said.

"Yes?"

"People be tripping over it!"

"Again, right," Ben said. "Other students were always stepping on her jump rope, and Bria was constantly arguing with them. She was always in trouble and a lot of people wondered if she was going to make it here."

Ben paused for effect.

"Then, on March 9th, Bria Patterson turned up missing."

Silence. No one moved, and Ben knew this was the critical point in the story. It was the place where anyone with a shred of common sense could poke a hole as wide as a highway into the logic of the plot. It was time to really sell here. Ben walked a few steps toward the Social Studies room. He stopped at the corner of the first row of desks and personalized the question to a dark-skinned boy with bucked teeth, black goggle glasses, and big pink albino splotches on the side of his neck.

"I know what you're thinking. If a girl was M.I.A., why didn't anyone hear about it?" He turned to the class. "It is a good question, and my answer is this. Ms. Johnson is connected. She has her own radio show and she talks to Oprah on a regular basis, I'm not kidding. She knows the mayor and the chief of police. The news only reports on people that don't have the money or the muscle to put a stop to the tattle, you see what I'm saying?"

"I know that's right," someone offered softly.

"And I'm telling you, when a powerful person like Ms. Johnson doesn't want any bad publicity, the news does not make it to the boob tube. Bank on it, folks. Ms. Johnson used her relationship with the police to cover this up. They investigated it in secret and when they came up with no new leads, Bria's mom went crazy. She moved down South and no one heard from her again."

He went back across to the entrance door, opened it a crack, and looked out into the empty hall. He could see the students leaning toward him out of the corner of his eye. He turned and spoke in a low whisper.

"Right out here, by this door, is where the horror most likely started." A boy near the back of the room buried his head under crossed arms and a couple of girls had their hands drifting up toward their ears. Ben walked slowly back to the center of the room.

"You know the alcove at the top of the stairs out here, right? That's where the juniors have those four little rooms all to themselves that everybody is so jealous of. What you might not know is that this place used to be an old factory, and that space wasn't fixed up in the first year the school opened. Back in 1999 the alcove wasn't four neat little rooms, but one big, dark room. It was filled with busted pieces of drywall and boxes of old, moldy shipping papers. There were stacks of splintery wood and piles of twisted sheet metal all over the floor. The ceiling was a maze of decayed pipes and dangling wires. There was a padlock on the big black doors out front, and everyone knew it was against the rules to go near the alcove, let alone in it."

A few sets of eyes drifted upward. This was perfect. The alcove was right above them.

"Don't look, for God's sake!" Ben hissed.

A couple of girls made the high-pitched "eek" sound. A boy was biting his fingernails, and a girl who had been sneaking corn chips out of her book bag had all four fingers in her mouth up to the middle knuckles. Ben sauntered back to the teacher's desk and moved aside a plastic tray bin filled with lab reports about the Ecosystem. He leaned his butt against the edge and folded his arms.

"Oh, they questioned everybody," he said. "Just because the news didn't get a hold of it doesn't mean they didn't try to discover the truth of what happened to Bria Patterson. You know the security guards here have sections they're responsible for, right? You know that Mr. Rollins has the second-floor high school rooms. Nowadays, old Mr. Harvey has the landing, the stairway, and this bottom area all the way to the lunchroom, but back then, it was under the watch of a guy named Mr. Washington. He only had two suits and both were this neon lime green color. Everyone called him 'Frankenstein,' because he was so tall and goofy, and he walked kind of pigeon-toed like a zombie."

Ben stepped away from the desk and imitated the walk for a minute. A couple of kids broke wide smiles, but most were smart enough not to trust Ben 's short moment of humor. He stopped.

"Mr. Washington was the last to see Bria Patterson. He thought he saw her standing up by those black doors, on the landing in front of the alcove. When the police went up there, they saw that the lock on the black doors had been stolen."

Ben supported his elbow on his forearm and pointed his index finger straight up.

"They took in their flashlights and floodlights and chemistry cases, their ballistics materials, DNA sample packs, and high-powered magnifiers. They dusted the place stem to stern for fingerprints, and do you know what they found?" He stopped. He put his hands in his pockets and shoved them down so his shoulders hunched up a bit. "The most frightening thing in the world of crime. They found that the evidence was inconclusive."

"What's that mean?" a paper-thin Hispanic boy with long black hair and braces said. Ben stepped into the aisle between desks. He could feel kids shying away a bit as he passed.

"It means that Bria Patterson was most probably killed up there in that alcove, and then her body was removed." He made a quick path back out from the desks and back over to the classroom door. He pushed it open and it squeaked beautifully. "See the Cherry Street entrance door here?" he said. The kids stretched in their chairs for the view. Two in the back stood up, thought the better of it, then sat back down quickly. He let the door creep back closed. "Many believe the perpetrator got access through that door, and it is common agreement that the door was open in the first place because of some member of the faculty who wanted to go catch a smoke. There are only two entrances to the building. There's this door right out here and the main doors up by the secretaries. If you wanted to sneak a smoke would you go all the way up front past the secretaries, who talk too much anyway, and smoke your cig right out there on Broad Street where Ms. Johnson could see you through her office window? Hell no. The theory is that this teacher or janitor or TA or lunch assistant slipped out through the Cherry Street door, stuck a pencil or something in at the bottom so the thing couldn't auto-lock, and went back to the teacher's parking lot for a quick fix. By the way, don't smoke. It's very bad for you."

No one laughed and Ben didn't mind at all.

"And so, Bria vanished. We all think someone got in through the Cherry Street door and we all know that Bria Patterson was standing up at the top of the landing. How the stranger approached her, whether she ran back into the dark alcove, how he killed her, and where he took her, all remain…"—he looked from one set of eyes to the next—"inconclusive."

A few kids let out their breath. Two girls looked at each other, leaned in to whisper something, and then glanced at Ben. They decided the better of it, and both straightened up. This was Ben's favorite moment in the story, because it was the false climax. They thought it was over. Now, it was going to get really personal.

"So," he said. "You know that in 1999 we only went up to ninth grade here, right? When I was hired in the year 2000 to teach the new tenth graders, there had to be a space for us. That summer Ms. Johnson had construction men to fix up the alcove, and yes, you guessed it, my room was through those black doors, first room on the right. I was there for a year. Since then, you know that I have moved into 209, the eleventh graders inherited those four little rooms, and the seniors lucked out with the fancy extension they built up front. Still, I am telling you, I never want to teach in that alcove again. In fact, if Ms. Johnson told me to go back there right now I would quit. There is something evil up there. Still."

Ben had never quite had this sort of focus upon him, certainly not up in the high school. It was more than strict attention. It was a submission that was almost divine in nature. They were lambs. There was an incredible cross-current of fear and trust. They were locked in with him, frozen, terrified. But he was a teacher, right? It was his job to keep them safe, right? They would all laugh when it was over, wouldn't they?

For a brief moment Ben considered derailing. For a moment he pictured the girl in front of him, the one with the hearing aid and the wide forehead, she who possessed only four of her top adult teeth, huddled tonight under the sheets in a blind state of fear. Bria was under her bed, scratching up to grab an ankle. Bria was in her closet slowly creaking the door open, on the chair staring at her in the dark, head lolled to the side, a silhouette in the doorway, arms extended, hair still dripping the dirty water from the Schuylkill River where her body had been dumped.

He thought of more than a few angry parents calling Ms. Johnson and asking why some substitute was telling high school stories to sixth graders. He dropped the storytelling voice.

"Do you guys want me to stop?"

"No!" The chorus was nearly unanimous. Nearly. There were two girls in the back who had not responded, in addition to a boy in the end chair, second row, left. Was it apathy? He couldn't tell. And again, it was too late now to make a difference.

"I brought my stuff in a week before classes started," he continued. "I've never been much of a decorator, so I had my parts-of-speech posters, a couple of pictures of Langston Hughes, an exploded version of a Maya Angelou poem, my file case, you know. And just when I am tacking up the verb-adverb board, I thought there was something in the wall. Something moving. I mean, have you ever heard something so faint that thirty seconds after it happens you wonder whether you really heard anything at all?"

Heads nodded solemnly. He walked to the wall.

"I could have sworn it sounded like this."

He made his fingers into a claw shape and scratched his nails down the plastered surface. A few kids squirmed in their seats.

"So, I run out into the hall like an idiot, because I thought someone was playing a joke on me. But it was just an empty hallway. Later, when I went down to get my lunch, I asked one of the other teachers if they played practical jokes on people here. It was then that he told me about the alcove, about the cover-up, about Bria Patterson. I didn't believe him. But when I went back upstairs to finish setting up, there was something sitting on my desk. It was something that hadn't been there before. It was a girl's blue cross-tie, laying there unbuttoned."

Lots of uncomfortable shifting. A boy was clawing his nails into his cheeks, eyes wide as saucers. A girl with multicolored beads in her hair had her knees knocked together and her hands in a finger web around the front of them. She was rocking and mouthing something unintelligible.

"I didn't want to touch it. Even though my common sense knew someone must have just stuck it there for a joke, my heart knew there was something unholy about it. Like it had come from the grave."

Someone was making a high-pitched moan up in her throat, but Ben hardly heard it. He had to finish and he had to nail this one. Damn the consequences, damn the torpedoes, damn everything.

"Now, I know for a fact that each and every one of us has a low-grade level of E.S.P. I'm not talking about dumb stuff like bending spoons and reading minds and making flower pots fly across the room, but think about this. Have you ever been at The Old Country Buffet, or even in our crummy lunchroom, and you could swear someone was staring at you from behind? And then you turn, and they *are* staring, for real, for real?"

Heads nodded.

"That's the way I felt. I turned quickly, and I could swear that I saw the edge of a blue uniform skirt whip past the doorway. Then there was a swishing noise out in the hall. Like a jump rope dragging across concrete. I walked over, turned the corner, and she was there. I could see through her. She had blonde pigtails, and no eyes, just dark spaces. There was a line of blood coming down the corner of her mouth, and she was running that jump rope back and forth across the floor. She was moaning in the voice of the dead,

"'Mommy...'"

Ben was dragging the imaginary rope, playing the part, eyes far off, mouth slightly ajar. Here was where the story always ended. He had never figured out a proper conclusion, and he normally broke character, smiled and said something like,

"C'mon, guys. I was just kidding. You didn't believe that crap, did you?"

He did not get the chance. The fire alarm went off. Loud. It was a buzzer that was so overwhelming down here it actually made his skin vibrate.

Girls screamed. Boys jumped up from their desks as if there were snakes crawling on the floor. Three girls in the back row stood up, hands pressed to their mouths. They were hyperventilating. A tall girl with white stockings had rushed to the corner of the room, pulled out her blue sweater at the neck, and buried her face in the void as if she was going to puke into it.

Ben was terrified. Surely, he would hear about this from Johnson.

"Guys!" he shouted over the numbing buzz. "Out through the Cherry Street door! Go ahead, it's just an alarm! And I was only kidding about the ghost..."

No one really heard. They scrambled for the door. A boy was crying and rubbing the base of his palm against his cheek in angry shame. A girl with thick glasses and blackheads clustered around her nose was furiously punching numbers into a cell phone. Oh, Ben was in a shitstorm now. He wondered if he would be fired. He hadn't looked at his résumé for years. This was bad. The last thing he wanted was to be thrown into the system and assigned to a regular Philadelphia public school. They doled out positions by seniority. Charter schools did not rack up points, and he would probably wind up at some ghetto middle school where the kids took apart your emergency phone on the first day, ran in and out of the classrooms like mental patients, and found out where your car was parked before it was time for recess. Ms. Johnson ran a tight ship here with this charter, and he was lucky to have the position he did. He had never really been in trouble with Johnson, but he heard she was merciless if she had a cause. He supposed he could beg. At least he had that.

He walked out into the sunshine and crossed Cherry Street. It was tennis weather. Construction was going on down Broad Street and you could hear a dull pounding complemented by a slightly sharper ratcheting noise associated with cranes and oiled chains being rolled onto big pulley wheels. The kids were gathered in front of a row house with empty planters in front of the dark windows. There were faded white age stains shadowed up the brick. A couple of his tenth graders had migrated over and were sitting on the concrete steps one residence down. Ben waved to them absently and started working his way between children, pleading his case. It was lame and awkward and necessary. He had to do some kind of damage control no matter how slipshod it appeared.

"I was only kidding, guys. You know that, right?… I made the whole thing up. I tell it to my tenth graders all the time.… It's a silly story, really.… Didn't you see that I had no ending for it? Yes. It was just a joke. No girl like that ever went here at all."

Mr. Rollins got on a megaphone.

"Drill's over. Move on to your last-period class."

Ben had not worked the group in its entirety. He had gotten to the hyperventilators, joked it up, and earned a round of cautious, weak smiles. It turned out that the girl with the blackheads was simply supposed to call her mother at the end of seventh period every day and she had almost forgotten. Big relief there. Still, he hadn't made it to the crying boy or the tall girl who'd almost vomited into her sweater. There were a lot of loose ends here.

Ben went back inside with his head hung down.

This time he might have actually blown it.

His homeroom was up next. The brown tables were folded up and pushed to the back-left corner of the lunchroom. There were rows of chairs set up in front of the steam table and the student council had put up crêpe paper streamers. There were some new plants suspended from the drop ceiling, and old Jake had hooked up a sound system. Ms. Newman's homeroom had just completed an oldies thing featuring the Electric Slide that the students laughed at and Ms. Johnson obviously preferred. A guy pretty high up on the food chain at Temple University sat with her at the judge's table, along with a man wearing thin rectangular dark glasses, and a long black overcoat.

Johnson had not called Ben in to the office today, thank God. He knew there was an unspoken code in the high school not to snitch about the wild stuff he pulled up there, but he had not expected the sixth graders to be so discreet. It had taken all his will power not to tell Kim about it like a confession when he got home yesterday, and he had woken in a cold sweat three times during the night. But he was pretty sure by now that everything was going to be all right. Ms. Johnson did not bide her time when she had to get something off her plate, so no news at this point in the day was certainly good news.

Laquanna walked to the center of the space, and the other girls followed. There was a hush. The boys filtered in and took their positions. Malik walked to the front, and there was a rousing cheer speckled by only a few boos from the small crew of guys from the "C" section that he had beaten in a parking lot rap battle last week. He looked over at Jake, and the music blasted on. The kids exploded in movement, and Ben grooved a bit where he stood. He was going to miss this homeroom next year. They had been a lot of fun.

Someone was pulling his sleeve. He looked down. It was a girl from the elementary school, short, probably fourth or fifth grade, long hair curled in sausage shapes and pulled back by a pink satin ribbon tied in a floppy bow. Her eyes were wide with terror.

"What?" he said. "What's wrong?" He had to nearly shout to be heard over the music.

The girl said something and he could not make it out. He leaned down, and her breath came hot in his ear.

"It's the dead girl. She's in the bathroom."

Ben pulled back a bit and raised his eyebrows.

"What?"

She made her lips frame the words in the deliberate manner one used when speaking to the slow or the deaf.

"Our teacher went out to make copies on another floor. Help us. It's the dead girl. She's in one of the stalls moaning, *Mommy...*"

Ben pushed past her and marched out of the lunchroom. The music was cut to a haunt the minute he turned the corner, and he felt his face going hot. This was *just* what he needed. Some jackass sixth grader squatting up on the toilet seat so you couldn't see her feet, then groaning "Mommy" like a wounded doorbell when a younger kid tried to take a piss. Wasn't this always the way of things? He was so sure he had dodged a bullet, and now in this strange backlash, he was still going to get nailed. He could picture the meeting right now, the teachers all at their tables looking innocently at each other, Johnson up at the podium.

"It has come to my attention that some middle school children have been frightening the elementary school students in the bathroom. Evidently, a story about an abducted third grader has been going around the school, and I would like to know where this started. From the bits and pieces I have heard, the story seems rather sophisticated for a student. I want to know what teacher was involved with this. I want that teacher to come forward and take responsibility..."

You know the drill.

Ben reached the end of the hall and made the quick left. He paused, but only for a bare second. He had never been in the girl's bathroom. He walked through the archway (there were no doors for bathrooms at People First), and before passing the brown steel divider that blocked the sightline, he called out,

"Teacher coming in! Excuse me! I apologize!"

The bathroom was empty. Besides the strange lack of urinals to the left, it was the same as most institutional boys' rooms. Tiled floor, drain grate in the center surrounded by a shallow puddle of water in a shape that vaguely resembled Texas. There was a row of sinks and each basin had a mirror above it, the reflective material more like tin foil than glass to avoid cracking under the variety of incidents that were often far from delicate. The soap dispensers each had spots of blood-orange residue pooled below on the sink tops where quick hands had missed, and only two had been converted to the newer white units that rationed out foam by palm activation. There was a Fort James paper towel dispenser by the entrance just above an industrial plastic yellow trash can surrounded by the damp, crumpled sheets that had been poorly tossed. There were four stalls, the first three standard issue, and the last sectioned off in its own private area that spanned the width of the space. All three of the doors on the regular stalls were open, but barely. It seemed the floor was pitched in a way that kept them resting an inch or two in off the lock plates. The handicapped door was half ajar.

Ben pushed open the door of the first stall with the middle knuckle of his index finger. Vacant. The bowl was unflushed from what looked like nine or ten sittings, all number one thank God for small favors, and on the wall someone had written, "Shaneeka sucks monkey nuts." Stall number two was in the same relative condition, and number three, of course, was filled with a deposit Ben could not believe someone had the guts to leave out on the surface of this earth. He backed out, breathed in deep, held it, shouldered into the thin stall, and reached for the flusher with the sole of his shoe. When it whooshed down, he pulled back quickly. These institutional mechanisms were sometimes loaded with such strong jets that they kicked up a bit of backsplash off the suction.

After the rush of the initial violent whirlpool, there was that hollow, pipe-like refilling sound, and just underneath it, Ben heard a voice. From the handicapped stall. It sounded as if it was in tow just beneath the running water, an echo, a faint ringing. It sounded like a girl's voice. Before he could really make out words, it blended with the receding sounds and thinned out to silence.

Ben walked into the handicapped stall. There was a runner bar along the wall, another behind the toilet, a private sink, and a separate towel dispenser.

To the right there was also one of those tinfoil mirrors, and he saw something move in it. His breath caught in his throat. It was blue, and it had seemed to shoot through the mirror like liquid through a distorted syringe. He moved closer to investigate, and sighed. It was his shirt, picked up in the light and worked through the microscopic steel grooves in an hourglass effect. How did the girls adjust their makeup with these funhouse things? The boys had them too, but he thought the female breed would have demanded better. Personally, he always used the faculty lounge up front by Johnson's office. It was worth the walk.

The hair on the back of his neck was up.

He turned.

There was a hand coming out of the toilet. The seat was up and there was a hand gripping the rim.

Ben grit his teeth and smiled, despite the knocking his heart was still making up in his ears. It was one of those dollar store, plastic dead hands you could affix to door rims and bed edges. So here was the dead girl. Ha ha.

He levered down a fistful of towels and approached. The artwork wasn't even good on this thing. The sores had red spots half covering the indentations and spilling over about a quarter of an inch. Probably a misaligned factory stamp. The nail polish on the scabby fingers had already flaked partly off, and at the edge of the wrist, the press that had molded the rubber most probably had a small void, since there were two renegade nodules sticking off that needed to be pruned. Ben reached down to pluck it off the rim and stopped.

There was writing behind the toilet. It was written faintly on the wall tile in the spidery, uneven, block letter style of a young child,

"Turn a promise to a lie, and you will be the next to die."

"Fuck," he muttered. The written message had suddenly reminded him of a missed obligation. He grabbed the joke toy, held it off to the side a bit, and walked it out of the stall. His feet made hollow echoes across the floor. He had forgotten to put in a good word for the boy who had been looking at the dead frogs. It would have taken two seconds. He tossed the rubber toy into the yellow bin and sighed. His word was his bond.

Something splashed in the handicapped toilet.

Ben put his fists to his sides and stalked back to the stall. Enough already. He stopped when he turned the corner of the doorway.

There were two hands gripping the rim of the bowl as if reaching up from deep within it, palms down, fingers over the edges. They were girl hands, rotten and burst at the knuckles with yellow-graying bone sticking through. The skin was mottled, water-shriveled, and blue. The fingers released, and the forearms slipped back into the water, the hands following, down to the fingertips. Gone. There was a faint gasp, like the exit of breath.

Ben approached the toilet. "I did not just see that," he said to himself. His legs were numb, his mouth ajar. There was a brown ring at the surface edge of the water, and there was still the hint of faint ripples dancing above the submerged, funneled pipe orifice.

Something from the drain-hole exploded.

Ben saw a flash of dirty blue and white checkerboard just before it whipped across the bridge of his nose. The cold toilet water that sprayed him in the face was eclipsed by the sharp snap of pain. His glasses flew off to skid along the tile into the next stall. Ben's left eye had been struck bald and it was squeezed shut. The other was half open in a squint, and through the blur he saw the elongated jump rope whirling mad figure eights, its alleged wooden handles still buried in the depths of the drain. Dirty water snapped to the sides, spattering the dull yellow concrete block wall and the steel divider to the left. Ben put up his hands in a defensive posture, but the rope was quicker. It snaked out and hooked him at the back of the neck.

It spun mad spaghetti twirls and peppered drain water up his nose. He clawed his hands at the front of his neck and couldn't get his fingers under. The taste in his mouth was hot copper. There was a yank, and he was brought a foot closer and a yard lower. He kept his feet, but he was losing this tug of war.

Black spots danced in front of his eyes, and his lungs started screaming for air. He tried rearing back, but the pull was too great. He opened his eyes for the last time, and saw the toilet bowl rush at his face. And the last thought

Ben had on the face of this earth was that the promise he had broken was far more fundamental than a forgotten bribe to a kid who was messing around with a dead frog in a jar.

[This story first appeared in *Weird Tales Magazine*, the "Uncanny Beauty" Issue, Summer 2010, and was then featured in *The Year's Best Dark Fantasy and Horror*, Prime Books, 2011.]

Cross-Currents

Even though Esther was six years old she knew what "NO TRESSPASSING" meant. She could read middle school books like *The Giver* and *Drums, Girls, and Dangerous Pie,* thank you. Her big brother Isaac was nine. He played chess. He could do algebra, and he wasn't going to go listening to his kid sister when he was out making mischief with his friend Rickie-Jay over in the restricted area.

Esther walked along the dividing line made of rickety sand-fencing. Between the posts the boys looked jumpy like an old-fashioned movie, and Esther halted, grabbing two of the fence slats and putting her face in between them. Down near the surf, both boys had their shirts off, sand caked on their legs and ankles like slave-mud. They were trying to yank something straight out of the darkened beach floor. It looked like a big game-board made of old wood or charcoal-gray stone.

Something breathed on the air, and far out to the right the sky bristled. Lightning splintered across the horizon and Esther's eyes glistened. It was a magic picture of a crooked crab tree dancing on the back of the water. Thunder boomed out over the ocean, and Esther screeched with glee, bunny-hopping in place.

Down left, the boys looked like howling monkeys, spikey stick figures dashing across the sand and hopping over the part of the fencing flattened down by the surf. They charged past Esther back up to the beach house.

Rain swept in across the dark water, a marvelous witch's brew filled with invisible kings in their lacy robes diving into each other. They roared in some strange ancient tongue, and the downpour came on in a rush.

Esther closed her eyes, turned her face upward, and held out her arms. The rain felt like a million angels, a million kisses, a million whispers bursting with the secrets of the sea. Mommy was going to be mad. She had told Esther to "Go get the boys," and that meant not getting soaked, not having her tuck-bun come out, her summer dress clinging. Mommy was a weirdo. She made Esther sad sometimes, because she was either mad or unmad, never happy like a smiley emoji. Mommy played solitaire on her laptop. Mommy watched CNN. Mommy worked on drawings with STRAIGHT LINES on her drafting board in the loft, and she sometimes took off her glasses, looked at Esther, and sighed. It was a nice sigh, because it meant Esther could crawl up into her lap for a hug, but Mommy never laughed, EVER.

Esther took a last, loving look at the shore. The low waves were tumbling in closer than before, and they backtracked leaving the sand flat and dark. Over where her brother and his friend had been, the object half stuck had been left at an angle. Esther blinked. She was sure the shape had been that of a game board with squared edges, but now the top had corners that curved. It looked like one of the tomb stones in the old cemetery they'd gone to for gravestone rubbing last month at camp. She'd left her sneakers on the bus so she could walk barefoot, and she'd gotten a rash.

She moved down to the place where the fence potato-chipped down the sand. Daintily, she tip-toed between the splintery posts, careful not to step on the twisted wire ties, and super careful to avoid the shining edges of the shells that were pointy.

A wave slithered up the sand covering her feet and then receding, making things pull like the world was balanced on the head of a pin.

The object sticking up out of the sand moved a bit in the direction of the water's retreat.

Huh?

It was loose, and it was also no tombstone. It was an old boogie board. Esther took tiny steps forward, and stopped at the edge of the crater her brother and his friend had worked into the sand. It was smoothed at the edges now, a murky puddle popping rain drops. The object leaned against the far edge, bobbing. She bent her knees, put her hands on them, and squinted. Scratched into the age-spotted Styrofoam, it said,

I liv in the oshin

mi name is jimmy

Esther put both hands over her mouth and held in a mischievous giggle. She wasn't supposed to talk to people she didn't know. She reached for the board, pursed her lips, and yanked it out of the hole. The surf came on, tumbling up to her ankles, and she gave a joyful cry, prancing back up the beach ten paces, splashing through the water as it drew back making the world reel again like a carnival ride.

She dropped to her knees and laid the board flat. The bottom of it had wavery marks shadowed on it like the ceiling in the sun room last year when it had "water damage." Esther had frowned when Daddy had called it that, too. She liked the shape of it, pretty, like river-ripples.

She poked her tongue out the corner of her mouth, and scratched into the board,

Esther.

Picking up the board was hard because it sucked to the sand for a second, but she popped it free, wrapped her arms around it, and ran down to the water. Rain thundered around her. The board was almost as big as she was, and when she gave it a hurl, she almost toppled over.

It fell to the roil of dark waves and floated, close, then away.

"Esther!"

Mommy. Esther looked down at her feet. She was in trouble.

The shower had been love-a-licious, rain washing rain, ha. After dinner, Mother had braided Esther's hair silently right there at the table. Daddy moved to the living room and folded himself into his chair, slowly crossing one long skinny leg over the other, opening his magazine importantly.

"Choices," he said. He looked across back at Esther for a long meaningful moment and then let his glance fall down to the page.

"Yes, bad choices," Isaac added. He was lying at his father's feet on the floor in front of the television. He was on his stomach with his shins up behind him making an "X" shape. He was playing Scrabble with himself.

"Enough," Mommy said, "we've discussed it."

Esther crawled out of her lap and padded in to her usual place behind the sofa across from the stairs so she wouldn't have to see Isaac. There, she sat with her ankles tucked under her and she bent over her iPad plugged into the wall with the charger thing so she could play *Peppa Pig: Paintbox* and pretend she wasn't listening.

"But she's such a *liar*," Isaac said.

"She's imaginative," Mommy said.

"Not the issue," Daddy said. "She should have delivered the message to come into the beach house to her brother more expediently. And her mother shouldn't have given such a directive to a six-year-old."

"Third person isn't necessary, dear," Mommy said softly. "I'm sitting right here."

"Then it's settled then," Daddy said.

"Yeah," Isaac said, "but she's such a *liar*."

"Am not..." she muttered.

"Are so!" his voice said with a laugh in it. "Your ocean-boy, Jimmy? Yeah, that's funny. A kid died last year, pulled in by rip currents. He was a first grader named Jimmy Sweeney. You can Google it. I'll bet she did. Ma, can you check the browsing history on your laptop?"

"She wasn't looking in my laptop, honey."

"How do you know?"

"She's not allowed."

"Oh my *God*," he cried. "You let her get away with *everything!*"

He stomped past and moved off up the stairs. Esther smiled savagely. Then she stopped, that was mean. Thunder rumbled outside, and her mother was saying something about punishments versus creativity. Then something about rewards, and Esther immediately pushed up and bounded out from behind the sofa.

"Rewards?" she said, beaming. "Can I have Slime?"

This earned her looks from both parents, dining room, living room, both different flavors, yet both saying "no." Esther pushed out her bottom lip and stared at her toes. For some reason she thought she was going to cry.

"May I go upstairs?" she said, lifting her head cautiously. "I want to listen to the rain."

"Of course," Mommy said. "I'll be up in a bit to read to you."

Esther nodded and made for the stairs, going heel to toe like a tightrope walker. Mommy wouldn't "be up in a bit." She was drinking wine. Daddy was drinking out of the glass shaped like an upside-down triangle, and once Isaac retreated to his room, he rarely came out, like an ogre lurking in a cave.

She was going upstairs to listen to the rain.

Then she was going to get Mommy's laptop, sneak it back to her room, and take it under the covers like a secret in a tent. She hadn't Googled Jimmy Sweeney like Isaac had said.

But she was going to now.

<hr/>

Esther had the covers pulled up to her chin in the darkness. She'd used Mommy's code, her birthday numbers, to look in the computer for the boy Jimmy Sweeney. There had been a picture. He had yellow hair that stuck out like straw, a ton of faint freckles, bucked teeth, and a mole on his neck. He died swimming by himself in the waters off the public part of the beach three blocks away, where you needed a tag to get in or a lanyard. The Google said he'd loved soccer. And horses.

Esther had unplugged her Goodnight Moon nightlight and left it on the carpet. The dark was like a big painter's canvas…a picture frame she could fill with the face of the lost Jimmy Sweeney. What did his voice sound like? Was he smelly like her brother? Why couldn't he spell "ocean?" Did he ever ride a horse, or did he just like drawing them or watching movies about them? Did he play soccer or was he just in love with Alex Morgan like everyone else?

She smiled wistfully. What was it like to live in the ocean? Did the sea-grasses wave to you when you floated on by? Did the fish all show off for you their beautiful scales flashing rainbows? When you slept, did the currents swing you gently like 'Rock-a-Bye-Baby?' The air conditioner was making noise as it usually did, but in the black backdrop it was different somehow, making rich watercolors ebb and flow across the darkness like waves.

Esther had almost surrendered to the rhythm of forgetfulness, when her eyes fluttered open. It was disturbing, the same way it felt when Isaac crept up behind her and clapped his hands hard.

She'd had a *thought!*

And oh, how she hated thoughts, especially when they surprised her!

Suddenly she'd remembered dance class for some reason, "Ballet 4 – 7" it was called, in the room above the music store that smelled like cobwebs and books. It hurt her feet and the teacher was mean. Mommy had said it would "take time," and Daddy had said the floor there was "forgiving," made of "semi-sprung" wood or something, but it hadn't felt like forgiveness when she fell on it.

She smiled again. In Jimmy Sweeney's "oshin," the floor was soft sand, and you only fell in slow motion. The water hugged you, protected you, made you graceful. Esther pictured herself doing pique turns and pirouettes "en pointe" amongst the coral reefs shaped like statues and honeycombs. So pretty and peaceful and she fell into the silky current of dreams.

———

She woke up when she heard something. Outside her door, something that bumped, or knocked, she wasn't sure which. Everything was strange, like being lost at the mall. The bed felt big in the dark, different than before, as if she was a peanut in a kangaroo pouch with no floor or walls.

"Isaac?" she said. The air conditioner hummed. Calming. The tide.

It wasn't just endless darkness, not if you looked to the sides instead of straight up as she'd done making picture frames in what seemed like years ago. The air conditioner had a tiny yellow light on, meaning Daddy had to clean the filter. Above it, you could see the barest outline through the shape of the blinds. On the other side of the room, up on the bureau, the clock said "2:19" in squared-off red numbers.

She went up on her elbows and saw that there was a thin bar of light under the door.

Then, there was a shadow in it.

Middle, a few inches right, it was Isaac, it had to be, going up on one foot, trying to scare her. It was his favorite ghost story, "The One-Legged Scissor Man," but Esther knew he'd gotten it wrong when he tried re-telling it back home at Boy Scouts in the den when she'd been making pump-kin spice cupcakes with Mommy, standing on the kitchen chair pressing handprints in the flour on the cutting board. She knew it was really "The RED-Legged Scissor Man," an awful German poem that Ms. Brittany, the substitute, read them a month before by mistake at the Play 'N Learn. It was a story about a monster-man who cut off your thumb if you sucked it, but Isaac made it into a one-legged groundskeeper with a set of extra-long hedge cutters who chopped off your leg because he got his caught under a ride mower. STUPID!

The shadow under the door moved. Slowly, to the left. It was smooth. There was no bunny-hop.

"Isaac!" she said. "How did you *DO* that?"

She turned to her stomach, pushed her feet over the edge of the mattress, and did the slow-slide off the side of the bed. Even though she was mad, she remembered at the tipping point to make her hands into claws. That way she could rake them into the contour sheet so the last six inches to the floor wouldn't be so surprising.

After landing, she straightened her nightgown. The mattress was blocking the view of the door, making it seem as if there was a hole in the darkness. She took a deep breath and walked to the front of the bed, letting her left-hand trace along the edge. At the corner, she saw that the shadow under the door had vanished. It was just a bar of faint light now.

Esther approached, expecting a dark shape to suddenly appear on the other side, her brother standing on one foot wearing a scary face and holding a pair of big garden hedge cutters. She got to the door, went up on her toes, and turned the knob. Pulled and backed off so the door could sweep open.

No Isaac.

The hallway was dim, shadows stretching across the walls. Down to the right Mommy and Daddy's door was closed as was Isaac's, and the bathroom light was on like it always was from around the sharp corner of the laundry room. Esther didn't like it in there, and she always held her pee until morning. The washer and dryer were stacked on top of each other and at night they looked like a person.

Esther turned to the left.

There was a soccer ball at the top of the stairs.

"Jimmy?" she said. Moving closer, she saw that the ball was scuffed, its pentagons and blacked-in triangles faded, the rest muddied and watermarked, but she could make out the black and gold lettering, *"Brine – Phantom X"* near the bottom.

She approached and tried to pick it up, but she kicked it before her hands could clap shut. Normally that would have sent her into a fit of laughter, but the bouncing ball wasn't funny. It hit the fourth step down making an awful "boing" noise and rebounded so high it almost hit the ceiling.

It came down with front-spin, kicking off the stair second from the bottom, doing a ricochet in the alcove off the cloak closet door and the bottom of the banister, next rolling out into the living room.

Esther gasped.

The front door was open. But that was WRONG, because Mommy said it wasn't allowed! The soccer ball quivered. It must have been the wind. The

42

rain had stopped, but Esther could hear the whistling in the archway. A door clapped open down the hall, far right; it was Isaac. She froze, hands up by her neck. He was wearing his shark print jammies and he had the heel of his hand in his eye, rubbing it. He thumped down to the bathroom without noticing her, and Esther looked back down the stairs.

The ball was gone.

She stared, closed her mouth, rubbed her ear. Then she made her way down, gripping the posts one by one under the handrail. At the bottom she usually hopped off the landing into the living room like a broad jump for a prize, but this time she lowered herself with a little lady step, walking carefully on the slate gray decorator tiles where *"shoes always came off!"*

Through the doorway the clouds looked black, the moon behind them a pale sleeping eye, the sand like the moon, both marbled and pitted. She slipped outside and went to the edge of the porch. The sunning chairs were sunk in so you couldn't see their legs and the badminton net had sagged in the middle. Down toward the waves, the soccer ball sat on a small mound of sand and Esther giggled into both hands. It looked like a planet on a dune saying, *"Mommy, I'm lost..."*

It started moving, just a wiggle at first, next rolling off, skittering along the beach to the right. It wasn't magic, the wind had picked up, and as the ball changed directions skipping along the sand the other way, then a foot back and five forward, Esther felt the breeze mimic the pattern on her face. The waves tumbled softly onto the shore; everything was dancing.

The ball rolled close to the waterline.

Esther leapt off the porch. The sand was cool and hard, good for running. Her steps were darts, but not quick enough. By the time she got to the place where the texture of the beach dampened with saltwater, the soccer ball was bobbing in the current. Twice, it almost came back to the shore, but twice it withdrew farther, each time ignoring Esther's calls to please, please come back to play tag with the wind. Soon it was a speck. Then a memory in the darker part of the ocean, and Esther grabbed the hem of her nightgown in her fists, trying not to cry.

Before her then, about fifty feet out, the waves changed. It was the foam, the white bubbly part, churning and whirlpooling into a shape. It was an outline at first rising out of the froth, just points that became flickering ears above wide glass-ball eyes on either side of a muzzle with big flaring nostrils. Seawater dripped off of its broad barrel-ribs, and it rose on long and powerful legs, stamping its hoofs, a great white horse with a majestic long flowing mane.

It started to come forward, splashing the skin of the water, not in a trot, but a princely march. Esther stood spellbound upon the cool sand just out of reach of the current, and by the time the magnificent beast came ashore, she'd noticed that it bore a strange rider on its back.

It was a skeleton, limp arms dangling, and she hadn't seen it at first because it wasn't sitting upright, yet lying on its tummy where the saddle would be, draped along the spine. Its skull lolled and bumped softly on the horse's front shoulder. Its fingers were splintered. The bones were spotted and caked in places with what looked like those "calcium deposits" Daddy muttered about when he soaked the shower head in that lemony stuff. There were threads of seaweed hanging off the ribs. One of the eye sockets had black algae oozing in it, and his big cracked teeth looked bucked-out and smiling.

"Jimmy?" she said. He smelled strongly of sea-life.

The horse strutted past, close enough to touch. Esther didn't, but as it passed, she reached after it, turning, seeing nothing behind her now but sunken beach chairs and a sagging badminton net. Her heart was racing, eyes shining, and she ran back to the house just bursting with stories.

Nobody believes me...

Determined, Esther had crawled out of bed, skipping her day-nap. Mommy and Daddy and Isaac were out front having beach time. Mommy had the tri-fold face reflector-thing and the lotion that made her look shiny. Daddy had brought out the umbrella and had on his socks with his sandals because even in the shade he said the tops of his feet burned. Isaac had brought out his summer reading packet, but as always, he was probably just playing *Fruit Ninja* on his iPhone.

Esther was sitting with her legs tucked under her in her special place behind the couch, drawing. She'd found a tablet of oversized construction paper at the bottom of her closet, and she was using a Sharpie to make a picture of Jimmy and his horse. She'd never been very good at art, but here, in her private nook, hunched over the bright yellow paper, she'd amazed herself with her creation.

The horse's ears were slightly too big, the muzzle too long, but the legs had come out *PERFECT,* especially the lower parts just above the hoofs below the knees that were angled back instead of straight as if spring-loaded. The nostrils were slightly uneven, but that made them look as if they were billowing! She'd almost messed up the mane, initially sketching the strands coming too high off the neck, but she worked the mistake into a flowing effect of what seemed a combination of water and flame.

The boy Jimmy was more - a stick figure. Since he'd been draped to the horse's back it had been hard not to double the lines, so she just drew a mis-shapen skeleton head, his boney feet, and his dangling spindle-fingers. Esther was pretty sure he wouldn't think it rude that you had to fill in the rest of him with your imagination. He was a ghost after all…

She pushed up to sit a bit straighter, cocked her head, and added a couple of dots to be the foam, a few falling off the wide chest and some off his tail. She smiled. *Now,* they'd know she wasn't making it up! It was the best thing she'd ever, ever drawn, even though she had pressed her palm onto the paper a few times, leaning, making it waffle a little and crease.

The door came open. Sounds of seagulls and surf and feet on the foyer tiles. The conversation was in the middle somewhere.

"She's eccentric," Mommy said.

"Autistic is more like it," Isaac said.

"Keep your voice down. Go check on her, please."

Isaac's feet pounded up the stairs, thumped above, thumped back, and thudded in return down the stairs.

"Asleep with the covers over her head like usual," he snorted. He moved off to the kitchen. The fridge door opened, and Esther's face burned. It was super-hot upstairs, so they always kept her door closed to conserve the air conditioning. He hadn't even opened it, she'd have heard. So should have her parents who clearly weren't listening.

"I'm concerned," Daddy said softly.

"No need," Mommy said. "Jerry Cohen is on the board. He can arrange for her to be identified immediately and they'll look after her, I'll make sure of it."

"She's not special ed."

"Maybe, maybe not, but she's peculiar. And if you run enough testing something's bound to come up. Everyone does it nowadays as a matter of course, and I'm going to make damned sure she gets every advantage."

"They pull her out of class and the other kids will know."

"There isn't that kind of stigma anymore, in fact, it's the opposite. Twenty nine percent of the district gets services for children with disabilities, it's on the website."

"Disabilities."

"Of course, yes, but please dear, you tend to be blunt. The studies say we should establish an atmosphere of sensitivity. Table-tact. Never use the words "disabled" or "damaged" or "handicapped." Our precious darling is 'special' and she doesn't need to hear anything else."

They moved off to the kitchen.

Esther's face was wet. Slowly, she let her hands fall upon her drawing. She crumpled it into a trash-ball and pushed it under the couch.

———

Isaac suddenly realized that he'd left his reading packet outside, probably flapping all over the beach like a wounded goose. He scraped back his chair, elbowing the table by accident, and making the juice in the glasses move.

"Linoleum," said Dad. He was reading *The Wall Street Journal.*

"Manners," Mom added, thumbing through her phone. Her reading glasses were perched on the end of her nose. Neither had looked up. Isaac bolted through the living room, opened the door, and stepped out onto to the porch.

The sun was blazing. The gentle ocean shimmered, and Isaac could have sworn he saw a fire-white horse wading into it twenty feet out, making a path straight away toward the skyline.

He squinted hard and put his hand across his brow like a salute. There had been something on the horse's back, a figure draped along the spine as if sleeping. The details of the shape were hard to make out exactly, but there had been a pinkish tint to it, the same as Esther's favorite knit summer dress.

Both Isaac's hands were up at his eyes now, one draped over the other, palms curved making a tunnel.

There was no horse.

But there was something pink floating on the water. It disappeared beneath the surface, and Isaac tore back into the house. He clumped up the stairs and raced down the hall. He had been asked to check on his sister. He hadn't, of course, I mean, why the heck would he? She slept like a log and acted like a turd, so why risk waking her up, yo...

He ripped open her door.

Whew. She was there like she always was, a lump with the covers pulled over her head, whew. At least he wasn't going to get into trouble.

His breath caught in his throat. The shape under the comforter was bigger than Esther by at least half a foot.

And the room smelled strongly of dead fish and saltwater.

[This story appeared in *Penumbra*, Hippocampus Press, 2020.]

The Girl Between the Slats

1961

Madeline Murdock crept to the edge and leaned over it with her hands clamped up at her chin. The snowflakes looked like little angels falling into the darkness of the pit, replaced by their sisters the moment they vanished.

"Walk the plank, idiot!"

Madeline's mouth puckered down to the hideous frowny-face Mommy was trying to help her manage, and they were all laughing at her now like they had in the classroom, the gym, the beginning of recess. She waggled her hands in front of her chest as if she'd bitten into something red-hot, so unfair! She just liked to touch things and taste them, that's all. It wasn't her fault that the cobwebs under the radiator in the choir room felt like the soft mane of some baby unicorn. She wasn't the one who made the kickballs look like big cherry jawbreakers.

"Stop calling me names," she said, turning back toward the group of third grade girls gathered on the other side of the caution tape. "At my old school they were nicer!"

Brenda McGilicutty pushed her black glasses up the bridge of her nose.

"Your old school had you in a resource room! My mother told me. And you went there every day on the dummy bus, with extra padding on the walls and the seats."

"That's not true!"

Rhonda Schlessinger walked to a Porta Potty over by a padlocked tool chest and pile of timber. She took off her glove and slapped the side of it like a judge rapping the gavel for attention, and for the millionth time Madeline wondered why doing things like touching the filthy wall of an outdoor toilet was any different than tasting puddle rainbows, or chewing on elbow scabs shaped like half-moons, or licking those orange traffic cones that looked so much like candy corn.

"I believe you, Madeline," Rhonda said, making everything slow down, like a movie, like a snow globe. "Go ahead and walk across. I'll be your best friend, I swear. Then you can be a part of our boy-hater's club." She batted her lashes. "But you have to hurry so we don't get in trouble."

"Yeah, don't be chicken," someone piped in.

"Don't you like us?"

"We'll tell you secrets about everyone, even the Principal!"

Madeline couldn't see anything behind them through the wooden slat fence, but down below she could hear the teacher's aids roaming the playground, starting to break up the game circles in order to collect footballs, Frisbees, and hula hoops. It was almost time for the bell and if she didn't move soon, they were going to get caught up here off school property amongst all the *dangerous equipment:* the bulldozers, trash drums, saw horses, and border posts with little yellow warning flags.

And of course, there was the humongous hole surrounded by caution tape, the one with the plank going across it. The one that was so deep the little angels got lost in it.

Madeline looked down at her shoes, both mud-spattered now, especially the right one with the skinny black buckle-strap that was worn to threads where the prong went through. She'd gone pigeon-toed because she was afraid, and her stockings itched. She wanted to rub her legs together but she was terrified the girls would think she had to wee, that she was the weird girl who licked things plus the stupid retard who still did a first grader's Indian dance when she had to make water.

So, what was it going to be: dimwit or daredevil? Porta Potty or snow-globe?

She stepped forward with a squeal and made a run of it, clicking her shoes along the grained and splintered board almost tippie-toe, all the way to the middle where it bowed down with her weight and went wobbly, where the wide black hole yawned on either side of her and flakes of sediment filtered from the bottom of the wood into the blackness that was still swallowing snowflakes. Madeline froze there, terrified, lost, and then she focused on a knot in the plank before her that seemed just like one of those almonds her mother saved for her in the cabinet above the sink, alongside the flour, brown sugar, and extract.

"So pretty," she thought, and the voices of her new friends drifted off to the background. Madeline Murdock wanted just one taste, just to see. She made to go down to her knees and her foot slipped off the edge. The board came up fast and angry, whacking her in the mouth and driving a tooth straight through her nasal cavity. She loved that moment before pain, that sliver of an instant that felt royal and tasted like Red Hots and pennies.

This was a good one.

The sky did somersaults, and when she hit bottom, they all heard the snap.

—

Mike Summers reviewed what he'd just scrawled into his notebook, cursed, and ripped out the pages. He was no fiction writer and it showed. First, he was unsure of the rule concerning "voice" and "point of view." He was in Madeline Murdock's head, but was he supposed to stick solely with a third grader's lingo? The description of her running tip-toed across the plank was well executed, but he seriously doubted a nine-year-old girl would use the words "sediment" and "filtered."

He ran his thumb along the steering wheel and gnawed at his lower lip. He liked the movement of the piece, but the background characters were disappointing, especially Rhonda Schlessinger, the toilet-slapper. He had pictured her in a light blue winter coat with an Eskimo hood…big nose and spot-freckles, one above an eyebrow and two below the left ear, the bottom one raised like a mole. She had pale skin, imploring eyes, and a practiced sort of sincerity woven into her speech based upon a soft, well developed intra-personal intelligence her parents praised and nurtured to the point of ridiculousness. She would wind up being the one who was always elected to speak for the friendship group when they got into hot water, the one who sang with gusto and danced poorly, destined to be the star of the fifth-grade choir extravaganza, yet merely a high school understudy when looks and talent started to mean more than heart.

But he'd gotten none of this across whatsoever. Rhonda Schlessinger was a stick figure, and while Hemingway promised the audience would fill in the balance, it was easy to mistrust the process when you were in it knee-deep.

Mike got out his cell for a time check and then looked across the parking lot. He still had ten minutes or so before he was due inside for this multi school in-service training, and he cringed thinking about Knickman choosing Saint Mary's Elementary as the central location, in fact he cringed just thinking about her in general. Even before she was named department head at Kennedy High she was the type to *volunteer* for those God-awful curriculum committees, where they pored over mission statements describing English as *"a beautiful and necessary universal human discipline, merging the triad of cognitive development, historical interpretation, and cultural meta-diversity,"* or some such lame horseshit. Blah. Her students hated her as did the rest of the English staff; a roll your eyes – look at your watch kind of thing.

And Knickman had most certainly chosen this old relic of an elementary school for the sake of contrast, making her "state-of-the-art" ideas seem all the more "bold" and "innovative," delivered in this antiquated facility run by a dying Arch Diocese where they still kept the girls in plaid skirts and rows, chanting their parts of speech and copying notes off the board.

Of course, Mike had misread the instruction section of the email, making him arrive here a half hour early, hence the notebook and the story attempt out here in the lot. Pure boredom. It was either that or chance doubling back up Dutton Mills Road to the McDonalds for a Sausage McMuffin with egg. But there was the possibility of getting caught in a line and Mike Summers was more for relishing his guilty pleasures than rushing them.

It was the perfect setting for a horror story though, wasn't it? The building before him was made of old church fieldstone with dark bay windows and doors with high arches. There were outdoor floodlights in the upper corners covered by wire mesh baskets and basketball hoops without nets. The playground had a jungle gym, a slide that leaned left, and an ancient carousel that revolved ever so slightly when the wind picked up.

To the left up the hill was a construction site barred off by wooden slat fencing most probably erected by property owners more than two decades ago, all dark gray and weather spotted, rambling along the rise in an alternating rail pattern that let slivers of daylight squeeze through. It was difficult to make out anything on the other side of it really. Mike knew it was a jobsite from the crane. They were building a new facility meant to replace the dinosaur down here, at least that's how it seemed. And with a half hour to kill, Mike Summers had made his first attempt at writing a short piece of fiction. So called. He crumpled up the three sheets of notebook paper and jammed them into the compartment below the radio where he discarded his dry trash. He'd stick to discussing the classics with a rather boyish enthusiasm, going easy on the grammar, and making the kids laugh once in a while. Stick to what he was good at.

He shut down the engine and opened the door. It gave its usual little metallic yowl, but there was a distinct transition here from the rather friendly and bumpy sound of the motor to the creepy whisper of winter wind coming over the hood. If only he'd been talented enough to truly capture that kind of thing with his writing! He stepped out, checked his zipper with a practiced mechanical surety, and moved those long Hollywood bangs off his forehead. He was skinny and slump shouldered, but never forgot to mousse the top and dangle the front, doll it up a little. No, he wasn't advertising. He hadn't saun-tered over to Home Ec. and asked Brandi Cohen out for drinks, even though she smiled at him shyly over her cup of herbal tea every time they sat across from each other in the teacher's lounge. He hadn't offered to help Jennifer Dooley set up her bi-annual CPR session on her prep, even though everyone and their mother knew it was a chance to be alone with her in the weight room when she'd typically wear those stunning pink shorts. He hadn't even clicked the box on his Facebook that offered photos and profiles of "Mature Single Women in [His] Area," nothing since Stephanie died. He just had nice hair. And wouldn't it be a piss-poor example for his little Georgie to start bringing strange women into the house? Granted, it had come awfully close to falling apart for a while, too close, but Mike was a fighter, a role model, and his three-and-a-half-year-old son brought him far more joy than any patch of fur ever could.

He opened the back door to reach in for his bookbag and there was sound from behind, floating down through the pattern of the wind. It was a suckling sound, coming from up on the hill. He turned, stepped a bit wrong, and wrenched his ankle in a way that he was sure he would feel more tomor-row. Up on the hill there was something moving, there in the fence between the slats. Something…

—

"Well?" Professor Mike Summers said. "Comments?" It was a small fiction writing class, yet one with surprising gusto. Trudy Bell had short butchy hair, wire frames, a nervous laugh, and a scarf, always. She was quick as a whip though, really good with timelines and structural stuff. She was the typical literature major, well used to ruling the roost in these electives where you earned your "fun and easy" credits, and she was wrapped up in a quiet, yet obvious sort of war with Mackenzie Dantoni, with her tight yoga pants, straight blonde hair, big eyes (heavy on the mascara) and this startling abil-ity to unpack characters and follow them down to the bitter ends of their neurotic little life journeys. The other three were lower classmen and bench talent: Nicholas Donahue, a thick kid who wore shorts even in the middle of winter, and the Stellabott twins, Donald and Daniel, both in dress shirts and ties, both rather shy, both experiencing the mild discomfort of landing in a course where grammar and expertise with the MLA or APA disciplines didn't matter anymore.

Professor Summers gently crossed one leg over the other while his students gathered their thoughts, and he looked rather blankly at the pages before him. There were some unwritten rules in university life. When tutoring in the Writing Center, you never told the students that their papers were "good," because anything their professors assigned below an "A" would be your fault. You didn't change rules on the syllabus unless it was in the student's favor, and you didn't bring in your own work for classroom review. It smacked of juvenile conceit and most often shook out to a clear lose-lose scenario. If it was dazzling, the students felt they could never live up. If it was a "work in progress," they wouldn't respect you.

But here, Summers hadn't really a choice. He had expected at least a roster of twelve and had built the course around the idea that they would review student drafts. The first two weeks had been magnificent, but he'd already exhausted their two pieces of flash. He'd gotten critical responses for five stories from the 30/30 anthology, and they were in the dead zone between that initial rush and the ten to twelve-pager. He'd needed something for filler.

"I liked it," Nicholas said, putting his ankle up on his knee and playing absently with the Converse All Star decal that had started to peel. "I mean, I think you were good as a high school teacher, Professor Summers, even though it got a little clunky and boring with the technical stuff the department head lady was into."

"Knickman," Trudy said dryly. He looked at her sideways for a second.

"Whatever. I got lost in the jargon."

"It built the character."

"Seemed forced."

"I thought it worked," Mackenzie said. "He countered all of the theoretical language with words like 'God - awful,' 'Horseshit,' and 'Blah,' letting us know his expertise with it all and at the same time his..." She fought for the right terminology, and then smiled rather triumphantly. "... disdain and dismissal." Trudy stared at her fingers clamped white across the front of the knee, clearly uncomfortable that she was in basic agreement with her rival.

"I liked his hair," she finally offered in a rare moment of sardonic remittance, and Nicholas chuckled. Playing it, Professor Summers "casually" moved those random (yet perfectly) placed strands off his forehead and then looked off, thoughtfully stroking his salt and pepper goatee to complete the cliché. That got a laugh from the whole group, and Daniel, the more rigid of the two brothers, cleared his throat.

"I...uh...know this sounds silly, but that little girl scares me."

"You haven't even really seen her yet," his brother argued. "Not as a ghost, anyway."

"That's the point," Mackenzie said. "You have to hide the monster." Trudy folded her arms coldly and spoke without looking at anyone.

"There's more than that here. The narratorial echo makes it so the author can build her in levels. In a way it's a cheap move, allowing him to add material from his brainstorming lists through his inner monologue about the writing process. But notice, he pays more attention to Rhonda than Madeline Murdock. He plays a trick with the trick, and that makes it interesting."

"And the fence is a perfect barrier," Mackenzie added, "because there's a chance we'll only see her in flashes and flickers. If she walks or floats behind it, she'll just be this dark form moving between the slats."

"Yes," Donald said, "and things could pop out from behind the fence." Everyone turned and gave him a glance when his voice cracked on the word "behind," but he pressed on bravely. "I could imagine the teacher inside the school for his staff development, and out of the corner of his eye he sees movement out the window. Then, from up on the hill, there's something coming over the fence, bouncing in slow motion toward the parking lot with the snow fluttering down all around it. A red kick-ball."

"Wouldn't be slow motion," Trudy said. "It'd have to be in real time or it would give the implication that the Mike Summers character has lost his mind. If that's the author's intent, it's too soon."

"A tongue!" Nicholas said, so loud it made Mackenzie jump in her chair and put her hand to her chest. "Sorry," he muttered. "Anyway, the slats of the fence make it so she can stick her tongue through, darkening the wood, maybe picking up splinters like a pincushion and leaving a trail of blood and saliva."

Silence.

"That was a little too good, Nicholas, but thank you for sharing," Professor Summers said, and everyone smiled. "In what other ways could we utilize the fence as a masking element?"

Another silence, but a good one. Summers hadn't expected that they would necessarily add to his fragment of a tale, but if this was the way it was meant to go, you let it. Teachable moment, right? Daniel loosened his tie and folded his hands, next doing the thumb twiddling thing.

"You could have the Mike Summers character march up the grassy incline and grab two of the slats in order to pull close and put his eye right up to one of the voids."

"Right!" his brother chimed in. "And just when you think something will poke him in the pupil, another set of hands, dirty with the mud of the hole, grab his knuckles from the other side!"

"I'd save that for the climax," Trudy said. "The real question we should ask is what the suckling sound is."

"Her tongue," Nicholas said. "Licking the fence 'cause it looks like an elongated Kit Kat or something."

"I don't think the sound can be licking," Mackenzie said. "The teacher is down in the parking lot and the fence is up on a hill, far enough away for the girls to convince Madeline Murdock to walk the plank without being heard by the aids on the playground."

"Playground's further than where Summers parked."

"But still…"

"Maybe it's her head," Trudy said. "When she hit there was a 'snap,' right? Of course, we could assume it was a leg or an arm, but consider the alternative. Maybe she broke her neck clean off the spine and when she moves now, her head sloshes around. That would be louder than licking if she's really rolling it across her shoulders."

"Maybe it's a sexual sound," Nicholas tried. "Like a symbolic echo of the intimacy Mike Summers struggles to recall from his dead wife."

Silence yet again, but the thick kind now. Professor Summers's wife Stephanie had actually died three and a half years ago almost to the day while giving birth to their son George. Nicholas clearly hadn't gotten the memo. Professor Summers felt his eyes dampen, but he kept his voice smooth and professional.

"My apologies, Nick. I should have at least changed the names. We write what we know, often bringing up personal issues in dichotomous contexts, maybe for a bit of self-misdirection." He smiled. "No cry for help intended; I just needed to build a character. I'm fine with it at this point, but I must insist that it goes in the hopper."

"In the hopper," the rest of the class echoed. It was their code for a piece of writing that was too close to the vest to be scrutinized. Nick nodded and rubbed his nose.

"Well I like the 'monster' here regardless. She has good back-story and she's scary."

"Definitely," Mackenzie said. "Way scarier than the girl in 'The Ring.'"

"I don't know about that," Trudy said.

"Really?" Mackenzie returned, head cocked so that mane of blonde hair hung down behind her like some velvety curtain. "Girlfriend was totally tame and utterly dependent on the effect that made her jump camera frames."

"The hair in the face was disconcerting."

"Please. She needed a brush, a hug, and some foot cream."

"Ha!" Donald said. "For her rotted, waterlogged toes. Ha!"

"So insightful," Daniel said, rolling his eyes.

"Yes," Professor Summers interjected. "I was aware of the possible similarities between the two characters, but I had more reservations about the idea that Madeline Murdock had severe special needs."

"Since when are we so worried about political correctness, especially in horror fiction?" Trudy said. Summers pursed his lips and shook his head gently.

"You misunderstand. The Summers character wasn't meant to be a boy scout. Moreover, I had most of the fellow instructor-characters from Kennedy High worked out in my head, and none of them were meant to play moral compass either. There was an intellectual snob who would insist it was not in her contract to teach a research paper, an old biddy who was afraid of the move toward holistic grading techniques since she had gotten by with focus corrections and minimal output for years, and a bald grammar Nazi named Matthew who drilled subject predicate and dangling participles even to seniors." He paused. "The point is that Knickman's big announcement was to be that they were on the verge of adopting the trend of dumping all the special ed. kids in the same classes, thirty at a time and excusing it by throwing in a special needs instructor to co-teach. Mike Summers was going to be furious...seeing it as a transparent short-cut that bypassed inclusion and turned him into a zoo keeper. That was his connection with Madeline, and it was an ugly one. Contrary to a "good-guy" scenario, he only saw those with disabilities as roadblocks, annoyances, strains of a virus that would do nothing but tarnish the paradigm of "cool teacher" he'd so carefully constructed throughout his tenure."

"Sounds good," Donald said, his brother nodding in agreement.

"But does it not sound like something else that's familiar?"

"Like what?"

"Like Jason."

"Who?"

"Voorhees!" Nicholas said. "Yeah. A kid with special needs that the campers tease and the counselors ignore."

"Too similar in plot and theme?" Professor Summers posed.

"Definitely not," Trudy said, pulling her feet up onto her chair and drawing her knees in. "The whole *Friday the 13th* thing was never even scary, except for a few select moments in the first."

"I agree," Daniel said. "You never actually have a feeling of trepidation watching those. You just cheer his kills." He looked around uncertainly. "If that's your thing, anyway."

"It's true," Mackenzie said. "*The Girl Between the Slats* doesn't spell kill-fest, at least not now as it stands. It's creepier. More mystery, depth, and suspense. More a focus on people and their intricate struggles, at least if it goes the way Professor Summers seems to intend." She looked at him shyly. "Sorry for the third person reference. Not trying to be weird or anything."

"No," he said. "Not at all, Mackenzie. I truly enjoyed this class and I look forward to seeing you all back here on Monday. And since there isn't anyone else here in the alcove with an office hour during our class time, I think it's better to reconvene here in the lounge. It's cozier with the six of us, don't you think?"

They mumbled agreement. Usually, Trudy stayed behind to discuss some elevated principle, but today she left with the rest of them. Professor Summers pushed up and made his way across the lounge to his office with the limp he'd recently inherited. In the elevator this morning he'd stopped the door from sliding shut with his ankle because he had his bookbag in one hand and a latte in the other. The co-ed who had called out, "Oh please hold that!" was grateful, and the awkward moment was rather humorous he'd thought, more her embarrassment than his, and a chivalrous deed well done in the end. But now, he'd developed a bit too much of a hitch in his giddyap, and he hoped he wouldn't have to put a call in to his primary over it.

He made it to his door and had just gotten out his key, when he heard something bump in his office. He stepped back instinctively, winced, then shuffled off left past the corner to look down the carpeted foyer. Professors tended to leave their doors open when they were using the space, yet Pat's door was closed, as was Tara's, Robert's, and Dianna's. Besides, they were too far away. His office was at the entrance to the alcove, and the sound hadn't come from fifteen feet down the hall. It had come from just inside of his door, there was no mistaking it.

He repositioned himself back in front of his office and paused. Was it Yvette? They hadn't shared the space for two years, ever since he'd attained full time status, so he didn't think it was her that was poking around in there. Besides, they had held class right here in the lounge for the last two and a half hours, and he'd been in the office right before it to throw his coat over the chair. He would have seen her go in.

He brought up his key, inserted, turned, and gave the door a push.

There was something on his chair.

It was a mud-stained kickball that had moist spots with strange etchings around them. They were bite marks, and the only inconsistency in all the whitened impressions was the missing front right incisor.

—

Dr. Michael Summers shut his laptop, leaned back, and ran his palm over his smooth, bald crown. He hadn't taken a classroom assignment in years, and he missed it. He hadn't tried to write anything creative for just as long and that had been worse somehow, as if some fundamental connection to his current position of Dean of the College of Arts and Sciences had been corroded and severed…the inspiration for all of it lost in the scatter of time. He had started on this path as the young tenth grade English teacher with the moussed-up top and Hollywood bangs, all bright-eyed, bushy tailed, and pure piss and vinegar. He'd understood kids, their clumsy passion, their insight and anger. But as a result of all the silly and destructive boardroom politics he'd moved on, earned a second Masters in order to become the lowly adjunct professor slumming between universities until a full time position opened at Widener where he moved all his books to the third floor of the Kapelski building, first office on the right in the alcove where he set up camp for a good while, where his hair went partially gray, where he grew a matching goatee as if it was his plan all along, where he taught lower level rhetoric and the occasional fiction class out in the lounge.

After the doctorate, there was a chance to move up the ladder and he took it. The decision wasn't an easy one and he'd called his father about it, actually. A retired professor himself, he'd claimed that these kinds of opportunities only came around once in a while, and even though it was clear that his "rebel son" didn't like meetings and mission statements, it was better to dictate policy than become no more than the hired help architecting someone else's vision of the landscape.

In the end Dr. Summers didn't despise it as much as he'd anticipated, but it wasn't the classroom with its teachable moments and glorious student epiphanies. In fact, the most contact he had with underclassmen of late was as mediator in a string of plagiarism cases, and for the first time in his career he wasn't in their corner. There were grade grievances and lawyers, policy meetings and enrollment projections.

And this was his cherished Christmas break, his time to relax. He'd made a personal vow not to check his email to go putting out fires, and he'd gotten out his laptop to unwrap an old guilty pleasure, that Big Mac at the drive through, that *Friday the 13th* sequel you'd never admit you got off of Netflix.

Writing fiction was like getting back on a bicycle, right?

It had gone well in more ways than he had anticipated. He liked the falling snow as background motif just as much as that weather-worn slat fencing that leaned and rambled across the hillside. He hadn't had to stretch all too far to "see" it either; the window in the third-floor den overlooked his sprawling back yard where the Feinberg's ancient alternating rail barrier divided their properties. It was an ugly, outdated piece of construction, but had become a part of his collective subconscious, his background mural, and he found it comforting somehow. The flurries just made it that much easier to write about.

In terms of problems and logic errors, he felt that he'd come out of this rough draft with a "pass-plus" or so. He agreed with his "Nicholas" character that the curricular phraseology in the first Mike Summers section in the parking lot was too rich, ringing of "Momma, look how good I'm writing here, huh?" and that it would have to be trimmed. The physicality of the office lounge in the fiction class scene was rather incomplete, yielding a muddy sort of impression of the logistics, and the biggest disappointment was Mackenzie Dantoni, the blonde bombshell with a brain whose type he knew all too well but somehow couldn't draw with any sort of credibility. First off, he'd initially sold her as an expert in character dissection, yet merely delivered a detail hound, sort of borrowing from the "Trudy" character's skillset. The blonde hair hanging like a curtain was a clumsy metaphor, difficult to visualize, and she was more a cliché than the girl who sat across the aisle and took your breath away.

He'd vaguely wanted to make her akin to a young Stephanie and had wound up painting this poor dear in a startlingly unflattering manner when compared to her better. But his deceased wife was a tough act to follow, her memory still haunting him in life and in fiction. In reality, he had married Stephanie Walker in 1984 straight out of college, and they'd put off having kids while they built their careers. He taught at Kennedy High for the rest of the decade, worked his adjuncting shuffle through most of the nineties, his full-time stint up until the Phils won the series in '08, and that's when they'd thrown away the diaphragm.

Stephanie was forty-seven when she died giving birth to his Georgie. All the charts and graphs warned that it was too late to try, but she'd still seemed so young and so strong. She was tall with daring eyes and beautiful knees, *God,* she looked good in a skirt! She was a senior lecturer at Temple for seventeenth century poetry and she'd still hushed a room when she entered it. She was the type who could wear stiletto heels to a department function and get away with it, drinking white wine with the vice president of the college and saying things to her like, *"What an exquisite elder faerie you'd be."* She sang rock and roll - opera style in the shower, she was one of those nutcases who wore face paint at Philadelphia Eagles home games, and she made sitting under a tree and reading a book seem like art.

Dr. Summers carefully used his index fingers to wipe under the rims of his eyes, then made a loose fist and bumped it against his lips. To say that he missed her made the feeling sound trite. It was horrifically empty now in the hollows of his heart, in the corridors of this house with its grand banisters and elevated ceilings.

All empty except for his Georgie, his love.

"Daddy!" the boy called, as if on cue. "Come look, come now! Please Daddy, come see back yard, come see, come now!"

Dr. Summers pushed away from his desk and made for the hall. Georgie wasn't supposed to be downstairs by himself, especially at night. He was probably looking out through the sliding glass doors, watching the snow. In fact, considering the muffled nature of his son's plea, it was probable that his nose was pressed right up against the glass, his breath-clouds advancing and receding like misted little spirits.

Dr. Summers rose and pulled firm his robe-tie, marveling (and not for the first time) over the odd acoustics of the place. Georgie could pad down the hall to the bathroom up here and Michael wouldn't know he was there until the flush. On the other hand, the boy could be building a Leggo castle in the living room or playing "Teletubby hockey" (Tinky Winky was the puck) out in the back den, and you could hear him puttering around as if he was next to you.

The stairs had a long sweeping curve to them, and tonight Dr. Summers wished he'd had one of those silly rail riders they advertised on the same channel that plugged the walk-in tubs, hearing aids, and call button neck-laces you used when you'd fallen and couldn't get up. In his hurry to leave the house four days ago, he'd cracked his ankle at the base of the coffee table, and the 600 mg. Ibuprofen wasn't helping that much. He limped down the stairs, and his son's voice carried to him,

"Hurry Daddy, or you're gonna miss it!"

God, what a gem. If Stephanie only could have seen what she gave to this world before leaving it. True enough, Dr. Summers coddled him but how could he help it? Georgie was the model boy, soft blonde hair curling at the top, crystal blue eyes, heart shaped smile welcoming the world. He had a smidging of chubby-cheek syndrome, but it was the last of the baby fat he was shedding. He was gorgeous, and it wasn't just "Daddy" saying it with the equivalent of a loving parent's "beer goggles." Georgie was just that boy you wanted to put your arms around and squeeze. Everyone said so.

Dr. Summers almost tripped over the lip at the edge of the kitchen. He'd initially been against having a rise there going from carpet to hardwood, but the installer had said this was the type of tongue and groove that warranted a step. It was the way royalty did it in one of those Middle Eastern countries Dr. Summers couldn't remember at the moment, and when he was tardy lifting his knee his toe grazed the edge almost sending him sprawling. There was that moment before pain that felt plush and high, and then the shooter through his ankle made him bite back a shout. Blasted contractors. They'd been a nuisance, and he'd succumbed to suggestions he'd been against simply because guys with tool belts, suspenders, and leather knee pads always seemed so damned sure of themselves.

He limped across the floor, past the island with the pots and pans hanging on the square rack above it, and when he got to the back den he froze in the archway.

There was his Georgie, pressed up to the glass. The lights were off, but the auto-floods in the back yard were shining, doubling the snowflakes with their shadows and casting a pale wash over the figure on the other side of the transparent door, twinning him. It was Madeline Murdock in Catholic School clothes, broken neck, head leaning so far to the left her ear was pinned to her shoulder. They were playing mirror, hands splayed out to the sides, but she was taller, making the image of the cross gain two levels. Georgie was stretching his neck, trying to pull his head down to the side, but couldn't manage to get it quite parallel.

"This is my special friend, Daddy," he said, "and this is my special hug so I can be just like her."

She started to lift her head off her shoulder and it lolled around like a zoo balloon on a stick. Shadows slanting down from the roof overhang moved up and down her face, and her smile came up in flashes and glare. It was a circus creature's grin with lips bloodied and swollen, broken nose pushed to the side with a tooth rammed straight through the nostril.

Georgie was doing his best to mimic her, but the way that her head dangled and flopped on its stalk was impossible to duplicate. Frustrated, hands still pinned to the glass beneath hers, Georgie started shaking his skull back and forth, so violently it seemed he was going to hurt himself. Dr. Summers burst through the room in shuffles and hitches. He reached out and screamed, but was too late.

Georgie slid open the door. It took everything he had, but the little guy was just tall enough to flip the lock, reach the handle, and pull the apparatus across.

Madeline Murdock had vanished.

The haunt of her frost and her snow swept through the archway, enveloping Georgie Summers and making whirlwinds around him. Dr. Summers grabbed his son by the shoulders, trying not to scream when he turned him and the head bobbed unnaturally, the boy's eyes rolling in dim recognition, lips bruised and bloody, front right incisor rammed straight though his nostril.

—

The man paged through it all one last time in helplessness or disgust, it was difficult to tell which. There were pieces of copy paper filled with slanted scribble and a stack of sheets written upon in haste and then ripped from a spiral bound notebook leaving the confetti-frills on the side, Post-It notes both yellow and rainbow colored, a few napkins, a piece of toilet paper.

"Mr. Summers," he said.

"Mike, please."

"As you wish." He gave a half-hearted attempt at rearranging the strange medley and removed his reading glasses.

"I just don't know what you expect me to do with all this."

"I want you to help him, father."

"I'm not a priest. I'm a therapist."

"And you can do nothing for my boy?"

The man made his way over from the desk, sat in the chair, and carefully rested the points of his elbows on the cushy arm rests. Slowly, he sat back, simultaneously crossing his legs and linking his smooth fingers in a little bridge before his chest.

"I'm not his therapist, Michael, I'm yours, and I believe this is to be our last session."

"But..."

"Michael. You're tired. You're sleep deprived. You have not eaten a square meal in three and a half years, and if you think it is at all positive that I play into this delusion it just represents a set-back too extreme for the tools I have available here."

"He's possessed, can't you see?"

"Michael..."

"No," he said. "My Georgie is a beautiful boy."

"Of course he is, Michael, but you must affix that to the way that he is, not some fantasy about who he could have been under other circumstances."

"He's intelligent! He's a gem! He's going to play lacrosse, get straight As, and go to the prom with the Homecoming Queen! And when he graduates summa cum laude from Cornell, Harvard, or Duke, I'm going to buy him a Ferrari!"

"You won't, Michael, and it's actually come time to talk about the business-end of things since you've opened that door."

"You're talking finances? You're kidding. I'm the Dean of the College of Arts and Sciences at Widener University for Christ's sake!"

"You're not, Michael. Not anymore. You lost that position three years ago. You never recovered from Stephanie's death, you refused to get Georgie professional help, and you wore yourself down to a thread. You lost the house and Margaret informed me that Blue Cross Keystone hasn't received a premium from you in six months. You can't even afford to drop him off at the center at this point."

"It's a lie! I just got a late start today and - "

"Regardless, I believe we should discuss aid from the state and possible institutionalization."

"I'd never *ever* put my Georgie in a nut house!"

"I meant both of you, Michael. Separately. For your safety and his."

"That's ridiculous."

The man let his hands fall atop the knee ever so softly.

"Michael," he said, "Your son George has severe obsessive compulsion, sociopathic tendencies, and a highly impressive sensory disorder."

"How dare you."

"You have spent the last three and a half years trying to reason with a damaged human being whose special needs warrant professional attention."

"No."

"If you don't take action, he could fatally harm you."

"It was an accident. I banged my ankle on the edge of the coffee table."

"You didn't, Michael, and I won't support your denial. Your three-and-a-half-year-old son got out of the crib you still keep him tied down in, found the tool box, brought in the ball peen hammer, and smashed your ankle as you slept in one of those fitful twenty-minute naps you try your best to sneak when you can. He wanted to hear the sound of crunching Kit Kats, he'd said."

"It's not true!"

"It is," Dr. Kalman insisted. "And you're going to have to face up to -"

The door burst open and Georgie Summers darted into the room, screaming at the top of his lungs, hands flailing before his chest as if he'd just scorched himself. He was wearing a neck brace and halo because he'd so liked the dizzying feeling that accompanied a constant violent shaking of his head, the doctors had feared he would suffer from brain-bruise and whiplash. He had a mouth guard that was fastened all the way around his skull, because he'd lacerated his tongue licking the splintered back yard fencing, and had torn his lips to ribbons from the constant biting and sucking that he claimed tasted like Red Hots and pennies. Inside his mouth he was missing his right front incisor, surgically removed from his nasal cavity after he'd purposefully run straight into the edge of a sawhorse the landlord had set up in the kitchen to cut a board while he was fixing a leak under the sink. Georgie had claimed that when he bit down hard it tasted like the almond extract he'd stolen from the cupboard a week ago, and if Daddy wouldn't give him another bottle, he was going to make his own juice. Mike had told the emergency room doctor that his son had tripped over a kickball and hit the corner of a playground slide.

Margaret hurried in after the boy, her hair loose on one side.

"I'm so sorry, Doctor, but it's not in my job description...."

They were all on their feet now, Dr. Kalman frowning, hands in his blazer pockets. Mike Summers limped after his son, walking cast making clumping sounds on the floor. His eyes were reddened at the rims and his face sagged with grief. Georgie had gone flat on his stomach and was banging his mouth guard against the crown floor molding, screeching incoherently. Margaret's hands fluttered up to her face like frightened birds.

"Dear God, make him stop. He's trying to lick the outlets."

Mike Summers was on the floor now wrestling with his son from behind, looking up at his doctor, trying his best to avoid the meaty little fists flailing back at his face.

"There's got to be a reason," he said. "There's got to be." Georgie started banging his forehead against the wall. Mike assumed the restraining position they'd taught him at the Children's Hospital, arms over arms, the body beneath him writhing in spasm, and he pressed his lips to the side of the headgear, as near as was possible to his son's sweaty temple.

"Buttercups," he whispered tenderly in his son's ear. "Buttercups Georgie, I know...Daddy knows. You think the outlets are white chocolate buttercups."

[This story appeared in S.T. Joshi's anthology, *Searchers After Horror*, 2014.]

The Sculptor

There's mist on the football field.

To the right is the small construction site they fenced off between the Annex and the Writing Center, and there is a mound of brown dirt next to a stationary wet saw and a work station under a canopy.

There's a squirrel skittering along the low branch of a spruce with drooping leaves. Below that, two female professors are having a conversation by the steps that lead to the library. The stocky one is smiling. She has square wire frames, a big nose, a nondescript dress, and thick ankles. She nods in agreement a lot. Her expressions are animated, and it is obvious she has made a name for herself with her ability to empathize.

There's an eyelash under my fingernail, and I figure it came from number twelve, because she was a blonde.

I walk over to the guard shack at the far corner of the ROTC dormitory, hit the keypad, and enter. I write on the log that I am on shift, and I take the small radio out of the charger plugged in by the microwave.

"2579842 present," I say.

"Check," comes back through the tinny speaker. I slide the sunglasses off the top of my cap, bring them carefully to my face, and hide my blank expression behind them. A pair of freshmen with a dented steel bucket walk by and purposely look away, as if I don't know that they plan to upkeep the tradition of egg-bombing the nude statue that stands in the fountain between the cafeteria and the Quad. Clever boys, but they've got it all backward. It is not their identities that are important, but rather the fact that part-time security guards wearing aviator sunglasses and blank expressions stay faceless.

I watch.

And no one watches me doing it.

If I fall in love with you, I might want to make you immortal.

It's easy to fall in love with a girl, each a storybook graced with God-given introductory pages that are written upon, edited, and rearranged into later chapters of beauty. Their journey is a splendid blur of mascara, lipstick, liner, bows, bands, ringlets, and flips . . . locks tucked thoughtfully behind an ear or hanging loose to the shoulder, freckles, coy grins, sharp cheeks that redden when you cross the line just a bit, and eyes that do that brief sparkling dance if you tell her she's pretty at just the right moment.

And so many flavors!

There are strawberry blondes, and ash blondes, and flaxen, ginger, and honey blondes, there are chestnut brunettes who come off soft, warm, and girly, and those sharp copper redheads who use a lot of rust and green around the eyes for seductive distance and brazen coquettishness. There are jet-black bangs and sable braids, teased-up auburn and wet tawny on the beach, there is the willowy girl working the library reference desk that you can't help but envision on the bed in her underwear on a Sunday morning, knees drawn up to her chin and painting her toenails, and the haughty cheerleader you ache to turn into a "good girl" who folds her hands, arches her back, and nods earnestly when you tell her things. There's the long-haired girl with the button nose and big charcoal eyes, and the platinum blonde with the white-rimmed sunglasses and cappuccino tan who was just born to be captured on Fanavision at the ball park.

Delicious.

And let us not let go unmentioned the serious artillery, the pleated skirts, the jean shorts, the low-cut blouses with silky folds and buttons unfastened, the black thong-straps positioned above the low waistlines of tight hip-huggers, and the long sleeves tight to the arm and extended to the middle of the palm. And, of course, there are the legs, the long legs with that vertical line accenting the thigh, the muscular legs that make you believe you could fuck like some spectacular athlete, the smooth legs you are dying to run your fingers across like exotic glass, and those legs the lightest blondes let go unshaven, making you swell inside because it's just so darned personal somehow.

Still, this is all window-dressing. No matter how the given female has prettied up the package or grown into her curves and lines, it is her inno-cence that finally draws us. She can be knowing and closed and clever and calloused, but in the end, she wants to let her eyes soften and melt into yours. It is unavoidable. Women are the warmth of the world.

And I am their sculptor.

There's a steady rain drumming along the roof of the truck.

I own my own side business called *Pressure Washing and Steam Cleaner's Inc.* It is a bland name, an industrial, indiscriminate label, and my truck is an old mid-sized moving truck I bought at auction, sandblasted, and repainted this old battleship gray. I have a twelve-foot ladder lashed down to the roof with bungee cords, but the ladder is for show. So is the truck. While there is indeed a pressure washer back there in the trailer, and an Emglo compressor to power it, there are no steamers, no wet/dry vacuums, no spare hoses, no replacement filters, no detergents, no pickle barrels filled with rags, no old leather tool belts and power drills, no miscellaneous fasteners, no brooms, and no squeegees and mops for the run-off.

Just one cold box eight feet long by thirty-six inches high held down by yellow polyester ratchet straps, one power washer tied down in the back-right corner next to the compressor, and a fifty-foot length of heavy gauge exten-sion cord. I don't need anything else, because I only have one customer. The local supermarket. Every two weeks or so I power-wash the wall on either side of the pharmacy dumpster, and of course I do it for free. What else would they expect from a faithful part-time employee who moonlights as a college security guard on his off-days? Gosh. Someday regional might even grant me overtime, or even holiday hours in return for the favor!

I park, adjust my name tag, exit the truck, and turn up my collar. The door squawks when I slam it shut, and for the millionth time I wish I could operate out of a van. But vans and mid-sized Penske movers and U-Haul units are designed for homeowners who don't like using high ramps. I need fifty-two inches from wheel's bottom to deck, just like a sixteen-wheeler.

That way I can access the loading dock.

My title at the supermarket is officially a "Closer," a part-time, interme-diary evening manager, who comes in at 8:00 P.M. to break down the product stacked and shrink-wrapped in the back-room storage area across from the three trailer bays. Then I wheel the grocery and non-food items on U-frames out onto the floor and into the appropriate aisles. At midnight, when the store officially closes to the public, I am alone, doubling as the stand-in Night Time Crew Chief, since my boss is out on disability. Lots of packing-out for one guy, and some would complain about being the lead player in this one-man circus.

Not I.

When the clock strikes twelve, I can finally go to receiving, cut the red plastic tie, and yank the chain hand over hand to crank up the ribbed steel garage door. There is a sheet on a clipboard hanging on a hook, and I will jot down the date and time that I broke the seal, writing in the "Reason" space, *Freezer maintenance.* Not that it really matters. I could write *Check,* or *Police dock area,* or *Verify timed lighting,* and no one would ever read it or care. The clipboard sheets are fail-safes to match up with the seal numbers in case anything is stolen.

But I'm not taking anything out of the supermarket tonight.

I'm bringing something in.

Cold box.

A flat-top freezer on rollers, eight feet long, three feet high, sometimes adorned with two sliding glass doors as cover panels, other times left bare and open-port. There are three freezer tubs outside on the dock apron that have gone down. They have required a tune-up for a week or so now, and I am always the first line of defense upper management "puts right on it," before they call in Redco with a real work order.

I bought my own freezer last year from an Acme that went out of business in a suburban location seventy miles west of here, and my used cold box looks exactly like the cold boxes out on the dock apron and the seventeen others positioned all through the store. There are twenty-three surveillance cameras on premises, yet there is only one camera that covers the loading dock area, set outside above the bay door and facing the woods behind the property. The apron yawns thirty-two feet off to the right, like a big lip hugging the wall. The dock is accessible to trucks at its far-right edge, so the camera records what goes in and out of receiving, but cut from view are the trucks themselves, let alone the three or four odd freezer units lined up at the far edge waiting for a tune-up.

When I go out, get my truck, back it in, and finally roll my personal freezer unit from the back bed and out across the apron, it will look as if I am bringing in one originally from the dock area. I have covered the top with a black cloth, since the grainy recording from the surveillance camera will simply make it look as if the shadows are playing across an empty cavity.

Not empty.

I move out to make my way to the employee parking area. Moments later, I am thankful that the security camera doesn't have sound, because the dock plate I left outside makes a sharp clanging when I drop it down between the dock bumpers and the rear side of the truck that I just backed in. It's dark inside my rig, and I undo the straps, feel my way to the back of her, and give a push, walking her out of the truck and back across the dock lip.

Once I am in, I pull down the bay door, shut the padlock, and tie a new red seal to it. I bend back down and push my cold box past the receiving shack, and through the red swinging doors of the meat room. It's cold, and that's good. It feels like work, like good work, like solid work, the type that grounds you. I put on a smock. I put on my goggles.

It's time to make a new doll.

—

Stainless steel work tables and cutting boards five inches thick. Sharpeners and scales and the auto feed mixer/grinder, and the poultry cutter and the patty former and the packaging unit that's always running out of plastic.

And of course, there's the industrial meat saw. I love the hulking, off-silver thing. Looks like something that came from a collector's basement, and I am attracted to the *nostalgia* of it, the way that every time I see it, that song in every grandmother's favorite musical comes to mind: *"Let's start at the very beginning. A very good place to start."*

Industrial meat saw.

To the eye of the amateur it could go in any metal shop and stand in as a stationary band saw. And while I certainly do appreciate the throwback look, the ripping blade scrolled onto it and the song in my head, I am just as thankful for the floor beneath it, all smooth red brick with a drain twenty feet long down center, rectangular grates, and seven-inch cork inlay surrounding it. After the work is done tonight, after I wipe my brow with a sterile cloth and soak the trade materials in my triple sink arrangement (clean, rinse, sanitize), after I fill the gun reservoir with concentrated industrial acid cleanser so strong it dissolves hair build-up in zoo animal cages, and after I blast the machines and blitz that smooth floor-brick with the wall mounted, gooseneck pressure sprayer, and finally squeegee the waste to the floor drains, I will have long removed any traces of DNA that might have been hanging around. Board of Health wouldn't have it any other way.

Meat saw.

I adjust the upper guard to accept stock up to nine inches. Overkill, I admit. Her throat is barely six inches in diameter, poor skinny thing, but I wouldn't want her to catch and snag. It is a real pain in the ass to have her by the waist and the hair, and get stuck in this preliminary, crude pass. Once it bucked the blade and caught up on her cheek. Yes. Number three, my only miscarriage.

I lean down and peel off the dark cloth.

Her name is Melissa. Lucky number thirteen. I haul her out, and she almost slips through my arms because I had her oiled and surrounded by forty-five Igloo Maxcold ice cooler bars. I adjust and walk her over to the saw, King Lear carrying Cordelia.

After I remove her head, I am going to eat her eyes. It is ritual. I don't particularly enjoy it, but certain obligations must be fulfilled; windows to the soul preserved. Feels right, like a hard lesson. Like morals. For the removal of these precious orbs I am going to try using the three-and-a-quarter-inch boning blade tonight, even though it will be like surgery under a rock. The serrated spoon doesn't really cut worth a damn, and it's annoying to get the remains of the extra ocular muscles caught between your teeth with no chance to floss right away.

Yes, there's a pop and burst, like a cherry tomato. No, it doesn't taste like chicken. Yes, I am careful when I do this because it's really gross if it flies out of your mouth and you have to eat it off the floor.

—

Now, with the preliminaries done, it is time for creation. It was a clean cut, no danglers, and the headpiece is up on the table. I have arranged my cutting tools biggest to smallest, and in three groups—Breaking and Skinning, Lance and Fillet, and Carving and Slicing—and I bring her head before me to move the damp hair off her lovely face. I tie it back in a ponytail for her, this long, loose, curly redwood perm with gold sunset highlights. The cavities where her eyes were seated stare out in pure, childlike wonder. She has straight teeth, sharp cheekbones, and featherings of wine-blush to accent them. Beautiful.

I reach for my first instruments and hold them over her for a moment, poised, ready, teetering on the brink of it. In my right hand I have the ten-inch breaking knife curved up like the weapon of some oily thief in a third-world desert marketplace, and in my left I hold the five-inch skinning blade, angled slightly, picking up gleam. A conductor about to start his symphony. The painter standing ready with two brushes instead of just one.

I lean in and set to work.

And the colors are spectacular.

—

I attended art school back in the day and studied Pointillism: small distinct dots applied in patterns that form images best seen from varied distances. Georges Seurat developed the technique in 1886, a branch-off of Impressionism, and it was quite popular until computer animation made it all rather obsolete. I suppose the most practical example of the thing nowadays is newspaper print, the dinosaur that can't be killed, but what has been lost in modern artistic relevance has been revived through metaphor.

We are too close up to our world nowadays to really "see" anything. Existence has become so ultimately accessible through virtual search engines that we have become a generation addicted to freeze-frames and short climaxes. We are egotistical self-hunters, obsessed with admiring the heads on the wall, our lives no more than the blur we ignore between texts and Facebook postings and shock-clips on YouTube. We have become background to our own theatrical presentations. Lifetime scrapbookers.

Time for some distance. Some breadth. Some perspective. Some awareness throughout the routine between poses.

Some wow down in the trenches.

—

There are gulls in a V formation, flying toward the promise of morning sun still hiding behind the horizon, the mountain tunnel, and the power station.

If I was pulled over and the trailer was searched right now, the given officer would find a very dead girl named Melissa Baumgardner lying rigidly in my used cold box, her face rearranged in what would seem random cuts, gouges, and ribbons, head clearly removed then sewn crudely back on, a thick wooden dowel lovingly inserted so far up her rectum that our good officer would be able to see the business end of it in the back of her throat if he or she took the time to force open her jaws.

Actually, the dowel is one of those antiquated window poles that janitors at my local elementary school found in the basement and threw out last month. And the cuts, gouges, and ribbons, the lacerations and the gradations I could only get right by wheeling in a deli meat slicer and making five passes, the second set of eye craters, the back-up nose hole and twin mouth-orifice I dug out of her left temple, cheek, and jawbone, all that would seem the grisly work of a madman.

But I am not interested in the view of the officer, nor in the report of some criminal psychologist. I know very well what I am.

I am an educated man who holds menial jobs like the rest of us caught up in this Trumpian, thinly disguised, middle-class recession...a creator, a messenger aiming his craft at your transitions, the times between movie shorts, the dead minutes that are the real moments of your lives: the trips to the bathroom, the times you make breakfast and fill out the Post-It Notes to stick on the fridge, the moments at work when you look at the clock, those stretches in the car when you drive between "meaningful" destinations.

I have mastered Pointillism, an art that can only be properly registered from a distance, and the cuts and gouges on Melissa's face are anything but random.

Today I am going to use this abandoned jobsite that has a dozer, a gargantuan pile of gray crushed stone, a walk behind saw, and a crane. I am going to park my rig as if I belong here, walk around the truck wearing my hard hat and safety vest like a veteran, haul out my masterpiece, and mount the end of the smooth stake I impaled her with into the unmarked flagpole base I stole from the ROTC storage garage back at school. It's a *Wizard of Oz* moment, yet a haunted one, because Melissa isn't a scarecrow with hay sticking out of her neck and a goofy smile cut through the burlap, but she is rather a blurry, bloody form under plastic.

I untie the bottom. I look both ways and see that the highway is momentarily clear. I reach up and unveil her.

I don't hesitate even for that last hungry, parting glance reserved for maestros and lovers. I put my head down, get back in my truck, and haul my ass out of there. The sun is about to break over the horizon.

According to the traffic patterns I studied, most vehicles frequent this stretch of road between 5:28 and 7:40 A.M. Early risers. Go-getters. My work will have left its mark long before this. I drive off at 4:55 A.M., and just as I round the curve that changes the sightline three hundred yards up, I look in my rearview and see headlights.

I smile.

My first customer!

According to what I have heard on the news, there will be an average of two hundred witnesses before rush hour, and around a hundred and fifty more before the police can make it out to the crime scene and take her down. The latter observers will just see a horribly scarred victim hanging limp on a pole, yet they are not my concern. It is the former, the virgins, the ones who speed by before traffic comes to a standstill, the early birds listening to their favorite radio stations, caught in the soundtracks of their lives, not thinking, not living, not really looking at the road before them because it has been memorized and placed into some fuzzy, collective background as they zone into the comfortable fabric of their respective transitions.

At a pass of fifty-five miles per hour, Melissa will offer a coy smile and mouth the words "love you" as her image in the rearview becomes a scarlet seductress fluttering off a series of winks, puckers, and kisses. At sixty-three miles per hour, she will crease her forehead, and then air-whisper the phrase "To arms!" to the receding image in the side-view of a crimson Native American princess, striped with war paint, shouting after you in a wide-mouthed cry of betrayal. And at anything over seventy-two, she becomes the red mask of terror, face rippling with G-forces, head slowly turning with you as you fly by, black eyes going from half-lidded semi-slumber to widened awareness, lips forming the words "mine forever," the image dwindling in the glass a petrified witch-queen, lips raised up and curdling.

Rest assured that each time I have left a doll, I have hit the next exit, circled back, and tried to film her on my cell phone in passing. No go. Thankfully, there is something about the craft that makes it camera shy. Even the steadiest hand yields nothing but muddy blurs of gore. Know that my art is pure, and that on some level religion is probably involved.

My girls are fashioned for bald observation, to form ghosts in the mind, phantoms guaranteed to wander through your dreams and appear sporadically in the fabric of your everyday routine as empirical memory. The real stuff. No instant replay, no secondary sources. Transitions become important again, and there is something to talk about. The scrapbooking, at least for a moment, takes second fiddle to a reality played out in real time.

Fear.

Live.

It is really a simple equation.

Pigeons flap into the air and then settle back down around the green monument modeled after some Age of Enlightenment guy with a powdered wig, stern eyes, flaring nostrils, and a long furling coat.

There is a brook and a walking bridge. There is a war memorial surrounded by decorator spruces and a garden with a fountain. Across the park due north, a larger cobblestone avenue stretches uphill to the law library, the amphitheater, and the bell tower. To the right, the park is bordered by 5th Avenue, which features a number of red brick buildings making up the University Health Center and a line of light poles, each bearing the school flag. This is a huge urban university, population more than thirty thousand, and their football team actually played a bowl game on ESPN last year.

It is my day off, and I am sitting on a park bench at the edge of the walkway. A male jogger goes by, and three janitors cross from the other direction, one of them pushing a gray cart with a bunch of spray bottles and an eighteen-inch floor broom sticking up out of the deep corner well. I see a security guard drive by on a ten-speed, and I note that like all the officers on foot I have observed, he wears a gray button-down jersey made by the same company that manufactures the three hanging in my closet at home. Of course, the circular shoulder patch is different, but I can buy a duplicate in their university bookstore's sports and decal section, then simply sew "SECURITY" in silver stitching along the bottom curve below the icon. The bike rider is the thirty-first security guard I've noticed on campus, and I walked it for a mere twenty minutes before sitting on this bench and watching the pigeons. Clearly the philosophy here is to flood the territory, create a uniformed presence, and it is likely that most don't know each other, especially the ones working the different eight-hour shifts. Finding the seam in those shifts and walking the shadows as "one of them" will be child's play, striding cap-brim down with "casual fatigue" beside my ten-speed, unmounted, as if my shift just recently ended. No questions, no worries.

And beneath the brim of my cap I'll be watching.

This is a perfect hunting ground: lots of trees and alleys and side streets and lots, construction areas with dark walkways bordered with tarps and scaffolding, and subway tunnels connected by poorly lit entrance stairways. This is a teeming labyrinth of lecture halls and cafeterias and auditoriums and apartments, all with easy access if you're smart enough to know where to find the service entrances. It is as easy as walking your ten-speed, identifying the blind spots between cameras, choosing your mark, and learning her come-and-go.

It is the top of the hour, and the park fills up with students. There is an Asian girl walking next to a tall nerdy guy with wild curly hair, a long neck, and big ears. He is a disaster and she appears not to notice, nodding in quiet support of his exaggerated exclamations, and yielding shy smiles when he clearly jokes poorly. She has straight black hair tied back with a thin green ribbon that matches her eye shadow, and she wears a black skirt. Slim hips. No backpack; she hugs her books in front of her chest. She has on black tights, and her legs are thin, toned, and strong. She walks like a dancer. They are five feet from me now, and he hits a home run, blurts something relatively clever, and she leans in toward him, turns up her face, surrenders a genuine smile that reaches her eyes, then the sun, the whole world.

I die a little inside and fall head over heels in love with the girl. I want to know her, comfort her, and find out her dreams and how she feels about her father. I want to caress her cheek with the back of my knuckle and hold her in front of a hearth fire.

I want to make her immortal.

Often when I am in the Target looking for cheap sweaters, or on the third floor of Macy's checking out coffee makers, or at Staples trying to find the right printer cartridge, people stop me and ask if I work there. I smile and gently admit I do not. Then they forget me. I am someone and I am everyone. I am the clerk at the service desk, the guy in the blue jumpsuit checking under the hood, the one who cuts your spare key at the hardware store, the man stocking shelves at Home Depot. You give me access to the pipes down the basement and always let me in to read the water meter. I run your credit card at the rental place, check your coat in the lobby, and bring up room service.

And you never bother to notice me.

[This story first appeared in *The Weird Fiction Review #2*, Centipede Press, Fall, 2011. It became the centerpiece of my fourth novel, *The Sculptor,* which will be published by Night Shade Books, fall, 2021. I am currently half done writing the sequel.]

PSYCHOS

Puddles

Doris Watawitz didn't like touching trash, and she didn't appreciate the fact that the Reading boys let rainwater sit in two uncovered Rubbermaids across the back alley for a week last month, next floating trash bags on top, poorly knotted. When the township garbage men left the stinking bags right there in their bins, ripped open by chipmunks no less, the older one had come out in shorts, an Iron Maiden retro tee-shirt, and black flip-flops. He'd re-bagged some of the remains and pushed over the trash bins, dumping the filthy moisture all over the uneven asphalt. He sprayed it off with a garden hose, but it did nothing but spread the brown, stinking water farther down the alley connecting the backyard fences and small garages of everyone who lived on Elmwood and Byberry Streets. There were chicken bones, rotted cherry tomatoes, and rank pieces of spotted lettuce littered into the crevice made by Jenny Walshberg's back garden bordering stones, and hair clotted cue-tips and cotton balls floating in a trench that ran behind Hugh McMenomay's grill area framed off by railroad ties with those pretty little planters on the top edge.

The Reading boy had tossed the new bags back into the cans and hauled them up the alley one at a time. He probably dumped them in the blue container they had at the park up the street, right next to the water fountain and the jungle gym. The alley smelled like disease for days, and though the stench had finally blown off, Doris still considered the asphalt of the back alley to be contaminated. As a result, her own trash and recycling ritual had become rather involved, and each few days she'd added a feature even though she knew it was all rather obsessive. First, she had to snap-on the plastic disposable gloves that brought up images of embarrassing physical exams, serial killers, and New York City perverts no matter what generation you hailed from. Next was the sacrifice of her pink Laverne and Shirley sneakers, banished outside now under the short overhang so she wouldn't track Reading germs back into the house, and then just for good measure, she'd started rolling her jeans to the knee so the cuffs wouldn't drag out there.

Tonight, she added a hairnet. She looked ridiculous, but who would be looking? She was just the nutty old broad across the way, and her son Michael hadn't been a regular visitor since his father died five years back.

Doris tied up the Glad bag, pulled it out with that particularly disgusting little wheeze of suction, rested it against the wall by the door, and then grabbed the mono bin with the bottles and plastic from under the sink. She strode across the kitchen, set down the bin, flipped the lock and pulled open the back door. Next, she had the trash bag in one hand, the recyclables in the other, and she gave the storm door a hip. Thunderheads had broken the four-day heat wave, but the air was an assault of humidity, all ghosted by a dark mist. It tasted like wet hay, and Doris broke a sweat. She shuffled out to the stoop, slipped her feet in her sneakers, and padded down the steps, arms spread like Jesus.

She'd have to wash off the door lock in there now, because she'd touched the Glad bag before flipping the catch. She'd also have to take a shower if the trash bag or recycling container happened to brush her clothing out here because of the same twisted logic that made her wash her hands after throwing out the plastic gloves. Part of her knew this made no sense whatsoever, but she'd long surrendered to the fact that her will and intuition were both better served blindly than with what she offhandedly considered "masculine reasoning."

Doris made her way down the walk. She angled right to avoid the butterfly bush spilling onto the ancient, turn-buckled pavers, nudged open the wooden gate, slipped through to the back alley, and then she stepped in a puddle.

For a bare moment it did not compute. There was no divot back here deep enough to hold this landmine of rainwater, for God's sake, she had walked through here thousands of times before and never had an incident. The water was tepid, going about an inch past her ankle, and Doris bit back the scream that had been building inside her. Back here the lighting was especially poor, and she couldn't really make out the booby-trap her foot had landed in, only that the surface had moving blotches, floaters. She pulled out and could feel something sticking to her bare Achilles heel. She dropped the bag, forced herself to set down the small recycling can as gently as possible, and reached down to pick off the leaf.

Her glove touched her heel and she gave a short shriek.

She approached the shadowed line of trash cans and fumbled through the rest in a blur. She pulled up the trash can lid, groped back for the bag, threw it in, and reset the top. She snapped off the outdoor recycling container's wide cap, groped desperately for the little bin, now lost down in the shadows, finally found it, and dumped the contents, hating that loud glassy clunking that made her seem like the neighborhood lush.

She returned the top to the container and stepped back. She was breathing heavily and her whole body swarmed with what felt like thousands of microscopic vermin dancing in and out of her pores. All around her were vague shapes, rough chalk-like outlines colored black and deep gray, houses rising up in the background, Billy Franklin's basketball net looming to the side like a dark praying mantis. She lurched for the gate, and her right foot made squelching noises. Oh, these sneakers were as good as thrown away already, and she would put these clothes right in the washing machine. Then she would shower with the water turned as hot as was endurable. Suddenly, it came to the forefront of Doris's mind that she never directly washed her feet. Nor her calves, she usually went down to the knee. Well, tonight she'd sit her frail, bony ass down flat in the tub and even soap between the toes. She'd use steel wool if she had to.

On the way back through the yard, Doris began thinking of all the things she would have to clean now, all the traces she'd need to eliminate.

Even if she left the sneakers outside to be tossed later, there was no way she could get into the kitchen without tracking in a bit of that puddle, so she would have to mop the floor before going to bed. On her way to the downstairs washer, she had to cross the corner of the den, so it would be necessary to get a fresh trash bag and tie it around her foot so she wouldn't have to wet-vac the carpet. She would bring a second bag in hand, dump the first one in the basement can she emptied the lint trap into, strip down to her bra and underwear, throw the clothes in the wash standing on one foot, tie up the second bag, get upstairs, get up to the second floor, set the second foot-bag in the bathroom trash, and hop into the shower with the pristine left foot. After washing off three times, she would walk the tall, thin, bathroom can down to the kitchen can, dump the small can with the foot bag, wash her hands, march back upstairs, and clean the tub out with Soft-Scrub. Then, one more shower for good measure and bed. Finally.

By the time Doris finished this dog and pony show, it was 1:17 in the morning.

At 2:19, she stepped in another puddle.

She had woken in the darkness with a start, not quite recalling the dream, but still feeling its potency. Something had been wrong, the world tilted. There was guilt involved and some impending doom at the edges, wild animals pacing and growling, her father, horn rimmed glasses buried somewhere in his fat, greasy face, cursing in Yiddish and storming around their small Brooklyn apartment adorned with the bright stained-glass lampshades, lots of marble and ritzy glassware, clowns with frowns juggling dead puppies, something.

She threw off the covers, swung out her feet, and rubbed her cheek. Her feet pigeon-toed in toward each other and she sighed. She'd never brought up her iced tea for the night stand, as the modifications to one ritual had overshadowed the execution of its subordinate. She ran her palms once over the skirt of the nightgown covering her skinny thighs, stood, put her hand to her back briefly, and walked toward the front corner of the bed. Right by the window by the bureau, she stepped in it. Water. Luke warm. And it reeked like trash.

This time Doris screamed long and loud. She gave a half turn, stumbled backward in the general direction of the bedroom doorway, and covered her mouth as her wet foot, the left one this time, made splatting sounds against the hard wood floor. It seemed like forever to get to the lightswitch.

The room flooded with brightness, and Doris blinked. Everything looked harsh, sharp-edged, menacing. Limping a bit, as if it would make her soiled foot infect the floor less, she made her way back around the bed, hand still frozen up at her mouth. When she came around the corner that led to the scene of the crime, where the bed and the wall made a short alley way to the nightstand, she saw it picking up a dull gleam. It was an oblong puddle of dark wetness about a foot long, and it had a squiggle of dirty sediment floating across the top like a snake. She gasped. There was also a leaf-stem in there, bobbing slightly.

And the smell was absolutely putrid. The closer Doris got, the sharper the odor came off the dank spill. This was trash water, Reading water. Doris darted her glance all around the room, her sharp face jerking into different positions. She felt she should call somebody. She looked up at the ceiling for a water stain, but it appeared to be bone dry. Her hands were clasped up by her throat now, and she crept a bit closer to the puddle. She gave a big sniff just to be sure, and Lord have a mercy, it was bad! In what seemed like centuries ago she'd worked in the Overbrook Delicatessen as a cashier, and had been sent to the walk-in box to get a few onions for Andy, the short order chef. She had reached into the pickle barrel on the shelf behind the steel whipped cream canisters and come up with brown mush between her fingers. At first she thought it was one of those jokes they all liked to play on the new girls, you know, like "Go get me a bucket of steam," but this was no prank. It was a rotten onion, and that pungent, rank odor was somewhere in this puddle, amidst what seemed akin to old, spoiled Lo Mein in one of those white take out containers with the dried, petrified sauce stains shadowed up under the top interlocking covers.

Doris went numb, went to auto-pilot. The cause, origin, and "possibility in the first damned place" of the puddle surrendered to this series of long-learned and deeply engrained motor functions involving her set of yellow Johnson and Johnson dishwashing gloves she left by the basement utility basin for emergencies, the bathroom can, two rolls of paper towels, some old contour sheets with paint-stains that she hoarded in the basement cabinet with the light bulbs and extension cords, her mop, the bucket that always seemed to collect hair in the bottom of it no matter how many times she scrubbed it and left it to dry upside down on an angle, a few capfuls of industrial-strength floor cleaner and some good old fashioned bleach. When she was finally finished, her room smelled like a hospital. Her fingers were red and her eyes, glazed. She showered for twenty minutes, skin still tingling as she toweled off afterwards. At 4:46 AM she crawled back under the covers, body aching, head like a stone.

At 7:56, she awoke to the smell of rancid trash mixed with sewage and an invasive sound, something odd, something that had interrupted the nearly imperceptible hum of the central air she'd paid an arm and a leg to have installed. The noise was coming from the bathroom, a slurping, slopping sound edged with that particular, echoed plinking that made one think of pipes and porcelain and dirty toilet bowls. She was lying rigid on her back. She rubbed her face with both open hands, and the noise stopped. She sniffed.

Something still stunk.

Doris pushed out of bed and looked down sharply when crossing the area where the puddle had been by the window. The slats of the blinds made bars across the place where the bleach had lightened the wood. She stepped over it and padded across the front of the bed. By the time she got to the doorway, she was holding her nose. By the time she turned the short corner to the bathroom, she was gasping for breath.

She could almost taste the smell, thick on her tongue, a molestation of her lungs. Suddenly, she realized what an absolute disaster area the bathroom was even *leading up* to the toilet. The floor tile was designed to "cover" as some salesman might say, or more particularly, hide dirt in the same manner as a youngster moving peas into the patterns on a dinner plate. There was a light layer of dust on the board behind the light fixtures on the medicine cabinet, and the soap dish built into the sink to the left of the faucet had traces of filmy residue topped off by a bobby pin with a few strands of hair twisted in it. The toothbrush holders were coated with the remnants of old paste on the inner sides of those little ovals, and the three-way pull out mirror was water-spotted. And what about the bowl brush and plunger casually left to the rear of the tank on the floor? How many times had they been submerged in water riddled with waste, and then simply stuck back there to fester? This whole room was getting a once-over, and a good one!

She edged up to the toilet, raised her eyebrows, went up on her toes, and looked over the rim.

The water was filthy gray, bubbles coating the surface, slightly darker scum crusted and settled at the edges. There were dark spottings under the bowl rim that had begun to drip back down like dirty tears and floating in the surface skin was a gob of what looked like a half pound or so of regurgitated mashed potatoes. In the center of it, just to the left like a cherry on top, was an object of firmer substance. It was a half-buried pine cone.

Doris almost vomited.

She also had to go. Number two. Now.

Doris stretched out her hand for the flusher on the far side of the tank, and then paused. Would the pipes handle the extra baggage in there? She had never tried to send down solids like this. Suddenly an image of an overflow came to mind, and she almost squatted and emptied right there on top of the mashed potato goop. There was no way she could handle, in this condition, that gray-brown sludge rising and flooding over the rim to the floor. First, it was the only bathroom in the house, and she would have no choice but to soil herself. Or go in the sink or the tub. And the possibility of the toilet refuse covering the floor, maybe seeping out to the hallway rug, plus feces in her underwear or partly sent down the drain where she washed her body or brushed her teeth was simply not a consideration. It just would not happen. It couldn't. God was not that cruel. She reached, held her breath, and flushed. There was that deep sound of water coming through the jets beneath the rim, and the mass lolled into its first revolution.

"Down," she thought, remembering not to bring the hand that touched the dull silver spoon-shaped steel to her mouth area. The angled side streams broke the dirty spots on the inner facing of the bowl and the whirlpool formed just below. The gob in the middle began its spinning act, a carnival Tilt-a-Whirl favoring one side, the pine cone following like some eager dog.

The load went down. There was a horrible moment where the bowl stood dead-empty, then gave a short cough of up-splash about two inches in height, (it made Doris jump), then a hesitant re-fill. It only came up with a half-bowl of semi-clear water by the time the mechanism had gone to its hollow, moaning phase.

A half-bowl. The silent sort of protest that let you know you almost had an incident, but the little invisible toilet soldiers went on overtime down there pushing the top-heavy load through the system.

Good enough. The cramps in Doris's stomach had gone to "code red" heaviness, and it was now or never. She dropped her underwear, flipped up the nightgown, sat hard, and let it come, praying she wouldn't have back-splash soil her upper thighs or worse.

Her Haines silk underwear with the soft pink flower shapes was touching the floor tiles. She would have to stick them in the wash now. Also the nightgown. Then, she was cleaning this bathroom soup to nuts. Then another change of clothes.

She heard something beneath her. A sputtering or bubbling, then silence.

Doris held her breath. Was that her waste dropping, or something else? She hadn't felt anything come out just now; she was in that in-between phase where the first portion had exited like a run-away train, and the second round was playing hard to get, aching a bit in the background and gathering itself for a final run.

She was vulnerable here. Suddenly she thought of those idiotic bimbos in horror movies who went down into dark basements in nothing but their panties. Ha. Child's play. Here Doris sat, thighs and privates laid bare to an open, exposed pipe-orifice, shielded by nothing but a thin veil of water. How idiotic was that? Who thought this up, some maniac? It was not like the fear she had as a young girl, that some scarred and water-rotted hand was going to come up from the depths of the drain and grab her where it hurt the most, but more, an adult's trepidation about sewage and drainage structures, and industrial accidents that hawked and belched and eventually exploded upward through the toilet - a fountain of brown, filthy, infectious waste product...yes, where *did* the poopy-khaka actually go when you flushed it down and out of mind, and what really stopped it from all rushing back home?

She squeezed. It hurt, but the relief would be...well, a relief. For some odd reason, her literature professor from Russell Sage came into mind, years and years ago, talking about dramatic structure, climaxes, and camel humps. It was sort of like pooping. Discomfort, pain, climax of release, then resolution. There was some Freudian connection here, mixed with a backward explanation of art imitating life, but when she focused on it the meaning eluded her and it turned into a chicken and egg scenario she didn't have time to bother with. Besides, she was done. She wiped, seven times, then flushed it all down the drain.

There was no incident. And the bowl filled back three quarters of the way this time. It was a sluggish surrender, but at least the water was clear.

Doris marched back into the bedroom with her nightclothes pinched between her thumb and index finger making the "OK" circle. Into the hamper they went. After turning back to the bathroom and washing her hands, she returned to the bedroom, flung open her bottom bureau drawer and got out the battle uniform: old loose Levi's with the back left pocket torn and curled down, her Philadelphia Eagles tee-shirt with the hole under the arm, and the cherry red bandanna with the white paisley designs. She dressed and put her hands on her hips. It was going to be a cleaning day.

She felt better already.

Down in the basement, she found the wooden horse brush with the hard nylon bristles and a spiral wire flue cleaner Frank had used to take rust off a handrail outside their old place in Overbrook Park. This was serious business. Lips pulled thin, she took the mop bucket out from its resting place by the red tool box and dehumidifier, strode over to the washer and dryer area, and flipped on the hot water spigot in the utility basin.

It gave a long groan and then there was a knocking that came from deep inside the pipes running behind the white veneer storage cabinets. She backed off a step, and the faucet piece actually bucked and jogged in its mount. Then it vomited out a dark fetid fluid that splattered along the bottom of the basin and kicked up to the left, spotting the swivel-face of her Swifter mop, the handle of an old corn broom, and the pockmarked cement wall they both leaned against.

Doris reached instinctively for the faucet knob with her face half turned away. She shut it off, but there was a last burp and fart from the bowels of the basin and a hard burst of brown discharge that shot-gunned downward, cascaded up off the wet bottom, and spattered syrupy gobs up into the air. A warm drop of it plopped right onto the end of her nose.

Doris Watawitz fell back two steps, she clawed at her face, she screamed, and stumbled upstairs, past the cloak and pantry area where she knocked her black cap with the sunflower on the brim off its hook to the floor. She rushed straight for the kitchen. She reached her hands in front of herself like a blind woman. She flipped up the handle of the faucet, cupped her hands under, and brought the affair to her face.

Immediately, she choked and sputtered. The liquid that had come from the spigot was denser than water, more a glutinous slime. She drew her hands from her face, and the substance stretched like phlegm, yellow-spotted with dark specs and flakes. Doris screamed long and loud. She wiped her face with her sticky hands and flicked the residue back into the sink. She snatched paper towels off the circular dispenser and pawed, then wiped, then rubbed so it hurt, she moaned, it smelled, she threw the soiled towels in the trash and groped for the phone on the wall. Tommy Preston, her plumber, was on speed dial, and she selected it through the scatter-picture that her tearing eyes presented. The smell was everywhere, trash, Reading refuse, ancient spoiled liver, maggot infested fat scraps, meat bones with driver ants crawling in and out of the rotted marrow in the pockets and joints, old emptied cans of white clam sauce with worms swimming lazily in the sickly green oil left in the crevices. She barked at his answering machine,

"This is Doris Watawitz at 227 Federal, you get over here right away, there is trash in my water and I have been contaminated, please, get over here right now, please."

A calmer, but no less shaken, Doris Watawitz spoke to her plumber Tommy Preston an hour and a half later in dulled, shocked disbelief and defeat. She sat at the kitchen table trying not to touch anything including herself, even though she had cleaned off with the four bottles of Deerpark she kept in the fridge. She had used the nine bottles left in the case by the back door to clean off the sink and then the residue spattered down in the basement basin. And that was the point, now wasn't it? Even the spots on the wall had come off too easily; they didn't even leave ghost-outlines. All the rags she had used were in the second rinse cycle by the time Tommy showed up, and the paper towels were in the trash outside. Of course, Doris could have walked him out there to open up the bags, but the freckled-phlegm from the sink had pretty much been the same as the dark basin sludge. Extremely soluble. He stood there now, fumbling with his red pipe-wrench.

"Like I was saying, Doris, no charge. I flushed the pipes, checked the connections, and snaked the toilet. You're good. There's no trace of this muck water you told me about, and besides smelling like disinfectant, there's no odor in here. Really."

Doris just stared. Usually, she enjoyed Tommy's visits. He was a gentle soul and he was cheap, usually nothing over a hundred and fifty. And he always cleaned up after a job. A lot of these blue collar workers would fix the shower head, but leave their boot marks in the tub. Tommy was considerate. He was of her son Michael's generation, yet not so tragic, more accepting of his lot in life. There was a smudge on his cheek that Doris dearly wanted to scrub for him, but she no longer trusted the sink, her perceptions, or her ability to interpret social codes. She looked at her raw, red hands, then back up.

"The sink water is clean now?"

Tommy shrugged.

"I can't say it was ever tainted, Doris. Look."

He walked over to the faucet and flipped it up. The plume of water that came down was that beautiful, silvery clear she had come to love and depend on.

Doris paid him fifty dollars anyway. For the trouble. At first, he would not accept it, but finally caved when he seemed to realize it was more important to her than to him. He left with his head down, ducking under the kitchen archway, studying his work boots on his way to the door.

And five minutes after his exit, she smelled trash again, faint somehow, as if coming from two rooms away.

Doris set her jaw, scoured the house, and couldn't find the source. After checking all the garbage cans, she smelled the sink water, then got on her knees and sniffed in the toilet. She stuck her nose in the basement wash-basin and took a whiff up under the hot water boiler, earning herself a smudge of floor grit swashed along her cheek and a peppering of dust bunnies up across the left side of her hair bandana/bonnet. Nothing. The smell was distinct yet remained distant. In fact, when she nosed in toward the particular water outlet being investigated, the smell seemed to recede entirely, giving way to the more standard rust, cleanser, pipe flux, or soapy fragrances normally left to linger around appliances and fixtures connected with running water.

By the time Doris was done her stink-hunt, she was filthy and dead on her feet. She hadn't eaten in almost twenty hours, hadn't slept more than three last night, and had neglected to start the day off with her habitual shower. The smell had backed off now to a mere whiff, but at least the water was clear. She went up into the bathroom, stripped down, and showered without incident. Afterward, she tossed her old clothes into the hamper, again washed her hands, dressed numbly, and went downstairs to make herself a sandwich.

Before she could even get out the Miracle Whip, she smelled it again. Faint, yet present. Not from another room, but rather...

No, it couldn't be.

Doris began sniffing herself: hands, insides of the elbows, up under the arms. She even sat hard on the floor and struggled her feet up to her nostrils.

Frank had gone through a period during his last seven years or so during which his body omitted a salty yet horrid odor, like bad seaweed, old man smell. Did she sense this on herself? Was it faint because she was used to it by now, only picking it up at the farthest fringe of perception?

No. Her body seemed to smell just fine, Ivory and Dove invisible solid, quaint and pretty.

But when her nose wasn't buried in a body part so to speak, the faint and lingering trash smell came back, off to the side, just out of reach.

Wait.

Wait just one minute.

Moisture was the theme here, right?

Doris looked around as if suddenly under scrutiny. She was still sitting on the floor, and she slid the bottoms of her feet so her knees were pointing up. She hunched down, squinted her eyes, and spit into her hand. She sniffed, and it gave off no odor at all, in fact, the already faint trashy smell faded to near nonexistence. She pushed up with the other hand, padded over to the sink, washed off her hands with a double pump of dish soap, pulled off some paper towels, and dried.

Then she smelled it again. Present, then not, pronounced, and next the shadow of an odor. She looked at the sink, then darted her glance to the fridge, catching the whiff, then losing it, back and forth, clearly a pattern.

Then she had it, though the family doctor wouldn't believe it.

She didn't like it.

Oh, she didn't go for this one God-damned bit, in fact, she tried to actively deny it with every fiber of her physical and emotional being for the next three days, lasting all the way until Friday at nine or so in the morning when she just couldn't take it anymore. Tuesday wound up being the day of denial, regression right into the cave with a William Lashner mystery novel she just couldn't finish, a Lifetime movie about a husband cheating with his therapist that she could barely stomach, a half hour of the Barefoot Contessa making something with carrots and celery that came off simply vile, and a last ditch run at the computer, surfing for shoes. Then she was up all night.

Wednesday, she stumbled around the house rearranging the bedroom and moving the furniture in the living room. She went for a walk, came back, cleaned the entire basement including the short, dark area under the stairs and the corner by the fuse box, then went out to the garage to throw out a hoard of rusty gardening tools, holiday decorations, and old papers in plastic storage bins hiding behind stacked lawn chairs, a yard umbrella, and her grandson's abandoned Kettler tricycle. Doris ended the day by looking through antiquated photo albums with only the vaguest of recognition. Finally, she tried to shut down by polishing off a bottle of Inglenook she saved for emergencies, but it only made the night thicker, her thoughts darker, and her breath shorter. She went the night without one wink of sleep, and rose the next day with a galvanizing headache.

She worked it off. She pulled down the submarine stairway that led to the attic, moved the old cedar chest and hickory crib they never got rid of over by the dinosaur of a computer they fought with back in the early 90's, the love seat with the stuffing coming out of the left arm, and the broken twenty four foot step ladder, just so she could get at the dirt and pollen and spider webs that had gone so long without being disturbed that it felt as if she was in some museum from another world. She hauled up her cleaning supplies and vacuumed and dusted and washed and polished, and her bones were aching, and her joints were screaming, and her head felt like lead ball. It was 4:47 Thursday afternoon.

She maneuvered down all of her cleaning materials. She washed the buckets, shook out the brooms, hot-rinsed the brushes, and threw the various rags away. She showered and stretched out on the bed.

And each time she moved, the smell came back.

She willed herself to take a nap, forced her eyes closed, denying with everything she could muster that the villain here was the one source of moisture impossible to get to.

She thought she slept for four minutes somewhere around midnight, but she couldn't really be sure. The evening lasted forever, and she actually observed the entire sunrise as fingers of light slowly crept across her room the next morning. Amazing how drawn out the process actually was. Somewhere deep down and far off she wondered if the novelists and songwriters should have been forced to be real witnesses to this phenomenon before writing and singing about the so-called romantic value and collecting royalties, but the ugly whiff that suddenly worked into her nostrils erased all desire to play art critic.

Doris looked back up at the ceiling she had been staring at most of the night and the smell vanished. Her head ached and her eyelids felt like tombstones. She closed them, and the smell drifted back.

Enough was enough.

She staggered into the bathroom and showered, sitting on the floor of the tub and letting the water thunder all around her. She toweled off, dressed, and went down stairs. Put on a hat and her Nike walking sneakers.

Time to solve this.

She walked out into the oppressive mid-summer blanket of heat.

To go to Home Depot.

—

Stevie Healy drove home from work exhausted, goofy orange apron rolled up and tossed in the back seat of his vintage Camero. He didn't like being questioned by the cops. It was all too close to the way those narcs had gone up one side of his twenty-four year old piece-of-shit brother and down the other last year when they had busted into the house, stormed the basement where he had been playing "Call of Duty: Modern Warfare," and found three pounds of weed under his beanbag chair. But the lady that had bought the appliance this morning had been weird, easy to remember, and the Sergeant promised that Stevie's obligation would end after a detailed description of the transaction.

She had bought an industrial grade ShopVac, the biggest and strongest model they had on the floor, highest amperage, the most CFM, a picture on the cardboard crate's side panel of the nozzle sucking up a bucket full of number twelve by three inch machine bolts. He had wheeled it to the parking lot, and muscled it into her car for her.

Weird.

She had on jeans that were too short at the ankles, a wrinkled blouse, and a hat with a sunflower on the brim. Her face was red from more than the heat it seemed, and her fingers were raw. It looked like she hadn't slept for a week, and her eyes kept tearing. She was glancing all around the vac aisle like a crazy person, wiping her nose, and dabbing at her eyes with this old hankie. Then the really creepy thing happened.

She held forward the damp, wrinkled handkerchief, and asked Stevie to sniff it. She wanted to know if it smelled like garbage.

He hadn't known whether to laugh or to barf, but he'd recovered with some lame excuse and rushed off for the forklift. He had gotten down the vacuum, purposely engrossed in the process so he wouldn't have to look at her, and he remained similarly embroiled while sticking it on a hand truck. The rest was a bit foggy in his head until he stuffed the thing in the back seat of her station wagon from God knows what year and turned down the dollar tip she offered.

She said "goodbye," then, as if they'd known each other for more than twenty-three minutes. He had tipped an invisible hat, and walked off, hands in his pockets.

The cop said Doris Watawitz's son found her an hour later after she blew a circuit that caused a blackout that spanned a one-block radius. "Get ready for your Greek tragedy," he had said, Officer Burns was his name, and Stevie had no idea what he was talking about. Still, the image of what Burns next divulged *would* stick with Stevie Healy well into the night and the next couple of weeks. It would, in fact, haunt him even when he thought he'd moved past it, making his eyes tear up. It would become a thing with him, a condition, an annoyance that would hound him for years.

She was found sitting on her kitchen floor, dead of a heart attack, vacuum attachment still in the grip of her red boney fingers. Her head was drooping to the side, her mouth ajar, and there were black craters where her eyes had been. They were later found in the belly of the vacuum.

There were thick trails of blood striped down her cheeks, and a note left on the table.

"In the end, we are alone," it said.

And next to it, was a pair of dishwashing gloves and a plastic bottle of Palmolive cleanser.

[This story first appeared in *The Weird Fiction Review #1*, Centipede Press, 2010.]

The Exterminator

Evan Shaw was lanky. He had a lean face and boyish sandy hair he kept long across the eye so he could clear with that haughty jerk of the head when it suited him. He was a tee shirt and skinny-jeans kind of guy, sweaters and moccasins, hoodies and retro-Keds, a casual guy, the kind of twenty-seven year old that had joked his way through high school, breezed through college with a degree in communications he had no use for, and put himself on track to become a thirty-something man's man, king of the golf outing, lord of the watering hole. He was the phone-tanker at a power tool distributorship in West Philly, and it bored the hell out of him. He rented in the 'burbs and cooked a mean paella. He often painted on Saturdays. Guilty pleasure. Oils on canvas. He never showed that stuff to his co-workers, but he and Eddie Boylan, the shipping assistant, sometimes held bachelor parties for no reason.

He had a 2009 tan Toyota Corolla passed down to him by his mother, and he always had his stuff tossed around in there because it was a shit-heap. There were empty Deer Parks strewn in the back along with a few brown jugs for re-fills at The Iron Hill Brewery, a backpack with a busted strap, a couple of ref's jerseys for weekend Flag Football, a dirty squeegee, a broken umbrella, and his Santa Cruz Shark Dot forty-inch long board.

It was the day before Halloween and Evan was driving sort of fast. Clemson was playing Florida State starting at 6:00 Eastern standard, and he'd forgotten to tape it. He'd originally intended to cut out of work early, but Horowitz had pinned him at the loading dock with questions about how to properly tag some repairs. It held him up for thirty-five minutes. Evan prided himself on the fact that he got along with everyone: diesels, wise-guys, dumb-asses, and even the sensitive intellectual types, usually electricians and specialty carpenters. Still, his sincerity with Horowitz had come off a bit condescending. He would have to work on that.

He hawked up and spit out through the open window while curving past the bowling alley.

Then, fuck, his nose started bleeding. He recognized it immediately; hotter and quicker than snot, and he could feel a runner drip over his lip. He sniffed in hard, tilted back his head, and felt along the seat for a tissue or something. He'd had a half-crushed Kleenex box with the cartoon rat from that old Disney movie on it, but to the best of his memory it had migrated to the trunk, God knew why.

He strained his eyes down at the road and looked for a place to pull over. He had just passed the D.M.I. Home Supply, and the parking lot for the commuter train was on the far side of the street, no light for the left turn, yeah flippin' stupid! The trees were a red and orange blur and the asphalt was a slick black mirror with leaves stuck in the wet gutters like paste.

Evan pinched the bridge of his nose between his thumb and index finger, and as he passed Ardmore Avenue, he felt a sneeze coming. This would be an interesting test. Sometimes he had a bleeder for just a minute or so, but now it would be determined whether or not he was going to have a gusher. He moved his head down a bit, studied the road, memorized his position as opposed to the oncoming vehicles, and let his mouth come open.

His nostrils flared out, his eyes squeezed shut, and he sneezed.

No blood, no gusher. He would have felt it immediately.

He opened his eyes to check and possibly realign his place on the road, and he saw something in the afterimage left by the sneeze. It was right on his eyes like a brand. Behind the image, the road was clear through the windshield, but this thing, this "crazy face" stayed superimposed for a few good seconds, sharp and detailed.

It was the head of a circus clown with fat cheeks that had blush-dots on them. The thing was wearing a big cone-shaped party hat with tinsel bursting out of the tip like a park fountain, and its wiry hair was painted in rainbow colors.

It had wide-set black eyes that protruded the way they did on spiders or lizards or birds.

There was no nose, just a furrow with two seed-shaped breathing holes slanted inward, and its grinning mouth was crammed with wriggling worms. The image stood on Evan's eyes for a moment, then started to fade.

He shook his head hard. He blinked twice and widened his eyes. He touched his nostril, checking for blood almost as an afterthought, and banged a right on Bryn Mawr Avenue. He passed the hospital and the library, then doubled back a block on Lancaster. When he parked in the handicapped spot in the Staples lot, he realized he was sweating.

What the fuck *was* that? He wasn't one to like carnivals, and he'd never actually been to a circus. He knew that clowns were also a cliché horror thing with a cult following, but they had never really interested him in that way either. Political thrillers tickled his fancy more than those jack-in-the-box slashers. He shut the car off and put both hands up on the steering wheel. He'd never paid attention in psych class back in high school, but he wondered now how this thing with wet black eyes and greasy-looking worm teeth had made it into his awareness. For something to come into the conscious, didn't it have to be planted somewhere in your experience?

He opened the door and pushed out of the vehicle. He stepped in a puddle and soaked his sneaker. He cursed softly. Then he laughed. It was warm out for this time of year, drizzling so slightly it felt more like mist. He ran his free hand through his hair and it comforted him, the memory of the image already tapering off. Maybe it was the gentle breeze on his face. It felt good. Sweet and damp. Evan loved the autumn. It meant burning leaves, and Thanksgiving, and bare trees scratching portraits into the gray, naked sky.

Made you want to stop for a moment, cross your arms across your chest, and marvel at the wonder of things.

He pushed back into the vehicle, turned the key in the ignition, and started thinking about change, about possibilities. Maybe he would take a class or something, go back to school, go into teaching.

He went for the back exit of the parking lot because there was a traffic signal there after you wrapped around. Was it slower than just banging a left on Lancaster against the flow of traffic straight out of the Staples lot? For sure. Was it worth it to go the long way? Of course. He'd already missed kickoff and ESPN showed a lot of the big marquee games later anyway.

He passed the Viking Culinary Center, pulled up, and waited for the light. Across the street in the Walgreens parking lot, a woman with blonde hair braided in long pigtails got out of a maroon Dodge Caravan. She was wearing a white back-ring halter top, jean shorts cut high enough to see the pockets, and gladiator sandals. She dropped her keys and bent over. Something in the background moved, and Evan's eyes drifted upward.

There was something across the street in the second-floor picture window. Movement. Colors.

Evan had the sudden desire to do the cliché thing and rub his knuckles in his eyes. The Walgreens used to be a Barnes and Noble bookstore. The second floor had the sports books alongside the children's racks, with the low brown tables, mini-chairs, and the reading rug. There was also a gourmet coffee shop that was surprisingly dope, but the whole floor had been left vacant when the drug store took over the property.

Except now there was a clown up there. He was in the window. This one had a big fireman's hat and a mop of bright orange hair frizzed out to the sides. He had a huge, red bulb of a nose and a reflective collar piece that curved up behind the back of his head like that of melodramatic old-school French royalty. He was wearing a baggy tinsel-green jumpsuit with oversized buttons that had propellers that moved. His shoes were enormous duck-foot cushions with coiled circular twirlers on the toes that gave the optical illusion that they were disappearing into themselves and simultaneously growing as

108

they spun. He had on a skull cap, white face paint, and big curving arches drawn high above the wet black eyes that protruded.

There was a man with him, pudgy and balding, small in comparison. Looked like a clerk or an accountant having a bad day. He was wearing pleated Khakis, a sweat-spotted dress shirt, and a surgical mask even though the statewide requirement had been lifted ages ago.

Boyfriend's problem wasn't the Coronavirus.

His problem was the psycho-clown towering over him, making to grab him from behind.

But Pudgy-face pulled an amazing move out of his back pocket at the last moment, faking-left and then bursting to the right out of sight deeper into the space. The clown bear-hugged thin air, straightened, and put his hands palm-up in a big shrug. Then he leaned down a shoulder, dug at some imaginary dirt with the sole of his foot, and galloped out of sight into the darkness.

A moment later the pudgy dude was back at the glass, heaving for breath, making the surgical mask mock the shape of his lips every other half-second. He glanced back and tried to suddenly run left for real this time, but the clown emerged suddenly and grabbed him by the back of the collar. Clotheslined, the dude's feet kicked out from under him. The clown tried to yank him back across like a sack of rags, but he lost his grip for a second. The dude fell toward the glass and caught his balance just in time to press up against it. His eyes were wide with terror. He pounded the window with his open palms, Evan saw it shake with the contact.

The woman who had just gotten out of the minivan did not hear a thing. She closed her door, adjusted her purse, and reached up the sides of her ribs to straighten her bra with an exasperated little tug and twist with both hands. Evan usually took his time to savor that particular move, but was compelled to glance back up at the glass. The pudgy dude was facing sideways now, trying to run, clawing at his neck as the clown had regained his hold at the back of the collar. With his free hand, the huge circus creature drew something from the back of his jumpsuit. It was a meat hammer. He raised it up and looked right at Evan. He nodded his head as if they were sharing the cutest little secret, and then he brought the weapon down.

The head of it disappeared into the dude's skull. Blood splashed the window, and sprayed the clown up the cheek. A black tongue squirted from the thing's mouth and lapped at the splatter, leaving blotch-lines ghosted in the face paint. The dude was going through convulsions and a milky discharge was coming out of his mouth. The clown yanked out his weapon, and slyly looked out at Evan. One black eye winked. Then he lowered his face to the back of the dude's head and let the worms in his gums start the feeding process.

The light turned green and Evan hit the gas. He screeched across Lancaster Avenue, bumped into the parking lot, took up two spaces on a slant, and jumped out of his car like a plainclothes cop in a bad TV movie. Still, the moment he passed through the doors of the store his courage withered. He was going to blurt out that there had been a murder up on the second floor, but he had not planned for the change in atmosphere. The dark sky and wet streets lost their mystery in here under the fluorescents. It was like watching old "Twilight Zone" episodes in the living room with the lights off, then having Ma come in, flick on the overheads, and start grilling you about fourth-period calculus.

Up one of the aisles there was an elderly man wearing an arm cast that was dirty and yellowed at the edges where his fingers poked through. He had his head tilted up so he could look down through his bifocals, checking out the laxatives. There was a plump African American woman in a caramel-colored pants suit waiting in front of the photo counter. She had on heavy foundation and jumbo triangular earrings that kept jangling back and forth as she spoke in an angry grin to a bow-legged teen who wore a Walgreens vest and was passing by pushing a mop in a bucket. There was a small grouping of mainline moms over by the pharmacy having an animated conversation in a blur of yoga pants, ponytails, sunglasses, and cleavage.

Up front, there were two counter girls in blue smocks with name tags, but the shorter one with all the face piercings was counting her drawer. The plainer one with auburn hair tucked behind her ears was managing a line five customers deep.

What was Evan supposed to say?

"Hey y'all! There's a dead dude upstairs with his head bashed in, yo! The clown with the worms in his mouth did it!"

Couldn't you get in trouble for bringing out the cops for what seemed like a prank?

He walked toward the middle of the store and noticed that his wet sneaker was squelching. The blonde woman with the short jean-shorts and gladiator sandals was squatted down on her haunches, sifting through the beauty products on a low shelf. Close up now, Evan noticed that she had pretty fingernails, half blue and half white, with silvery trim.

"Hey," he said.

She pushed up and balanced the thin steel handles of the shopping basket on her forearm. She had nice eyes, heavy mascara. Her nose was a bit too long, but she had that hourglass thing going for her. Evan suddenly wondered if there was any blood left on his upper lip. In all the excitement he had never checked in the rearview.

"So tell me you didn't hear someone pounding on the window out there," he said.

"Say what?"

"When you got out of your car. You dropped something and someone was banging on the second-floor window. You're telling me you didn't hear anything?"

She stopped chewing her gum for a second and put all her weight on one leg. With her free hand, she took a long, braided lock of hair and tossed it behind her shoulder.

"Fucking stalker."

She brushed past and Evan felt his face redden up. He balled his fists and moved to the back of the store. They had only really used about a third of the ground floor. There was new drywall in the rear by the auto parts, and a steel door with diamond wire in the window-glass. Evan tried the knob and it was locked. He moved in closer and could see a thin darkened hallway and a row of temporary lockers. If there was a stairway back there it was not in this sightline. And Evan could not remember where it had been in the Barnes and Noble anyway.

He strode back to the front of the store and approached the counter. The girl counting bills didn't even look up.

"I'm closed."

The curved barbell ring in her eyebrow looked painful. Her hair was tied back and thrust through a leather Concho, or whatever you called that oval piece with the stick running through it.

"How can I get upstairs?" Evan said. He bent down a bit. "Hello?"

"You can't."

"I left my jacket up there."

"No ya didn't."

"Yeah, I did. Yesterday—"

"It's locked and they knocked out the stairway. Ya got to take the elevator and it's out of service."

She looked up and cocked her head. She had a sharp face and electric jade colored contacts. The nose stud was subtle, but the horseshoe lip ring was just a bit much. She smiled a little.

"Watcha want, anyway?"

Evan was suddenly attracted to her and he did not understand it in the least. He sensed that she sensed this and he looked away, past her shoulder. His eyes settled on a folding chair, behind her to the right beneath the cigarette display. There was a green jumpsuit laid across it and on the floor was a big fire hat with frizzy orange hair stapled to the brim. She turned to look where he was looking, her eyes staying with his as long as possible. When she turned back she had her mouth opened slightly. She was curling her tongue around the silver stud that was pierced through it.

"It's a return," she said. "The kid said it was too baggy."

Evan went up on his toes and leaned across a bit. The suit was nowhere near big enough to have fit the thing he saw in the window. And this hat had a golden label on the front that said "Engine 52." The one he had seen did not.

Maybe someone stuck on the label for show.

"Can I see that?" Evan said.

"Sure."

But as she turned he changed his mind. The momentary pull she'd had on him was gone, and he didn't want his fingerprints on that thing on the chair. He walked toward the exit and looked along the ceiling for surveillance cameras. He didn't see any and it did not really matter. The guy didn't come in through the front entrance and he probably wasn't even up there anymore. If the counter worker was unaware of an access point, the escape would be just as invisible as the entry. There was probably a ladder back by a cutout behind some piping near an old emergency exit or something.

Even if the thing cleaned off the window and took the dude's body with him there had to be some trace of DNA left up there. Evan knew what to do. He'd get in his car, call the police on his cell, and anonymously report what he had seen. He'd just ignore the question of why the pudgy guy was up there in the first place. He'd just leave out the part about the wet black bug-eyes and the moving worm-teeth. He'd let the professionals figure it out for themselves.

But he never called the police.

He swerved back onto Lancaster Avenue, maneuvered around an old bat in a Mini Cooper going about three miles an hour and got stuck in the turning lane two blocks down. Just before hitting the last digit in 911, something made him glance to the left.

What he saw in the dark windows of the building across the street was not of this earth.

It was a violent infestation.

It defied rational definition and made his skin crawl.

The huge windows were sectioned off by what appeared to be three-by-three white square frames. Through the glass portions, Evan could see that the "things" covered the floor ten to twelve feet high and wall to wall about fifty feet across. They were man-sized and swarming over and across and underneath and between each other. Evan had once seen news footage of rats that had overrun a section of a downtown junkyard, crawling across the bodies of their mates, and this was the same plague on a larger scale. The movement was a constant and violent blur of bright satin colors, arms intertwined and writhing through legs mixed in with flashes of red painted smiles and stretched balloon party pants. There were ball noses and squirting joke flowers and bowler hats being crushed and popping back into shape and French berets slipping in and out of the cracks along with white gloved fingers and leggings with stripes on them all knotted up and wriggling between and around wristlets with bells, neck frills, gaudy vests, and ruffled-up cummerbunds.

There were people walking past on the sidewalk, and no one was noticing.

Evan jerked the wheel to the right, hit the gas, and sped away down the avenue. He knew he wasn't crazy. If he had gone insane he wouldn't recognize all the normal stuff. He'd be in fairytale la-la land, dribbling on his shirt, picking at his hair, and believing he was someone like Gandhi or Kim Kardashian.

This was something different.

There was a rip in the fabric here, bursting with vermin.

The face of Rudi DiDomenico flashed into his mind. Rudi was a counter customer who came in with a batch of homemade wine every year around Easter. He was short and always wore overalls and flannel even in the summertime. Rudi drove a van with a model of a huge bug on top of it. They called it the roach-wagon. Rudi was an exterminator, and Evan had worked out a deal with him where the guy bought his extra long straight shank carbide bits in bulk at thirty-five percent above cost.

Rudi had once said that the key to stopping an infestation was to find the "point of entry."

Evan raced through the intersection at City Line Avenue and sped back toward West Philly. He wouldn't be home for a good while.

—

By the time he got to the tool house, opened the front gate, and pulled it shut behind him, it was almost dark. Mr. Jarvis had given him the building's alarm code for the sake of emergencies, but that was a year and a half ago. He hoped the boss hadn't changed it.

He walked past the red bay doors and rounded the corner of the building. The steel door to the shop had a small window made of safety glass. There was no light coming through it, and the overhead halogen in the back parking area was off. Good. Sometimes Joey Sanantonio liked to stay late and tinker with his vintage Mustang out under the corrugated overhang so he could save money on garage space. Tonight he had cut out at closing with the rest of them.

Evan took a last look around. The back of the lot on the neighborhood side was bordered by cinderblock walls with razor twine curled in at the top. Back roadside next to the entrance, there was a plot choked with weeds and occupied by a couple of arrow boards they tried to rent to PennDOT every now and again, and back across Grays Ferry Avenue, the power station was dark and quiet for all but a nearly inaudible hum. He could smell someone burning trash. He opened the door, disarmed the alarm, and turned on the back-office light in the repair shop. The dull glow made long shadows come off the plastic invoice trays, the red repair bins stacked in steel racks anchored to the wall, and the calendar with the girl in short-shorts and work boots posing in front of a miter saw.

Every mechanic had his own work station arranged with various power tools on long wooden slabs, each with a shop vice anchored to a corner. Evan walked over to Paulie Frehley's bench and picked up a Metabo four-and-a-half-inch grinder. He flipped it over. It had an eighth-inch cutting wheel on it. OK. So now he would have to go into the first aisle and get a grinding wheel as well as the other stuff. He grabbed a flashlight and went out into the warehouse.

When he returned to the bench he set down a jigsaw with a metal cutting blade, a four-and-a-half-inch grinding wheel, some rivets, a handful of number twelve self-drilling screws, and a fourteen-inch diamond blade still in the cardboard. He unpacked it. He put it in the bench vice. He reached across for the mallet and a file with a thin end on it, and he started knocking off the segments. They were only good for concrete. When he had a bare edge, he put on a pair of goggles and plugged in the grinder.

After burning up three abrasive wheels and trashing seven jigsaw blades, he was ready for welding. He went out by the forklifts and approached the scrap pile to the side of a pallet of generators. He found a length of two-inch-wide pipe that was about five and a half feet long. He brought it to the shop and got back to work.

By the time Evan pulled up in front of his apartment the moon was at its highest point, and some DJ was talking about how you could do late night radio in your underwear with a fifth of Jack Daniels by your elbow without management ever knowing it. Evan shut off the car, gathered his stuff, and went up the short stairway. He entered his apartment and left the lights off. He didn't need them anymore.

━

"Hey, ma."

"Why ain't you at work? It's eight o'clock in the morning."

"I called out. I had to take care of some things. Did I wake you?"

"I was reading my horoscope. What kind of things?"

"Shopping."

"What, do you need money?"

"No, ma. I'm good."

"What's that mean, you're good? You want to talk to your father?"

"What's he doing home?"

"His back went out again."

"Naw, that's OK. Tell him not to believe everything he hears."

"What's that mean?"

"I love ya, ma."

"What?"

"Dad needs new shoes. Last time I was over I saw him limping, favoring the right."

"Hey, are you sick or something?"

"Bye, ma."

Evan Leonard Shaw looked around his apartment. He hadn't slept. He didn't remember not sleeping, but had no recollection of lying down. He had no recollection of anything.

His fingers were aching.

His tubes, solvents, hog's hair brushes, and pallets were littered across the black dining room table that he bought two years ago at IKEA. The red canvas director's chairs that went with the long black table were shoved into his coat closet along with his down comforter, his four pillows, five trophies (one back from his nine-year-old little league team, The Angels), and thirty-seven novels that had recently shared space with the trophies on the inlaid shelving by the fake fireplace. There was paint on the bed sheets. Lengthwise, there was now a pair of eyes, a bulb nose, and a grin. The forehead was cut off by the rectangular limitation, but the tongue was continued down the side of the bed so it could spill out onto the carpet.

The inlaid shelves, those that had been one of the primary reasons he took the place for such a high monthly, were now bare. They helped form a picture of a clown-giant as if seen from under water, huge balloon-like feet across the bottom, then legs with ruffles at the knees, all pyramiding up the slats like waves until the head was but a dot on the front edge of the top mantle.

The exposed bottoms of the pots hanging off the rack in the kitchen were covered with dots and smears. At first it looked like random, yet somehow organized, paint splatter. From the stove five feet away, however, it was a close-up smiling Bozo, red hair bursting to the sides, wide eyes, and a grin that stretched along the bottom frying pans. From the dishwasher at the far edge of the space, however, the nose became a medal hanging around the neck of a hairless clown wearing a chef's hat and flipping red pizzas. In the bathroom, there were clowns riding bicycles on the three sections of mirror, but when the two outer pieces folded out, the reflections joined to make a smiling elephant clown that turned into a frowning hippo clown if the angle was altered a fraction of an inch.

The television was on, its screen painted over in thick strokes that formed a smiling clown with deep dimples. The inside of the mouth and the eyeballs were not painted in, so the moving images beneath made it seem as if he was communicating with the wall clowns across from him. They wore striped shirts, suspenders, and white flood pants and they were painted on either side of the stereo unit, each with a sledgehammer raised in the ready position. The rest of the collage filled the balance of the wall space, one portrait bleeding into the next. There were clowns with big bow ties and clowns with red smiles. There were clowns with checkered bibs, and clowns that were pouting. There were Fedora hats and police hats, and little British hats, and pirate hats perched on bald heads and those with wooly hair sticking out over the ears. There were fat clowns and thin clowns, and clowns with teeth and clowns with mini-trumpets that had little rubber squeeze bulbs on the ends.

He did not recall painting them.

They stared at him and he knew what to do.

He went to the bathroom and got out his beard trimmer. He removed the comb-head attachment. He shaved off his eyebrows and then used his razor to erase the stubble. Then he began to remove the hair above his ears. First, he had white-walls, then a Mohawk, then a burr. He picked up the razor for the second time. When he was finished, he started painting again. They wouldn't even see him coming.

⸺

The clown strutted down Lancaster Avenue, and when he passed the college kids who spilled out of the Subway sandwich shop, all four of them cheered.

"You da man!" Andy Pressman called. He was a sophomore, philosophy major, red hair, wire frames, head shaped like an egg. He was known to cross his legs, click his pen up by his ear, and in the silkiest of tones deconstruct whatever paradigm the professor had just spent a half hour building in seminar. Even his friends admitted that they thought he liked to hear the sound of his own honey-voice too much. Tonight, he was dressed up for the Halloween party as a cowboy. He'd borrowed the Stetson and the brown chaps from a techie in the theater department. He had just eaten two large Italian hoagies. There was going to be grain punch with dry ice in it later tonight, and he didn't want to party on an empty stomach.

Mandy Rivers was wearing a black leotard. She had straight strawberry blonde hair, funny teeth, and an ass that had gotten a bit bigger this semester. Too many late nights reading for her Modern American Lit. survey course, and too many jumbo bags of peanut M & M's to get her through. She was wearing cat ears and had drawn whisker lines on her cheeks. She had painted the end of her tiny, upturned nose silver with product from a cheap makeup kit that she picked up at the Acme, and she tried not to think about how badly it itched.

Terry Murphy, the Murph monster, had gone the economical route. He had on a corduroys blazer, jeans, and a cap. He had drawn in a square, black moustache above his lip, and around his waist was a wire stuck through a potato hanging in front of his crotch. On his back there was a sign that read "The Dictator."

Rachel Silverstein surprised them all. Throughout the semester she had always worn baggy army pants, oversized sweatshirts, and dark black eye makeup, real Emo, for all but a mane of curly brown hair that would have made any female country singer jealous. A lot of kids thought she had an eating disorder. Tonight, she was wearing a nun's habit, a tight halter top, and black hot pants. Skinny yes, but all legs, hips, and muscle. Andy Pressman couldn't take his eyes off her.

Except when the clown strutted by. That got everyone's attention. The four partiers spilled out onto the street to cheer. Mandy held up her soda spiked with vodka and spilled a bit on her pink ballet slippers. Across Lancaster Avenue a group of suits elbowed each other and laughed out loud, while a woman wearing ear buds, a fanny pack, and a sun visor turned her baby carriage around, squatted, and pointed.

Later, back in the Subway Hoagie shop, Andy Pressman would tell the police that the dude was born to be a clown. He was made for it. He was lanky and humorous. He was strutting and swaggering. He would take two steps forward, and one step back. He would prance in circles and wave to onlookers. He did the "Farmer-John-Doe-See-Doe" thing with his elbows, yuck, yuck, and made all the exaggerated facial expressions. He had his entire head painted bright white. He had a Charlie Chaplin hat about half the size of his bald crown cocked to one side. There were blue brow-arches painted all the way up to the top of his forehead. He had black liner around his eyes and they made big teardrop shapes at the outer edges. He had a red nose ball that honked when he squeezed it and fake ears that were about nine inches long. His jumpsuit was Christmas colors, you know, red and green, with buttons down the front shaped like horseshoes.

And of course, he had that sick executioner's axe. It was humongous, with a five-foot handle and a fourteen-inch blade cut in a half moon. It was covered with crinkled tin foil, as if there was cardboard or something like that underneath, and it had a red ribbon tied around the shank in a big bow.

He was the scary clown, perfect for the Halloween party in the McDonald's next door.

When asked why he followed the clown, Pressman said that he saw something strange. When the dude passed by, Andy noticed that there was a small rip in the tin foil on the blade of the play-axe. But the material underneath the rip was smooth silver, not cardboard brown.

When asked what he saw when the clown entered the McDonald's, Andy Pressman took off his wire-framed glasses and rubbed his eyes too hard. He took an extra second to collect himself, and then said that before the doors shut behind the dude, he could hear the screams of children. The scary clown-thing, you know? Then, through the dark windows sectioned off by those three-by-three white borders, he saw the guy raise up the axe and bring it down in a rush. It flashed. It seemed as if he split a white-haired lady straight in two, forehead to crotch. Pressman thought he may have even caught a glimpse of the inside of her head for a second, marbled T-bone steak in a half-shell kind of thing, as she was turned sideways on one leg still standing for a split-second while the other half of her fell like a domino. Or maybe it was a trick of the light. It was really hard to see anything with the angle and the glare of the low sun. Then Andy had hustled back to the sandwich shop to dial 911. He could have done it out on the sidewalk, but his instincts told him to get inside while the getting was good.

His cowboy hat was now behind his head, the rubber band stuck under his Adam's apple. He rubbed his nose on his index finger and then asked the cop if anyone made it.

Officer Scott McMullin went under his cap with his pen and scratched his forehead.

"After we put him down, we found four survivors," he said. "Three of them were employees who hid back in the break room, and there was a six-year-old girl dressed like a fairy godmother. Like you said, son, he was born for this."

He looked down at his notebook in a quick review.

"Is there anything else you saw?"

Pressman shrugged.

"Not really, just a flash of something. I'm waiting for it to fade, but I don't think it ever will."

"What exactly?"

Andy Pressman looked off vacantly. His usual "voice of silk" was hoarse, shocked, and dull.

"After he did the old lady, I watched through those windows for an extra second before I ran. I saw them all trying to get away. And for a second they didn't look like people anymore. They were bristling all over each other, like bugs when you upend a rock in the woods." He looked Officer McMullin in the eye. "He made me forget all the stuff that we pack on to make ourselves into complicated geniuses. He made me revisit the fact that we all urinate like dogs no matter what kind of fancy porcelain we make the bowls out of. He reminded me that we hate for no reason and shit on each other more often than we pause to offer one of those 'how ya doin's' that we don't really mean."

Pressman looked at the officer square.

"He tricked my eyes, don't you see? Just for a moment, he made me look at kids and grandparents as if they were a swarming disease. Then he erased them, and I'll never forgive myself."

He looked down at his hands.

Can I go now?"

"You can. We'll be in touch."

Pressman pushed through the door and the little bell at the top tinkled in a small fanfare that followed his exit into the night.

[This story first appeared in *Seven Deadly Pleasures*, Hippocampus Press, 2009.]

Quest for Sadness

I ordered my butler to fetch me a shotgun. To this he raised an eyebrow and revealed the trace of a smirk.

"Uh huh."

"Just do it," I said.

He stuck a long green blade between his teeth, even though I had told him not to chew grass in the house. He hooked one thumb under the dirty blue strap of his overalls and used the other to push the Marlboro cap higher up on his forehead. He smelled of Pennzoil and gas-powered gardening tools.

"Winchester or Smith & Wesson?" he said.

"Something with a kick. Meet me by the west wall and don't tread dirt on the foyer carpet." He was usually careful, but it never hurt to remind him. I strode toward the main staircase and had just rested my hand on the banister.

"Hey there," he said.

"What!"

The old coot stood under the high archway and stroked his beard.

"Whatcha want the heavy iron for? There ain't nothing in the west wing but breakables."

"The glass," I said. "I am going to shoot the stained glass."

He sunk his hand into his deep pocket and scratched the back of his right calf with the left boot tip.

"The whole wall is gonna be rough there, fella. That glass is thick as a swamp and stands ninety foot high by seventy across. Took them artists six months of hard labor to install and it won't come down easy."

I flexed my jaw.

"Bring extra rounds."

The madness began yesterday on my private six-hole golf course. I was ten feet off the green and chipping for par when the gun went off.

That cocky old swine. He brought a .44 Magnum today instead of the starter pistol.

With a slight frown, I stroked through the ball and landed it in the cup, touch of backspin.

I turned.

"You fired late."

He didn't respond. He just sat there in the golf cart, feet up, toothless grin, firearm aimed to high north with gray wisps of smoke floating around the mouth of the barrel. My voice was patience.

"I told you that the most sensitive point of concentration is needed an inch before contact with the ball. You shot on the follow-through."

"Well of course I did," he said. "By now, you've come to expect it like an old hog waiting on a slop-bell."

"Then we need a new game," I said.

"Looks like it."

I slid my seven iron back into the waxed cotton duck canvas and leather bag and crossed my arms. He scratched his temple with the muzzle of the .44.

"Can we think of nothing else?" I said. He leaned over the coffee can he always brought with him and spit a long brown runner into it. He wiped his mouth with a sweaty flannel sleeve and smiled at me.

"Let's play Antichrist," he said.

"What?"

He nodded at me slowly. The smile stayed.

"You know."

"No, I don't. Explain. You're no Antichrist."

"'Tain't about me," he said. "Every dime-store book of prophecy says the Antichrist comes to glory by age thirty-three. Seems time for y'all to be doing the thinking."

My thirty-third birthday was in two days, and the glint in his eye was constructed of things other than jest.

"You are permanently dismissed," I said. "Be off the grounds by five or I will have you bodily removed. Start packing."

He did not stir.

"I'll call the police right now," I said.

I went nowhere.

He tossed the pistol to me.

"Go ahead," he said. "Aim and pull the trigger. Put a slug right in the center of my forehead."

I did nothing. He pointed his crooked finger at me and wagged it for a second.

"Now you must ask yourself why," he said. "Why do you choose not to fire the weapon? Is it because you give a damn about your fellow man? I don't think so. Y'all got more money than God and don't feel nothing for no one. Only way you keep ties with a man is by owning him and you won't pull the trigger because it makes no sense to toss away your property."

"That's ridiculous," I said. "You are my employee, not my property."

"That so? Did you hire me or buy me? How much does it take to purchase a soul? What's your definition of slavery?"

I had no answer for that. He had been a patient in one of the long-term care facilities I had sold off. He was harmless. Mild signs of pre-dementia, good with machines. His eldest gave me power of attorney almost immediately, and the old geezer had had no complaints.

"Give me back a life and a pair of work pants and I'll do it for free," he'd said.

I viewed it as a gesture of charity, the start of a strong bond of trust between a pillar of wealth and the salt of the earth. Now I was being forced to view it as something else. I studied him closely, my butler, my handyman, my lone companion who sat in the golf cart, the one who was brought on to expedite my will, he who would do anything for me because I owned him. I felt a sudden whisper of fear up my back.

"So, I bargained for your loyalty," I said. "Why is that so wrong?"

His smile vanished.

"Because I'd break the knees of a baby or take a bullet in my side for you. Go on, now admit who *you* are."

"No. You're the one with the problem and there's really no challenge in this. It is too easy to prove that you're wrong."

"Then do it," he said. "Prove me wrong." I hesitated and he went on with words that seemed treasured and rehearsed. "Children of Satan don't feel sadness, friend. They are incapable of any sense of loss. Tell me one thing that makes you feel sorrow for another."

I shifted my stance and crossed my arms.

"Game's too easy. I could lie."

"Why would you lie to me? I'm nobody."

"And I'm not a machine. I feel like everyone else."

"Do ya? When's the last time you shed a tear?"

I had no response and the fear whispered back, in my spine, my neck, the back of the skull. Weeping was one particular release that helped define the human experience, I knew that, I had certainly read about it, seen it in film, observed it on the news. And though I had never actually come face to face with woe, I just assumed all along that this kind of thing existed in those more connected.

What does sadness feel like? The impact of a difficult moral choice and its effect upon others?

You'll never know. It has been fully unlearned and now remains too easy to buy off with your money, more money than God.

I stormed off the golf course. Though it was too early, I retreated to the confines of my second-floor study to fix myself a vodka martini with three anchovy olives.

What am I?

Things I had known about myself were altered in this twisted context. Apathy seemed cruel. Lack of emotion seemed evil. Calm, cool, and collected seemed sociopathic. And why did I not just have my butler thrown off the grounds, no more questions asked? He was obviously disturbed.

You knew that from day one. You bought him so you could keep him as property. Now you refuse to let go what you own.

It ate at me all afternoon. It was an unsolvable round-about.

You have enough money to buy off sadness. Enough to purchase souls.

Wide-eyed in the dark that night, unable to sleep, I searched for feelings of pity about anything. There were none. I did not give a damn about the homeless, not one shred of grief for the starving, not a single crumb of ache for any of the damned living outside of my isolated world.

What am I?

I was going to find out. I was going to scratch up some kind of humanity from deep within. I was determined to prove the accusation false.

Those lovely, massive windows.

I aimed high and the first shot back-kicked my shoulder so hard I almost fell to the floor. The large face of the Virgin Mary shattered into a thousand sharp glass raindrops, most of which landed outside on the grass. Others smashed the marble floor before me, skidding and spinning. Morning sun stabbed through the ugly void and the glare lanced off the steel barrel as I cocked another round into the chamber.

My butler followed as I moved behind the display of Persian vases. He was laughing. I went back on my heels, steadied myself against the wall, aimed low at the wide reproduction of The Last Supper and let the buck-shot fly.

The second *thwack* of gunfire seemed louder than the first, but it did less damage. In somewhat of a rage, I grabbed the other shotgun and pumped five successive explosions at the stained glass mural, bursting it out at the bottom in thick sprays of calico shrapnel.

The entire middle section caved and we both dove for cover.

A huge chunk that was most of a thirty-foot version of the fourteen Stations of the Cross toppled inward. I sneaked up a look just as it crashed down on my antique Ford, mint condition, museum quality. It crushed the roof, blew out the windows, and flattened the tires in a roar of destruction.

Smoke churned in the air and spare tinkles of leftover falling glass mixed with the faint calls of birds outside. I got up and approached the wall that was now no more than a vacancy with jagged edges. My shoes crunched in the glass, my gun dangled down toward the floor.

It was still there.

In the bottom left corner was the little treasure, originally hidden within the larger piece. I had spotted it a day after installation, I do not miss much. It was a tiny, nearly microscopic picture of a woman's head made with fragments. Below it and barely legible without a magnifying glass stood the letters, "Mama, R.I.P."

I brought up my gun and blasted that little piece of history into oblivion. I turned to my butler.

"Clean up the glass, get an exterminator, tell the security company it was a false alarm and make arrangements with a local contractor to temporarily patch the wall until the stained glass can be replaced. Now, you will excuse me. I have a phone call to make."

I was convinced his reaction would make me feel regret. The artist. The one who custom-made the stained glass wall piece by piece and spent the next half year of his life installing it.

When I told him of the senseless act there was dead silence.

"Why?" he said.

"I wanted to destroy a piece of your art. And I felt the need to obliterate the testament to your mother. How dare you include that within something I own. She will never rest the same."

"So, why call?" he said. "You want your money back or something?"

"No, I want you to fight for your mother's memory! I took it, and it can't be replaced."

He laughed.

"I'll buy her a park bench or plant her a tree, asshole."

He hung up. I stared at the phone, listened to the silence, then the dial tone.

Art meant nothing. It was merely a way to get paid. The authenticity of memorial was illusory; blind ritual, dumb obligation. The importance of "the mother" as some sort of "icon" or "monumental symbol" was no more than a mirage. This was going to be even harder than I had thought.

I told my butler to bring me a deer.

I watched.

He drove it onto the south grounds in a horse trailer, ignoring the car path and rolling straight onto the open lawn before the hedge gauntlet. Even through the expansive pantry window, I was close enough to hear the animal bucking and kicking in its mud-stained steel prison. Locked in the dark. Frantic.

Don't fret, love. You'll be set free soon enough.

Bowlegged, my butler ambled out of the pickup and went around back to lift the drift pin that held shut the trailer doors.

They blew open.

Headstrong and frenzied, the deer galloped upon the smooth metal bed, slipped and banged down its proud white chest on the tailboard. It jerked up then and lunged out to the grass. Like a statue it froze there.

I raised my Nextel.

"Leave us," I said into it.

The transmission must have been loud on the unit hooked to my butler's belt, for it broke the spell cast over the deer. It bolted and my butler shook his head before driving off. He did not specifically understand and I did not need him to. Yet. All he had to know was that he was shielded if he had attained the animal illegally. Simple fact: through political contribution I supplied the police most of their radar devices, firearms, and computer equipment. It kept me well protected.

But there would be no protection for the animal-thing. The south lawn's forty acres were fenced in, it would not get far.

I palmed the leather grip of my Proline compound bow and ventured out into the sunshine. There were birds in the warm breeze, squirrels in the trees, beings of beauty, God's creatures.

Lower than you on the food chain. Insignificant in the vast scheme of things.

Were they? I thought I had formed an alliance with anything that lived or breathed. Or was that all inbred by the mass media, inserted, incubated, and sculpted over a lifetime in order to form a false system of values? Was I conditioned? Had a mental parasite with an exterior of high morals eclipsed my true being?

I was going to find out. Though my butler was required to provide me bi-weekly instruction on various styles of weaponry, I had always shot at targets. As far as I knew I was against killing for sport.

Really?

The only way to know for sure was to do it. To become involved in the act and gauge my responses. To hope the (power of God) execution brought on feelings of remorse.

Like a traumatized dog that pawed up to lick the boot of the one who kicked it, the deer had circled back to its original point of release. It stood about thirty feet away now, and I reached and slipped an arrow from under the hood of my bow-mounted quiver.

It was an XX75 tipped with razorback 5, needle-sharp point amidst a cluster of five steel arrowheads all arranged in a circular pinwheel. Straight on, it looked a bit strange.

Like a five-pentacle star.

Odd feather out, I mounted it on the string, careful not to pinch but just hold gently between the fingers. I drew back on the eighty-pound resistance of the pulleys and my butler's voice twanged in my head.

"Let it go easy, don't snap away your finger pads. And go for the vital area behind the front leg. It's the best way to a fast kill."

But I did not want the thing to die quickly. I wanted it to suffer. Carefully, I aimed at its stomach and in my ears the outdoor sounds seemed to magnify behind the drum of my heart.

I let go the string.

The arrow split the air, a silent merchant of doom. It struck the deer flat in the paunch and there was a smooth sound of penetration similar to a hatchet sunk hard into a wet stump. The thing lurched with the contact, sprang high into the air. It was beautiful.

Wrong emotion!

I bit my lip, not willing to face my inner rush of joy as the deer shot across the lawn in its ecstasy of pain and confusion. The arrow shaft stuttered and bobbed from its flank and grass divots kicked up from beneath the blur of its hoofs. The beast tore straight away and then smashed through the pantry window.

Damn. Not in the house.

I drew another arrow and walked to the side door. Upon approach, I heard a riot of clapping hooves amongst crashes of wooden shelves, trays of silver, and stacks of fine china. By the time I entered the fresh rubble of my pantry, the thing was lying by the far wall in a state of jerk and spasm. I set the bow down and stepped forward, trying to fend off the nag of annoyance I felt as a result of the damage done to my kitchen.

The deer died with a guttural moan and I stared into its lifeless gaze.

I felt nothing.

There had to be something: guilt, sadness, anything. There was nothing, and I moved slowly around the dead thing. The fatal wound had spattered green intestinal juices and it stank. Were this a two-dimensional presentation on television, my reaction might have been different, might have been, but all I felt was disgust.

What is wrong with you? Look at it!

The blind stare. The tongue hanging out of its muzzle, the rich blood that seeped across my Pietra D'Assisi beige ceramic floor tiles, all visually and intellectually pathetic. So where was the pity? The feelings of shame?

Nowhere. Considering the damage it did to my kitchen and the stench, I was glad I killed it.

I pulled the Nextel from my belt.

"Get in here and clean up the mess," I said.

The tone of my voice barely hid the panic rising up in my throat.

I ran past the garden to the yard's south edge. Inside I felt scorched, blackened.

What am I?

I stopped to catch my breath. My nostrils were flaring and I looked down at my shaking hands. They seemed huge, smooth as bone, manicured nails, baby-smooth skin.

Flesh that thinly covers a dark beast whose inner eye just opened.

No! It did not mean anything, couldn't have! Lots of people hunt!

You don't.

I squared my jaw and marched down the grassy knoll toward the building I frequented the least, my butler's tool shed. I needed to see his domain, the castle I had built for him, the cold, hard proof that I had done some good for a fellow human being and blessed him with purpose, *time bombs of dark purpose waiting for ignition,* that I had rescued him from an existence of despair, *purchased his soul,* and made him into the kind of man, *Devil's henchman,* that he wanted to be.

Tool shed.

An ugly word that drew up images of work benches, dirty blue rags, grease guns, and a cracked, oil-stained concrete floor.

Devil's playpen.

A place where men, *salt of the earth,* reigned supreme and broken machines became female. The frozen hex nut that would not turn was a *bitch.* That stripped screw that refused to budge was a *whore,* and the engine that blew an o-ring was dubbed a *fucking cunt!* For the first time in my life I felt something like lust. The feeling was ice, far from the warm touch of remorse I so desperately yearned.

The door was open. Just outside on the grass, there was a scattered array of railroad ties, framing lumber, gas compressors, and high-powered air nailers, as it was my butler's latest project to build a gazebo to be erected abreast the outdoor pool.

The door to the shed stood open. Inside was discovery. A single flood light poured its beam to the floor leaving to the sides a periphery of gloom.

I was hesitant to enter.

I was hesitant to walk between the long shadows of shelved equipment and stand in the spotlight, afraid of what would be illuminated there. My mind streaked to its farthest corners in search of a direction, a guidepost, some testament of how to start and where exactly to begin, a visible cornerstone to dent the steel shroud that lay cold on my heart.

I needed a symbol.

I fired up the compressor as I had seen my butler do and picked up a large framing nailer. With the hose snaking behind, I bent to set two thick wooden planks at perpendicular. I depressed the gun mouth down and fired a three-and-a-half-inch nail through the beams. It banged through to flush with a sharp pop. I set five more nails into the same general area.

Now I had a huge wooden cross.

I dragged it into the shed, leaned it upright and stood before it, desperate for answers before this vision of purity.

I felt nothing.

No sparks, no quench of enlightenment, nothing.

Instead, I thought of the graphic crucifixion it represented, the vision of pain we had twisted to a commercial science of love. In literal terms, we celebrated the murder of a man, he who was nailed to a cross with a javelin stuck between his ribs. We framed the picture. We propped it over the fireplace, made it into earrings, and hung it off the rearview mirror. A man was nailed to a pair of dirty wooden beams, left to die in shame, and the scene filled our minds from our tender beginnings. We were impressionable children looking up with open faces at an extreme representation of violence that was made to be transformed somehow to the pious and the beautiful. I blinked. Suddenly, the cross looked wrong.

Top-heavy somehow.

Of course! I am not the one who has gone numb! I am the one who has come of age, become aware! We have all gotten too used to the image this way! Though the Lord's death must have been ultimately painful, he could have been punished... more effectively.

I pushed forward and wrapped my arms around the cross. Careful to lift with the legs, I slowly turned it upside down. I backed off and stared. Now it seemed right, a rack of pure torture as it should have been from the beginning. I pictured the pain of having the ankles spread at bottom and hands, palm over palm nailed overhead like a victim in a medieval witch chamber. This is where sadness could live. This is where woe could be born.

I needed to feel it now more than ever. I was so close to the pain that would come from this...more *potent* crucifixion. So close to true remorse, face to face, and ongoing.

I told my butler to get me a girl...

[This story first appeared in *The Leopard's Realm,* 1993.]

The Matriarch

I ain't scared, asshole.

It's not like I ain't changed a tire before, right? It's just that the bulb light is shot and I got so much shit in the trunk I can't find the jack. The cold rain is blowing in from the left across the median in dark wailing sheets, and I'm reminded of Jesse James, this little black guy who works in the warehouse moving pallets. We break his balls 'cause his mama named him Jesse, and he ain't even no sports player like Milton Bradley or Coco Crisp. But mostly, we give him shit because he uses these old school sayings like "stop coming at my neck," and this is sweeping, machine gun, Forest Gump rain, coming right at my neck and all down my back, straight through to my drawers and I ain't laughing now, brutha.

I got an empty box for a hubcap in here, a dented toolbox, a fly reel, an old mini step ladder missing a stair tread, and a blanket with a design of mooses and elks on it. My mama got it for me when I was seven, and for some reason I dragged it around all these years. My mama was Lenape Indian. She used to tell me I had the spirit of a warrior, but my feminine side made me cautious. She said this blanket had my dreams wrapped up in it, and that someday I was gonna make some powerful woman happy.

I work with men. I'm six foot five. I got a granite jaw and deep carved lines around my mouth like judgments. I fix gas compressors, slab saws, and power tools. I keep dirty magazines under my workbench, and I wear a blue canvas monkey suit with my name stitched in an oval on my chest.

A truck is coming; I can tell by the drone. Eighteen wheeler. International cab-over shitbucket with a 6V-53 most probably. The lights come over the ridge and wash across, and when I look down to the side I see the reflections in the long black puddle snaking along the edge of the breakdown lane, rain making needle dashes in it. He can see it too, I know he can, but the hillbilly-fucker roars right on through, sending up a sheet of gutter flush and road grit.

Prick!

I stalk out to the middle of the highway shouting into the roar of his back-spray. I put up both middle fingers and almost hope he screeches those Firestones, fishtailing and halting there like a ghost-ship on a black sea, exhaust making twists and threads in the air like serpents and omens.

He does kiss the brakes actually, but I ain't scared, asshole. Rearviews distort, but don't lie. He don't want no showdown between the slick reflection of his tail lights and my long, slanted shadow, this big silhouette standing out here on the double yellow, arms hanging down, long black hair sketching patterns of rage into the driving rain. No thank you, right? Safer up in the cab there, ain't it brutha?

I'm back at the rear of my vehicle, wind rising and moaning, black clouds cutting across the moon, and I see that it's not just the back left tire that's pancaked, but the right one as well, pulling a monkey-see-monkey-do, starting to belly down and bulge like some pregnant little immigrant. I only got one spare, but I ain't scared, asshole. I can ride that bastard for at least a few miles before its sunken down to the rim like its twin, maybe a bit after that. Enough to get off Route 476.

Hopefully.

I lean back into the trunk and will myself not to start throwing shit around. Last time I had the jack out, I think I threw the tire iron back by the dented tin that once had three types of popcorn in it. I should have tucked the little black bitch away in the triangular leather pouch that goes in its place under the false-bottom particle board covering the tire well. But I didn't, and it was irresponsible. That was my nickname growing up: "Irresponsible." Through dark magic and psychological power of attorney, Mama appointed it Godfather to my chores, my hygiene, my attitude, my study habits. I have tattoos that brag of convictions, but I don't believe them. I have trust, but it's an old corpse. I have a soul, but I loaned it to the church. I hear they keep it in a basement cage so the robed ivory behind the first floor podium looks more polished and pure by comparison.

I lift the particle board and have to put my back into it, considering all the parts stored under the blanket with the mooses and elks on it. Stuff shifts and tumbles off left making muted sounds in the rain, and I paw around in the dark recess. No pouch. Only what feels like a catcher's knee pad, a gas can lid with old caterpillar webs caught under the lip, and a moldy Garfield toy I won at the Dillsburg Community Fair three years ago, tossing wooden rings into bowls slicked with Wesson Oil.

I ain't scared though, asshole. I'm going to have to drive this shit-can as it is, bumping along the dark highway just the three of us, a pancake, a pregnant immigrant, and one drenched soldier, pressing forward like a band of brutha's riding this wounded stallion straight into the hardpan. I try to dig for my keys and I can't get my fingers in, 'cause leather pants fall in love with you when they're drenched. There are lights coming over the rise now.

They ain't white and glowing.

They're circus red and neon blue, rotating in sick pulse up along the slow rise of the craggy rock-face and making the road signs flash like mirrors. Now I'm groping in my pockets a bit more desperate-like, and I'm looking in the trunk, shadows moving off and back like the gauzy wings of some dark beast.

I see the popcorn tin winking through the advancing streaks, the catcher's knee pad with a broken buckle and "Macgregor" written across in white flaked cursive, some empty Deer Park bottles in the outer crevices, a stepladder, a pickle barrel, a length of frayed manila rope, a spade shovel with paint drops splattered up the shaft, a ripping saw, the crinkled edge of an oversized aluminum loaf pan, and an old blanket with mooses and elks on it, wet with more than the rain, only partially covering the parts underneath it now, the most noticeable - the dainty hand with the pale curling fingers sticking out from under the edge by the lock release.

I move the blanket back over her, thinking how much she'd looked like Mama, with those penetrating eyes and imperial shoulders.

They all looked like Mama.

I pull the trunk lid down, but it catches on something, the edge of Mama's blanket perhaps, and I hear the hiss of her laughter buried in the sounds of the recoiling hinge pistons.

I have been irresponsible.

The blue and red lights wash straight across my back now, making the landscape grin and laugh and revolve like some lunatic carousel. The engine cuts off, and I hear a door open in the rain. Then there's the distinct wet grit of boot soles finding purchase on the blacktop, approaching footsteps, the snap of his poncho in the wind, and I can imagine him pulling down the brim of his hat with one hand, while the other unclips the strap across the top of his firearm, The Lone Ranger, Superman.

A ripping saw makes for a poor attack weapon.

I never could find that tire iron.

My secrets are naked.

And I'm scared, asshole.

[This story first appeared in *Schlock Webzine,* Volume 3, Issue 28, 2012. It then became the first Pre-Chapter in my third novel, *Phantom Effect,* Night Shade Books / Skyhorse, 2016.]

TOOLS & TECH

Soul Text

August 2029: The Big Reveal

"Good evening," said the news reporter. "I'm Katherine Gray, live at the offices of Micro/Tec Industries, where they are about to roll out the device that will render your computers obsolete and turn your laptops to bookends. All the Facebook-Premium, Twitter 2, Instagram-Plus, and Digital Vignettes platforms will be reanimated. In other words, we're talking – makeover."

The camera started its slow dolly back.

"This new device," Katherine continued, "is revolutionary because Micro/Tec has found a way to directly connect the Internet to human neurons. We become the power source. I am here with Marty Wallingford, the creator, and I suppose the general public will first question whether or not this makes us slaves to our machines."

"It has nothing to do with slavery," Marty said, lab goggles up on his forehead. "On the contrary, it has everything to do with liberation. There will be no more toting around a cell phone or laptop, no more hunting for a charger. Access will be round-the-clock and instantaneous." He gave a pert nod. "Slavery? How about baptism. The only issue our customers will have is how fast they can take in and enjoy the flood of information available at the tips of their fingers."

"Or rather, a thumb," Katherine added.

"Absolutely," Marty said, "and thanks for the segue. The Micro/Tec 'Thumb Screen,' model 77AB, and the micro-lens spectacle accessory you need to read it, will both be available tomorrow morning at 6:00 A.M. at your local electronics stores, retail $595.00 for the package. Of course, the 77AB is offered in children's size and adult's, both easily grafted to the thumbnail and inter-fused by any primary care physician right there in the office. And the procedure is covered by most health care plans."

"However," Katherine said, "I have attained information from reliable sources that you have not just been streamlining virtual access in the form of this new mini-screen powered by human energy. I heard that you are making available certain "data" that we never thought possible. Can you explain?"

Marty's eyes narrowed, who leaked this?

Didn't matter. And there was no use trying to put genies back into bottles, especially on live television.

"We're developing a program," he said carefully, "that would allow users, with consent verified by an exchange of access codes and PIN numbers, to mentally join with their 'partners,' in order to experience their thoughts for a brief time period. Like being a guest in another's mind, reading his or her story firsthand. We're calling it 'Soul Text.'"

"'Soul Text...'"

"Yes," Marty said, "Tough to picture, I know. Just try to imagine the police officer that is suddenly able to mark a given target from multiple vantage points. Picture all the lab techs that can now connect seamlessly with manufacture and distribution...the mechanical engineers working in teams that can simultaneously pool knowledge and gain immediate access to their respective colleague's untapped potential."

He paused. Folded his arms.

"No more politics," he continued. "No lukewarm compromise, and this isn't just limited to law enforcement and the sciences. In terms of the military, I am not at liberty to discuss future contracts, but in the public sector, schools will benefit exponentially. Group learning will become a tool through which we can teach to multiple intelligences simultaneously, and differentiation will be as easy as breathing." He smiled a bit, face coloring. "And even though the Behavioral Psych. and Civics Division works out of a different building, it would be unfair not to mention the social implications. Rivals get to understand one another, friends get to be better friends, and romance takes on a whole new dimension."

He cleared his throat.

"But let's focus on the Thumb Screen for now," he said. "Mechanism first. Super-content, TBC."

The camera zoomed in to Katherine Gray's close-up.

"A few years down the road then," she said. "Truth and connection. Full disclosure." She flashed her signature smile. "For now, however, Internet access twenty-four seven, never on shut-down, powered by pulse in the form of a Thumb Screen. I'm Katherine Gray, here at Micro/Tec Industries, reporting for Eye Witness News."

November 2032: The Thumb-Screen

"She's a third grader who can read Shakespeare," her mother said hotly, "and you're telling me she needs special ed. Services. It's not only astounding, but ridiculous. If she gets accommodations of any kind it should for the gifted, not the disabled."

Dr. Tucker, the Principal, looked over at her spec. ed. Chair Reba Hatboro, and to this, Reba leaned forward, lips pursed. She poised her fingers on the desk like she was about to move poker chips.

"Mrs. Billingsly," she said delicately. "Joan. We have tests that confirm that your daughter Marla has what we now call 'severe inter-connective disabilities.' Her allergic reaction to the Ocular Diamond has forced her into wearing Google Glass headgear, and it was phased out for a reason. It's bulky, and without constant precision adjustments at the nose bridge and ear contact points, it makes a poor tool for learning."

"We get it fine-tuned once a week. We're paying outside of our insurance."

"We're sensitive to that," Reba said gently, "but our hands are tied. Results are results and the numbers don't lie."

Joan looked off toward the classroom's American flag hanging off its pole by the listening station.

"The Ocular Diamond is a cruel device," she said.

"Not to most children," Reba countered. "After the adjustment phase it sits at the edge of the left eye unfelt and unnoticed like an earring or nose stud. Studies show most of the kids forget that it's there after a month or so." She folded her hands in front of her. "Please accept the fact, Joan, that Marla has consistent adverse reactions to the instrument, similar to the peanut allergies of past decades. She doesn't need clunky, outdated technology. She needs special instruction."

"But she can read Shakespeare," Joan insisted.

"And that is admirable," Principal Tucker said, "but this is a new age. Reading is a preliminary skill that does not require the mastery of abstract concepts we once affixed to the works of Shakespeare and the other literature in the antiquated canons and curriculums. The new state mandate is that children learn to access information quickly and efficiently, gaining the ability to navigate and manipulate virtual data at an impressive rate." She sat back in her chair. "Simply reading a story or a play and pontificating about subtleties and symbols doesn't make for a valid education anymore. It's like being able to build a fire out in the wilderness. It's a nice ability to have in your stable, but it doesn't do you any good in the real world if you don't know how to turn on a light."

Joan put her knuckles up beneath her nose for a moment.

"It's as if you're telling me that because my daughter is allergic to a jewel surgically placed at the edge of her eye, she's retarded."

Reba and Principal Tucker eyed each other warily. Joan looked back and forth between them.

"What?" she said. Principal Tucker got a box of tissues and handed them over. Joan took them, set them down absently, and again said, "What?" but this time her voice was mouse-like and hushed.

"It's more than the allergy," Reba said. "Even when the manual eyeglass device is fixed at precise angles, our testing has shown that Marla has trouble manipulating the thumb-data, often lagging behind the rate of expected pagination, enough to make the Thumb Screen freeze."

"I don't understand."

"We didn't expect you to," Principal Tucker interjected, "it's a generational thing, but in short, you are aware that finger-touch manipulation of data has been made obsolete, and all gaming controllers and cell phones with texting options have basically vanished. In terms of Thumb Screens, you take in information as I do, Joan, reading the given page and blinking twice in order to access the next one. But what children are doing now is not simply reading their Thumb Screens really fast. They are moving the text with their eyes, a feature Micro/Tec embedded in the program specifically for those with newly developing optic muscles and nerves that can be groomed and trained from a primordial standpoint. In other words, Joan, our eyes are too old for the rigorous training, but the kids can do it, in most cases almost naturally. A child's intelligence is first measured now by the 'MEM Quotient,' which is an acronym for 'Metacognitive Eye Movement.' Marla only looks for information in a linear manner, experiencing massive failure levels when she needs to backtrack, go circular, or access a pull-down menu. It is what is popping up on the grid nowadays as a form of severe modern dyslexia."

"I want her re-tested," Joan said.

"I would advise against that. Marla's been tested enough."

"Well, do it again."

"No, we will not!"

That came from Gina Barnes, Marla's classroom teacher, silent so far, but emotional now. "She needs specialized help," she pleaded. "She can't keep up with the rest of the class and she's becoming a behavior problem, jumping up from her desk and running around the room for no reason. She hits other children, scratches herself, and claws at her own eyes, for God's sake!" The room echoed with it for a moment, and Gina put her hand to her chest just below the hollow of her throat.

"Please help us help her, Joan," she continued quietly. "Nowadays, the average beginning reader falls off the viewing plane two or three times per minute. Marla has trouble staying on-screen for five continuous seconds."

"What's the cure?"

"There is none," Reba said. "But there are programs for medication that we can try. Side effects might include moodiness, bad dreams, skin rashes, and headaches, but we are willing to—"

Joan put up her hand like a stop sign.

"No," she said.

"You *have* to!" Gina spouted. "You absolutely *must* get her help, tutoring, and accommodations. She can't continue this way in front of her peers. She's teased constantly, and I have forty other students in the room I have to attend to!"

Joan's eyes were wide.

"It's your job," she whispered.

"Then help me do it!"

"She reads Shakespeare..."

"It doesn't matter, Joan! Marla can't function in public!"

"I don't accept that. Not today, not ever!"

Gina opened her mouth as if the hasty retort was right there on the tip of her tongue, but she held it, smiling tightly.

"I'm sorry if this all sounds harsh, Joan. We sympathize. But we are in the world of the blunt and the literal now, information and speed, not poetry and metaphor. Euphemism is death in a modern age." She reached out and took Joan's hand, that which the woman surrendered grudgingly. "But I get it," Gina continued. "I'm an old-fashioned girl like you, so I'll put it figuratively. When it comes to moving information across the screen with the eye, adults like myself, you, Dr. Tucker, and Reba have good old-fashioned, fine-tuned pointers. Kids nowadays have the advantage over us, employing high-tech mouse and cursor systems. Marla is trying to do all this with nothing but an old pair of blurry glasses and the end of a busted crayon."

You could hear everyone breathing.

Joan Billingsly removed her hand from Gina's and reached into the tissue box.

—

December 2034: Soul Text

Frank Hall stood in front of her facing away, backed in hard against her, hands spread so she couldn't move. His expression was one of absolute blankness. He was the Vice Principal at the People First Charter School in downtown Philadelphia, and he thought he'd seen it all. The girl behind him in the stairwell was wearing a winter coat. The coat had slashes in it. If her attacker had come at her stabbing forward or jabbing downward instead of swinging out with wild swipes, this would have been a different story altogether, oh yes, *quite* different. Frank was a year away from his retirement, and right now he had containment. He was a short, stocky man with a gray moustache, a bald head, and a band of fat on the back of his neck. The police would be here momentarily and he had to keep contain. His face was a blank. The subway came screeching into the tunnel below, and kids passing by were trying to get a look at the girl.

"Move along now," Frank said calmly. From behind him the girl struggled and tried to do a duck-under. Frank adjusted. She screeched in rage and he ignored it. The open-air stairwell smelled like old rust and urine. It was raining and there were puddles on the concrete by his shoes. He had not had the opportunity to radio security, but he was fairly sure Gerald Richards had run back to the school. That meant reinforcements if the police took too long. Gerald Richards was a snitch and that was a wonderful thing. For now, Frank Hall had contain.

Two girls were clapping up the stairs from the subway tunnel, both in uniform, so at first glance he knew they came from People First and not Franklin across the street. That was good. From what he had gathered there were girls involved from three other schools, but he couldn't suspend or expel those he didn't have a file on. One of the girls was wearing sunglasses. The other was in the process of taking out her earrings.

"Turn right around and go back down those stairs," Frank said. "It's over."

The one with the sunglasses had tears streaking down her face from under the dark rims, and the moisture had pooled in the creases of her nostrils.

"Bitch!" she spat to the girl behind Frank. "You scratched up my sister and when I get yo ass out from behind there I'm gonna fuck you up like you was a nigger with a dick!"

The girl behind Frank Hall went nuclear, punching and struggling, pushing and kicking. He put all his weight into it shoving back hard, and her head clumped the wall. Liability. But it could have been far worse, and her mother would have to understand that her daughter had attacked another girl out on Broad Street five minutes after school let out, coming up from behind and ripping out part of her weave, raking her face and neck with the spike-hook fingernails that were the latest fashion, and punching her repeatedly on the right side of her head. The victim's friends, two from Franklin and one from George Washington up the street, had been over in front of the Korean hoagie shop, and in a hail of screams and profanity they'd swarmed in like a gang, the one at the forefront weilding the knife.

The girl had broken free and made a run for the subway. Frank had seen the whole thing from the top of the steps and had managed to trap her just behind him on the first landing in the stairwell. To get contain. Her name was Mia Jenkins. She was thirteen years old. And the girls who had attacked her for attacking one of their own were not strangers to her.

They were all thick as thieves, a big friendship group including the one with the sunglasses named Paula Butler and her second cousin Melodi, both of whom had heard about the incident down below just before boarding the express train to Market Street and had rushed back up the subway stairs looking for blood. Ironically, they were Mia's very best friends as far as Frank knew, constantly hanging out with her along with Ashley and Asia and Dominique, messing around in the hallways, practicing pep squad cheers at lunch, and cutting class in the bathrooms, being loud. They were always in a state of relative chaos, talking about one another, laughing, keeping secrets, stealing one another's boyfriends, the usual. But Frank Hall had never seen anything like this. Not since Twitter got popular—and that was nothing in comparison, not even close.

From behind him, Mia had recovered, gaining back strength, screaming and choking out a string of expletives that were crazed and incoherent.

He should have seen this coming.

He had heard about it through the rumor mill, but he'd been buried with other duties, refusing to believe in the end that the use of the new technology would get so heinous so quickly, especially since Micro/Tec had advertised its product as containing a package of such heavy and "fool-proof" safeguards.

But he'd been around long enough to know that it didn't take a genius to pick a lock. And he'd just lied to himself by thinking he'd shrugged all this off because he was busy. He had seen it coming a mile off, but in truth he hadn't known how to run the meeting, getting all these girls in a conference room and letting them hash it out. The whole issue was so grossly inappropriate it seemed even *knowing* about it could have meant his job, his pension, his sterling reputation. No, sir. He'd opted for pretending that this was kid stuff, none of his business, and something that would simply blow over.

Evidently, Paula's twin sister Brianna had Soul Texted Mia Jenkins late last evening, faked a sign-off, and ghosted her. Mia had then pulled up her favorite Thumb-Sketch music video, the one with pop sensation Brett Wallace without his shirt on, and she'd masturbated there in her bedroom under the covers. Brianna recorded it, hit "send," and publicized the experience to everyone in their "Soul Group," including three thousand five hundred and thirty-nine user-participants. Within minutes it had gone viral, national. By now, it had probably spread worldwide.

Contain, hell.

This was just the beginning.

And he was way too old for this shit.

September 2038: Infiltration

With all the new laws and regulations a girl would have to be super-talented to gain this kind of access, but please... Annie McClinty was all that. First off, she could run a scope of up to three hundred thumb pages in less than a minute, and now that they'd finally squared off the viewing screen with fool-proof bordering, it was just too damned easy.

The real trick, however, was her ability to manipulate screen changes without looking, all of it performed with her inferior oblique lower eye muscle like some crazy contortionist. Since it was a misdemeanor to Soul Text outside of the house and an actual felony to do it in the company of others in public domains, it would take someone like Annie to pull this off. Last night they'd toasted her with bong-shots of Purple Gorilla Plus and offered her a half-gram for free. She was a star. So how could she refuse?

Professor Filmore was a total prick anyway, he had it coming. No one in the class had above a C and seven of them were failing, all because he wouldn't allow them to cut and paste even in their technical programming papers. He wanted them to be "writers" and use "proper grammar," like out of their heads and shit. He had this theory that the act of lifting script from one source to another in a simple celebration of the rate of extraction was a modern evil, eventually destined to shatter our world because a copy of a copy of a copy of a copy lost its resolution to the point of linguistic manslaughter over time or some such lame horseshit.

But who needed Comp 101 anyway? You learned to write for the Heaven Center (once known as "The Cloud") in all your other classes in blunt declarative sentences of the literal. You only needed rhetoric past 101 if you were going into journalism, and even in community college, people had the sense to avoid classes doomed to be dropped from the roster. There was no such thing as "the news" anymore—you just "Souled" right into the "flow."

"Good morning," Professor Filmore said. "Today we are going to talk about tense, pronoun antecedent, and a couple of other issues I keep seeing in your connective drafting." He was standing beside a small podium. He had on a sweater even though it was 87 degrees outside, and he was a bit ashy between the eyebrows. His gray hair was sticking up kind of wiry, but that was his usual.

The desks were those old-fashioned things that had the flat teardrop shape to write on, yet Annie had swiveled hers away to the side, front row fifth from the left. Oh-so-casually, she drew her feet up onto the chair evidently making herself cozy, arms around her knees holding them together, sneakers spread beneath, slightly pigeon-toed. She was wearing a gray cross-fit half-shirt and silk short shorts. Annie was a redhead with a swimmer's body. She had a lot of freckles, but she knew from hacking Filmore's school profile and sneaking a split-second soul-probe last night, that he liked texture.

When she'd pulled her feet up on the edges of the chair, her shorts between her legs had shrunk down to the thinnest of strips. She wasn't wearing underwear, and she hadn't waxed. Total beaver-walnut.

Filmore didn't miss more than a beat, glancing at it briefly, pausing slightly between the words "murder" and "they," accenting the latter as the offender in the sentence, "If one commits murder, *they* should get the death penalty," and then turning to write it on the board.

To hide his erection.

But Annie had hacked him and recorded what he felt looking at her barely covered vagina, briefly imagining himself fingering aside that band of cloth and cramming himself into her, rocking his hips, and pushing those pretty knees back nearly to her ears.

In vivid, living color.

Without looking of course, she twitched "send" and let four thousand nine hundred sixty-four of her followers look at her pussy through the eyes of Professor Ray Filmore, along with the entire student body of the community college and all its staff, including maintenance and food service.

Ray Filmore was put on leave the next day.

Annie McClinty wound up getting an A in Comp 101.

October 2039: Freedom of Soul

There was a massive rally at Temple University out in front of the Johnson and Hardwick dormitories. Participators and observers were jam-packed all along the courtyard going back past the Annenberg building and out front as far as the Liacouras Center and Diamond Street up the other way, north. There were people with signs and glow sticks and beach balls and air horns, people in knots, people with sign boards, people climbing light poles for a view, and others sitting on rooftops.

There were people drinking and pushing and smoking and shouting, and someone was blaring music from shitty speakers that might have been coming from the alleyway between Pi Lam and Sigma Pi, but it was hard to pin down with the echo, making everything hazy and surreal. At the center of it all in front of the dorm lobby doors were the virtual purists on a cheap wooden stage, all dressed in army fatigues as if to prove they were in this for keeps, holy war, and they weren't giving speeches. They were chanting, over and again, louder and stronger, megaphone for megaphone, fists raised and pumping.

"We want to fuck!
We want to fight!
We want the real truth,
that's in the heart and mind!"

There was a massive group Soul Text, and before the police could fortify their positioning, there were two marriage proposals, twenty-six inquiries for dates, seven hundred fifty-three dirty propositions, forty-six fights, twenty-two rapes, nineteen stabbings, and seventeen shootings.

It streamed to eighty-three percent of the world population.

Neighborhoods emptied into the streets to discuss.

—

October 2039: Lock Down

"This is a recording. Anyone found doing a soul-trace on this voice will be arrested. Anyone performing a soul-search for the identity of this vehicle's driver will be arrested. Stay in your homes. Curfew is twenty-four hours and surveillance will be constant. Food rations will be brought to you, so make sure the area by your front door is secure for delivery. Anyone reported making contact literally or virtually with a distribution attendant will be arrested. Poachers will be shot on sight.

"Residents are required to cover their thumb-screens. Articles found to be acceptable are duct tape, electrical tape, and adhesive bandages. You are not permitted to use sports mesh or anything with a degree of transparency. You are required to cover your thumb-screens. There will be raids. They will be random.

"It is your patriotic duty as American citizens to do your part in this emergency campaign of suppression and temperance. The responsibility is yours. This is not a drill. Your immediate cooperation is mandatory because Soul Text cannot be shut down.

"Repeat, we cannot shut it down."

[This story appeared in Nicole Castle's *Ghostlight* anthology, Fall, 2015.]

The Grave Keeper

I'm telling you, Professor, I'm gonna catch the bastard red handed and you ain't about to go talking me out of it.

No one's talking you out of anything.

Well, you don't have to say it. I can feel it the way you're sitting there staring out the windshield as if some ghost is floating there between the headstones.

Jonathan, I'll humor you with this nonsense because I feel that tonight we've become something like friends, but the ridicule isn't necessary. It is no secret that this makes me uncomfortable.

Why?

Why do *you* think?

Hmm. I think that up there in your classroom, in front of them first year students gawking at you, especially the coed-types twirling their hair and popping their gum, it's easy to talk about graveyards in *stories* and such, like that fella who always made the children into beggars and had the streets overrun with soot and with fog .

You mean Charles Dickens.

Yeah, Dickens. You think I didn't know that? I went to school. I know Dickens and Shakespeare and Hemingway and all them English *gentlemen*. What I'm saying is that when you read about stuff it's one thing.

And when you do them, you could go to prison.

We ain't breaking no law.

But we could be easily blamed for the actions of the phantom you want to catch simply because we're here on the premises.

It's my job to be on the premises, Professor.

At two in the morning?

Well sure. What if Percy books four burials tomorrow instead of three? Sometimes you got to dig at night, break out the braces and struts and the gas-powered Ditch Witch, get dirty.

Isn't that kind of loud?

Who'll hear all the way out here?

Don't you get tired?

I work best at night, I told you. Shit, you asked me all these questions when I first made to bring you out here. Is this some kind of teaching trick, like you want to test how set I am on catching this guy by making me repeat my reasons or something?

No Jonathan. I assure you that repetition is not something I favor. I'm just nervous, that's all.

For what?

I don't know.

Sure you do. You just don't want to admit that some wacko digging up graves and filling them back in scares the mess out of you.

Would I be sitting here if I was really that frightened?

I don't know. Would you?

Stop it.

What? Being rhetorical?

Yes.

You didn't think I knew that word, did ya?

No, I didn't.

Learned it in church.

Well, God bless.

No need to be sarcastic, Professor.

I wasn't being sarcastic. I was being ironic.

Christ! There he is!

Where?

There, by the flush memorials!

I don't see him.

Don't you have eyes? There now, crossing in front of those decorator boxwoods, the garden gate, now…shit, I lost him 'round the corner of the columbarium.

I want to go back.

C'mon, I was just kidding, Professor. Ain't no ghosts out here, just a lot of grinning skeletons.

What if he does show up tonight? What if he sees us?

He won't.

How do you know?

The lamp from the shed tosses a glow on the windows here. We see out, but he can't see in. We're safe. No one will know what we're doing.

What are we doing?

We're waiting to find out why this sick son of a bitch keeps digging up my handiwork…why I have to have this shit job excavating trenches in the elements in the first place and getting no credit for it while Professors like you sit in your ivory towers making all the rules.

Well, I do grade a lot of papers.

That ain't the point. And now you're making me mad, sitting there, hands folded in your lap all delicate, grinning that little grin like you know something I don't.

No one's laughing, Jonathan.

Well it feels like you are.

I either laugh or I don't. There's no middle ground. (pause). But Jonathan...

Hmm.

How do you know someone is really doing this?

Shovel marks on the backfill. I ain't no pedestrian.

Nice use of vocabulary.

Thanks. But you know what time it is, don't you?

No.

Professor...

I don't want to go back. I want to sit with you and play detective, where it's safe out here in the truck.

Game's over. And if I don't put you back in now, I'll still be sitting in the backhoe when the sun breaks and we can't have that, now can we?

It's dark down there and cramped and gritty.

Now, now, just hold still. I'll use the power tamper and pat you in snug as a bug.

I'm afraid your pun doesn't quite work, Jonathan. The bugs made their way through me a long time ago. It was quite offensive.

Yeah, you smell offensive. Let's go.

Jonathan?

Yes?

Will you adorn my crest with shovel marks?

Now, you know that's the signal! I can't go digging up the same grave over and again, 'cause it'll wreck the integrity of the cavity. Tomorrow is Mrs. McGill's turn over in the Covington Grove section. That's the game. We're family, all of us.

Family.

Right.

Games.

It's all we have. Now, let's say our goodbyes here where it's comfy. You know I don't like to have our voices lost out there in the wind. Goodnight Professor.

Oh fine. Goodbye.

Oh no, yourself, Professor. I prefer, 'See you soon' if you please."

[This story first appeared in *Schlock Webzine,* Volume #4, Issue #2, January 2013.]

The Tool Shed

I'd always been scared of the tool shed. My father built it back in 1962, the summer before Ma ran off, setting the base-concrete on four inches of crushed stone at the back edge of the property that was roughly bordered by a spread of thick public woods. We used to poke around back there behind the shed, my sister Sara and I, skirting the short clearing where Father set his traps, and slipping into the shadows between the trees to go looking for treasure. We found trinkets in the rough sometimes, a wallet chain, a mud-caked figurine, a rusted tooth-tipped skeleton key.

I was scared of the tool shed like any eleven-year-old would have been.

We lived on a four mile stretch of logging road that was isolated and therefore didn't have street lights. Miles away back through the forest and past the train depot there was a junkyard flare tower that burned methane, but that faint, oily illumination somehow just put a dull glow on the sky and darkened the tree line. When Father told you to go out and fetch him a hacksaw or one of his good Rigid pipe wrenches, you had to take a flashlight with you.

It wasn't just a tool shed.

Father worked the night shift at the chemical plant in Fulton County, but he made extra money doing odd jobs and masonry work for small businesses, as well as selling animal pelts to James "Badger" Jones, this old timer who ran the Thunderhead Trading post next to the gravel parking lot tourists used to gain access to the Aroura caverns to look at the stalagmites. Most of the time Badger sat in a rocking chair on the front porch, mouth puckered-in like a scarecrow, whittling, spitting tobacco, and hollering in at you that you'd better stay away from the display case with the firecrackers and cigarettes, and that maybe you could buy something for once after looking over the polished stones, fossils, and arrowheads. Father's sinister-looking fox and rabbit and squirrel hides were pinned to a board on the wall behind the cash register, but I liked the place anyway. While some of the shelf-stock was dust-coated junk to me, every now and again you found treasure, like a bright silver key ring with a whistle on it, or a no-date Buffalo nickel, or a bone tribal pen knife with a blade and a scissor in it.

Father used a "cape skinning" method that kept on the animal heads, and he floated the muscle tissue in a bucket of water and hydrogen peroxide, never chucking out the waste product until the tanning process had been completed for a bunch of them. Ever see an animal head without the skin on? The rodents look like black-eyed buzzards, and the foxes, like oversized blood-sucking rats. After a tanning, the shed smelled primitive, like animal fat and death long after Father buried the bones and innards in the yard and cleaned off his fleshing knives, leaving the doors open all day.

Even with the sunlight slanting down through the archway, the tanning table looked evil, like a torture rack with wide oak legs, taking up most of the floor space, with the cans of Borax, wood alcohol, and turpentine cluttered underneath along with the tubs of muriatic acid he used when he got a side job removing efflorescence from the masonry at the rec center or the municipal building. On the shelf to the right he had his baking soda, water jugs, and salt bags, but most of the wall space was covered by his power tools, hand tools, and accessories hanging on nails and pegboards like they were on display at one of those fancy hardware stores with a key-cutting station or one of those new-fangled paint shaking machines.

When Father sent you out to the tool shed he wasn't kidding about it, making you poke around for a bucket of steam or a left-handed smoke shifter. He timed you. For each minute you were gone he'd slip his leather belt out a loop. His Levi's had six of them, but if he hadn't changed out of his work clothes before supper he'd just undo the button-catches of his leather suspenders, four in the front and two in the back. When he wasn't wearing the belt, he kept it on a hook next to the stove. It was a brown tapered double pronged lizard print with a wide buckle shaped like an American Eagle. He didn't smack you with that part. He used it as a grip with his index and ring fingers down in the wing divots. When he grabbed you by the collar and gave you a whooping, his pants would slip off his hips through the process. When they got to his knees, he laid off. The limitation "kept things measured," he said. It was also a sin to have your drawers visible too long in front of a child, and Father was a God-fearing Baptist.

Thing is, I wasn't scared of a good lashing. Didn't need to be. I rarely completed a "go-get" in more than two loops or button-hooks, because the tool shed was haunted. See, the dead animals shrieked at you in there, all muffled and horrible like they were being gagged, or more as if you'd caught the moment the fur was being pulled off over their faces. It happened as soon as you opened the big double doors, and it seemed to be coming from the cement floor, from up-under the screw-jugs, pickle barrels, and dented steel drums under the tanning table.

Last week we were eating late because Father had been held up at the factory fixing a machine with a faulty rail-grease dispenser, but he was sure to remind us that he'd still taken the time to rustle us all up some corn and a few slivers of blue fish. His hands were clean especially around the nails, but the imprints on his face shaped like safety goggles made his eyes look wrathful. When the heater downstairs suddenly clacked and banged like it had just given up, he pointed his knife at me.

"Go out to the tool shed and fetch me my claw hammer. And also bring the long-handled slot drive screwdriver and my sixteen-inch tongue and groove pliers." He slipped the key from around his neck and tossed it on the table. "Hurry now."

165

I snatched it up and stretched out my legs to get it in my pocket. Sara put her fork down carefully so not to make noise. Her hair was up like static because she wasn't allowed to wear her wool knit cap at the table, and she looked at me first, then Father, chewing hurriedly with her mouth closed. That made her look like a bunny, and like always, it made me feel sad. She was precious to me, a delicate little bunny rabbit living in a dark house that had hard floors and sparse furnishings. She deserved better. Softer edges or something.

"Can I go with him?" she said.

"No."

Then he changed his mind, shrugging, unhooking the first catch on his work-suspenders.

"Yeah, sure," he said. "Double quick, now, the both of you."

We burst from the table and made for the back door. The Rayovac was hanging by a string next to the pot rack, and I went up on my toes to slip it over the nail, pausing only to flick it on and slap it hard like a man was supposed to, making the batteries snap to attention. I gave a quick glance back, but Father's eyes were too hot and bright, so I let my head sag between my shoulders and followed Sara out into the darkness.

Our feet made sounds in the cold grass like snakes. Thirty feet ahead, the image of the shed bobbed and started in and out of the light beam, and that's how I knew how fast I was running. Under the Maple, Sara skipped over the long ditch our sneakers had dug-in when we'd had a tire swing, and then she stopped dead in her tracks. I pulled up beside her at the edge of the cinderblock walkway, and she linked her arm in with mine at the elbow.

The doors were open, one flush against the wall, the other- an arm's length askew, creaking back and forth an inch or so in the wind. I put the beam of the flashlight between us, and we looked at each other, faces washed pale. Father never left the shed unlocked at night, let alone standing wide open. Ever. His power tools were too important to him, especially the wall stock. When he bought a new one he let us look at it in the living room first, propped there on the wood block table like it was a relic in a museum under glass.

But the shed doors were open just the same. I shined the light down and saw the pad lock for the ground-surface cane-bolt sprung open, lying there on the walkway. Then inside the shed there was a sound. Something muffled and shrieking. From under the tanning table. It was vibrating the bottom of some of the steel jugs making them buzz. I wanted to run away, but Sara held onto my elbow.

"Sounds are sounds, but the belt is real," she whispered.

She pulled me with her and we stepped through the archway. My mind was frozen, and I felt like my body was going through the motions on auto-pilot. We edged the corner and got to the long side of the tanning table, single file in the dark, the musty air tasting like dust and old mower-grass. A scream erupted from the floor to our left, sounding like a muzzled coyote with a knife in its throat, and we felt it in the concrete, I swear it. I was too scared to look down there so I kept to the task best I could, my flashlight making crazy swipes that cut into the dark, flashing across circular saws, power drills, diamond blades, and masonry trowels, some new and polished, others wearing spatters of cement or paint spots or tar streaks.

I somehow managed to steady my hand and focus the beam on the back edge of the tanning table where there was a bench vice and a battered red tool box. I ran to it, with Sara whispering to watch out for the exactos and fur knives Father might have tossed in there without retracting the blades. I also had to remind myself not to rush, because the bottom was so crammed that the tray wasn't even close to being seated flush. Didn't want to spill the whole kit and caboodle now, did I?

The floor shivered with a harsh screech that erupted from under the tanning table, pressure-filled and choked, and Sara and I rushed around to grope and thrash through the tool box, all caution be damned.

We found the screwdriver and pliers immediately, but hell if we could lay our hands on his claw hammer. We routed through the box again to no avail. I scoured the walls with the shaky beam of the Rayovac, but when I lit on the hand tool section by the hoses on the far side of the shed, there was a clear gap between the crimpers and the pry bars, you could see the empty U-shaped hook that would support the hammer head's neck, and the C-bracket that would have housed the base of the grip.

I moved to check out the far-left corner of the shed where he had some of his bigger tools propped up, and the second the light hit his walk-behind grass-seeder, my foot slipped in something.

It had to be blood.

"Run," I said quietly. "Now."

We ran. We crossed the lawn like thieves, and when we burst back in to the harsh light of the kitchen, Father was just reaching for the two back-snaps of those work suspenders. He saw what we'd returned with, and told us to go upstairs and strip to our skivvies. He went outside. He came back in, we heard him. He fixed the heater, we heard that too. When he came upstairs, he was kind enough to tell us where he'd found the hammer. It was under the tanning table. We each got a whooping. Didn't even feel it much. Too scared. Of what was in the closet we shared. It was our clothes, but more specifically, our sneakers. We hadn't felt it because the cold had made our feet and hands numb, but when we'd come upstairs to disrobe for our beating, both our pairs of old Keds had the soles burned clean off. Wasn't blood we were stepping in.

Wasn't muriatic acid either. It was *supernatural* muriatic acid, and I didn't put two and two together until the next day after a sleepless night, when I was looking for treasure at the Thunderhead Trading Post. Right there in the middle aisle on the two-sided gondola by the fishing rods and Christmas ornaments, I saw it. Bigger than I remembered, big as my palm. It was an earring Ma wore, this yellow, red polka dot, polyethylene art deco thing, shaped like two pyramids with the bases stuck together. I think technically it was an equilateral polygon, or maybe a rhombus, but I was never good with the geometrical shapes past plain squares and triangles.

I didn't remember it until I saw it and remembered it, if that makes a damned bit of sense. I didn't really remember my mother. When I was four and a half she ran off – out West our Father said. Her bright cartoonish art deco earrings were one of my first forgotten memories, and somehow that connected with one of my conscious, remembered first memories, and that was looking out my bedroom window into the back yard. It was three weeks after Ma left, about five days after me and Sara came back from Aunt Helena's trailer where Father had dropped us off for a couple of weeks so he could get papers and things in order. The tire swing was still on the Maple, and the Sheriff and two of his deputies were having fun digging holes.

Father said it was "procedure" and he told us they were making sure he'd buried his animal carcasses the right way…something about laws and property violations, but standing there in the Thunderhead with Ma's earring in my hand made me think differently about the whole thing.

I walked out through the door, and Badger looked over, seeing what was in my hand, his face like petrified wood. There was a long silence between us, and then he started laughing, coughing hard, bending over, saying "Oh, Jesus effin' Christ" a few times in that bone-gravel rasp. Finally, he got himself together, tightened his grip on the arms of the rocker, and hawked up a good one that seemed to have been rattling around somewhere deep in his chest throughout the affair. He rolled it around his tongue a bit and leaned to spit it over the porch-rail.

"You gonna buy back your own property?" He had turned back to me, sort of glancing over his shoulder. It looked like he was going to break into another fit, and I said bluntly,

"When did you get this?"

He settled in his chair and he squinted.

"Yesterday. Your paw brought it in. Brought a whole box of old stuff. He said he was cleaning the attic or something, and I paid him two dollars for all of it."

"Where's the other one?"

"The other what?"

"Earring."

His mouth made a funnel shape.

"Don't know," he said, finally.

But I did.

—

I told Sara about it and we waited until the next morning. We ate our sugarless oatmeal and pretended to walk the road two miles to school like we always did. But just past the dog leg we dipped into the woods and cut back toward the house, hiding there in the wild grass until we saw Father pull off in his pickup truck. He was working a double at the plant. We had plenty of time.

To dig for treasure.

We struggled over the biggest rock we could find in the brush and dropped it on the padlock locking the cane bolt seated in the ground sheath. That part took the most courage. But now that the hasp was scuffed, we'd passed the point of no return anyway.

We broke the lock in three tries.

It was impossible to push the tanning table out of the way because it filled most of the interior and wouldn't fit through the doors. Father had built it in there, so we tipped the monster up on its side, struggling so you could see the cords in our necks. Finally, we got it past the balance point, and it bashed over into his pegboard display sending some hand planers, tin snips, and jab saws flipping up over our heads. We quickly moved all the cans, jugs, and steel canisters to the side, next to waddle over a big bag of mulch that we set at the bottom just in case the table wanted to start skidding on us. We rested a second. Got ready for step two.

We tried to haul over the big jack hammer, but it was too heavy. I could hardly even lift the steel for it to tell you the truth, and we were lucky that we found a smaller chipper with a D-handle nearby. The first extension cord didn't work, and we tried two others before realizing that it was the outlet that was fried. I unplugged his bench grinder, stuck in the twelve-gauge prongs, and dragged the smaller breaker hammer to the center of the floor.

He'd done a good re-pour. You literally couldn't see the lines. I thought the breaker was going to be like a battering ram, but it wasn't. It didn't start "striking" until you leaned on it, so it sluffed away the cement instead of bashing at it.

I didn't have to go far. About three inches down I found treasure, and when I pulled it out and dusted it off, I could swear I could feel my dead mother's heartbeat inside it.

Her other earring, of course. Made with polyethylene, all art deco with these girly red polka dots, but it was anything but "girly," and nothing short of pure genius. See, Father's muriatic acid might have been able to take care of Ma's skin and bones and muscle and fiber, but it couldn't do too much to this kind of plastic. That's why they kept the dangerous liquid in a polyethylene container in the first place! And I don't know what chore she forgot or what menial task she was too slow getting done, but it was clear that Father had it in for her, big time.

He'd sent us to Aunt Helena's trailer for a couple of weeks. And Ma didn't see her friends all that often, as she was stuck four miles down an isolated logging road, trapped in a cheerless, dark house, jarring preserves, shelling peas, doing laundry. It would be near a month until she turned up missing, so father had one hell of a window.

He had all the tools and materials. He killed her, probably right there in the shed so he wouldn't have to move her, except to the corner when he busted a hole in the concrete. Then he got on his rubber gloves and chemical mask, and dumped her in what was most probably a hazardous waste drum made of blue plastic, taken from the stock yard at the plant, and it was likely it didn't take him long to dissolve her to nothing in it.

The next part took patience, I'm sure, but there had to be a filtering process where Father sweated it out playing chemist. I looked it up in the library later to confirm my initial suspicions, and found out specifically that to dilute muriatic acid, the ratio is a half pint to a gallon of water, and an eighty-pound bag of cement gets three quarts. When he had a good mix, he filled the hole back in nice and neat. Did a resurfacing of the whole floor too, just to cover all of the fissures. The concrete chunks that got busted out to form the original void wouldn't have even looked a bit strange in the back of his pickup, and he carted it all off to the dump as if it was nothing.

His original tanning table from a few years back was a portable job that had folding legs; rickety as all hell from what he had said. He'd built the big oak tanning table when I was born. It was his holiday gift to himself as the story went. I suppose that's when he decided he was going to murder my mother a few years later, dissolve her, bury her in the floor, and cover it all up with the table nobody in their right mind would think about moving, trust me, tipping it up on end was no picnic.

Father had a good decoy. When the Sheriff and his two deputies came, they brought their spade shovels. Though it wasn't an all-out excavation with dump trucks and backhoes like you saw on the news when they thought they'd landed themselves a serial killer, the three of them dug there all day. Dug up his animal carcasses to the right of the shed and the bigger grave over where the grass was dead by the lattice fencing where Ma had tried once to grow carrots and cabbage. They only found animal bones. They checked his truck. They checked his time sheet at the plant. They never checked under the tanning table.

I held the dusty plastic earring in my hand, feeling its weight, fingering the edges. Like I said, it was big as my palm, and I had to wonder two things about that, the first one – a scenario easy to fill in the blanks, and the latter, the most horrendous thing you could possibly imagine.

The first issue was how Ma managed to sneak it out to the shed, and I imagine the scene began with Father standing in their bedroom doorway casting his black shadow across the floor, telling her to strip down. I didn't like to think of my Ma doing such a thing because it was wrong and I could barely remember what she looked like to begin with, but I was intent on painting the truest picture I could.

Father wouldn't have watched. He'd have given the order to her and closed the door leaving her to it. Scarier that way. It also let her work through her nerves in private, making it so she could build up a game face. Not that

Father would have cared how brave she made herself look, but he was smart enough to know it was less probable she'd try to scratch at his eyes or go for his groin once she'd made up her mind to make an exit all proud and honorable.

But when he closed the door, I don't think she was shaking and whimpering, trying to work through it all. I think she was careful to be quiet and methodical about taking off all her things, her wedding band, maybe a brooch-pin, the whole nine yards, and I think she took the big plastic earring from her jewelry box and hid it under her thigh. So she could palm it after Father came back to make the final check of her ears, hair, and fingers. Because she knew he had muriatic acid out in the shed. Because she thought that someday someone might notice one of the earrings was missing.

But he'd see her closed fist when he stood her up, you say? I don't see it unfolding that way. Father was a big man who drove big vehicles and worked big machines. He was a beast who took matters into his own hands, and I strongly doubt that he guided her out of that bedroom like she was a quaint little lady. The way I see it, he banged the door hard against the corner-wall, barged in, forced her mouth open for a quick last look, grabbed at her fingers, and ran his rough hands through her hair like he was checking some wild animal for wood ticks. Then he threw her over his shoulder, giving her the chance to slip the plastic accessory out from under her leg in that split second his eyes were cast down. Careless of him you say? Maybe. But flinging her around like a ragdoll would have satisfied him, deep to his roots, and he prided himself in his flair for dark theater.

The second part of the scenario, however, the horrendous part, is what must have happened in the shed once he got her there. See, I don't think he killed her right off. I think he tossed her in, closed the doors, and pushed down the cane-bolt. To make her wait. In the dark. Six minutes, like one per belt loop, except this time he probably used a stop watch instead of the kitchen wall clock.

Couldn't she have gotten a weapon, you say? Well, sure. But it was dark and she was scared and she knew that when he pulled up the lock and flung open the door he'd be ready for it. Better to die trying, you say? Could be. But maybe she was too small for that or too naked and cold. Besides. She'd

173

already planned her revenge. The horrendous part is how hard it must have been making herself swallow that earring.

I think she fumbled around in the pitch black until she found a rat tail file or maybe Father's three-sided architect's ruler. I think she put that wide clumsy object in her mouth and shoved it down her own throat, making it bulge, making her shriek in a savage pain that was muffled like an animal screaming into its own fur being pulled over its face.

How exactly Father killed her is incidental. I would think he opened the doors and executed the mechanics in a manner that was cold and efficient, no talking, no distractions, like the way he did business, like the way that he beat us. As for the murder weapon, I would guess it was a heavy blunt object; a knife meant more blood-spill and guns could be heard even four long miles down a logging road.

Like a sack of grain, he hefted her up and dumped her in what was most likely a fifty-gallon plastic drum meant for bio-hazardous waste and such, and then he dissolved her. Next, he worked the diluting process until he had enough purified water to make new cement, and he filled in the hole he'd busted in the middle of the floor like the true handyman that he was. Following that, it was a question of moving everything out off the floor so he could re-finish the surface, and all the secrets were silenced forever.

Except for the fact that my Ma's ghost kept calling out to my sister and me from under the tanning table until I got wise and did my own demolition.

I stood there in the shed, holding my dead Ma's earring in my hand and looked over at Sara. When we talked later it was clear we'd come to similar conclusions about the remaining unknowns and puzzle pieces, but there were two things we didn't agree on at first, trivial as our differences of opinion might have been.

First, why didn't Father just scatter the diluted acid out in the grass or somewhere deep in the woods? To this, I was initially pretty convinced that he didn't trust the dilution process completely, I mean, no matter how many times he did the transfer container to container, you had to think there would be some concentration of the burning agent left swimming around, and I'm sure he didn't want to leave singe-marks. He had no idea the Sheriff and his deputies wouldn't call in the Feds to comb the forest, so he did his fancy cement burial leaving the evidence right there a few feet from his animal boneyards, masked in plain sight and all that. Sara's spin on it was that he mistrusted the dilution process in a different way, as in the idea that maybe he wasn't able to assure himself that there wasn't some bone meal at the bottom of the barrel that didn't quite get absorbed, or a microscopic piece of tendon or something. I didn't disagree all that wholeheartedly. It was like that saying, "six of one, half a dozen of the other."

The second thing we saw differently, however, was the question of why he didn't see the polyethylene earring floating in the mixture between pours. I mean, the strange artifact was almost palm-sized, and that's no small bit of bone meal or microscopic tendon you'd miss! My answer was and still is that it was a combination of darkness and science. I am convinced Father killed Ma at night, and there is no way in hell he had a light on in the shed during the dissolving and diluting operation, no way. He would have had to leave the doors open, and even a small utility lamp would have lit up the world in there. It was the contrast, that dark tree line behind him, and trust me, even though the nearest neighbor was more than two miles removed, Father wasn't about to risk putting on a show for some passerby out on the road. No. He did it by moonlight, whatever filtered into the shed. He didn't hear the earring when he poured barrel to barrel, because large volumes of liquid are loud in the transfer, especially in a partially enclosed space, and he didn't see it settled on top because some polyethylene is denser than water, depending on the factory mix. It sank to the bottom each time he poured. It was dark, and he missed it. Sara was more of the belief that he hurried through and got subconsciously careless on purpose. Because of guilt. Nowadays, Sara is a renowned psychotherapist, and I am sure she has a boatload of books and scholarly journal articles that would indicate she was right all along.

But I still beg to differ. Father didn't know guilt. He only knew order. And even though the State Prison didn't allow for shoe strings or belt loops, I'll bet he felt right at home, moving gate to gate and buzzer to buzzer. I often wondered if any of his daily obligations had six-minute cut-offs, like shower-time or bed checks or taking a piss in the community john. Of course, that would have been the prefect irony. Or maybe not. His being on the wrong side of the limitation didn't necessarily mean that he was intimidated by it. Familiarity can translate to a sort of comfort regardless of your perspective. And any window they gave him longer than it would take a frightened young boy and his sister to run out and grab a few hand tools out of the tool shed, would have seemed to him a grand sort of bonus.

[This story appeared in Jason Henderson's *Castle of Horror 1* anthology, July 2019.]

Toll Booth (a novella)

Anemia: a condition in which the blood is deficient in red blood cells, in hemoglobin, or in total volume.

M y name is James Raybeck, and if you are reading this message, I am already dead.

It most probably took about two weeks to work through all the light-weights trying to make it all night in the booth just once for the thrill of it. It probably took another two to put feelers out past Westville and come up absolutely empty in a serious search for long-term toll collectors to work the graveyard shift. I would estimate it was another three or four working days to rush through the paperwork issuing the green light for removal, and a few more for the dismantling, the demolition of the concrete pad beneath, and the excavation of the ground under that.

It is no secret to the townspeople of Westville that the Siegal Group claimed back in '74 that the footer under the base was never properly surveyed and assessed while Runnameade Engineering gave the quicker OK for the construction of the pad, and later, the single toll booth at the base of the exit ramp off the Route 79 overpass. Everyone and their mothers knew that Siegal never really cared so much about that initial pour (small beans) or the possible flaw in the footer (a technicality to be used for leverage). Their real interest was in the contract for an entire toll plaza, a complicated network of lighting systems and road signs, a restaurant complex, a gas station complete with plumbing of its own, and a double-yellow two-way straight through to Main Street. It was Goliath's vision. Risky, gargantuan costs up front, and when it all came down to whose bid was chosen, Ed Runnameade was the now late Mayor Smitherbridge's second cousin, and his middle boy was just starting out on his own with Runnameade Concrete, Road Systems, Builders, and Wreckers. The easiest (and most expeditious) solution was dumping in the backfill, pouring the concrete, and enjoying the highest initial profit margin that a simple guard shack, traffic signal lamp, and barrier gate arm would bring despite the horrible things that happened right there at the edge of Scutters Woods.

Since the present-day removal of the booth itself will be the first item of business (the current governor is married to a Siegal) and certain individuals in current positions of power downtown have been waiting for an excuse to move forward with the closure of this particular chapter in Westville history no matter what the cost, I would estimate you are reading this approximately five weeks after my demise, six at the outside. A new contractor recommended by the conglomerate now known as Siegal/TriState Industries, initially represented by some twenty-five-year-old kid with a hangover from last night's adventures at the Pleasure Chest Gentleman's Club out on the Pike, will have found this packet of writing long before his team has taken out the safety glass, disengaged the roof support channels, and used mini-grinders to cut through the welds bonding the wall panels.

He will have found this writing in its manila envelope under the storage cabinet that I bolted to the floor with wedge anchors last February. I kept the night-time stuff in that steel case, the lot consisting of a pair of Embury Luck-E-Lite Kerosene traffic lanterns, a Streamline Fire Vulcan flashlight, and pair of PF 500 power flares, meant to be of bland disinterest to the dayshift employees: Tim Clements Monday through Thursday, and Frank Hillboro the long weekend crew chief. And just in case one of them had gotten a wild hair up his ass, unscrewed the bolts, and moved the cabinet before I died of "natural causes"? Well, I do carry a Ruger LCP .380 for protection. I would have had no problem turning it on myself. It has been a long road, my friend.

Since the age of seventeen I have dedicated my life to this toll booth, this literal sanctuary, this metaphorical prison, Monday through Monday, 6:00 P.M. to 7:00 A.M. Cal Ripken's got nothing on me. If you entered the town of Westville, Indiana, from Route 79, down Reed Road and through Scutters Woods between the years of 1978 and 2021 after the sun dipped below the horizon, you did it on my watch.

I endure.

When this structure went up, the first toll collectors on graveyard shift initially complained of feeling faint. Then came rumors of severe palpitations, followed by stories of visions in the windows, always at the edge of sight, teasing the periphery of the given operator's view of the 360-degree sliding glass safety panels around him. Some claimed it was a boy laughing maniacally and then being decapitated from behind, while others swore it was a woman ripping apart a super-sized embryo. After two short weeks, the booth almost came down. I dropped out of high school to save it. I had no choice.

Within days of my first moments on the job, I started taking Geritol to up my iron and B vitamin counts. It was like a Band-Aid on an amputation. The visions were bad enough, but the blackouts were disastrous. In the first month I was woken up from a dead faint three times, twice by customers laying on their horns, and once in August when a young waitress from Kulpswood actually exited her vehicle, opened the portal door, and helped me off the floor. I approached my doctor and was refused medicine for anemia, which I showed no signs of in my life outside of the booth.

I thickened up my blood the old-fashioned way. I went on a "diet" including high-fat stuff like liver and whole milk. Since my late teens I have consistently eaten breakfasts made of a minimum of five egg yolks, three large links of Hatfield sausage, home fries smothered in onions, and Jewish hallah covered with butter. My lunches have been constructed of various red meats, and my dinners have always included drawn butter, fried side dishes, and cheeses. Between meals I've pretty much settled with deep fried Cheetos and good old-fashioned vanilla chocolate chip ice cream, but have been known to go off the beaten path with Hot Fries, Ranch Doritos, and Ring-Dings.

There is no physician worth his salt that would ever tell you that there is a correlation between cholesterol and anemic need, but please believe me when I say that you could not survive the booth with an LDL or triglyceride count under 330. When I started there I was five foot-eight inches and a cool one hundred and fifty-four pounds. Though I have quietly cheated any overt sort of obesity with a lightning metabolism passed down from my mother's side of the family, my small pear-shaped paunch and respectable weight of one eighty-four is deceiving. Stuff like this catches up with you, and I have been a poster-boy for a stroke, blood clot, or heart attack for some time now.

That which you are reading at this moment, I composed on my Dell. It took me four months to say it exactly the way it needed to be said, and since I wanted you to get the whole picture I put the thing in story form. I even added italics at times to express inner monologue and recent flashbacks. Though I am no professional, everyone knows that even a high school drop-out can up his level of discourse through reading. And I have had nothing but time on my hands. I have had time to read, to write, to mourn, and adapt.

Reed Road is a one-way thoroughfare that cuts through Scutters Woods for five miles and eventually opens out to Main Street. To use Reed Road up until now, you would have had to come off the Route 79 overpass and pay me a toll anywhere from fifty cents to two-seventy-five, depending on where you originally picked up the turnpike. So to all my customers, to my acquaintances in the past, to my mother God rest her, my relatives, and those of you that will hear of this through the media, know and try to understand my story.

And to you, my contractor friend with the hangover, he who has just found this packet under the bolted-down cabinet. I finally want to confirm something before you dismantle the walls, stack the safety glass, put my cash drawer and F9 500 POS touch screen on eBay, and start busting out the concrete pad below your feet.

The toll booth still erected around you is haunted.

I am going to tell you how it got that way.

This is my confession.

1.

She's a pussy-dog, and you know it, Jimmy.

No she isn't.

Is! She looks like a leprechaun.

She's half beagle and half fox terrier. That's why her ears stick up like that. And she's really nice.

Nice! Dog's ain't supposed to be "nice." They're supposed to be faithful. They're supposed to have big paws and lots of hair. They're supposed to chase after sticks, guard the house, and flush rabbits and pheasants out of the brush and shit.

She barks when strangers come...

She yips! She's a yip dog.

Well, I like her.

I know you do, Jimmy. Hell, I like her too. I was just kidding.

Really?

Yeah, she's awesome. For a gay, faggot, pussy-dog.

Kyle winked, pushed out of the pit, and crawled under the caution tape. On tiptoe I peered over the lip of our new hiding hole and watched him walk across the abandoned job site. He stopped by a stack of cinderblocks and a pile of long steel bars with grooves in them. He turned and scratched his head. He stroked an imaginary beard. He hawked up and spit into a red wheelbarrow with a flat tire, then spun away, spread his feet, and fumbled with his pants. He started pissing down the side of a dented fifty-gallon drum. His shoulders were shaking as were mine, and his stream went through a number of unsteady spurts in rhythm with his laughter. He started gyrating his hips and the urine that dissolved the old dust in shiny splatters became a pattern. He was writing his name.

"Kyle, don't."

He zipped up and climbed into the cab of a bulldozer.

"Don't what?" He started yanking on the gear handles. He was not quite tall enough to reach the floor pedals with his feet.

"Don't mess around."

"But Jimmy, this piece of shit won't move."

More yanking. Hard. His teeth were clenched beneath the thinnest of smiles and sweat ran through his dirty blond crewcut. The scene was becoming a familiar one. It was a hot summer day in Westville, we were thirteen years old, I was Kyle's new pal, and we were out making mischief.

"C'mon," I said. "You're gonna bust it."

He stopped.

"So? What are they going to do, take fingerprints? Next, you're about tell me that the Chief of Police is gonna connect some busted dozer gear with my name written in piss over there on that drum. You're a paranoid little jerk-weed, ain't ya?"

I shrugged. He shrugged back and we both laughed. It was the usual standoff. My base instincts screamed "foul" long before we chucked apples at the Levinworths' tin roof, or doused the church doorknobs with bacon grease, or lit up a bag of dogshit on the top step of Mr. Kimball's front porch. I was the worried voice of what could go wrong and Kyle would twist my words around to prove we wouldn't get caught.

I rested my forearms on the edge of the trench and looked for a place to draw pictures in the dirt. There was a half-buried tube of liquid nails and a scuffed-up red gas cap next to a fanned-out toss of broken green glass pieces. The bent-up Genesee Cream Ale bottle cap was a foot to the left, and I made note to possibly flip it at Kyle if the moment was right. I rubbed my index finger into the ground. It was good dirt. Soft, with pretty little mica specs in it. I drew a cartoon penis and a cartoon vagina. A stalk with a bulb and an oval with an upside down "Y" in it. Why did vaginas look like peace signs anyway?

"So," I said. "This is the big secret?" I looked up. "We rode bikes five miles just to trash some old dozer? You said you had some new surprise out here that was ultimate pisser."

Kyle put his elbow up on the steering column.

"Still drawing pussy instead of getting it, Jimmy?"

I frowned and rubbed out my dirty cartoons.

"So, how much kootchie are you getting?"

"Enough," he said. Just ask Billy Healy."

I had heard the stories. Supposedly, Kyle had copped a feel of Jeanette Wallman's crotch at the Thatcher Park Shopping Center in the back bed of a pickup parked behind the Overbrook Deli. The legend was that she was wearing tight white jeans and his dirty hand left actual prints.

"Got any gum, Jimmy?"

He was staring. It sort of hurt to look back at it. For the millionth time that day, I looked down, and to my dismay, started drawing in the dirt again.

"You know I don't," I said. My mom didn't let me have gum. She didn't let me have Twizzlers or corn chips either. She was a health food freak-a-zoid and stocked the house with granola, wheat germ, and soy products. She also did regular room checks.

"That's OK," he said. "I do."

He fished a square of Bazooka out of his pocket and chucked it to me. It fell a bit short and I reached out for it eagerly. It felt like Christmas when you could scarf up a freebie. I ripped it open, licked the sugar powder off the comic no one ever read anyway, and jammed the gum in my mouth. I had chewed it three good times before I realized that Kyle was still wearing that hard, blank expression.

"That's all right," he said. "I didn't want my half anyway."

My shoulders sagged. Kyle Skinner was the most wild and obnoxious boy that went to Paxon Hill Junior High School, but he also had these cast-iron rules of etiquette. Figuring out the boundaries was a constant source of pain for me, but it also fascinated me in some deep, secret place. Somehow, these were the laws of growing up your mom never told you about.

He turned away and gazed out at the woods that flanked the dirt road.

"Come up here and have a smoke with me, Jimmy."

"My mom will smell it on me."

"Huh?"

"My mom will smell it!"

"That's bullshit and you know it," he said. "Butt breath goes away in fifteen minutes."

"How do you know?"

Kyle bent his knee and slapped the sole of his foot flat to the bulldozer's control panel. He hiked up the bottom edge of his jeans and dug for the smoke pack hidden in his sock.

"Bobby Justice told me."

I was silenced. Just the fact that Kyle had conversed with Bobby Justice was an instant credibility. The guy was seventeen. He took shop classes half the day, majored in raising hell, and even got arrested once for selling grams of Hawaiian pot under the bleachers on the school football field. He drove a jacked-up black Mustang. He wore shit-kicker boots, and a chain hanging out the back pocket in that half-moon that said in its dumb, blind sort of grin, "Fuck off, Chief." Rumor had it that he once pulled a sawed-off shotgun out of his trunk at a Hell's Angels biker party, somewhere between the tube-funnel beer-chugging contest and the motor throw, because some dude was wearing a Lynyrd Skynyrd T-shirt that he wanted.

And it was mind-boggling to picture Kyle extracting this information from Bobby Justice in casual conversation. The only reason this bully ignored kids like us was that we were still too young to beat up.

Kyle drew out the pack, ripped away the cellophane, and let it float off on the wind. With a mild sort of alarm I noticed that the brand in his fist was the filterless Chesterfields. Last time it was Marlboros.

He scratched at the foil cover and pinched one up.

"Come here, sit down, and have a smoke with me, Jimmy." He held it like a pointer for emphasis. "I'm not asking you to steal the change from your mom's purse like I did. I'm not asking you to go down to the Rexalls and tell the old fart that the butts are for your old man, neither. I've already done all that myself. The only thing I want is for your first puff to be with me. Ain't you my new best friend no more? Don't ya want to hang out with the big boys?"

I climbed out of the trench, my face burning, my mind racing. In the past two years friendships had suddenly twisted around by definition, and it was like I hadn't been paying attention in math class or something. The "cool" kids had access to *Penthouse* and *Gallery* magazines, and stuff like Pop Rocks, cherry bombs, pump BB guns, and exploding gag cigarette loads. They were building monster album collections with the complete works of Zeppelin, Sabbath, Kiss, and The Who, while the only things Mom let me have was this shitty eight-track, a tape by Helen Reddy, and a commercial, pop anthology you ordered from TV called *Autumn '73*.

I walked to the dozer.

Kyle scrambled from the big bucket seat and sat on the dozer's thick tread strip between the two side wheels. He slapped the area next to him and I took my place at his side. Our weight bowed the track pad down a bit and I put my hands between my knees. His arm was across my shoulders.

"Now listen," he said. "Don't suck it down like you're gulping a Pepsi. And don't use your teeth. Take a small puff, hold it in your mouth for a second and then breathe it in slow. And when you blow it out don't try to do smoke rings. That shit is for girls."

I nodded.

"Go on then, Bozo. Take it," he said. He was holding the pack out with my cigarette jutting up about a half inch from the others.

I reached for it. My fingers were shaking a bit.

"Breathe," he said. "Breathe, baby. Stay with me." In a far-off way I noticed that his arm had disengaged itself. I put the cigarette between my lips. Took it back out. Wiped off a little drool. Reinserted. "OK, OK," he said. "Here we go."

He struck a match, cupped it, and brought it across. I leaned in going cross-eyed. Close up it looked beautiful and deadly. I sucked in carefully and got braced for the hot, nasty swallow.

It was awesome.

Sharp, it hit the back of my throat and rolled into me like a chocolate cloud. It was potent and rich. Forbidden. I blew it out and watched the gray smoke make art on the air. My head spun a bit in a friendly sort of a way, and I knew I could handle this. I was older now. Better. I spit my gum out and took another deep drag.

"Now you're ready for the surprise," Kyle said. He was studying me, smoking one himself now. His eyes were thin, but his expression was otherwise neutral. I leaned back.

"Show me."

He hopped down, went to his knees, and reached behind the dozer's front roller. I couldn't see his arm from my angle, and I had the sudden premonition that he was going to fake like something grabbed his hand. He would open his eyes in wide surprise and jam his shoulder into the front of the dozer, giving the illusion he was being yanked really hard from something lurking in the shadows under the load bucket. Of course, this didn't happen. If it had, however, I would have been ready and it made me smile. I really was changing for the better.

He came back up with a cardboard box about the size of a car battery. It was old and stained, and the front had a sticker that said "16D."

"What is it?" I said. He carefully set it down on the tread a few feet to my left.

"This here," he said, "is a fine example of why most grown-ups have shit for brains." He took a deep drag of the smoke he'd been lipping, then pointed to the box with the lit end for emphasis.

"Notice, James, the '16.' This stands for three and a half. The 'D' stands for 'penny.' Put them together and the '16D' means three and a half inches of nail. But please explain to this dumb-ass kid what 'D' has anything to do with 'penny,' and what 'penny' has to do with hand nails which are so obviously made of steel and not copper."

I let go a nervous laugh.

"Where did you get—"

"I clipped them from my Pop's tool box," he said. "Look." He flipped open the top, dug up a nail, and held it outward. It was bent and a bit jagged.

"Why's it all screwy?" I said.

"When my Pop's done framing a house, he walks the job and yanks out all the bent nails."

"Why?"

"He brings them all back to the tool-house and pulls a major bitch and moan. Gets paid back for each and every one of them."

"Then he'll miss that box!" I said. I had jumped to my feet, and I chucked away the smoke. "Geez, Kyle, why did you go and do that? He's probably going to kill you and then come for me!"

His eyes narrowed.

"I ain't that stupid, James. I found the empty box in the garage two months ago and stashed it in the closet behind my old board games and Lego garbage. I've been filling it up one nail at a time. Cripes, don't be such a fucking dipshit!"

I forced a wounded grin.

"You're the one with a dipshit pal and that makes you a total bonehead."

"Yeah," he said. "I must be freakin' bonkers." He was smiling but I found it hard to mirror. Just because Kyle knew how to handle his old man didn't mean I'd figured it out.

Mr. Skinner was Westville's definition of a good ole boy. He drove a mud-splattered, light brown Chevy pickup and always had the back bed filled with ladders, lumber, upside-down wheelbarrows, and power tools. He had an American flag on the hood-side opposite the antenna and a bumper sticker that talked about ripping his pistol from his cold, dead fingers. On the driver's door was his company logo, "One-Truck-Johnny."

I sat back and kicked a bit at the dirt.

"So, what are the bent nails for?"

Golden question. Jackpot. Kyle was glowing.

He brought the box to head level and gave it a shake. The nails clacked inside and he moved to the sound in a sarcastic rendition of the

"Do-Si-Do" we learned in gym class two winters ago. His head was sort of sideways, one eye regarding me in a sly sort of observation. He was doing a circular motion with the box now like the Good & Plenty choo-choo boy on TV. He shuffled past me. He stopped. He pulled up the box top, drew out a nail, and tossed it into the middle of the dirt road that cut through the job site.

He turned back with raised eyebrows. I was sorry to disappoint.

"What are you doing?" I said.

He shook his head, took out a second nail, and flipped it to the road from behind his back. He grabbed another, lifted his leg, and chucked it up from beneath. That particular one landed with its sharp point angled straight to the sky.

I shot off the tread.

"You can't do that!" I looked back to the Route 79 overpass that spanned the horizon to my right. "If someone takes a wrong turn off the highway you know they'll be trucking, shit, they're gonna run over those nails and pop a tire!"

Kyle looked up at the sky with his arms spread out.

"By George, I think he's got it!"

The taste in my mouth was electric. Three months ago the construction men had blocked off exit 7 up on the overpass while completing the off ramp, but the job got delayed before the new extension could be finished down here. Dirt road city. The plans for pouring and paving had come to a dead halt and long since, all the road barriers up on the turnpike had been stolen or moved. It was an old joke by now, that bum steer on the overpass and everyone knew not to take the deep, unmarked turn. Everyone.

Unless they weren't from Westville.

Every now and again some goober took the exit by mistake and barreled down the ramp to the dirt road. It was a major pain too, as the rough detour stretched for five miles through the woods before hitting the outskirts of Westville Central. Bumpy ride. Slow as all hell.

Soon to be stalled out and stranded.

I looked up at the overpass and, from behind its triple guard rail, heard the cars shooting past. They couldn't see us and we couldn't see them. A double blindfold.

"Pick 'em up, Kyle," I said. It sounded like a command backed at least by a shred of confidence, and of that I was glad. Kyle replied by flipping another nail into the road.

"You sound like your mother." His voice rose to falsetto. "Let's talk about you and how you feel about yourself, James. Let's have a big pow-wow."

His tone went back to normal.

"Damn, Jimmy. Your ma just won't leave you be, will she? The lady has you turned pussy is all, hell, why does she have to know everything anyway? She don't even give you an allowance."

"What does that have to do with—"

"Well she don't, *does* she? Does she?"

My eyes felt hot and bloodshot.

"She gives me money."

He snorted.

"Exactly! But ya got to ask for it every time. That's how she keeps tabs on what you're going to do with it. Don't you see? Anytime you want to buy something fun she gets to shoot it down. She wants to keep her little baby-boy, don't she? She won't let you have secrets. That should be a crime or something."

He nodded at me meaningfully.

"I know you're a charity case, Jimmy. That's why I want to help ya. That's why I *like* ya." He held up a crooked nail. "This ain't gonna cost nothing. This here secret is gonna be a freebie."

My mouth opened and I shut it. Like always, Kyle had twisted my mother right into the crux, and though the correlation was clumsy, the effect was damned potent. Most of my friends were starting to get out more, like after dusk and all, but I still wasn't allowed. I had to stay home with mother so we could talk. Talk-talk, some nights she had me at the kitchen table until eight o'clock, asking about the details of my day and hanging on the words.

189

She was lord, judge, and jury, always cramming my head full of her *interpretations*. Oh, she was a regular code-cracker all right.

So yeah, since Dad left it had become a big responsibility being the man of my family. A responsibility I was starting to resent with or without Kyle Skinner.

He pushed the box out toward me and gave it a shake.

"Go on, Jimmy. Do a nail, man."

I scooped my thumb and index finger into the box, drew out a nail, and underhanded it out to the road. My nail looked like a crooked finger, pointing.

This was not the way I imagined I would turn out.

I took a step forward so I could grab back my nail.

"Too late for that shit!" Kyle said from behind.

There was a *shhhuuuuckkk* sound to my right followed by a flock of shadows spinning madly across the road. A shower of nails pelted down to kick up a scatter of dust.

The lane was covered.

I thought of picking up the nails one by one, but I stopped myself right there. I wasn't the one who dumped the whole box. It wasn't my idea to leave someone stranded out here with a flat.

I decided to let him get his own Goddamned nails and pick mine up in the process. What did I owe him? A Chesterfield and a piece of gum? I didn't care. I wasn't going to do this. I had enough guilt dumped on me at home.

I turned to tell him all this, but Kyle wasn't looking my way. He was staring at something off to the side. Something absolutely mesmerizing.

I followed the line of his gaze and saw the car coming down the ramp.

It was coming fast, and the air suddenly tasted rusty and harsh. Kyle grabbed my arm. My stomach was a lead ball, my ears hot as branding irons.

We scrambled behind a red dumpster and there was the gritty sound of a car bumper banging from roadway to dirt. Kyle dropped to his knees for the low view and I stayed up high.

Sharp sun lanced off the chrome and plastered a hot glare to the windshield. It was a dull orange Honda Civic, already swerving, plumes of dirt spitting up high behind it.

My mouth was working the word "no" silently.

There was a series of sharp "pop" sounds. The car did a rapid back-and-forth, left to right to left to right, then shot straight toward us. Like a yanked sheet the glare on the windshield vanished, and I was eye-to-eye with the driver.

She had straight blonde hair. I thought she was wearing one of those plastic, red, three-quarter-moon hair bands that formed her bangs into their own separate little statement, but I couldn't be sure at the moment. Her face had a sharp sort of beauty that was almost regal, and of that I was quite sure. Then the moment was gone. She overcompensated for control and yanked the wheel the other way. Now I saw the back of the car and the huge oak tree rising up ahead of it to the left of a jobsite trailer.

There was a hard clap. The butt end of the car actually jumped, and small fragments of bark and glass burst to both sides. The car bounced and settled, and the raised dirt blew off into the woods.

The car horn sounded.

Its steady wail fingered its way into the afternoon sky and spiraled up to an accusing, hot summer sun.

2.

We both spoke at once, and then took a moment to absorb what was voiced by the other.

"Run," I said. This was Kyle's problem.

"We killed her," Kyle said.

We.

One of those nails was mine. We were in this together.

But I still thought we could run. I didn't have time to consider what the slightly older boy I was on the verge of growing into would call "social responsibility," and what the boy I was on the verge of leaving behind would call "owning up." The car horn was a danger. Though we were five miles from Westville Central, there was bound to be someone passing by on the overpass with the windows down. And perpendicular to the dirt road, through the front leg of Scutters on the other side of a shallow, wooded valley of sorts stood my own house. Was it a quarter-mile from here? A half? Was Lucy out on her lead, up on her hind legs, front paws scratching at the air in response to the sound coming from this side of the trees?

I opened my mouth to argue what I thought was the obvious, and was denied the opportunity. Kyle was walking away. He was not running, but walking with casual purpose in the last direction I would have expected.

He was walking toward the Honda. His hands were in his pockets and his shoulders hunched in just a bit. He gave a cool glance to the side and I saw his future. In one hand he had a crowbar and in the back of his waistband was a Colt .45 with the safety flipped off. The Honda's horn was the alarm in a jewelry store downtown after hours with a shattered storefront window and three smashed display cases inside. Kyle casually glanced down both sides of the avenue to see if the cavalry was onto him yet, and approached the getaway car. And he didn't approach it on the run. He walked toward it with casual purpose.

I expected Kyle to look through the window of the Honda and give himself a "one-two-three," but he didn't. He simply yanked open the door and leaned in. Through the short rear window I saw his elbow piston backward, and the horn stopped as if it was cut by a blade. He backed out, slammed shut the door, bent, and puked into the dirt.

I suddenly wanted my father. Mom couldn't help me here. Mom pushed morals and preached lessons and soothed stomach aches and provided verbal simulations that *proved* mean people were insecure on the inside, but this was out of her realm. It wasn't even in her universe.

Before their divorce, when I'd had man stuff to talk about I used to approach Dad and beg for "Boy's Club." As busy as he was, he always seemed to make time for these moments, most probably because it both excluded Mother and also helped him see himself for a moment as "Dear old Dad" with the pipe and the confident smile you saw in fifties movies or the sugar tins and cookie jars with Norman Rockwell prints on them.

Once, back in fifth grade, I asked his advice after breakfast when Mom went to check the laundry downstairs. It was Saturday.

"Dad," I'd whispered.

"Yeah, Skipper." He turned down the corner of the paper and peered over it. My eyes were wide and earnest.

"I have to ask you a *question!*"

"Right." He put the paper down, folded it in thirds, and looked at his watch.

"Let's go."

We slipped out through the sliding glass doors and went to our spot on the log bench by the tire swing. I proceeded to tell him that yesterday when I went back to the school to get a social studies workbook I'd left in my cubby, I caught Spencer Murphy stealing Mrs. Levitz's science test from the top drawer of her desk. It had me frozen in the doorway. I looked over my shoulder for a janitor and saw nothing but empty hallway.

"Hey, dork!" Spencer said. He was a tall, thin boy with disheveled reddish hair. He had what seemed a permanent cowlick on the back left side of his head, early acne, an upturned nose flooded with dark freckles, and ears as small as quarters. He was wearing a light blue shirt with the Copenhagen tobacco logo written across the chest in cursive. There were sweat-stains under his arms. His face had paled, and the pimples on his cheeks shone out like stars. He took a menacing step toward me, the test between his thumb and index finger.

"Tell anyone, Raybeck, and I'll say you were in on it. I'll tell Principal LaShire you dared me to do it, I swear."

Mom would have hit the roof. She would have called Spencer's parents, demanded a meeting with LaShire, rounded up all the other kids involved, and lectured them all about "ethics." I would have been labeled the world's worst snitch and banished to the special ed. lunch table for life.

Dad just got out his calculator.

"What's your average in science so far, son?"

"Around a 95."

"More a 93 or a 97? Be precise, Jimmy."

I closed my eyes. The in-class report on the nervous system didn't go so well last week. I hadn't gotten a grade sheet for it yet, and I had been riding a 94 up until then.

"Maybe a 90."

"How many questions are on this test Spencer *borrowed*?"

"Fifty, I think."

He punched a bunch of numbers into his calculator.

"You're going to get eleven of those answers wrong. Make it every third or fourth, then clump a few together in a row. That'll leave you a 78. Considering it's a big one at the end of the marking period, I would imagine it might be worth fifteen or twenty percent. You'll wind up with a 'B' for the semester that you'll have to live with. If Spencer gets caught you never knew anything about it."

He tousled my hair.

"You're my tiger."

It was pure survival in its most practical form, and I needed that kind of logic in the here and now. I needed my Dad to hit his calculator and map me a way out of this.

Kyle wiped off his mouth with the back of his forearm and came over to me.

"Now listen, Jimmy, and please listen good. We have to get rid of her. We have to make her vanish like fucking Houdini. See, yesterday Barry Koumer called you a pussy while we were checking out his dad's compound bow, and to defend you I told him we were coming up here today to raise all kinds of hell. If someone finds this wreck, Koumer the Rumor is going to point it straight back at you. So there ain't gonna be any running, Jimmy. Stop standing there with your mouth open and start picking up nails."

I could hear myself breathing.

Nothing left but me, Kyle, and the street logic.

And we were under the gun to hide a dead body by sundown.

3.

The nails were everywhere. A small colony of them were in the strip between the dumpster, the dozer, and a few stacks of three-foot piping, but the Honda had scattered many of them into trickier nooks and crannies. I found two under the rack of a gas generator and seven in the shadow of a huge compressor that said "Emglo" on it. There were storage boxes and gravel troughs gated off near the green construction trailer, and I found six nails playing chameleon with the bottom of the chain-link fence. There were three nails hiding under a long roll of razor twine that had caught on a wooden surveyor's marker with an orange strip-flag on it, and I cut my middle finger on the withdraw when I finally managed to coax out the third bent nail.

I'd filled all four pockets and I widened my sweep. On the far side of the trailer, toward the oak tree now directly to my left, I found a good many clever ones that had bounced into the dead grass that split the dirt road from the woods. I found five more in a patch of wild ivy below a trio of birches and then I backed crawled back to the dirt road. I took my time with the bloody horror only a few feet away. I sifted my hands back and forth for leftovers beneath the dusty surface. Sweaty hair dangled in front of my forehead.

I heard Kyle open the car door a second time, then muffled shifting and knocking about.

"Jesus Christ," he said. "Get the fuck *off* me!"

I looked up and got to my feet.

The passenger side of the car was smashed in, and I really had no window to look into. Not like I wanted to study the damage or anything, my eyes just sort of fell there at first. I moved wide around the back of the vehicle to get to Kyle's side of it, and coming into view I saw his ass in the air; he was buried in the driver's opening all the way to the waist. The car was rocking a bit, and it was clear that he was struggling with something on the floor.

He backed out and his face was a twist of aggravation. A smear of the woman's blood zigzagged across the chest of his T-shirt and a wipe of it stained his left cheek in a shape like the Nike logo that came out three years before. He shrugged his shoulders like the dope I must have looked like, and then he threw up his hands.

"Well, don't just stand there," he said. "Try helping me out over here."

I came forward to the back corner of the car and paused.

This was it.

Whatever Kyle expected of me it was sure to involve the dead woman, and I wasn't ready and it wasn't fair. While I had been picking up nails, Kyle had already hurdled a stage or two ahead of me, graduating with fast honors from pulling the dead thing off the wheel and puking, to pushing at it and yelling. I hadn't managed my first solid glance yet.

I took a step and looked down-right into the back-seat area.

There were a few paperbacks, one missing its cover. On the far side there was an upside-down bunch of dried roses tied with a rubber band. Deeper in on the floor it there was a pair of yellow flips-flops, a squeegee, a record album by Jackson Browne, and something with blue streamers. Could have been a kite.

"C'mon, Jimmy!"

Right in my ear. I jumped and brought my hands to my throat. Kyle grabbed my elbow and pulled me around to the open door.

"I can't throw the clutch and bang it to neutral because my arm can't reach," he was saying. "And the bimbo is stuck right in the middle. The passenger side is crushed and I can't move her, ya dig?"

I did not "dig." We were right in front of the open door and I could feel the cab's sticky heat. Throw the clutch? Bang it to neutral? I knew he was talking about the gear shift, but wasn't sure whether the clutch was on the floor or by the steering wheel. My mom drove a Toyota and it was automatic.

"Neutral?" I said. I avoided the car's interior by focusing on the top rim of the door. Kyle sat down Indian style before me and pushed his hand in toward the floor mat.

"Yeah, neutral so we can move the car. When I push down the clutch pedal I need you to switch that gear shift to neutral. Pull it to the middle and just waggle it a second to make sure you're back to home base, all right?"

Easy for him to say. He had to fumble around with a pair of shoes down there, but I had to go in right over her lap.

"C'mon, Jimmy!"

I held my breath and bent into the car. The heat was an assault. By instinct I turned away from the close form beneath me and the harsh sun came through the windshield in splinters, a webbing of fractures that flowered out from the dent pushed into the glass where her forehead initially made contact.

I let out my breath in a burst and gagged.

Caught between two scissored shards was a piece of her skin. It was big enough that I thought I could see a freckle on it.

My head swam. I could taste the aroma of her perfume on my tongue mixed with the heavier scent of shock, violence, and what might have been shit.

I bent in farther to accomplish my task in swift combination. From what seemed another planet I heard Kyle ask what was taking so long, and I fell a bit forward. I put my left hand down to the seat for support and it pressed the woman's bare thigh.

A scream whistled up in my nose and I groped to find the space between her legs. I stretched in with my right and pulled at the gear shift, watching my fingers go white with the struggle as if from miles away. I yanked it as hard as I could downward instead of across and got nowhere. I jiggled, threw a shoulder into it. I almost toppled in. I tried using some finesse and just wristing it. The bar went into its groove. It snapped in to rest at center, and I nearly tripped over Kyle in my peeling scramble away from the vehicle.

The hot wind actually felt cool for a second. I crossed the dirt road and went hand to knee before a square stack of bricks. I breathed deeply, then advanced to standing fairly straight with my hands on the back of my hips. The brick pile was waist high and covered with a ratty blue tarp. The taut, roped-down surface was water-stained and covered with sticks, mud curls, bird shit, and a few acorns. Ordinarily, I would have liked to have chucked those hard little nuts at a sign or something just to hear the "ping." Ordinarily, I could have been distracted at any moment to jump up and see if

I could touch a high archway, or tap a ball against a wall four hundred times for a record, or race someone through a field, past the last phone pole with the tar marks on it, and all the way to the little walking bridge over the creek that sat between Pennwood Park and the back side of the shopping center. Ordinarily. The word didn't exist anymore.

I wiped the back of my neck, looked at my hand, and almost threw up. Her blood and my sweat combined in a red slime. I rubbed my palm on the leg of my jeans until it burned. I thought of Kyle reaching in for the pedals between those hard, impersonal shoes while I had the open wounds in my ear and the bare thighs of a corpse on either side of my prop hand. I thought of his telling me to hurry up from the safety of the open air outside of the cab while I was stifled in the hot box, and I suddenly wondered if I could take him.

Kyle was bigger. I floated between one-o-eight and a hundred and fifteen pounds or so, and I would estimate he was about a buck forty-five. The problem was that I had never seen Kyle fight. Some guys were built for fighting and they dressed for it: guys with the silk shirts and gold chains, the guys with motorcycle jackets and boots, and the guys with crewcuts who looked like they already pumped iron. Kyle was the closest to that last category in appearance, but didn't need nor bother with the actions that usually went with it. Where tough guys seemed to look for the weaker breed to build a footing on, Kyle made a living gathering troops of all shapes, sizes, and colors against the older generation. He was never challenged because he always had everyone on his side.

There was, however, the thinly smiling (but not at all smiling) aggression everyone could sense beneath the broad grin of the ever-present wise ass, and I believe Kyle sometimes gave a demonstration or two, of course masked as a joke, just to make those with an ugly side think twice about crossing him. At the end of seventh grade, he brought a tape measurer with him into the hallway and bet Ronnie Shoemaker that he could put a two-inch dent in a locker with one punch. A crowd gathered in the traditional semicircle at the end of a line of thin lockers we called "The Gray Mile," and watched Kyle wind up, bash the steel, crimp it in about an inch and a half, and fall to the ground in gales of laughter.

At the end of the same year, Kyle became the hero of metal shop by cutting off the tip of his pinkie. I heard that they listed it as an accident on the school report, but I was there. This was not incidental. Kyle had been at the station with the portable band saw turned upside-down and propped to an angle in a set of huge bench vices, filled in their creases with metal shavings, dirt, and WD-40. His project was a four-post lantern shell and he was supposed to trim the scrolls down from twenty-four inches to a foot. Before doing so he walked the room with a whisper in a given ear at the soldering and welding bench, a hand to a shoulder at the drill press, face to face in front of the bench grinder. Protective glasses were propped up on foreheads and safety shields were put in open positions. I set down my file. Kyle approached the Portaband, flicked it on, and turned a sly smile to us. He then ceremoniously raised his hands above his head, the triumphant prize fighter. He next held the tip of his left pinkie in between the pads of his right thumb and index finger. He lowered it all slowly and then leaned into the whine of the machine. We craned our necks and went up on our toes. No one had a good angle for a visual past his shoulder, except, that is, for Junior Macenhaney over by the dual industrial wash basins who suddenly put a dirty work glove up to his mouth and pointed.

Kyle turned around. He was still smiling. A thin, spotty line of blood had splashed up his cheek and over the left lens of his goggles. He walked up to Mr. Ruthersford, who was bent over the tool drawer, and shouted,

"Hey dude! Want a Chiclet?"

After being rushed to the nurse and then the Children's Hospital out past Rutherford Heights, they sewed the tip back on for him. You didn't even notice the tiny scars nowadays unless you got right up close and personal with it, but he still got mileage from it. He claimed he couldn't feel it anymore, and on a dare right before last Christmas break he put it over a flame in science lab long enough to burn the nail black.

You would have to assume a guy like that was a vicious competitor if forced to fight. Some guys boxed real well, and others even laid down rules like no eye gouging or crotch shots, but Kyle gave the impression that he would do anything to beat your butt if he had to. I pictured kicking, bites, scratches, and worst of all, props if they were handy. What would stop a guy who cut off his own fingertip for a thrill from grabbing a rock and bashing your cheek with it, or snapping off a car antenna and jabbing your eye, or breaking a bottle and swiping it at your jugular?

I was no weakling myself, but my skills didn't apply here. I could wrestle pretty well, and had earned a spot on the B team last year. Though there was an ace at a hundred and ten pounds named Barry Cutlerson who knew all kinds of fancy ways to stack you up, put your head where your ass should have been, and twist you into a pretzel, I had my own reputation for being "a worm," rarely pinned, often winning my matches by a couple of points. But even if I could rush Kyle, get a single leg, and take him down, what happened next? What could I really do except hold him there? I needed to knock him out and run home, not tire myself out submitting him.

The cold fact was that I had to have the cold will to pick up a rock when he wasn't looking and sucker him. I had always wondered if those who bragged about keeping weapons handy actually had the gumption to use them. What did it feel like to murder someone if you thought you had the right? I looked down at my hands and pushed out a shaky breath. I just helped murder someone for absolutely no reason at all, and I deserved a bash on the head as much as did Kyle. A sneak attack just muddied and worsened the complicated equation.

"Hey Jimmy," Kyle called. "I want to show you something. C'mon, man, you're really going to like it."

I turned and spit into the dirt. There was blood in the saliva because I had bitten the inside of my lip without realizing it. Kyle stepped across the lane, took a position before me, and rubbed the sole of his sneaker over the place I had moistened. The thin streak of red mud blended, darkened, and vanished.

"What, did you cut yourself shaving?" he said. I sucked in at my lip to nurse the wound that was no more than a trickle. He licked his teeth, smacked his lips, gulped air a few times, and let out a tremendous belch.

"Whiplash!" he said. He then took a fistful of my shirt and dragged me across the road past the back side of the car. "Look."

We were on the far side of the road now, near the edge of the woods, and I saw nothing but a patch of wildflowers in front of a thick march of trees.

"What am I looking for?" I said.

"The doorway, man, the doorway!"

Now I knew. There was a space about nine standing men wide between two elms at the lip of the forest. A rough path pushed a short way in, quickly hooded and darkened by overhanging branches. The far side of the glade was a wall of ferns, vines, and brambles.

"Go in, Jimmy," Kyle said. "Walk through the doorway, make a sharp right, and find the surprise down at the end of the path."

I advanced into the shadows. I did not want to take the time to second-guess it. Dead vegetation crinkled under my sneakers and passed through my mind vague images of snake skins and insects. I shook it off. I had been in dark forests hundreds of times, hunting out salamanders, fossils, and arrowheads, and whatever was down here had to be better than what was waiting in the Honda.

The woods took me in like a cold womb. Stabs of sunlight slipped through at odd angles, and I turned right down the rooted path about twenty-five feet as Kyle had advised. And there it was, waiting in silence.

It was a place where the ground fell off in a twenty-foot arc. A deep, black hole.

It was going to be the woman's grave.

There were huge banks of dirt piled at the far side covered with what looked like low-cut open air circus canopies. There was a digging machine to the left, and a score of rusted shovels scattered along the perimeter. I dragged my feet to the rim of the pit and peered over the edge. The drop was so deep I could not see the bottom. Edges of roots pushed out of the near inner wall like the knobby fingers of jailed witches. I reached into my right front pocket and fumbled out a bent nail. I tossed it into the hole. Once the nail winked out of sight I did not hear it land.

The other nails followed, all of them, mate joining mate down the black well of silence. No one had told me to unload the evidence here; I just sensed it was right.

All on my own I was beginning to think like a criminal.

I forced myself to walk the border. Past the dirt hills and shovels the glen was busy with "stuff" that I passed on the roadway a thousand times and took utterly for granted.

There was a heap of crushed stone, and at the far side of the clearing there were two machines with massive inner coils and big, flat bottom-pads. They were turned on their sides like discarded bicycles near an apparatus that looked like a standing ride mower with a nine-foot chain saw at the end. Five rolls of orange construction fencing were lying in some overgrowth between two trash cans filled with wooden stakes, and the mini-bulldozer now directly to my left sat opposite the position I had just abandoned at the front side of the hole.

The machine had "BOBCAT" stenciled in block letters beneath some dried mud caked to the back panel. Around front, the wide bucket was full of the whitish crushed stone in a pyramid shape and the whole thing was raised out about ninety percent flush over the lip of the hole. I stepped in closer. It seemed as if the driver of the machine had stopped cold just before getting fully squared in position to spill the rocks, and there was a thick length of old chain now holding up the bucket. It was padlocked through a hole between the digging teeth and figure-eighted into the high steel mesh of the cab.

The Bobcat was obviously busted.

So was the chain. There was a broken link halfway up that was rusted through, cloven on one side and almost forced straight by the pressure of its neighbors. The whole affair was held together by what seemed no more than a thread.

"Do you know what this is, Jimmy?"

Across the hole, Kyle was standing with his arms stretched out wide. He had followed me down to see my reaction and then give a lecture. His old smile was back like neon.

"It's a footer, James. Before my asshole dad started his own asshole company he poured concrete for Molina Industrial. He always talked about footers and stuff. Bored me to freakin' tears."

The smile left him. He reached down to his sock for a cigarette.

"Want one?"

I shook my head. He straightened, puckered his face, lit up, and dragged.

"Footers are good, James," he said. "Footers are our friends. They pour cement to complete footers, and we're lucky we found this one half-baked. They dig these things for big columns that hold up bridges and stuff, and you can see that this one was a mistake. All we've got to do is put Blondie and her piece-of-shit car down the hole. We fill the fucker with dirt, throw on a light cover of crushed stone, and when the new guys do show up, they'll think the first team filled it back in a long time ago."

My nose flared out.

"What if they think it looks like it wasn't done by a real contractor? What if they decide to dig it back up?"

He snorted.

"Too much money, my man! Contractors are cheap whores by trade! Why would they dig around into a mistake when the help costs over twenty an hour? If they don't think the little bow we put on it is nice enough, they'll swirl around the rocks on top more professionally or something."

I crossed my arms in front of my chest. I was not good at this riddle stuff, especially considering that I was not as technically minded (or as willing to roll the dice) as Kyle. The apparent ease of all this was more than disturbing, and I still wanted to weasel some way of running off, or at least delaying any more interaction with the dead thing up there.

"What if it wasn't a mistake?" I said.

"It was."

"But how do you know?" I was pleading now. "It looks like they had every reason to dig here and the foreman or whoever just blew the whistle in the middle for some reason. What if the job starts up again and the same guys do come back and try to pick up where they left off?"

Kyle took a sharp drag. Blew it out hard.

"They won't."

"How do you know?"

"First, because you don't have extra-fine dirt ready on the side unless you brought it in for repacking. Look at the piles, Jimmy. That dirt didn't come from this hole. There are no rocks in it and no roots. Also, why the crushed stone? That stuff goes on top of a repair. You don't use it when you're going to put in a pillar. And even if this turns out not to have been a mistake originally, it won't be the same guys working off those old plans that never came together in the first place. It's been eight months since this job shut down. Look at it, Jimmy! I know you're not a diesel head, but look around. Doesn't this hole seem funny to you?"

"Yeah."

"And why?"

"Because it's in the middle of the woods. It doesn't fit."

"Right!" he said. "The guys digging the holes didn't work for the same company cutting the trees, or pouring the 'crete, or grooving the road. No one got along and no one ever knew what the other was doing. It was a big fucking mess and my dad used to laugh about it regularly. Every night. Believe me, I'm an expert on the subject even though I never wanted to be until right about now."

"Oh."

"Let's go," Kyle said. "We've still got a lot of fun stuff to do."

I walked around and put my back to the hole. Kyle's arm was around me immediately. The smoke from his cigarette struck a chord of familiarity in me, the sensory trigger of my concept of "friend," of "not mom," of "other," of the "not me" that was becoming more of the latest "me" every second.

Side by side, each absorbed in thought, we made our way back up the incline toward the open air. Below our feet, the roots along the path pushed up and across, and I caught a toe at one point. Of course, Kyle held me up. It was nice and at the same time crushing, since it reminded me again of his superior strength. We turned the corner and walked into the heat and the brightness through the two elms that made Kyle's doorway. We stopped. He flicked away his smoke. The car was waiting for us. I noticed that from this angle I had to tilt my head up slightly to look at it, as the path from it to the trees sloped downward ever so slightly.

"Jimmy."

"Yeah?"

"How ya doing?"

"'Kay."

"Do you think that you're strong enough to shove the back bumper and move the car by yourself? The right front tire is flat, but the other three are OK."

My answer was automatic.

"No. I'm not big enough, Kyle. I'm sorry."

"No problem." He turned me to him and put his hands on my shoulders. He looked at me with full, sincere eyes.

"I can move the car or at least get it going, Jimmy, but the rest of this is on you. Just promise not to fuck it up, all right?"

"What do you mean?"

"What I mean, James, is that this whole thing will be fine if you can pull through."

"How?"

He glanced up at the Honda.

"I'm going to push. You've got to steer."

My breath hitched. I blinked. The picture was clear, and it wasn't too pretty.

I was going to have to get in with her and shut the door. The space between the two elms was barely enough to fit the car through, let alone allow me the luxury of trotting beside with my hands reaching in to the steering wheel.

I was going to have to sit in her lap and feel her press against me while I tried to maneuver the entry, pull the turn, hold it steady over the roots, and bail at the last second.

Suddenly I heard something, faint and sneaky like a whisper. It could have been the wind or the traffic droning past on the overpass, but I knew that it wasn't.

It was the corpse. She was waiting for me in that hot vehicle, baking, letting a horsefly run over her crushed lip, the gash in her head, an open eyeball.

And on some dark wavelength that only existed between sinners and the vengeful dead, I could hear her say something. It flickered between us but for a moment, a message in the static, barely on the radar.

"I dare you," she said to me.

I swear it.

4.

The right corner of the Honda's fender was turned up and embedded in the tree. At first, Kyle wanted to piston out his foot and kick it loose with the sole of his sneaker, but there wasn't quite enough fender to kick on the outside edge. He tried wedging himself between the tree and the crimped hood, but the car was too close. We removed our shirts to be used as makeshift gloves for our fingers and actually crawled under the car. Kyle had the one-inch nub to the far right and I hooked my hands more toward the center where there was a lip in the steel to grab. We both straddled the trunk of the tree from under there like a horse, Kyle on ground level, my legs splayed above his. Something from the engine dripped on me three times, but it wasn't quite hot enough to leave burns.

We pulled together hard as we could. There was a squeal and a stuttery moan like a door creaking open. The fender had come loose. It gave about an inch. We crawled out from under the car and brushed off. After a couple of misfires and determined "one-two-three's," we really put our backs into it and managed to push the car backward a few inches more from the tree in a hesitant, lumpy sort of progress. Now that there was a bit of room, we both mounted the hood, backs to the tree, shirts now used as buffer cushions against the hard bark. We pushed with the soles of our feet and actually managed to extend our legs.

The new placement had the vehicle about two and a half feet from the tree's base, and I got a full-frontal view of the corpse from between the shadows of overhanging branches.

Her face was tilted down, hair hanging in front of it. Toward the bottom something protruded, her tongue, and she had a dangler, a spindle of blood that went down past her chin.

I stepped down, turned away, and crossed my arms.

"I can't do it, Kyle."

He stepped in front of me.

"You have to."

"No way. You do it."

"Go ahead and move the car one inch by yourself and I will."

My mind raced.

"Why just me? We can both get it going and then you could jump in to steer."

He pointed at the car.

"There isn't enough room. One of us has to bang a hard right on the wheel from the start or it will end up back at the tree."

"Fine," I said. "I'll take the back and you lean in to the front through the open door. You can work the wheel and help me get it rolling too. As soon as you hit the patch of flowers there, it's downhill. You could take it all on your own."

He looked at the ground and shook his head.

"Won't work. The guy who leans in the front don't have the leverage. The bigger kid has got to be at the back. And once it gets moving there won't be time to switch places."

I went to the back of the car.

"Let's try it my way first."

"Fine." He shrugged, put his shirt back on, and walked toward the driver's side door. "Just hurry the fuck up."

"Fine," I mimicked, as if the last word really meant something. I retrieved my own shirt, threw my arms through the sleeves, and took a stance behind the vehicle. I started getting ready to get set, and my heart sank a bit.

Kyle's not going to push very hard.

Didn't matter. I had to try. I bent down and pressed my hands against the back bumper. I started to draw deep breaths. I pictured the thing rocking a bit in the starting groove, then making lumpy advance by the sheer force of my will. Think it—be it. Easy. No problem.

I heard the car door open up front.

"Ready when you are," Kyle said.

I tightened up and got ready for the push of my life. I counted it out really loud so there would be no false starts off the blocks.

"One, two… THREE!"

Nothing. No way. Dead weight going absolutely nowhere. I pushed again with every possible piece of strength and my back screamed with it. My face prickled and my eyes went scream-wide. Nothing. Nothing at all.

"Ready when you are," Kyle said. With a final gasp I dropped to all fours and hung my head. I pushed up on my fingertips and dragged through my feet to cross them Indian style. I sat in the dirt and heard the approaching footsteps.

Closer, then halted.

"Door's open for you up there," Kyle said. "Now try it my way. Just to see, OK?"

I got up and brushed by him. Our shoulders knocked together a bit in passing and I held up my jaw. I was angry and enjoying the feeling. I was also aware somewhere beneath the surface that I was feeding off the anger to manipulate myself away from the idea of approaching the horror in the front seat. By the time I registered this idea I was there at the opening, so I continued as quickly as possible before the little that remained of the power of my anger blew off.

I stuck in my right hand. The steering wheel was hot and I curled my fingers tight. I braced my left palm in a pushing position against the door's armrest and had a sudden feeling that the woman was going to clamp down her broken teeth on my elbow and sink them in as deep as they would go.

The car started moving. Kyle had gotten it going on his own, and we bumped about two inches forward.

"Turn the wheel!" Kyle said.

I spun it hard to the right and heard the tires beneath me creaking and scraping in the dirt. The car slowly moved away. I sidestepped in to keep up.

"Aim it!" he shouted.

I straightened back the wheel and walked faster beside the moving vehicle. Every time the wound in the right tire rotated to the bottom there was a skip and a clump, and that combination was getting less and less pronounced as we gained speed. We bumped off the road and went through the wildflowers. I had thought this was just a test, just to see...

"Keep going!" he yelled.

Now I was running beside the car, almost struggling to catch up with it. The "doorway" between the trees was looming a few feet before me. All options vanished and it was now or nothing.

"Do it!" Kyle roared. "Do it for real!"

I did it.

I jumped into the hot car and reached for the door that was flapping like a broken wing. I found the void in the arm rest. I pulled the door shut, and all the sounds snapped off as if by a switch.

The woman was a hot envelope stuck to my legs and back. Her hair brushed along my right shoulder and my neck. I was moaning, bending in low for a view beneath the bloody cracks in the windshield.

The front end of the car made it between the trees for a bald second, and then there was a terrific yet muffled screaming sound as the flanks of the vehicle scraped against the bark on both sides. We jarred through and the light wiped dark. It felt as if we had gone under water, as the heavy smell of death and hot vinyl filled my lungs.

I jerked the wheel to another hard right and skidded a bit, just missing the thicket on the far side of the glade. I straightened back the wheel, and the woman's wet face fell against my neck. I screamed and the knotted branches of overhung trees rushed in and elbowed the roof. The car picked up speed down the rough decline and the roots underneath wailed hard on the tires. The woman and I shucked hard against each other.

The wide hole approached fast. It was time to abandon ship. I reached for the door handle.

My fingers found it, pulled up, and then tried to shove outward.

Nothing. The impact with the trees had crimped the door and jammed it. I made a weak play at giving it a shoulder. Frozen solid.

The hole was everything now, huge and black and big as the earth. I jammed down my foot for the brake and found a jungle of the woman's feet. I stomped down haphazardly, got nothing, and felt a discarded shovel bang up under the car.

The hole was upon us. I could not even make out the front edge anymore, only its wide rim at the periphery and its yawning, bottomless center. I brought up my hands. The front tires fell away into nothingness and there was a shock and a bang as the undercarriage scraped across the dirt cut-away. There was a final thump from the back tires and bumper, and then we were jettisoned into the black.

5.

The dead woman and I were flung off the seat, floating and bumping around in the black. My knuckles scraped on the windshield. The body beneath me slipped out from under, bounced away, and hurtled back in. Her hair snapped in my eyes and my head banged the roof. My legs forked out, my eardrums popped, and then we hit bottom.

"Holy fuck!" were the wild words I could actually see spelled out in my mind as the impact hammed the nose of the car. *"Holy fuck!"* as my head was hurled forward and the windshield ruptured above me.

I had a quick vision in the pitch black, a glimpse of what my face would look like after smashing into the hard rim of the steering wheel. It was no work of art. In reflex, I thrust out my hands to block. The heel of my left hand caught most of the wheel while my right barely got in a thumb.

It broke my fall, or at least put a major dent in it.

I hit face first.

There was a loud *smooonch*, a slap of bright pain. But what I hit could not have been factory made.

It was the woman's face wedged between me and the wheel.

My first kiss in the dark.

I choked, I scrambled, I flailed. It wasn't just my own blood in my mouth, and my nose felt as if it had been flattened. I couldn't breathe; I gulped instead of spitting. I twisted away and fell waist-deep into the vertical void between the wheel and the seat. I screamed, and there was a cool brush of air on my face. The impact had blown the door open.

I pawed for the shallow breeze.

I flutter-kicked, climbed, and doggie-paddled through the dark portal and tumbled out onto the bowed-out car door. I stood, wobbled, and grabbed at the wheel-well of the back tire. My eyes had adjusted to the deep shadows and I could see in grainy snatches. I chinned up past the driver's side opening, reached up, hauled in, and put my feet where my hands had just been. I soon found footing on the rear hood, almost slipped backward, crouched, and froze there for a moment.

"Are you cooked down there or what? Jimmy-man, quit jerking me off and say something, huh?"

The voice was faint and dreamlike. I stood up slowly and felt a brush of fresher air. Still, I pictured the woman's eyes suddenly coming open in the darkness below me. She would jerk and twitch and then gnash at the air. I could feel her desire to crawl out of the car in jerks and spasms, to reach up for a pant leg, yank me back down, and suck back the blood I had swallowed.

I had my hands splayed out for balance and I saw my best chance sticking out of the earth, just above the shadows. The re-grown roots that had pushed their way through the higher end of the pit's inner walls hung about a body length away and three feet over head.

I jumped.

I stretched out and my feet made insane bicycle pedals in the open air. I forced my right hand into a last-ditch, overhand sweep and clutched out for broke. I caught the base of the nearest root and just managed to turn a shoulder before crashing into the embankment. A burst of dirt showered around me and I held on. I twisted myself to face front and my left hand joined its mate. I pulled my chin to my fists and then grasped out for the next highest root. The heat of the open air teased my forehead and I strove for it, arms burning, just like on the pegboard anchored to the polished block wall in the gymnasium at school. I really had to reach to the side for the next root, and I almost slipped back into the hole. I got it by the fingertips, shimmied it into a fist, swung out one-handed, grabbed with both, and pulled. Sunlight bathed across the base of my neck and my back. I was *in* it now with my chin again parked at my clamped fingers, and I was going to make it, and when I raised up a knee for a last thrust to the top, there was a hard tug on my ankle.

I shrieked.

I struggled and kicked and almost lost hold. Of course it was the pawing zombie that had followed me up the wall to pull me back down into the shadows. It was the beast, the dead-alive thing hungry for boy-guts, she who wanted to rip me to ribbons and sniff at the remains for her shoplifted blood.

Of course it was just a root that had snagged on my pant leg. I tore loose, clawed up to the lip of the hole, and screamed again when a hand closed tight over my wrist. I was dragged up into the heat. The pit's edge scraped along my chest, ripped my shirt, and drove dirt into my underwear.

I was out of the hole. At the far end of my arm was a strange being that I believe on earth they once called a boy. He yanked me out the rest of the way and my wrist roared with Indian burn. His footing tangled and he let go of me. He fell flat on his butt and looked at me in amazement.

"What the fuck, Jimmy? You look like a monster from Mars! Is that all your blood or what?"

"No!" I cried. I jumped to my feet. The light was overly bright, tinged with afterimage, and Kyle was a swirl of the woman and the hole. I fell on him with flailing fists and he knocked me aside with an easy, backhanded pass.

"No!" I cried, finding my feet again, swinging at nothing. I was still deep in that grave, covered with darkness and kissing a corpse. "No!" as I stamped on the ground. "No!" as I clawed at my shirt.

He hit me.

It was a nasty, open-handed wallop that caught me full in the face. My head turned with the force and my mouth dropped open. The sting gave way to a dull throbbing that worked itself into the sobering sounds of the wood; the call of a bird, the shrill of crickets, the sigh of the wind. I was free and I was alive. The dead woman was no longer the entire world, but a series of frightening pictures that flickered by slower and slower.

I let out a grunt of exhaustion and sat down. I was breathing in dry sobs. My nose was bleeding, but it had petered down to the sluggish phase. I touched it on the bridge. Sore, but I didn't think it was broken. I hugged my knees and tried not to shake.

"Hey," Kyle said.

I ignored him. I noticed that he had moved closer, but not quite close enough to reach out and touch. I stared at his sneakers.

"Clean laces," I thought. I rubbed my arms to smooth the chill that stole over me. "Thanks for your help," I said to the sneakers.

"Don't mention it," Kyle replied. He had noticed my dry, toneless delivery, and his three-word retort clarified things. He was too proud to admit that he had not jumped down into the footer to help. "Don't mention it" meant, *"C'mon, Jimmy. Let's move on to bigger and better things. Of course I didn't fly after you down the hole. I probably would have landed right on your head and snapped your damned neck with my squeaky-clean sneakers."* "Don't mention it" meant, *"Let's not talk about it because I'll come up with a million excuses as to why it was better for you to go down there instead of me."* "Don't mention it" was Kyle's way of admitting that the two of us were never again to be friends.

"Help me fill it back in, Jimmy. We're almost done."

A spade-point digging shovel landed at my feet. It was an ugly, rusted old thing with the initials P.D.G. written on the wooden shaft in spidery black magic marker.

Kyle turned his back and walked up to a mound of fill piled at the far edge of the pit. He pulled up the stakes of the tarp canopy and yanked it off. Some of the fine soil had run off over time, but there was still a massive amount left in a shape that vaguely looked like a large camel hump. He picked up his shovel, sunk it into the pile, and tossed the first scoop of backfill into the opening. The sound of dirt that scattered across sunken steel was gritty and final.

The horror of it all was now somehow diluted, and I was left with a hollow grief in the pit of my stomach. I pushed up and dragged the shovel to my side of the hole. To the immediate left was a mound of fill with a clear plastic covering flattened over it and kept taut with tent stakes at three corners. I took a moment to peer over into the dark tomb, my expression closed and flat. She was not a zombie. She was no monster. She was a once-pretty lady whom two bad kids had to make disappear before dinnertime.

"I'm sorry," I said. It was an empty whisper. I pried up the plastic at one of the corners, dug in, and threw my first shovelful of dirt down the hole. There was a tinkle of soil across the wreckage, and that led to another thrust, and another followed by another. The sounds of our shovels were flat accompaniment to the memory of the unlucky soul trapped beneath us, and though the sounds were anything but musical, they were rhythmic in their dumb regularity.

It was hypnotic. I developed blisters on my hands that had been mildly alarming when they formed, annoying when they broke, and then an afterthought when they finally went numb. The afternoon wore on and spun itself into gray, gauzy, thoughtless purpose.

We were fully entranced when I dug up the watch.

This pile of dirt is different.

I'd noticed but not noticed. I was on overdrive, a machine, shoulders and back aching in a distant way that was not really "mine" somehow. My shovel was making a different noise. The pile had rocks in it and was filled with trashy stuff amongst rougher dirt. There was a busted cup to a field telephone with the bigger holes in it for the ear, small pieces of wire with the copper sticking out, an industrial rubber glove that was black on one side and yellow on the other, an old, opened pack for a Trojan condom, and a million cigarette butts. I pushed up and put my hand to the small of my back. Kyle had exhausted four huge dirt piles and I had managed three. There wasn't much left to dump. I sunk my spade into the pile and it made a gravelly sound. Something winked up. I turned the shovel and scraped the tip over the area.

It brought to the surface a Mickey Mouse watch with one of the bands torn off. The face was scarred by a jagged pair of nearly parallel cracks, and the colors and familiar shapes just under the deformities doubled like mirrors. The image brought up the trace of a smile. Red and black kiddie colors, big white gloves on those stick arms. The red second hand was continuous, and didn't do those little twitches across the background. One of Mickey's gloves was on the ten, and the shorter one was just shy of the five.

I jerked up and looked around in a wider view than I had taken a second ago. Had the cover of the forest screwed my sense of time flow that badly? It was not as if I was some expert like the explorers in adventure books who always seemed to know the time by the position of the sun, but I usually knew when the day was getting old. I looked back in the general direction of my house and then up toward the jobsite above us. The sun was filtered through the trees the same as it had been all day. Of course it was. The sun didn't go down until seven or eight at the end of the summer. I could have gone at least another hour and a half until I noticed any difference at all. My thinking was behind the eight-ball here, and I cursed myself for it. Worse, Ma had bought me a watch and I always forgot to wear it. My whole life was one step behind, and it was self-inflicted.

I threw down my shovel. Kyle had ceased digging as well and he was gazing into the hole.

"Looks almost ready," he said. "Almost."

"What?" I said. "Uh, Kyle, I just dug up a watch and it's getting close to five o'clock here." I took a good look into the grave and saw that we had actually filled it three quarters of the way. It seemed good enough to me and I suddenly burst into action. Last-minute business, chop-chop. I was dimly aware that I hadn't asked permission or advice, but the time factor had forced me to independence. Kyle stuck the point of his shovel into the ground, and leaned on the D-handle with his elbow.

I vaulted up the rooted path. The sun made me wince and I spread my index finger and thumb to make a visor. The Honda had left a trail of tire marks. I ran up and dragged my feet across the evidence. Dust rose. I coughed a few times. There were imprints running through the wildflowers as well, but I couldn't straighten all of the broken flowers of the world, now could I? With nothing leading up to the impressions they would be a mystery. An unnoticed one, I hoped.

I approached the tree she'd crashed into. There was no time to pick up every shattered headlight piece, so I kicked dirt across the lot of them. Baseballs under a rug. It would have to do.

The gash in the tree itself was impossible to hide, but I tried to give it the illusion of age by scooping up soil and rubbing it into the wound. I stepped back to study my handiwork. It simply looked like dirt plastered to a fresh gash in a tree. Again, it would have to do.

I walked back down to the clearing and circled the pit. I picked up a flat garden rake with steel teeth and smoothed over our sneaker marks all around the perimeter. Next, I raked over the tire marks at the base of the path. The front fender had kicked up a wide spray of earth on its violent entry into the space and left behind an angry furrow that was an extraordinary pain to repair. Kyle never helped. He simply stood at the edge of the drop with a cigarette. I didn't care. I took my shovel and tossed it by the rake. I was about to ask Kyle to give me his tool so I could throw them all in the dumpster up on the site when he asked a strange question.

"When do you walk the dog, Jimmy?"

Everything kind of stopped. My breath was loud. It had probably been loud all along, but I noticed it now, and noticed myself noticing it. A drop of sweat made a runner down my jaw, and I wiped it off with the back of my hand.

"Why?"

"Just tell me."

"For what?"

"'Cause it's important. Trust me."

My eyes narrowed. He knew I didn't trust him and I knew he didn't give one shit about my dog. Double lies. His open, sincere persistence made it interesting though, like sticking your tongue in a mouth-sore.

"Right before dinner," I answered warily.

"What if you're late? What happens then?"

"Mom does it."

"She walks her?"

"No. She puts her on the lead in the back yard. She probably had her out there all day, actually. Why?"

"No reason," he said. "Here's my shovel. Don't throw them away up there because it'll look too obvious. Trash guys pick through stuff. Find a place where it looks like shovels and rakes should go. Maybe scout out some others and make a little family, hmm?"

I gathered the tools and headed up the path. It amazed me that Kyle somehow guessed I was going to toss the stuff away, and I was still puzzled about his concern for my dog.

By the time I set the tools in the middle of a group of others that were leaning against the top crossbar of a long sawhorse, I realized that I didn't care what Kyle had to say. I strode back down the path. I didn't need any dialogue with my ex-friend, we were done here. I walked over to the Bobcat with every intention of banging loose the busted link in the chain that held up the bucket of crushed stone. I wanted to put a final covering across this nightmare and go home. I reached up to do so, and Kyle laughed.

"There's no time for that now, Jimmy. We'll do it later."

I turned.

"What do you mean, later? There is no later. I've got to get back."

He laughed again. Heartily.

"Like that? Jimmy, maybe there's no mirror out here, but I'm telling you there ain't no way you could walk through your door right now. You're covered with dried blood, man. It's in your hair and on your shirt and embedded in your pants. It's all over your face. Damn, how are you going to explain *that* to mother dearest, huh?"

I froze. Then I was the sleepwalker, stumbling off toward the path to look for a fountain or canteen or something to wash up with.

"Ain't no water up there," Kyle said after me. "When I was up here planting the nails yesterday I cut my elbow on some barbed wire by the trailer there. I hunted all over that damned jobsite searching for a cooler and a first-aid kit. It's bone dry. The nearest water is clear across town at Meyer's Creek and we can't chance someone seeing you like this."

I wanted to run up there and check out his claim, but the fact that my window of time was down to a hair made me put that suspicion on hold. And why would he lie about it? He wanted to get out of this as badly as I did. I turned.

"Maybe she wouldn't notice."

Kyle roared.

"Wouldn't notice? Have you lost your fucking mind? Christ, Jimmy. You come in from climbing a tree in the front yard and your mom checks your hair for ticks! We've got to do better than that."

Tears of frustration welled up in my eyes.

"I could sneak in and clean up."

"Are you serious? It's dinner time. The kitchen window faces the back yard, and even if she goes to the bathroom she'll hear you coming in. She'll be listening for you and you're going to be late as it is."

"How about the front door?"

He clapped his hands at me.

"Think, Einstein! That front door is one short room off from the kitchen. Her antenna is going to be up! You ain't gonna have the chance to get in, cross through, and run for your room. Those Fred Flintstone, one-floor jobs out on Weston Road suck for sneak-ins and you know it."

"Then what do I do?"

He walked over. Closed in.

"She puts the dog out back when you're late, doesn't she? In fact, Mommy never really liked little Lucy because your dad bought her for you way back when, right? She probably left that darned little yipper out all day so you could take her in when you got home your own damned self, right? Just to make a point?"

I nodded cautiously. That was Mom's game. It was my dog and if I was going to play all day, Lucy got banished to the back yard with the water bowl that wound up getting bug floaters and leaves in it. Old rule. Kyle came up a bit closer.

"Now, do the math. The way your house is set up, you can't get in unseen or unheard, but you would maybe have the time to race into the back yard and, say, touch the hose spigot and sprint back to the woods, now wouldn't you? I mean, even though she watches out for you through that back window like a hawk, she sometimes goes to put soap in the shower dish, or a bowl of nuts in the living room, or she slips off to the bedroom to take off that tight bra because it digs in a bit too much when she bends to do the dusting, ya copy?"

My eyes glanced away. I didn't like strategies predicting what my mother would do. It was first, much more complicated than this little map-on-a-napkin presentation, and next, it was personal in a way that gave me high discomfort up in the neck bone. Though Kyle made a living busting on my mom, she wasn't his to interpret, especially when he started removing pieces of clothing. It seemed impolite, even for him. He reached out and placed a hand on my shoulder. His left palm copied the other and he made me look at him.

"Jimmy, listen to me. If we walk through these woods no one will see us. It's a pain in the ass with the gullies and stuff, but we could make your back yard in seven to eight minutes, fifteen at the outside."

"What about our bikes?"

He pulled his hands off.

"To hell with the bikes. It's not like we're going to leave them here. When we're done we'll ride 'em back down the dirt road to Westville Central like we came and go the long way. If we hurry we won't be going in the dark. Let's go."

"Go where?"

"Through the woods! Your old lady has already put the dog out back. The high weeds at the far edge of your back yard will give us cover until the moment dear Mommy goes to another room. Then we can make our move."

"What move?"

He gave a short laugh.

"That's when we can grab the dog, Jimmy. That's when we can bring her back here and do what we have to do. If it looks like a roadkill there ain't a parent alive that would question the blood on you. The story is easy. We were out here having a dirt fight with the shovels. That's the cause of your blisters. But then we stopped when you realized how late it must have gotten. Feeling all guilty, you ran back and snagged Lucy, because you knew it was time to walk her. But she ran away and got hit by a car up on the overpass. It knocked her into the muddy ditch under the guardrail and you had to crawl in and get her. There's the dirt and the blood in a nutshell. And I know you'll be bawling when you bring her back to the house. It's perfect. You've always been a crybaby and your little tears are going to be just as real as the blood your ma will think came out of the mutt."

It made such a strange kind of malicious sense that at first, I could not work up the inevitable refusal.

"How?" I managed.

"Oh, I don't know," he said. "Does it matter? A rock to the skull or something. Anything that will do it quick. Then if you want to get fancy we could run her over with something up on the site with a wheel so it looks like a car tire did it. I would try to use this Bobcat, but it looks kind of busted, are you with me?"

I did not respond.

"Jimmy," he said. His eyebrows were up. "Are you with me? Time that we don't have is a-wasting."

I said nothing. He came toward me as if to give me a tickle.

"Jimmy, say it. OK? Are we ready? Check? Roger? Victor-vector? Ten-four?"

"I can't kill my dog," I whispered.

To this, Kyle threw his head back and laughed loud. He laughed as if I had misunderstood the whole thing and *boy,* would I be relieved when I finally got a firm grasp on the bottom line.

"Whew," he said, flattening his hands on his knees and shaking his head. "That was a good one!" He straightened and stretched. "God, Jimmy, no one would ever ask you to do *that*. Shit, you could never pull it off in a million years. All you have to do is sneak up and grab her."

His smile turned down to a thin line.

"And *I'm* the one who's going to kill her, Jimmy," he said. "I'm the one who's going to kill her."

6.

We wasted ten minutes in angry debate before Kyle gave up on me and tore off on his own for my house. I had tried to convince him that we could rub dirt into the bloody patches on our clothes, just enough to cover, but he gave a straight "no." I ripped off my shirt and tried it for show, but the dried blood rejected the ability of the dirt to really "catch" or rather "absorb." Then, I tried to convince Kyle to fly back to his house in the Common and bring me back a change of clothes. Straight refusal. His dad was waiting with a cold Miller in one hand and his chrome pitch counter in the other. Fall baseball was coming up soon, and before dinner every night Kyle had to hit a hundred balls off the tee in the basement. There was no sneaking into his house either. Kyle had sneaked out so many times, "Coach Dad" had nailed shut all the windows. And parked in the living room, he had full view of the entry-points: front door and the one on the far side of the kitchen.

But I wasn't done brainstorming, and I had even entertained the idea of burying the clothes and going home naked. Why not? Kyle was a joker, right? He would steal my clothes to razz me, wouldn't he? His response was to laugh in my face. Plainly, my mom would call the cops on him if he stripped me down in public, wouldn't she? Well, wouldn't she? Is that what I wanted? A plan that *invited* the cops?

He was not going to budge on this. In the end a lie was best worn out in the open, and I was going to do it his way or nothing.

I chose nothing. I just could not watch my dog get slaughtered, so I sat down right there at the edge of the pit.

"I'll stay here all night. Bring me the stuff tomorrow."

"Fine," he'd said. *"I'll get the bitch myself. See you in twenty minutes."*

I sat there in disbelief for a moment and it was not until he was nearly out of hearing range that I jumped up to follow him.

The woods were not friendly. I aimed in the general direction he had taken and barreled on through. Stubborn tree limbs swung in at me and I forearmed them aside. I ran through patches of deadwood. I tried to dodge big jumbles of prickers, and I hurdled large rocks, nests of tangled ivy, and mounds of thorny scrub that came in my path. I took crazy chances, running blindly into the brush and headlong through shadows.

My lungs were screaming, yet it ironically felt as if I had made up some ground on the sudden elevations hewn into the forest floor. There were a few rocky crags that rose before me with some obvious (and rather luckily placed) ledges for finger- and toe-holds, and two nearly identical bluffs in a row draped with thick, hanging vines that I grabbed, trusted with my full weight, and went up hand over hand, back parallel to the ground, feet kicking up bursts of loose earth as they slapped their walk up each bank. Kyle couldn't have made it through those obstacles that fast. He couldn't have.

Still, the flat-out stretches between made it a footrace and things seemed to jump in from dark places just as I began to get a rhythm.

There was a bad moment when a low-hanging crook of a branch crossed in from nowhere and nearly separated my head from my neck. I raised my forearms into an X and ran straight into it. Dull pain rang straight through to my shoulders and a flapping cluster of swallows burst upward.

I kept pushing.

I jumped over a rotted-out log with white fuzz growing in the bark and moss covering one end like a blanket. I had made the hill, and I caught sight of him down in the gully, scrambling across a wide ribbing of partly exposed steel sewer pipe. The thing in the ground looked like the knotted, rusted spine of some partly buried monster. Almost home. The misshapen landmark sat between two rises, the one I was on, and the far one that spread out of the forest and into my back yard.

I sidestepped down the embankment. My breath was a tired horse. Sweat ran through older sweat and dried blood, making sticky trails down my jaw and forehead. There were rocks in my sneakers.

I found the bottom, scrambled across the sewer pipe and sneaked up a glance to mark my progress. Kyle was waiting for me at the top of the rise, elbows bending in and out with each heaving breath, his eyes pinned to me with dark regard.

I slowed. Each intake of air felt like the cross of a sharp scissors, and the more I clawed an advance up the slope, the more my resolve weakened.

He waited.

The strategy was so cool, so unexpected and obvious that it stole any of my remaining fumes of courage. I had gotten nowhere with this. First, from his position above, all Kyle had to do was give one push and I would tumble back down the embankment. More practically, however, Kyle had quickly and effectively gotten us both right where he originally intended. Seventy yards or so from my back door. The victory for him was cold and absolute. I hauled myself up over the lip and there was no helping hand to pull me across. Those days were done.

I fell to my knees on all fours in front of him so he couldn't shove me in the chest just to teach me a final lesson or something. I looked down and took in sharp draughts of air, hating myself, hating the world and its cruel little realities, the twists and slants on fairness, the imbalances. If another kid was stronger, I was supposed to inherit the smarts. Those were the rules, weren't they?

Kyle spoke first, but just before, he snapped out his arm and gripped the back of my neck with clammy fingers. He pushed down a bit so my face went about four inches from the ground.

"Just come with me and take a peek," he said. "Chasing me down to fight is only going to get you beat up and the both of us nailed. See if you see it my way first, that's all I ask, all right?"

An absolute insult. He was quite capable of charging in on Lucy and grabbing her for himself. I was no factor. The only possible difference was that my dog trusted me enough not to make a ruckus on the approach. But why would that matter to Kyle? As long as Mom was in a room away from a back window Lucy's barking wouldn't mean diddly to her.

I suppose he wanted to get off scot-free, take from me what I loved the most, and do it with my approval. Maybe so he could sleep better. The fucker.

I had not responded.

"All right?" he repeated. He shoved my head down farther. Now the ground was a pencil's width away my nose.

"Let go first."

"Promise to help me scope out what's waiting for us in the back yard and I will. Nice and slow through the weeds. We'll spy it together. Make the promise."

Yeah, fucker. With your hand on the back of my neck and the dirt so close I can smell it I'm just a rat in a trap, aren't I? Like this I would swear the world is flat, school is a blast, and chickens have lips, but you're still going to make me say it, aren't you? Aren't you, fucker?

"All right," I said.

He squeezed harder and I gave a short yelp.

"Say it like you mean it, Jimmy. And don't even think about pulling a run and tattle. You're the one wearing the blood, dig?"

"OK, I get it, Kyle!"

He gave one more hard press, then removed his hand. Then he helped me up, but made sure it didn't really feel like help. He hooked into my underarm and dug right up in there as if it was the bottom of a window frame that was stuck. I came up and looked him in the face, but my eyes wavered first. His grip had been like iron. The message was clear.

"Let's go," he said.

He crawled his way through the high grass and I followed behind as I was supposed to. A swirl of gnats followed above us in a cloud. We pushed through a long stretch of high reeds, pussywillows, and long ferns that bent quietly before us, and when we passed over a damp patch we detoured off to the left. My mind thought of everything and nothing at once, circling back to an image of Lucy curled up at the foot of my bed every night, little paws under her jaw. I tried to scratch out alternatives, but came up with nothing.

Mutiny was not my game and the familiarity of the surroundings was distracting. We were on the outskirts of the world of Mom, the place in which I was nothing but a squatter. Here, uprisings were not tolerated and loud protests never given. I had never been a path blazer or a rebel, a fighter or even an underdog. I followed here. I followed and hoped one day to grow magically into my right to drum up alternatives.

Kyle was going to kill Lucy and I could not stop him.

The weeds were thinning a bit. It was happening fast now. Everything itched and my mouth was bone dry. We were at the edge of my back yard. Kyle took the last bit of camouflage, a stalk in the middle of a wide growth of prairie grass, and moved it an inch aside.

It was lucky that we had averted the muddy little run back there. If we had continued in that direction it would have brought us to the middle of the property and that is exactly where my mother was looking.

She was on the back deck, hands in fists on the hips. She stared into the woods just to our right. Her blouse was a soft pastel green, an absolute irony to the steel beneath drawn into high tension you could see in the tendons of her forearms, the cords in her neck. Strands of her reddish-gray, bobby-pinned hair had come loose and they flew around her face like sharp tendrils of smoke. Her nostrils flared and I immediately thought "dragon." Her shock-blue eyes looked both ice cold and blistering hot at the same time.

It was a bad sign. I was not permitted past the weeds and into the forest, and if Mom thought I was desperate enough to try a sneak-in from this angle, it surely meant dinner was long past burnt. How long had it taken for me to rake the area and dump the shovels once I had found the watch? How long had I argued with Kyle about strategy? How many minutes were lost in the wild sprint over here? I had not taken the Mickey Mouse timepiece with me to keep a running check, and it was one more piece of poor preparation.

A gust of wind swept across the yard and my terrier stretched out her paws. She was lying on her side at the edge of the patio with her snow-white chest aimed at the sun coming in from the left. She snorted a little breath through her nose and ran her tongue along her whiskers.

Mom ignored her. The nylon lead kept the dog out of her perennials and that was all she cared about. Lucy was out of the way, chained there.

Lucy was our best hope and it killed me inside. Kyle was right. There was no fooling the blue-jean queen at the door.

A sudden shrill, mechanical buzzing cut into the breeze and Kyle tensed up beside me. A sick rush went through my stomach. Mom turned toward the sound and made for the kitchen door.

The clothes were done.

This was it. The dryer in the garage had completed a cycle and Mom would be tied up for ten minutes or so, folding shirts and piling skivvies. The screen door swept shut behind her and Lucy barely noticed the exit. Her ear flicked. Kyle gave me a shove.

"Go," he said. "Now."

I paused. I couldn't.

"Fucking go, Jimmy! What the hell are you waiting for?"

I did nothing. He started to stand, and I grabbed his shirt sleeve.

"No," I said. "I'll do it."

I did not want Kyle Skinner touching my dog. I would take her myself. Hold her a last time.

I took one more second to look between the stalks of wild grass, and Lucy crossed her front paws. She opened her muzzle, curled her tongue, and gave a yawn.

I swallowed hard, and I rose up out of the brush.

7.

Lucy sensed me right away and sprang to all fours. Her ears perked up. I came across the lawn hunched over as if someone was about to strike me. It was a nightmare and a blur.

The silence about the house seemed to boom a sickly pulse. I could feel the threat in my throat. At any moment, Mom's face could swim into one of those windows, her surprise quickly spreading to a look of alarm. Then fury. Coming toward me, Lucy pulled on the lead. It caught on her water bowl and dragged it across the concrete patio deck for a few feet. She went up on her hind legs and pawed at the air.

I kneeled and she exploded into me, a flurry of paws trying to take me in all at once. She was jumping to get up onto my back. I grabbed at her collar and unhooked the lead. I had a moment of disorientation during which I saw what I must have looked like in symbol world. I was no longer a boy, but a demon with no face. Lucy started in with her licking and lapping. I had no face, and the void was filled the blood of a dead blonde. I almost threw up.

I gathered the awkward moving bundle. She was still trying to mash her muzzle against my lips, craning in, cold, wet nose. I turned and made for the woods. At any second I fully expected the squeal of that screen door, the sharp call of my mother, the footsteps in pursuit.

They never came.

I broke through the weeds and pushed down the hill, past Kyle, down the steep rise. I almost tripped and went headlong down the slope. I caught myself just in time and widened my steps. I heard Kyle's hoarse breath behind me. He was panting and I don't think it was just the rapid pace. I think he was excited as hell. Lucy was nervous now, nearly motionless for all but an occasional kick from a hind leg.

I reached the bottom of the gully and stopped. Lucy's nose was nuzzled into my neck and I could hear her curious sniffing. Her body felt warm with trust in the arms of her best companion.

My mind went red and I heard roaring in my ears. I could not do it, not in a million years, not ever. A hand fell on my shoulder. I shuddered so badly I almost dropped the dog. Kyle moved in front of me, smiling. He reached for Lucy.

"Hand her to me, Jimmy. You've taken her as far as you can go, I can tell. Give her up. It's almost done."

He stretched a set of grubby fingers to the fur on her neck and I exploded.

"No, you fucker!"

I tilted back my head.

I brought it down. The air whistled. My forehead made contact. A splatting sound. He was rocked back and my motion brought me just past his shoulder. In the corner of my eye I saw his palm race up to the middle of his face. I got my balance and took a good look. Bright blood squeezed through his fingers and dripped down his wrist. Got him square in the nose. Bull's-eye.

"Argghh," he said.

"Take that, you fucker!" I shouted back. I was fuming at a height so great and so new that the boundaries seemed endless. Kyle was hurt. I had caused it. Now *my* breath was starting to race and Lucy started to kick.

I held her tight.

Then I just dropped her. Maybe Kyle could chase me down in a dead heat, but he would never catch Lucy once she got going.

She fell between us and scratched for a footing. Kyle dove in at her and missed, landing hard on his forearms and pitching up dirt. Before he could recover I stamped on the back of his left hand.

"Run!" I hollered. "Go, Lucy, run!"

She skidded across the sewer pipe in a fast break for the far hill. Kyle clawed to his feet and spit blood to the ground. I shrank back and covered up. The rain of blows was going to be heavy and motivated.

But no punch was thrown, and by the time my eyes fluttered open Kyle was past the pipe and tearing up the side of the hill. He was going for Lucy. Fifty feet above him I caught a glimpse of her hind legs disappearing over the peak and into the trees.

And suddenly I knew.

I knew where she was going and Kyle did too. She was not running blindly. She was following our scent right back to the pit.

I put down my head and pushed my aching legs as hard as they could go in chase of the boy who was stalking my dog. My heart was pounding. My lungs started to burn.

This was all far from over.

8.

By the time I crashed through the trees and into the clearing it was almost too late. The unfolding scene was repulsive, with Kyle bent over and making a slow tiptoe along the far lip of the grave. One bloody hand was pressed to his face and the other was dangling down and out, thumb rubbing against forefinger. His breath rattled. His voice was a muffled "come hither" from beneath the bloody hand and kept repeating "Here, kitty, kitty," between more muffled curses from the back of his throat.

Lucy was not buying into it. Yet. Her tail was down and her neck hair was up. Every time Kyle got close, she pranced away. Then she would slow and stop, never escaping but always keeping a cushion of a couple of feet between herself and her coaxing assassin.

I ran long to the left where they were instead of where they were going and wound up at the edge of the circle across from the rooted path I had driven a car down in what seemed another age. My hands went to my waist, then my knees. My shoulders were heaving up and down, my lungs raw.

"Lucy!" I gasped. "Come here, now!"

She stopped fast and twitched up her ears.

"Come, Lucy, come," I said, suddenly hating myself for having let my pet roam for her entire life as a wild child. She was never the type to sit or to heel. She had not been taught to obey, and now it was going to kill her.

"No, Lucy," Kyle said. "Come to me, little honey-bunny, come to me."

His eyes darted back and forth between me and my dog. Lucy cocked her head and eyed us both in turn. She had moved off from Kyle, but had not yet committed to me. Her tail was wagging. She thought it was a game.

For a moment the three of us held our positions at the rim of the abyss, Kyle at due west, myself claiming south, and Lucy dead east.

Kyle jumped for me. I ran to meet him head-on. I ducked under the raised bucket of the Bobcat and it cost me a second. Kyle was coming hard. I passed under the steel tub and put on a burst of speed. He matched it, and we both closed in with such determination Lucy became a temporary afterthought.

We rammed each other chest to chest, and while his momentum was a bit stronger, backing me up two steps on impact, I was quick to recover and throw my arms around his shoulders. I bear-hugged him and tried to trip him, to bring us to the ground; I would have been stronger there. He wouldn't go down so I clapped his ears hard and pushed off. Our hands slapped out and gripped at the shoulders of the other. Heads buried in the crooks of necks as we grunted and pushed and tried to gain superior holds. The footing was bad. We were atop a small spread of rocks and the sound of heels raking across stone seemed to fill up the world.

He was strong. His biceps were iron.

I was desperate, my limbs slippery and quick.

He tried to shoot his arm under to clamp onto my shoulder blade. I countered by flapping down my elbow like a chicken wing and pinning his hand in my armpit. Our heads were mashed ear to ear and locked there by pressing fingers. I was holding my own.

He yanked loose the hand that was trapped and got a palm flat to my collar bone. He dug in and pushed, shifting me a quarter turn and a full step backward. I tried to plant my sneaker flat and it slid farther back along the rocks. Then suddenly it was not the whole sneaker on the ground. It had become just an arch and a toe. I was at the very edge of the pit and Kyle had almost succeeded in pushing me over. Loose pebbles cascaded down into the void.

I suckered him.

I pushed as hard as I could, gained back two inches, then released all my pressure. He came in to me hard. I nimbly leapt to the side, a half-inch to spare from the drop, put my hand on the back of his neck in passing, and helped him right into the motion he initiated with a hard shove. He took a header into the hole. I heard him swear and hit the dirt we had thrown in there. It hadn't been a long fall. We had filled it up almost all the way, and he would be back out of there almost as fast as he went in.

I turned to make a run for Lucy. I did not know exactly where she was, but I was pretty sure she would still be at the hole somewhere. The fight had only gone on for a few seconds and I didn't think she would have wandered yet. I saw her up by the edge of the rooted path, and when I ran to get her I stepped on the business end of a square-mouthed shovel. The thick wooden handle snapped up and I saw it snapping up, just not fast enough to avoid it altogether. I jerked my head to the side and it whacked me just below the hollow of my throat on an angle. I didn't want it to stop to me, I *willed* it not to slow me up, but it put me down to a knee. I saw red and black stars dance in front of my eyes, and a wave of dizziness threatened to drop me the rest of the way. I shook my head hard. It cleared. I turned.

Ten feet back, Kyle's fingers came over the lip. Then a dirty face, a palm placed flat, an elbow and an arm propped to make a perpendicular angle, a foot sideways and ankle down, and a knee pushing into the dirt. I grabbed the shovel and ran at him. I was holding the thing like a soldier going through a swamp with his rifle, flat across a bit above chest level on a slant, one set of knuckles out, one set in, but I was not moving slowly like a soldier pushing his knees through the muck. I was charging as if chasing the American flag down a hill in a blitz.

It happened fast.

Kyle gained his feet and I was on him. He was surprised. He threw up his hands and grabbed the shovel handle right before it blasted him in the face crosswise. His feet had no choice but to mimic mine and I ran him backward. A bicycle built for two, our feet in perfect synchronization with Kyle facing the wrong way. The Bobcat and its bucket filled with crushed stone came up behind us and when I rammed Kyle into it there were three distinct sounds that matched up with three graphic visuals. There was a rip, and Kyle's eye's jerked open wide. There was a light crunch as the bar of the shovel came in contact with his already flattened nose, and a piece of the bridge-bone tore through the skin. And finally, there was that sound that really has no fitting name, the flat and final sound known mostly to butchers, when something sharp at the edge runs through meat-product. The front of Kyle's throat bulged, the foreign shape pushing out the skin like a book shoved into the bottom of a trash bag. The last digging tooth on the right side of the bucket had impaled him straight through from the back of the neck. Everything stopped. Just like that.

I was amazed that I did not feel even the slightest bit sorry. I dropped the shovel.

He froze there like a doll. His mouth was a forced grin baring teeth in an eerily similar copy of the shape the tine made against the outer surface of his neck. I looked into his eyes for a moment. Blind as stones. I marveled for just a moment more about how something round like an eyeball could look so flat. Then I moved around behind him, put my palm against the back of his sweaty head, and pushed.

He went over in a rumpling cascade of elbows, knees, and head lolling around like a balloon on a stick. His blood streaked along the tine, marbled, and beaded. I had the vague impression that these claws would have been too blunt for this kind of event, and most of them actually were. This one, however, must have hit a big stone or two in prior journeys, because it was turned up to a sharp little edge in the middle and nicked worse in a divot on the outer corner that curled to a point like the end of a knife.

I was numb now. I was thinking in a far-off way, but not so far-off, that if the police felt their find was a layer deep there would be no reason to dig into the same hole twice. Could I actually explain away Kyle? Maybe. He tried to kill my dog, that fucker. And the woman? Never in a million years. I picked up the shovel and whacked the chain holding up the bucket. Dust and dried dirt gusted back in a small cloud and there was a "ping" when the broken link popped free. The bucket came down and dumped the load of rocks over Kyle in a flat roar.

It didn't get all of him. An ear, two fingers, and the cuff on one of the legs of his jeans protruded. I jumped down into the hole. It had to look like I panicked and tried to hide the body. There had to be something to *find*. I kicked rocks over him and smoothed the surface over one last time with my toe.

"Bye, Kyle," I said.

I climbed out and looked for Lucy. She was gone. I had nothing left now but Mother, my "story," and dumb purpose. I trudged up the rooted path to the jobsite to retrieve our bikes, because that is what Jimmy Raybeck would have done if he killed his best friend for trying to kill his dog and he wanted to cover it up.

The last lap was a tough walk, but I did it. Sometimes I wheeled Kyle's bike and simply let my old Huffy crash down the embankments like a wild marionette. At other times I couldn't help but toss Kyle's Schwinn, but I tried to baby it when I could. He had a sissy bar that I didn't care about and extended forks that I cared very much about. They were fragile, and I didn't want to lose the front wheel. Dragging the bike up the steep parts would be a lot harder that rolling it.

It was cold at the edge of my lawn and I was sweating. With the jobsite behind and my fate out in front it felt cold in the space between nightmares. I let Kyle's bike drop into the thick grove of weeds and pushed forward.

The sun was finally on its last legs, deep into the clouds closest to the horizon and the back yard was vacant. Garden in a rough square to the right of the patio. Moldy birdbath with the stone dish set unevenly to the left. Unconnected dog-lead. A harsh light from the kitchen window.

I let the Huffy fall to the grass. I walked forward and thought that in another life Mother would have scolded her boy for not putting what was his into the garage.

I opened the screen door to the kitchen.

Bulb light washed over me in an angry glare. The house smelt of burnt broccoli. The door clapped shut behind me and for the moment, Mother's back remained turned. She was reaching up for something in the cabinet over the utensil drawer. Yellow Pages. She hugged it in and then said to the wall,

"Young man, you had better have a damned good explanation for—"

She looked at me over her shoulder and her eyes went big.

"Jimmy?" A long strand of hair fell across her face and she ignored it. She finished her turn in slow motion.

"Mom," I said.

"Mom, I just killed a boy."

9.

I wanted to burst into tears, but I was empty. I wanted my old life back, but it was gone. My mother and I stared at each other like strangers. Jimmy Raybeck didn't live here anymore. She reached out and set the phone book on the counter.

"Mom," I said.

"Who?" she said. "Tell me who."

"Kyle Skinner." My voice sounded feminine, fake. Mom folded her arms as if chasing a chill.

"Where? Where did it happen?"

I shifted and tried to find a place for my hands. I had moved a step forward and Mom put her palm up like a stop sign.

"Where did it happen? Answer me."

"Through the back woods, at the Route 79 jobsite. By the overpass, but Mom, I—"

The stop sign flashed up again and she quickly whipped it back into the fold-pattern, forearms crossed above her stomach.

"How did you do it?"

I wracked my brain in an effort to come up with the right little spell for her, the psychological reasons as to why I killed Kyle, of how on earth I possibly *could* have done it.

"How, Jimmy? It's a simple question. Tell me. Knife? Stick?"

I swallowed, and it made the clicking noise.

"I pushed him. He banged his head against the metal tooth of a small bulldozer and it went through his neck. Then I was so scared I covered him up with rocks."

"You pushed him."

"Yes."

"You—"

"He was going to kill Lucy! I had to!" My hands were out in the begging posture. I pulled them back quick, but not before my mother had seen them. Then she looked at me, all of me, not just with a gaze leveled at the eyes, but more, for lack of a better word, *comprehensively.*

I could guess that a lot was decided in those two seconds, but I can't be sure *anything* was actually weighed or decided. As far as implications or accusations or suspicions you might have, I go on official record here stating that my mother, Judith Raybeck, said absolutely nothing in reference to further implications, accusations, or suspicions.

What she did was spring into action.

—

"You can't walk into a government building and speak to an officer of the law looking like this. Take your clothes off and put them in the bag. Do it."

She had let down her hair and rolled it into a knotted lock between the shoulders. Battle guise. The place was sealed, doors latched, shades pulled, and Mother had not so much as let me twitch during the preparations. She had yanked open drawers to crash around the silverware in their plastic tubs and then she rooted through the utility cabinet. By the time she found that old pair of dishwashing gloves her ears had gone angry red. I tried not to wince when those scum-hardened Johnson & Johnsons imitated big yellow spiders with my mother's fingers wriggling inside. She bent again and reached under the sink, breathing hard through her nose, never pausing until the Hefty bag made its way into the light.

Double ply. Mother only bought the best.

Close before me she let the bag unfold and cascade down to its full length. There was a slippery gnawing when she fingered for the opening, a loud *whack* when she whipped it down to fill it with air, and a look of divine wrath as she loomed above me like a great white shark in a red mommy wig.

"You can't walk into a government building and speak to an officer of the law looking like this," she said. "Take your clothes off and put them in the bag. Do it."

I paused. In the past there had always been a tenderness in my mother's face, a kind of long-term sadness etched there as if the things she had wept over as a girl had left traces. Even when she dragged me through the typical lessons that dictated why *my judgment had been poor,* there had always been an opening for understanding. Acceptance. It would finally show in the softening of her eyes when she let loose the hooks and said,

"Now we've both grown a bit, Jimmy."

Not tonight. No softness behind the steel glare, friends and neighbors.

I fumbled with my pants button and felt my face redden. Mom had not seen me naked for five good years. But I had made us regress. Mother held the trash bag front and away from her body as if I had lice.

"Sneakers first, Jimmy."

Of course. Footwear before pants, shit, everybody knew that. I bent and had trouble with the laces. There was blood caked in them. Blood assumed to be Kyle's. I worked at the hard knotting as best as I could and got nowhere. The double square on my right sneaker was frozen and I risked soiling Mom's shiny floor, I crashed to my butt for better positioning. I hauled up my foot by the heel, rested it on a knee and twisted. My sneaker jumped loose and bounced on the floor. A gravely spray of dirt followed it and I leaned to scoop it into a neater pile.

"I'll get that later," Mom said. "Put your clothes in the bag."

Sneakers, socks, and shirt went swishing into the sack. I scrambled up and attempted to work my way out of the pants. It took forever and I almost fell over twice. I smelled of earth, of old sweat, and death.

"The underwear too," she said. "Move."

I slipped down my dirty Hanes briefs and stepped out of them. I wanted to hide but there was no escape from my mother's cold stare. I sensed myself swing open before her, and my balls felt like two hard pieces of granite in a pouch with the slip-string pulled tight.

I dropped the underwear in the bag and felt horribly cold. I stepped back and covered myself with both palms. I started to shiver. Mother pulled the red plastic cords of the trash bag and started tying them.

"Go shower, Jimmy. Then comb your hair, brush your teeth, and get dressed. We have to go do our duty now."

—

When I came back to the kitchen in fresh jeans, my backup Keds, and a nerdy shirt with a yellow smiley face airbrushed on the front of it, I saw that the kitchen floor was clean. The yellow gloves had been put away and the trash can by the sink was empty. Mom was wearing her white summer dress. There were dark clusters of hair laying against her bare shoulders. Combed down, still wet. We only had one shower, so I assumed she'd washed up in the utility sink in the garage.

We drove to Westville Central and did not speak one word to each other for the entire twenty-six minutes.

10.

I don't have a good recollection of the Q-and-A downtown, mostly because I was lost without context in the cacophony of file drawers slamming shut, the ringing of incoming lines, and the static patch on the two-way radios. I was also busy playing the boy in shock (I think I still was a bit in shock really).

I dimly recall that the station was oppressive in a vaguely masculine sort of way. I remember a thin woman with a long face and a hawk nose working the phones from behind a half partition, but I don't remember where the set-up was in reference to the lobby. There was a ceiling fan turning slowly enough to make absolutely no difference and the shape of cigarette and cigar smoke hanging beneath it, but I don't recall what room that was in.

I do remember Mother walking me up to a counter and saying, "Excuse me, officer. My son murdered a boy and we would like to make a full statement." That particular policeman suggested that I be attended to in some kind of medical facility and that was shot down by my mother faster than you could say, "The queen bitch is in the house." She signed the waiver so hard it almost ripped the top sheet.

The rest is a bunch of grainy flashes.

The cop behind the counter was quickly replaced by another, then yet another, and we were moved away from reception. When I revealed the location of the incident there were wide eyes, buttons pushed on intercoms, and orders barked from hallways around the corner. I heard snatches of conversations that mentioned the mayor, a fear of red tape tying up "that mess out there" for another eight months, the new construction that was going live at 7:00 A.M. the next morning, and that a mere two black and whites and an ambulance would expedite the process out there better than the usual carnival.

At one point I was in a bright interrogation room with a detective who had combed-back black hair and an avocado blazer. I recall that he was rather dislikable. Snotty and irritating. He sat with his legs crossed, eyes often half lidded, and a slight, soft preference for his "s" sounds in a near lisp. He also used vocabulary in a way that made you think he felt working for the police department was beneath him, but I don't have a good recollection of where in the timeline this occurred as opposed to the questions asked at the desks in more public spaces.

I remember a coffeemaker on a folding table with a stained, red checkered plastic cloth, a big old kettle of a coffeemaker that smelled as bad and as old as those that cook all day in the waiting rooms of shops that change your tires and do alignments for no extra charge. I remember talking in a monotone, yet the *sincere* monotone of a boy in shock who had categorically given himself over to clearing the air with the absolute truth. I admitted that I tried at first to hide the body under the rocks because I was in a panic. I told of my immediate confession upon returning home, because I could not bear to lie to my mother. When asked over and again in a thousand different ways why I killed my best friend, I responded over and again in a consistent voice that he tried to kill my dog. My violent response was prompted by instinct and the result was a horrible accident.

When asked why he would want to do such a thing to Lucy in the first place, I remember having a bad moment. I was unprepared for the question. Hell, if you knew Kyle you wouldn't have even thought twice about his wanting to do any sort of damage for a thrill. Still, it wasn't my automatic assumption (and miscalculation) that my story-listeners would be as up on the background stuff as their storyteller that bothered me. My mind had been working on two levels, one answering the easy questions being asked out in the live, real world, and the other below the surface calculating the unattended variables that could get me pegged for the murder of the woman.

I had just been thinking about the pressure on the officers to be done at the site quickly, and the gash in the oak tree. Had it been dark yet when we arrived here at the station? I thought it had been on the cusp. Two black-and-whites meant that there would not be a flood of headlights up there, and whether or not they noticed that gash depended on which direction they approached from and where they decided to park. When the interrogator asked about Kyle's motivation to kill Lucy in the first place, I had just been reassuring myself that I had been at the station for a good while now with no interruptions, so I could only assume everything out at Route 79 was going according to plan, no questions about gashes in the trunks of old oak trees. It was then that I suddenly thought about the body of Kyle and had a pre-monition of the future question that was bound to be raised by those doing the autopsy. What would they say about Kyle's hands? Sitting there, I knew I would be able to fill in the blanks concerning the current question on the table, but what would I say later about Kyle's blisters? I had kept my hands palm down all night because I didn't think Kyle's initial idea about a dirt fight with the shovels was good enough. I hadn't thought about *his* wounds being exposed and it froze me.

Then I actually smiled. When Kyle initially mentioned the dirt fight I had assumed he was covering for both of us, but he must have been talking about my hands alone. He wouldn't have had the same problem. His dad made him hit a hundred balls a night off a tee in the basement. His palms were already calloused as hell.

I used my smile to my advantage, dipped down the corners of my lips, and made it the predecessor to a wry response. In the driest tone I could manufacture, while still staying respectful, I proceeded to say that Kyle tried to kill my Lucy on a dare he claimed another kid made to him. It was a kid he refused to name. Though we had spent most of the day racing the dirt road from Westville Central to the site on our bikes, there was a good portion of the time devoted to Kyle's mischievous genius.

Mom raised her eyebrows at me when I told about smoking the Chesterfield, and I think that helped my case all around. Then I spilled *"everything."* I told about Kyle's pissing on the fifty-gallon drum and his pulling on the gear shafts of the big dozer. I told about the way he stole money from his mother's purse, and how he lit bags of dog shit on people's porches. I revealed that Kyle set off firecrackers in mailboxes down in the Common, and I snitched about how he was the one who snuck the small piles of cow shit up in the drop ceilings of the elementary school last year, yes, go check, he still had a piece of the soft ceiling tile that he broke off for a trophy hidden under an old box of clothing in his garage. Another Westville mystery solved.

After an undetermined amount of time, yet a long and drawn-out undetermined amount of time, they let us go home. I got the feeling that most of the officers felt sorry for me, and I had the stronger feeling that the guy in the avocado blazer did not. Whether that translated to his not *believing* me was another issue altogether, yet either way I was not really worried about him. Sometime during the questioning, somewhere in the middle when there were a lot of interruptions and different representatives posing different versions of the same basic five or six routine queries, I heard him say six key words to a fellow officer in the hallway.

The dead make for poor witnesses.

Besides, the guy didn't even really look at me during his part of the inquisition, and this I recall better than all the questions, bright rooms, rattling key rings, standard forms, and long hallways that could very well have led to my destruction.

Avocado kept staring at my mother.

I think he liked the way she looked in that low-cut white summer dress.

The new construction is going live at 7:00 A.M. tomorrow morning.

I rolled over and set my alarm for 6:30. If anything was going to be found it was to be soon, and for that I was thankful. At least I would know. I would be spared days, weeks, or months, wondering when the hardhats would settle in, fire up the engines, and possibly unearth the "mistake" at the base of the rooted path.

The dead make for poor witnesses.

Yes, unless the equation added another dead body. Suddenly, the dead started talking loud and clear and people started looking back at the one left standing, wondering how he got that way.

If she was found it changed everything.

This line echoed in my head and became a numbing chant of sorts that I whispered out loud. Soon the combinations of the words gave in to the sounds of the letters, accenting the soft *shhh* in "she," the tender *fff* in "found," and the smooth exchange of syllables in "chhh... ai... ngggged" that floated over each other like silk.

My eyes drooped closed, gently shutting down the sight of my second set of clothes rumpled on the chair in the semi-darkness, next to a light blue Frisbee. The night in my mind spread and I curled down. In a far-off way my stomach ached, and in a further sense I felt myself weeping as I began to drift off. The tears felt distant and cold and I did not understand them because they seemed so disconnected. More familiar was the mild fragrance of cedar woven deep in the pillowcases and the whispery drone of the night bound cars on the overpass coming through my half-open window.

It all smelled lovely and tasted like tears. The strange flavor in my mouth painted the way. It forged a path, thickened the air, and kept me foggy right up until the dead ones came to visit me in my dream.

In my nightmare I was sleeping when I heard the strange noise. My eyes blew open and I jolted up in bed.

It was Kyle Skinner sitting on my chair.

He was shirtless, his body covered with circles of matted filth that grew outward in succession like rings you would see on the top of a sawed-off stump, of an oak tree to be exact. There was a void in the back of his neck gushing sheets of blood against the wall behind him in rhythm with the beat of his heart. The place on the wall being doused was where my crucifix had hung. With the exception of a few splatters that dotted and sprayed up to the ceiling, the stains of fluid made more horizontal patterns that were spreading to the other walls. They looked like a row of mountains, or from another perspective, piles of backfill that were positioned a few feet above eye level from my place on the bed. He was painting my room in a manner that put me back in the pit.

The noise had been a crunching sound.

Kyle was holding my crucifix and chewing on the head of Jesus.

"It's hot down here in hell, Jimmy," he said between bites. "Wanna see?"

His voice echoed off and he melted. His skin rippled, swam, dripped off, and gave way to a taller form, dark, a silhouette that gained shape and texture as if being brought into focus by some unseen artist of the grave.

It was the woman from the Honda, the way she looked right before hitting the oak tree.

"Wanna go for a ride, Jimmy?" she said. "In my car?"

Her face broiled and changed. Wounds ripped open on her forehead and burst with wriggling worms. Bugs jumped out of her ears. Her teeth broke off and she spit them to the floor. Both of her eyes exploded and smoked.

"Give me back my blood," she rasped.

I snapped awake with a holler caught up in my throat. I clenched my teeth and mashed my lips with my hand to lasso the scream. I darted anxious eyes across the darkened room to relearn the old familiar shapes which now seemed menacing and strange.

Everything was ringing.

I breathed heavily and let the dream's aftermath settle into the reality of my heartbeat, the soft sounds of night outside of the window, the ticking of my clock. Gradually the surrounding gloom loosened, worked itself off, and waned to the pale intrusion of the glow of the moon.

I swallowed dryly. I tried to cry and could not. I breathed through my nose, stared ahead, and wondered how long these ghosts would own the shadows in my darkened corner of the world.

Possibly a lifetime, depending on whether or not the construction men found something in the dirt tomorrow.

I closed my eyes and fell asleep wondering which of the scenarios was ultimately worse.

11.

I heard the sounds of chainsaws the minute I hit the bottom of the gully and shuffled across the rusted sewer pipe.

The alarm had blasted into a cheap, tinny rendition of Rod Stewart bitching to Maggie that he couldn't have tried any more, and I jumped up to dial down the volume. Mom's room was a door down past the den. I crept over to my chair and put on the same clothes I had worn to the police station the night before.

Mom's door was closed and there was nothing stirring around in there that I could hear. I padded past to the kitchen and out to the patio. I half expected Lucy to be waiting for me out there, cold in the crisp morning air, wet with dew, tail shaking so violently it moved her whole back end. Nothing but the yellow bowl still pushed to the side almost off the edge of the concrete. She was gone, so I put my hands in my pockets, pushed forward across my back yard, and let the high grass of the woods take me in.

Going at my leisure made me realize how difficult the trip really was, and I had to be careful going down the first incline. At one point I misjudged the angle of the drop and slid about five feet, but I recovered without going ass over tea kettle. Once at bottom, I paused a moment to search for Kyle's blood in the general area that I'd head-butted him, and then I heard the machines.

It sounded like chainsaws, but there were other sounds too, like big engines. Come to think of it, I could feel the ground rumbling as well, and I tried to discern exactly how it made me feel. I had gotten the start time wrong and woken up too late. On the one hand, I had missed their initial progress, and this was bad. They could have found the woman already and called in the boys in blue for an assessment. On the other hand, those sounds on top of the rumbling engines were definitely chainsaws, and if they were cutting down trees they were not worrying about what was lurking down in the rabbit holes, so to speak. On the other, other hand, I wondered if they had gotten to the oak yet and if anyone had noticed the fresh gash. I started up the other side of the gorge.

―――

I almost stumbled right into them because they had changed the configuration of the woods. The glen that had contained the footer and the rooted path had been cleared of all machinery and foliage both in front going up to the original site and about forty feet back. I took a position behind a cluster of trees on that far side, and spied out from underneath the hood of a long, low-hanging branch of a maple endowed with a wealth of fluttering leaves.

Everything looked bald, and I was relatively high up. When I had raced after Kyle into the woods to protect Lucy, I had not realized how steep the initial climb out of the clearing had been. Now with so many of the trees gone from the original rear end of the grove, I was even with the top of the rooted path across the way. It was now merely a short hill that looked almost no different from the rise naturally cut into the ground to the left of it. The trees in that patch of earth had already been removed, and there was a clear view of the main jobsite clear to the overpass. The oak was gone. So were the construction trailer, the fencing, the dozers, the dumpsters, and the scatter of old tools for the most part. What stood up there now was a highly organized line of flatbeds seemingly putting the finishing touches on removing all traces left by the failed workers of the past. Men with hard hats moved and snaked all around in pockets of activity, and the loudest sounds came from the three dull-yellow, pitted tree-shredding machines parked in a line at Reed Road's dirt road entrance that we had originally come through on our bikes yesterday.

And the footer? I briefly had to search for its location with the surroundings altered so, but after a couple of seconds I saw it. It sat smack in the middle of the larger, tilled crater, rooted path and rise on the far side, little green flags all around the perimeter (I was close enough to one of the flagstakes to reach down and steal it if I wanted to). What was so recently a hole now had a slightly darker face than the rest of the soil around it. Otherwise, it was uniform with the broader surface, and looked like a huge empty dish. They had filled in the dead woman's grave the rest of the way.

I was just starting to wonder what purpose the crater would serve, and what part the hole within the hole might play, when I saw the dump trucks, big ones, sounding their beepers that warned they were coming in reverse and backing up to the ledge of dirt between the upper site and the lower one. The gargantuan steel tubs started rising on their front hydraulics, and the new dirt started cascading out from under the heavy back tailgates pushed out and squeaking on their mammoth hinges.

They were filling in the crater, evening the ground from the rise, probably all the way to the green flags at my feet. The overpass ramp would now have a huge landing pad. There would be no more drilling or digging into the dead one's resting place.

I walked home with mixed feelings.

My pain was to be of the longer, slower, more internal type. Option number two.

When I came back through the kitchen door Mother was slicing up fruit for breakfast on a cutting board by the sink. We looked at each other expressionlessly and I went back to my room to change into fresher clothes.

12.

Feared. Shunned. Wall-shadow. Forgotten. What else is there to say about my social existence through the balance of my career in Westville's fine institutions of learning? It was a rough ride from the day I entered eighth grade to the moment I dropped out of high school in the middle of my junior year, but I do not think it is appropriate in this kind of communication to dredge up those details. First, it is all pretty obvious (with the small exception of whether or not some girl with a wild side actually got close enough for me to sniff during those difficult years, and the answer would be, not unless they had to) and second there is really no point. Does one really, finally care if a boy-murderer got a passing grade on his critical analysis of the structural issues in *The Catcher in the Rye,* or whether or not it was fair, or funny, or sad that he couldn't get laid?

I also do not wish to take up too much valuable time retelling all the little facts about the trial that one could look up in the back issues of newspapers. It would be more than easy to discover that Mom asked for and got a speedy trial for me in front of a judge, *"Only the guilty ask for juries, Jimmy."* It would be just as simple to find documentation proving that Mr. Skinner tried to file a civil suit to protest my verdict of innocent, and ran out of money before it really got going.

What is not in the papers or online is a measure of how difficult it was to live in the same town with such a hateful enemy. I never quite shed the fear that I would run into Skinner or his small, plump wife on the express line at the Giant, or sitting in the waiting room at Dr. Bransen's. That fear turned out to be a valid one, and this little thread of the tale has two halves, the first an incident that unfolded in May of 1975 just after the civil suit was dropped, and the second in the dead of winter, 1984. Here, however, I must split those two events and reveal but one now with the hope that you will patiently wait for me to unveil the other just a bit later. I know. Timelines are a bitch.

The first Skinner incident occurred right after the thing with the buried dead woman.

Right around the time the man was dropping his civil suit and I was thanking God school was almost done for the year, the construction specialists had shored up the east edge of the landing area from the Route 79 overpass. They'd done the primary and secondary pours and gated it off with Dura Flex safety rails. By Christmas of 1976, they would finalize the new construction of Reed Road, complete with overhanging streetlight poles every two hundred feet through Scutters Woods with a merge onto West Main Street five miles down. At the end of May 1975, however, right about the time when they were putting in the white shoulder lines on that wide landing, I had a horrifying experience.

I found her "spot."

I had wanted to do this for months, actually. I had recurring dreams of her exploding eyeballs, and on some level I thought showing the courage to stand right over her again might help. I also had a constant fear that they would find some reason to dig and check out what was really down in that hole within the hole after all, and I had taken regular afternoon visits to the site all that year, hanging off in the cover of the trees to make sure they did not bust out the pneumatic jackhammers and put a whooping party on the cement and dirt fortress she was lurking under. Up until May, however, I hadn't had a chance to actually walk onto the cement platform because the space was always crawling with workers. And I hadn't dared make a nighttime attempt. The darkness was her playground, and the dreams were bad enough in the safety of my bedroom.

It was a Wednesday afternoon. I walked my famous path over the sewer pipe, and when I pushed aside the leaves of my hiding tree I saw something that filled me with a sick kind of excitement. The landing was empty. There were surveyors marking off what would be the road paved through the thick part of the woods about a hundred yards away, but their backs were to me.

I approached. I got to the guardrail, climbed over, and had a moment of *déjà vu* when I crossed the threshold. It was hot and windy on the platform and I gave a quick study to the ground in front of me. I walked a number of

247

paces and then I saw it. About twenty feet from the guardrail, and fifteen feet south of the front end capped off with a three-quarter round cylinder painted in black and yellow stripes like a barber pole, was a small pair of grooves cut into the concrete. I looked up to get my bearings, and though it was difficult without the old landmarks, I was pretty sure someone had marked off where they had filled in that strange hole the rest of the way, now better than twenty-five feet below surface.

A feeling of fear ran up between my shoulder blades. If someone marked it, someone had a question about it. I would never be safe, not with these hidden ghosts always floating just out of the reach of my experience and authority, in boardrooms, with complicated plans spread across their drafting boards like tablets of fate.

"Hey!" I heard. One of the workers had seen me, and he was pointing a rolled-up piece of paper in my direction.

My face went suddenly red hot and my heart started palpitating. My hands felt like stones and I almost dropped right there on the hot top. This was not the fear of getting caught by the surveyor, now jogging toward me with his partner just behind, struggling to stick his sunglasses behind his pocket protector while on the move. This was different. The breeze came up around me in what felt like a whirlwind. At first it sounded like huge, beating wings, and then it moaned. It raced by my ears and made what could have been just an undeterminable gust like the one you would hear if you let down the back seat window of a car moving at a high rate of speed, or it could have been perceived as a couple of words.

"My blood," I heard.

My nose was bleeding.

I felt it run out and drip down-over the top of my lip, but it didn't quite feel like a drip. It felt like a pull. A dot of it splatted on the concrete, right into one of the little grooves, and I crumpled.

The voices of the men came to my ears. Then the temperature felt different, and I knew there were shadows over me blocking the sun.

"Hey, Doug," one of the shadows said. "Here's another one."

"C'mon, son," the other said. He helped me to my feet. I opened my eyes. They walked me over a few feet and then I ran for it.

"Hey! You!" they were calling. I scrambled for the guardrail, crawled over it, and sprinted for home. Ghosts didn't just hide in boardrooms. I suppose I could have interpreted *"Hey, Doug, here's another one"* as an acknowledgment that I was just one more kid who was dared by another to sneak onto the site, but that version didn't feel right to me. *"Hey, Doug, here's another one that passed out"* seemed more the fit. I knew it in my bones.

It was the first time she had spoken to me in the waking world, and she had been speaking to others before me.

I came through the weeds, trudged up the back lawn, and looked up at the face that came into the kitchen window. I didn't really feel the pull of those shock-blue eyes anymore, and I broke the glance. I turned and sat on the edge of the concrete patio, drawing up my knees to my chin. I stared out into the woods. What was going to become of me? What would I do if it became public knowledge that you passed out if you stood directly above the burial place of the neglected dead?

The doorbell rang inside.

I jerked my head up. It was a strange sound. Since the incident I had not been afforded the opportunity to invite over many "friends," and it was rare we had a caller. I pushed up and moved to the kitchen window. There was glare on it so I went up on my toes and made a hood with my hands for my eyes to peer through. I moved over to the left a couple of inches. I could not see the whole exchange because of the corner of the hall archway, but I had most of the front doorway in view. It was Mr. Skinner. He was wearing his Sunday best, reddish-orange plaid flood pants, a collared shirt, and a tan leather jacket that went down a bit past the waist. He removed his hat and held it before him. His hands were sort of wringing it. I could not really hear what he said even with the kitchen door standing open, but I could hear that his tone was soft.

I wondered what he could possibly want. An apology? A heart-to-heart? The civil suit had caved weeks before.

Suddenly I saw Mom's elbow pop into view. Her hands were obviously on her hips. Her voice was also unintelligible for all but the tone, but the pitch was of a sharper nature than that to which she had responded. She closed the door, came around the corner of the living room, and went down the far hall toward the garage.

I walked into the house and followed her steps. I walked past the refrigerator, into the utility hallway, and down the two wooden stairs. I stood outside of the screen door and peered into the garage.

Since the divorce, it had long been a woman's space, filled with gardening tools thoughtfully placed on nails in the walls, lawn furniture, a couple of mulch bags neatly piled on top of each other, and a spiffy workbench. There were soldering tools, shears, strips of lead arranged across the surface, and colored glass pieces stacked at the right front corner. Dead soldiers. The stale remains of Mommy's little stained-glass hobby that got ditched when I started having my "problems."

She was by the utility sink. Her long fingers were making the prayer shape, her thumbs tucked under her jaw and her nose pressed between her index fingers. Her shoulders were gently shaking up and down.

"Mom?" I said. I pushed the screen door half open and it squawked.

She ripped her hands from her face and jerked her eyes to the wall in front of her. She was wearing faded jeans and a white cotton shirt that had blue stripes across it. It made her look both cold and fragile. There were tears on her face, but she had cut that particular faucet off to the quick. Rain on marble.

"What is it, Jimmy?" Her face was still looking off at the wall in profile.

"Ma?" I said. I came forward an inch or two, then stayed in the doorway. "Mom, do you love me?"

She looked over slowly.

"I'll always love what you could have been, Jimmy. We'll always have that, I suppose."

I went back to my room and turned up my radio as loud as it could go.

13.

Before I give the violent details of my second and final run-in with Mr. Skinner nine years later, I think it is necessary to backtrack and talk for a moment about Maryanne. The woman buried in her car, twenty-five feet under the concrete apron at the base of the Route 79 overpass. Maryanne McKusker.

I found out her identity four days after her death.

Mom had not yet begun to drift from me, and we were in that mute aftershock that held loved ones together until the dust settled and they could really think things through. We were also still running on autopilot, our wheels in the grooves of our established patterns and habits. News had always been an absolute requirement before dinner so the both of us could go through life "informed," and with the hoopla surrounding my own case dying down just a bit, we had on NBC, the rabbit-ears antenna thrust all the way over to the fireplace that had on its mantel a picture of me and Ma smiling together at a church picnic last year.

I was watching Ted Johnson shift from one pile of notes to the other, thinking that his fake-me-out voice was more annoying than professional, when he said,

"This just in…"

He disappeared and a photograph took his place.

Good legs. Halter top. A woman in her back yard hanging up laundry, facing away, looking back at the camera. The white basket was perched on her hip. The sheets on the line, military gray, were frozen in time, furling around her in swells. Her expression was alluring in its gentle, girlish sarcasm, saying over the shoulder, *"Oh yeah?"* in a wry smirk.

She had straight blonde hair.

"Pictured here is Maryanne McKusker, a kindergarten teacher from Unionville who has been missing now for four days. The daughter of Minister Charles McKusker, she was last seen leaving her home in a rust orange '73 Honda Civic, enroute to Concord University for a training seminar in child psychology. Miss McKusker never made it to her destination, and her father claims she seems to have 'disappeared from the face of the earth.' The Unionville police have not yet officially made a statement confirming that there has been foul play, yet welcome any information leading to this young woman's whereabouts. Maryanne McKusker is five feet, three inches tall. She has green eyes. She is twenty-nine years old."

I glanced over at Mother without turning my head. She was staring at the television with the same general indifference as when Ted Johnson had talked about a four-alarm warehouse fire on Grant Avenue half a minute ago. If she suspected some sort of connection between Maryanne McKusker's last four days and the time elapsed since my confession, she was not letting on.

The good thing was that Unionville sat four towns over from Westville, up the Pike about twenty miles due east. The better thing was that Concord University happened to be three towns due east from Unionville, thirty or so miles in the opposite direction of where she'd made her final resting place.

She sure as hell was not going to any lecture.

And even though I was fairly convinced at that point that it would be amazing if they actually traced her here, this was an intellectual deduction that did not take into account my instincts and emotions.

I never felt safe.

And the nightmares did not get any gentler just because I knew her name. They continued once or twice every night with a horrid, almost mechanistic regularity. She haunted me in the dark and, in return, I decided to stalk her during the day. It was a defensive move. A coping device. I would *know* why she was headed in the wrong direction. It became an obsession, yet not one all that long lasting, as I learned the truth before I even completed my first ninth-grade research paper. Of course, I had the advantage over everyone else in that it was far easier to unveil the set-up when I already knew the punch line.

As the summer wound down and I awaited my "trial" before the honorable Rita Moskowitz a few months later, I collected newspapers in my room and followed the investigation. Over a period of weeks the biggest piece of evidence that the Unionville police had uncovered was, in fact, a newspaper.

In her room, on the bed, there had been a copy of the *County Gazette,* left closed and folded at the bottom edge of the mattress. The local police had dusted the paper and done every kind of test imaginable, but had come out with nothing but the statement, "At this point we have a number of possible leads, but we have so far found them to be inconclusive." Evidently, it would have been easier if the newspaper had been left open to a certain section, or something had been circled in magic marker, or she had left more of a wrinkle in the corner of a certain page. The inserts and leaflets, however, had been put back and rearranged in perfect order. And Maryanne McKusker's fingerprints were on every single page, all with the thumb on the front, top right corner, and the index finger on the back. Whatever she had been looking for had been mentally noted and passed. She was a subtle, yet thorough reader.

I went to the library on a Saturday in late September when the place was relatively empty and aimed straight for the periodical room. I found the thing, and placed it beside the most current copy they had of the *Westville Herald.* I kept looking over my shoulder. The last thing I needed was some librarian to wonder why Kyle Skinner's killer was so interested in the sole piece of evidence in the Maryanne McKusker case.

I scanned the more current paper first. The article on the progress of her case was shorter than the one I read at home the day before, and it was obvious that the police were letting this one fade to the unsolved file without much of a fight. They had completed their interviews up at Concord University, and were now "entertaining other leads."

In other words, the newspaper evidence had led them nowhere, and they were moving on to other cases.

I opened the copy of the *Gazette,* and spent a good while with it. There was only a couple of pages of real news—"Penny Becomes Scarce Commodity," "Amax Strike Drags On," "Local Industries Claim Coal Supply Will Withstand." I went through the various sections, spending most of my time with the advertisements and pullouts. Nothing. All dead ends. There were nature walks available in a national park, there was a special on the Johanson Company's supply of backyard pools, there were five pages of personals. I worked out some scenarios in my head, and though there were possibilities, like a female selling a used stereo, none of them made a straight line with Maryanne McKusker's place in Unionville and the Route 79 overpass. I made a second sweep of the *Gazette* and widened my focus to goofy stuff not so "evident." I came up with little else. In the back of my mind I had just noted the futility of the exercise considering the fact that the Unionville police had already made these deductions, when I ran across Rolling Joe's advertisement.

I had initially passed it over because it seemed so silly to be put even in the same paragraph as the person I had imagined Maryanne McKusker to be. Still, the place was local, so I took another look at it.

Rolling Joe was a Sixties dropout going on forty, who thought himself a visionary. He was balding and still holding on to a ponytail. His dingy shop was crammed with nudie posters, bongs, and other various no-no's, like rolling papers and canisters of nitrous oxide commonly known as "whippets." It was all perfectly legal, and most around these parts thought of Rolling Joe as the perfect asshole.

Business was limited, but Joe kept his going by feeding on teenagers. I had heard lots of high school kids tested the waters of rebellion and believed for at least a short period of time that it was cool to hang at the head shop.

Clearly, Joe was thinking bigger nowadays. His advertisement read,

"Rolling Joe's Shop of Dreams. Grand Opening Tomorrow! Monday Will Be YOUR Day of Psychedelic Rest. New Flotation Tank. Appointments Only."

Evidently, he came upon the new technology that wound up being later popularized mostly in myth by the William Hurt film titled *Altered States*. Oh yes, Rolling Joe was a trend setter!

Did Maryanne McKusker actually sign up for an appointment for this thing? I was about to wander out to find a phone booth so I could call and ask him to check his log book from a couple of weeks back, but I didn't. First, the police would have done this already, and second there was something about the ad that bothered me. Then I saw it. He called "tomorrow" Monday. We killed her on a Monday.

I turned the paper over to the front page. Of course. I didn't notice it before because the date at the top, just under the slightly perforated edge, had the month and day solely represented by numbers. This was a Sunday paper. That's why it had so many extra flyers. Maryanne had thumbed through it and failed to find what she was looking for. The next day she picked up Monday's paper, saw what she needed or wanted and went directly to it. She was already on the road and either tossed the paper out or left it in the car.

The police probably didn't jump to the conclusion I did because of those extra flyers. Everyone knew the Sunday paper had all the promotional stuff. Was it possible that whatever attracted Maryanne did not make the weekend deadline? Did they or he or she get a discount for having the ad or announcement or bid first shown in an edition with less circulation?

I twisted around and took a look through the doorway. The librarian was in the main lobby, eye glasses on the end of her nose and a pile of file cards a half-foot high in front of her. There was a small girl with her mother way over by the children's section and a guy in an army jacket asleep at the long table by the window. I crept over to the rack and slipped the next day's edition of the *Gazette* off the curled wire. I found what I was looking for in about two minutes.

It was an advertisement as subtle as the side of a cereal box, but to me, it was more than obvious.

NO NAMES NECESSARY

DR. GOLTZ GYN. M.D.

112 BYLINE RD., DEGGSVILLE

555-3865

She had been going to get an abortion. A kill of her own, and the more I thought of the ways that this might not be possible, the more assured I became that it was.

The father? Yes, where the hell was he in all this? Why had he not come forward to claim his right as a player? Was he a secret, ongoing fling, still under cover now because the disappearance would implicate him? Had Maryanne been on her way to see him in stealth? That did not play right somehow. First, why the secret, and second, someone at either end of it, his work buddy or her little phone-gossip friend or someone like that would have known. They would have come forward by now.

It must have been what they called a "one-nighter," or what Kyle would have referred to as a "pump and dump." They probably met at some crowded bar or some lecture she had attended in the past and gone and gotten a room. I understand and believe this now as an adult, and even at thirteen I had my imagination. It was not too difficult a stretch.

Maybe they had been drunk. Maybe recently he even recognized her picture on the news and had remained silent, ignorant of the pregnancy, sure of his innocence, and unwilling to arouse suspicions that would swallow his time, mar his reputation, and prove answerless anyway.

The fatal ride of Maryanne McKusker came to me with a hideous clarity. She did not want Dad the minister to know she was pregnant, so she anonymously called for directions from a mall or gas station telephone.

"Interstate 7 to Crum Creek Parkway. Make a right onto Exit 3 and follow the curve to Jukins Cross. Bear left at the 'Y' and continue on Byline Road. It is unmarked at that point, but you will see us a mile up on the right hand side."

Hell, Rolling Joe's was *on* Crum Creek Parkway and she probably passed it. But soon afterward she must have gotten lost. I do not believe, in fact, that she ever got to the clinic or much past Rolling Joe's, for that matter. I think she took a wrong turn at the "Y."

At the end of Jukins Cross there was a "Y" in the road all right, but it was not really a "Y." It was a three-pronged fork that had two major, unmarked arteries and an offshoot to the far left that looked more like a private driveway than a real street. Byline was definitely at the left of the "Y," but to the newcomer it would have appeared more as the center path of three, if you counted the little side-chute.

Maryanne McKusker's directions had specifically stated "bear left at the

'Y,'" and she did just that, even though the avenue in question looked generally untraveled.

The small patch of unmarked country lane was actually called Mulberry Street.

Mulberry Street led one way to the Route 79 overpass.

Maryanne McKusker had bumped along Mulberry Street, maybe fearing she might run over the amount of time she allotted herself for the false appearance at the lecture in Concord, fretfully searching for the clinic a "mile up." What she got was an ongoing, lazy panorama of seemingly deserted horse farms, barns, and meadows back dropped by trees. No gas stations, no general stores, just a confusing wind of back road stretching farther and farther to nowhere.

She was probably relieved when Mulberry Street curved suddenly and opened out to the overpass.

Civilization at last!

She would have passed under the big green overhead road sign that announced "Westville" in friendly white letters. She would have immediately understood her mistake at the "Y," regrouped, and opted for the first possible left turn allowing her to double back and try it again.

It was a mere fifty feet between the Mulberry street on-ramp and the fatal left turn. It is entirely possible that she, for that short period of time, was the lone motorist on the overpass and unobserved. It is fact that the triple guardrail kept her from knowing exactly where the left turn was about to take her, and it remains my own speculation that at this particular moment it felt right to her. At least it was a turn in the proper general direction.

Considering the "alibi" she told her father, the time was getting tight. She was probably pressing on the gas a bit harder than usual. She swung down that ramp and onto the dirt road faster than you could say *"death trap."*

She wanted an abortion and she got one.

Kyle and I killed two birds with one nail.

14.

The toll booth did not go up until the summer of 1978. There were legal snags, and Runnameade's proposals that received initial local approval were put on hold at the state level. For a year and a half cars simply came into Westville off the turnpike for free. Then in late '75 there were questions about the integrity of the original exit ramp, and they closed off the turn on the overpass for another twenty-three months.

Of course, I did not know all of the details concerning the finer details until years later when I could access all the documents, transactions, and bureaucratic maneuverings online. As a developing adolescent I was left to my own assumptions. I therefore took it upon myself to continue going regularly to the jobsite as I had begun doing as a thirteen-year-old, to hide in the cover of the trees and see if today was the day the hardhats started poking around again.

It turns out that Runnameade Construction won the bid with a simple, low-risk scheme to put a single toll booth in at the base of the overpass. In the Nineties, many referred back to this as "The Blair Witch Plan," not only because Runnameade's booth wound up being haunted, but more to compare it with the miniscule cost the creators of "Blair" put forth to make their blockbuster in the first place.

The Siegal people must have always questioned the integrity of that original footer, but those protests were probably trivial to them, more footnotes in fine print than the dollar signs that came across in bold. It was common knowledge that they wanted the powers that were to shoot the moon. Still, it never got past City Hall. They wanted the government to spend big, and plain and simple, the Siegal vision had a higher cost than what many believed would turn a profit. Through the years, as the running debate wore on, interested parties on both sides did traffic volume evaluations and Siegal's independent firms always seemed to come up with different results than those hired by the county. Go figure.

And when the single booth did go up in the summer of 1978, as predicted, it began turning that slow, faithful profit, like a low-risk, low-interest savings bond. Every time Siegal got to the table through the years, their bid was rejected for the same basic reasons.

The booth started turning a profit the minute it was put up.

We are a small town.

Your plan will cost millions in exposed funds that will take years to show dividends. As long as that booth stands, and continues to come up in the black on the quarterlies, there will be no plaza. Period.

That is why I dropped out of school in 1978, a year before graduation. After Runnameade installed the booth, no toll operator could bear to stay in it, at least not after the sun went down. I do not recall the names in the succession of those who tried to work nightshift there throughout that critical month, but I know it was more than twenty. The reported physical symptoms were "lightheadedness, heart palpitations, and minor bleeding for no apparent reason," but it was the psychological symptoms that really captured everyone's imagination. It was bad enough that some actually recognized Kyle Skinner's fleeting image just at the periphery of vision, laughing silently and snapping his head back and forth on that flap of neck-skin. The one that really scared me, however, was Maryanne's image, hair flying behind her in slow motion, eyes crawling with worms, a baby in her arms that she reportedly first caressed, next scratched, then bit into, and finally snapped back and forth in clamped jaws like a frenzied dog tearing at meat. Supposedly you couldn't really "see" her, since the minute you fixed your eyes on the particular glass pane she was occupying she switched to a neighboring panel, but I could not afford to take the chance that someone would actually recognize the face (or worse, take a photograph of it) and connect it to Maryanne McKusker.

When the trouble in the booth started there were also reports in the newspapers and the *Construction Times* (of which I had become a regular subscriber by then) that Siegal had heard about the complication and were stirring around again, probably going back to the footnotes in small print concerning the integrity of the otherwise unexplored footer where *"that boy died years ago."* Suddenly not so trivial. Could have been their angle to get their hands finally into the pie.

I actually read an article about that while goofing off at school, and I remember walking straight out of chemistry class and Westville High School for good. When I told my mother later that day, she accepted the news with quiet defeat. She brought the collar of her robe up under her jaw in a fist and slowly went back into her bedroom. No shock-blue eyes. She had kept them down to the floor. The blue jean queen had lost her power over me some time ago.

I was hired immediately. And while many initially saw it as some sort of sick prank that I earn my living literally standing directly above the spot where Kyle Skinner was killed, there were others who came to understand (or thought they understood) that this was my duty, my way to mourn, my method of healing that allowed me to give something back to society.

And I did give back. The trusty low-risk savings account. I was never told exactly where the money was filtered off to after I took the weekly take in fifty-pound strongboxes and helped pack them onto the armored GM van they also used for prison transport, but I suppose a portion was put right back into the city. I never came up with the cure for cancer, but we erected a huge bandstand down in the Common back in '83. I never discovered a way to solve world hunger, but I would bet dollars to donuts that the war memorial they put in the grove behind the recreation center in '95 was sponsored at least in part by some cash that came from my strongboxes.

Of course, this is all well and good, but I am not trying to fool anybody. If you are reading this you know exactly who I am, what I have done, and where it has left me. Working the booth has been no picnic, and I am not immune to the spirits that dwell there. I am fifty-eight years old and I feel like I'm in my seventies. I eat poorly, on purpose, and have been loading up on daily doses of F9 Blood Liquescence ever since it became possible buy your own smorgasbord of drugs on the Internet. As I said, I am a walking time-bomb, a guaranteed candidate, no, an *elected official* for a heart attack or stroke, but before I pass there are two more things I am obligated to disclose.

First, please know that my mother was always innocent of all this. For your information, she developed osteoporosis, broke a hip when she took a header off the stairway in front of the Staples on Willow Street, and died in the hospital of pneumonia last year. She was always ignorant of the breadth of my sins, and for that I am thankful.

Second, understand that it was not just the supernatural that targeted this booth. Through the years I was attacked a total of twenty-six times on the job. Most were drunk teens chucking empty bottles or rocks at the booth for a laugh, but there were some incidents born of more serious motivation. I was shot at three times. Two of the occurrences were arbitrary acts of hate by those in vehicles I could not identify, but the one in the winter of 1984 was anything but random.

I was reading an article in a teen magazine that discussed the differences between Eighties sleaze hair metal and new wave, when I heard a vehicle screech up to the gate. By the time I looked out, Mr. Skinner had already exited his vehicle. His hair was matted with sweat and his eyes were blood-red. He called something to me but the fierce wind swallowed the words. I was lucky he was so drunk. The other assaults I experienced during my tenure in the booth were drive-bys, but here, he really wanted to get his hands dirty. There was a double-plated bulletproof sliding glass unit above the half-door I exchanged cash out of, but I had left it up. Skinner only needed to walk four feet to have a clear, frontal shot at me.

He didn't. He staggered, took a position at an angle to the booth, spread his feet, aimed, and fired his weapon. It smoked and banged louder than I thought it would have. I had covered my face, and now slowly brought away my hands. The bullet had dented the safety glass of the panel to my right and glanced off into the roadway. Skinner was not visible.

I got out of my chair and opened the portal door. Skinner had slid down to his butt. He was shirtless and had on dirty overalls. He had snot coming out of his nose, and the wind blew it away in threads. He was propped up, back against the front right tire of his vehicle. He had one leg splayed out straight and the other bent at the knee. He looked at me with squinting, tearing eyes. He smiled crookedly, and brought the gun to his temple.

I just watched, hands dangling at my sides, breath coming out in steady little puffs that made clouds on the night air.

He started laughing. He laughed as he brought the weapon down, and laughed as he pushed to his feet. He offered me the gun, butt first.

"Eh?" he coaxed.

I just cocked my head a bit to the side and stared.

He turned and tossed the thing into the woods beyond the edge of the concrete deck. He started laughing for the second time, and I could still hear it as he drove off into the darkness. I never saw him after that night. He moved out of state and no one I knew ever heard from him again.

And so that concludes my story. When I am gone, the booth will inevitably fail and Siegal/Tri State Industries will finally control that section of roadway. They may even go back to the fine print, bust the shit out of that dirt-and-concrete tomb and finally exhume Maryanne McKusker. It will be poor closure for her. She will be remembered as a vengeful spirit and sensationalized as worse.

As for me, I suppose this story is my closure, but one must be human to feel that kind of thing. My soul was erased years ago. I was a boy with dreams and I made a horrible mistake. I do not for a minute think myself more innocent than Kyle Skinner because I only threw one of those nails, and I do not consider myself disassociated because I was unaware of the baby. I do not even feel there was righteousness in bringing fatal consequences to an unfeeling hoodlum who threatened a defenseless animal.

When you strip this down to its bare bones, I am the worst kind of sinner. From everything I read about her, Maryanne McKusker was a wonderful person. I turned her into a monster. I could have told somebody before now. I could have at least told somebody.

Maryanne, please forgive me. And in my last days, when I see you rise from the dead looking only to take back what is yours, please know that I understand.

For I have always been the horror here.

I have always been the horror.

[This story anchored my first collection, *Seven Deadly Pleasures*, Hippocampus Press, 2009.]

MARTYRS AND SACRIFICIAL LAMBS

The Echo

J F.K. is dead. Judy Garland, King James, Chaucer, Hitler, Shoeless Joe Jackson, Nostradamus, all dead like a trillion others. So am I, but don't ask if I've seen your long lost great uncle or anything. It's not like that. There's just foliage out here, vague images and dark outlines in the passing windows, a lot of roadway.

I drive an old Nissan Sentra, and it's a junkyard on wheels. Members of my family tease me about it: the pitted back bumper, the broken driver's side door handle that makes you lower the window and claw out to flip up the exterior release, the worn seat cushions marbled like dough.

Oh, and don't fret over the fact that I refer to my wife and kids in the present tense. I engage in this practice only because I think I am trapped in a moment that keeps being played out as if in live time, and my family is no more concerned about me than they were in terms of their "yesterday" or the day before that. And though I cannot be utterly sure in terms of hard proof, I am fairly certain that I am indeed deceased because I don't get hungry anymore. Moreover, I can only recall universalities. I know that killing is wrong and that getting a girl pregnant before you marry her can put a real dent in your plans. I know that The Who translated better to the seventies than The Beatles, The Stones, The Airplane, and The Kinks, but I don't remember what I had for dinner last night (if there is such a thing as an "evening" for me any longer).

As I alluded to before, I know I have kids, but can't recall how many. I know my wife is a pale brunette, but I can't recollect her laugh. I know she has sun freckles dusted across her cleavage, a nondescript suburban ass, and Mediterranean cheekbones she accents with lavender blush, but I can't remember her maiden name. My whole life, or past life if you will, has been reduced to wallet-sized black and whites, faded and out of order.

Thing is, I don't miss it. My life. Because even though it seems I am stuck for eternity in this shitty charcoal gray Nissan, there is also a feeling about me (or in me) that I am in transit to a destination. Now, please don't interpret that as something spiritual, like I am on some cosmic pilgrimage to meet the almighty. I am saying that the feeling about me (or maybe imposed on me) is one of casual indifference, like I am on my way to work, or the Crate and Barrel, or the driving range for a quick bucket, and it doesn't feel anything like "death." The window is open, my elbow up on the rim, and the sky is that pale broad canopy of the lightest blue that fills us all with hope and longing; images of sailboats inching along sun spangled waters…carnivals, picnics, graduations, promises.

Here's the thing. I can't exit the vehicle.

The first time it happened was quite by accident, pardon the pun, when I rear-ended a big dude in a red Dodge Ram, silver contractor's boxes bolted to both sides of the back bed. I'd been cruising along and had just passed an area where the roadside sound barriers flanked the near spread of woodland like the walls of some majestic fortress, and I had sort of realized in the back of my mind that I hadn't seen a road sign in a while. It was the first inkling I'd had that something was odd about this journey and the first hint that maybe I'd been on this road for longer than what I might have considered "normal," but just as I started to focus on that a green sign flashed by. It was bolted to an overpass, and I realized I'd missed another one, and then traffic before me had come to one of those sudden standstills, and I hit the brakes and screeched the tires.

I skidded, swerved a bit left, and plinked his back bumper. An insignificant little nudge, a Boston kiss.

"Fucking moron," I heard. Couldn't see him. His back window was tinted jet black, but I saw his arm from out the driver's side window, flannel cut off at the shoulder, beef-bull forearm. He jabbed his index finger up and over the roof toward the breakdown lane. It was an order and he wasn't kidding. The car in front of him moved forward a bit, and he pulled over, tires making chock 'n gravel sounds. I followed, stopped, put it in park, kept it running. My heart was thudding a bit and my face was ashen, or at least it felt that way. And I couldn't find my information in the glove compartment. It was a mess of papers, envelopes, expired insurance cards, parking passes, dashboard flyers to identify me as a parent for summer camp pick-up.

I reached out through the open window, flipped up the handle, got out of the car, and everything changed.

I wasn't on 476 or 95 or the Northeast Extension anymore and it wasn't the beginning of summer. It wasn't daytime either. It was after-dark, and it was late fall...you could tell because there was that smokehouse tang in the air like someone had been burning leaves, and the trees all around me were bare and crooked under a low moon. We were on a back road cutting through the forest, and the pick-up had its blinkers on, leaning right because the shoulder was an uneven ditch.

There was a rather brisk wind on my face and I walked forward, sure I was going to get a lecture or maybe even a punch in the eye. I was sweeping apologies together in my head, trying for the right flavor, and couldn't decide between the half-jest "sorry about that," or the sincere, "Hey friend, my fault, what can I do" kind of thing.

His door opened and his leg thrust itself out, work boot clapping down to the dirt.

"...learn to drive in a fucking girl's room..."

He pushed all the way out of the vehicle and slowly straightened, taller and then some, more than 6'5" minimum with long curly hair, a neck tattoo, and a hillbilly beard. He took a long moment to twist at the waist with his elbows up, first right then left the way a prize fighter would go about stretching his back. He pulled at his crotch to move the underwear and started making his way toward me, shaking his head like he was going to teach this little bastard a lesson. He looked up and saw me. His mouth dropped open. He slumped a bit, shoulders curling in and withering, knees knocking in toward each other like he'd just been whacked in the nuts.

"Uhh…" he said. He fumbled back for the open door, almost missed, and scrambled back into his vehicle.

Then I saw it, what scared him. It was only for a split second, reflected there in his back window. I only saw it out of the corner of my eye because I was so focused on his odd retreat, and it was only a flicker because it changed when he broke eye contact. For that one second, however, I was a horrid swamp-creature with twists of dead vegetation draped off of my skull.

I knew it was me because the silhouette was mimicking my advance. I could see it at the periphery of my vision, both hands extended out like "what the heck" in response to his cowardly retreat. When he broke eye-lock I stopped and looked at the black outline directly, yet it was just me in there now, short hair, pudgy face. I could even see my glasses with the moon reflected in the bottom rim of each lens.

I somehow knew that the rotted figure in the glass had been an image he'd picked up from some TV special he saw when he was six years old, after he stole his sister Melinda's Ranch Doritos and tip-toe'd down the basement even though it was past his bed time and if Daddy caught him, he'd warm up his behind something good. I saw the original horrific images washing over his face in pale lines and shadows just as clearly as I saw the flash forward to his wetting the bed for a year, lying in his own sour dampness with the comforter pulled over his head, breathing all cut and shallow through the little porthole he'd made for his mouth.

The pickup pulled off in a roar.

I blinked, and it was summer again. I was doing a lazy sixty-three miles per hour and the sky opened before me in that panorama of oceanic crystalized blue. There was sloping acreage to the right, wheat or rye moving with the pattern of the breeze, and on the left, there was a long meadow with antenna towers in the background. There were cars around me, but the occupants were nothing but forms, vague outlines, shapes.

And no road signs. When I concentrated, focused, and bore down, like my Dad used to tell me to do in little league when I couldn't find the strike zone, I'd see something ahead, that familiar rectangular highway-green with the white block letters. Then I'd get distracted at the last minute by a deer crossing sign, or a plane flying low overhead, or a truck passing too close.

After some indeterminable amount of time, I pulled into a Howard Johnsons to get directions, to get a handle on this, to convince myself that what happened with the contractor was illusory and that finally, I wasn't the creature from the black lagoon.

I didn't get further than the parking area.

Originally, the structure had seemed a familiar, charming little piece of Americana, offset from the highway by a grand sort of rotary with the restaurant at the far edge and a sprawling golf course in the background. Across the way was an antique furniture store and a glass crafter, both a short walking distance from the shopping center up ahead with the Wegman's and the movie theater.

But when I stepped out and shut my door, I realized I had been mistaken about the surroundings. Everything was gray, and to the left across the highway was an abandoned warehouse, windows darkened, weeds at the perimeter growing out of the cracked cement tire bumpers. Past the motel dumpsters on the far-right side, a swarm of cattails and yellow grass led to an area of marsh and tangled woodland. To the right of the place was a rusted cyclone fence with old trash blown in at the bottom, and beyond that, a drainage basin and an abandoned quarry, dozers parked up on the mounds. I remembered that the parking lot had seemed populated when I entered, yet now it stood empty for all but a black mini-van with a soccer magnet in one corner of the back window and a Garfield toy with foot suckers in the other.

I walked up to the vehicle and noticed that my forearms had run over with goose bumps. It was starting to rain, slanted darting drops, and the clouds that were moving across the sky were running thin shadows along the asphalt.

In the side-view mirror I could see the woman in the driver's seat, coral copper hair pulled back in a pony tail, sharp eyebrows, delicate face - beautiful like glass.

"Excuse me," I said. "Could you tell me where I am, please?"

I honestly believe she was about to turn toward my voice and acknowledge me, but a piercing scream erupted from the back seat. I didn't have a good angle to get a look inside past the lady's shoulder, but when I backed off a half-step I could see through the glass it was a toddler in a car seat, struggling, scratching at his harness, staring at me with wide, rolling eyes.

With Mom occupado, I bent to look in her side-view and saw the strangest, most frightening thing looking back at me on an angle.

I was a playing card, a Jack I think, and I couldn't tell if I was a heart or a diamond, but I knew for sure I was one of the red ones. My face was elongated, skull-like, shaped like the "Scream" mask, but the eyes were brilliant and savage, close-set and piercing. I was holding a flaming scepter, and my hair was a nest of wriggling snakes.

I stumbled away from the vehicle, out of the kid's sightline, and I was driving again, back in the burst of landscape unfolding into the bosom of flawless blue sky, warm and mindless, a vacant baseball field on the right, a red barn, a silo, grazing cows.

The boy's name was Jason MacGonigle, and his mother had been trying to teach him to play "Crazy Eights" while the tile man was laying a mosaic pattern on the floor in the sun room. It was the Jack of Hearts, and this robed nightmare with the skinny face and the big fire-stick had hideous eyes that followed Jason even when he pushed it across the table and told Mommy he didn't want to play anymore.

I knew that he dreamed about the Jack of Hearts that night, and that the dream character was far worse than the playing card itself, elongated, fluid and reptilian, a Disney cartoon gone horribly wrong, and the thing slithered through the cracks outlining the closet door and waited in the shadows for

Jason to close his eyes so he could claw his dagger-like fingernails straight into the boy's once rosy cheeks.

So, you see now, that I am everyone's nightmare. I wonder what I did to earn this title, but my past life is a blur. I do know that I am on a real highway with real people who don't have a clue as to my presence, not really. But how often do we really notice who sits next to us at a red light or cruises in the neighboring lane at sixty-plus? Looking would be rather impolite, like staring at someone in an elevator when we all know the rising or falling floor numbers are a mandatory study.

Plainly, this is my hell I suppose. I am to stay on this road for eternity, and if I veer off of it, or cause some sort of accident that disrupts my journey, innocent people, real people will pay. This is all a private outdoor prison that is secured by my morals, go ahead, go figure, chew on the irony.

I tried driving off the road and aiming for a tree once. It was in a stand of foliage with a high canopy that temporarily darkened the highway, and I got close enough to see two knots in the bark. I put my hands in front of my face and braced for the impact just to get beeped at for my trouble. You see, just before the impending crash, I was "sent back" a few seconds and I realized that I had merely drifted a bit over the double yellow. Instinct came into play, and I jerked the wheel to hard right just in time to avoid oncoming traffic, another irony, since I had just tried to kill my already dead self.

I've tried driving off bridges, causing head on collisions, making danger-ous 360 turns in heavy traffic, all failures. Nowadays I pull one of those just to wake myself up, for the fun of it, to remind myself that I was once a living being who wasn't stuck daydreaming for hours, years, centuries at a time, driving off to nowhere straight into the blue.

I've also caused a multitude of those minor, harmless accidents that get me "real contact," and I've scared the living shit out of more people than I can count. I do it because I have to, because being time deprived is a torture. I do it to remind myself that even though I am stuck in this endless cycle, I'm still real.

Do my victims remember me, or am I the shadow of a dream? Am I merely a bad feeling to recover from…finally, the explanation for unwarranted depression?

In what seems like years ago I cut off three high school girls on the way to put in orders for prom dresses. The red head with the turned-up nose and the ¾ moon Alice headband saw me as a dirty cop and feared an invasive frisk outside of the car, a hard rape across the front hood. The ash blonde with the nose ring and practiced sour-apple pout in the passenger seat saw me as her own father, drunk again, short sleeved dress shirt drenched with back sweat, shock of gray hair falling across his eye while he punched her like a dude again and pulled her out into the brush so she could *really* get what was coming to her for acting like her mother all these years. And finally, there was the little cookie in the back, rosebud lips, tiny tits, big teeth, black hair tucked behind her ears, who envisioned a maniac with a wandering eye, one strap of his overalls unhooked and dangling, taking her by the scruff of the neck and the back of her pants and throwing her into an old van sanded down on its sides to the brown primer splotches. It belched exhaust on the jarring, bumpy trip to his farmhouse basement where he had waiting for her - a cage and a specific type of torture porn involving steel clamps, oily puddles, heavy gauge cables, and car batteries.

Of course, I retreated, but I wonder if they swapped stories, arguing about my given appearance and calling each other "stupid" for being so paranoid. Did they remember being cut off at all? Was my "presence" known, or just "felt?" Or, here you go…did I ever stop them in the first place?

I need to exist more meaningfully in this realm I have inherited. I can't ride into the blue anymore, conscious in the unconscious endlessness of a never-ending blur going pleasantly and rapidly nowhere.

The question is, what do monsters do when they finally come out of the linen closet, or the attic, or from around the corner of the wood shed? When I was a boy, I was terrified that a nameless, hooded man with yellow eyes and a steel grip was to reach up and grab my ankle if I let it off the edge of the mattress. So, what if he grabbed the ankle? What if I screamed? What if he leaned in close and breathed death into my face? What would be next? Would he ask me my favorite color? Would we talk about God? Would he tear out my throat with his teeth and put me on a road leading straight to the bosom of blue?

Time to find out. I'm going to kiss a bumper, cut off a Kia, give someone the finger. Except this time, I'm not going to walk away at the first sight of transformation in the side view mirror. I'm going to get in the car and tell my victim to drive. Home. Into a life where the streets are named, where engines rest, and where demons, torturers, and rippers are finally granted a timeline, a purpose, a meaning, and an end.

This story first appeared in *Nameless Magazine,* December, 2012, and was also featured in Jason Henderson's anthology, *Castle of Horror #3,* Summer 2020.]

The Falcon

"Push, Rachel."

"It hurts so."

"Push hard or I'll slap you again. The chloroform slowed you."

"It's out."

"It's a boy, God bless."

"Turn him, Belinda. Hold him in the lamp light."

"What's that on his back? Oh God! Oh, my holy God!"

"I'm sewing them shut."

"You can't. 'Tain't natural."

"What ain't? You call what's in there natural?"

"But that's fishing line, Rachel. He's two years old."

"The skin's tough there 'round the slits. He'll live."

"Adam Michael Rothman, you come down off that barrel, now."

"I'm not standing on a barrel, mother. It's your eyes tricking you. Come closer."

"Down, I say, this instant!"

"Why? I like it. And it feels good to get them air once in a while."

"Someone might see, God damn you. Through the widow. You're tossing shadows. And don't go up to the rafters again, or so help me, I'll get the
short rifle."

"You're full of fiction."

"Really? Well, I'm sewing you up again. And this time I'm using the steel
baling twine. Try and stop me, I'll knock your skull. You gotta sleep sometime, and chloroform's got many uses, it does."

—

April 1892

On his seventeenth birthday, Adam Michael Rothman set off into the
Penn Woods to meet Katie Claypool, because she'd promised to show him
her bare legs all the way up to her privates. She was waiting for him in the
glen by their sitting stone. A shadow lay across her bosom and her breath
was high. The straight black hair she'd been growing since the age of ten was
twisted in a long braid down her back.

"Do you want to play *Fox and Geese*, Adam? *Hide and Seek*?"

"You wouldn't hide from me."

"I would." She raised her chin. "I've just had my bath, and I'm not wearing any undergarments. If you don't believe me, you'll have to go exploring
up my tea dress." When he didn't answer, she pursed her lips. She webbed
her fingers down curtsey style in front of her waist, turned her head slightly,
and looked up through her bangs and lashes. "But you'll have to catch me
first, Adam Rothman."

She was off then, running into the dark wood with Adam chasing
behind her. At the peak of the first rise a fallen oak blocked the path, and she
angled off right, down the knoll through the wild grass, and then she darted
across the creek, toes dancing along the dark, polished stones. Adam splashed
ungraciously across, followed her up the short craggy incline, and gained
ground along the long floor of pine needles. He reached for her once, grazing
the fabric of one sheer, puffy sleeve, and she zig-zagged off into the shadows.

"Not so easy for you, boy," she cried over her shoulder.

"You're a damned gazelle," Adam panted, and she made for the footbridge, dodging between a pair of birches too tight for Adam to follow her through. By the time he'd skirted to the left and hurdled a short crop of witch hazel shrubs, she had made it to the high clearing at the back edge of what had been the property of some rich wholesale grocer a century before. There was a flat cement square rough with creeping thistle and nut grass, and where a stable once stood were the petrified remains of a hitching post. In the background was the carriage house, all rubble but for the northwest corner still standing tall like some ancient monolith at the edge of the wood's darkest border. The moon came through the tangled nest of overhead branches in splinters, and she was waiting there for him, leaning against the old stone well covered at the bottom with moss and ivy and vine.

"Want to make a wish, Adam?"

He approached heavily and kissed her. It wasn't the first time, but it was certainly the most urgent. His hands were on her waist, and she'd indeed shed her underclothes, for he could feel her beneath as if touching her through the thinnest of silks, and when he fondled at her breasts she moved his hands southward where he could get up and under the hem. Then he kneeled, the cool April dampness soaking through the knees of his trousers, and he was kissing the outside of one sturdy thigh, and then the warmer insides of both, and he caught her fragrance, and buried himself there, making her bite off a screech that led to a husky moaning in the thick of her throat. He wasn't sure if it was all right to kiss her lips afterwards, but she was on to other business, and his sack coat was pulled off him, laid out in folds behind her to make a buffer against the coarse surface of the well. His trousers were at his ankles.

"Where?" he begged.

"Right there, that's it."

"But Katie-"

"You've got to push, Adam. It won't hurt me too bad, and I know you want to."

"Like that?"

"Hard, Adam. No…oh yes! Mighty Christ!"

"Should I stop?"

"God, no. Get through with it, rough if you need to, just finish."

Afterwards they held each other for a moment, and Adam whispered that he loved her. She kissed his forehead and said it in return, and then she felt something move. It was something in his back, and she groped a bit to the left and found its twin.

She didn't scream, and when he went to take her hands in his, she let him.

"I'm different," he said, "and all the time I've known you I wanted to tell you. Mother sewed them in when I was little, and she thinks the skin grew over them like scars." Hair fell across his eyes and he shook it away. "But there ain't no skin covering. I have slits, roughened around the edges, and what's inside I've trained myself to hold there. But when I get excited, and I mean *really* excited.…" He stopped. Couldn't go on.

"They move," she finished for him. She unbuttoned his shirt. Slid it off. And then he let them come free.

There was a wet suckling sound, steam coming up, and they rose from behind him, dark and oily, and he made them spread and made them work, and he rose off the ground before her.

When he descended, he let her touch them. They swore they would love each other forever.

What they didn't see was the figure hiding behind the remains of the northwest corner of the carriage house, breath making a thin vapor upon the air, half-lidded eyes staring through a pair of octagonal nose-pinch glasses with no sides to them.

—

"Where you been?" Papa said. He was at the table, papers before him. Light from the oil lamp played off his thick face, the soot of the iron works cleaned from around his eyes, nose, and mouth, the rest of him dark as the corner shadows. Katie clasped her hands behind her back.

"I was in the wood," she said. Papa took off his cap and rested it on his knee.

"You're not to go in there. Nor the train station, we discussed this." He rubbed his nose with calloused hands, clean at the knuckles, filthy beneath the nails. "And you're not completely dressed."

"Papa!" she said, eyes widened.

"Jonathan Claypool, that's personal to her." Mother came into the room, one of the twins in the cradle of her arm. "I'll speak to her myself-"

"No," Katie said. "Jean Marie lost Baxter again, gone into the wood all barking and loping after a field rabbit. She called to my window, and I only had time to throw on a dress, ask her."

"Sit down," Papa said.

"I don't want to."

"Sit, Katie. I need to speak to you of adult matters," he said. Mother had come forward and taken a chair. Katie shifted her eyes back and forth between them both for a moment, came forward, and sat quietly. Papa cleared his throat for a speech, and being that he was a man of few words it was going be dire news, Katie knew.

"Thorndale's closing down," he said. "Lord knows I've put my time in. Most of the boiler plates 'round these parts and five states-south bear the iron run through my shift." He took a deep breath. "Today, a new man, Jacob someone, a puddler's helper was taking out a buggy of hot coals. He slipped on a plate and fell with the buggy tipping toward him. Lucky it had a crust on, or else he'd have been covered with live cinder. Still burned him bad. Broke his arm and both ankles too. I think that was the final straw for Mr. Bailey. We'd been working for wages cut by twenty percent anyhow, and there'd been too many accidents, too much liability, let alone the lack of contracts. We were told at the end of the second shift that the doors will be closed by December. All to be left are the muck rollers and furnaces."

Katie pouted.

"You already take most my wages. And Mr. Drake won't let me work overtime until I'm eighteen, 'cause of some stupid new rule. You want my allowance too?"

Papa looked at his hands making dark shapes before him.

"I ain't talking about the spice factory, Katie, Lord if it were only that simple." Mother leaned forward, the baby's tiny fingers twisted into a lock of hair that had come free down her cheek.

"Things are changing, dear, you'd best understand it."

"Sarah, let me finish-"

"But if you'd just let me explain to her-"

"Quiet. I'll handle this." He looked up, eyes cold.

"I want to talk to you about Ezra Fletcher."

"What about him?"

"He's taken a liking to you."

She jumped to her feet.

"He's fifty years old!"

"Forty-five. Sit down."

"No! What are you saying?" He looked over at mother, and she nodded him on with her eyes. He tapped the table lightly with his thumb.

"You're to be wed. It's a favorable match. By the time you're thirty, he'll be gone and all he has will be yours. You'll be of middle age, but then you can do as you please. The decision's been made."

She had her arms rigid at her sides, fists tight.

"But Papa, I don't like him! He's spindly and crooked, and all those times I went to his store he was eye-balling me over the edge of his glasses, looking at my bum when I bent over to get the molasses, or staring at my bosom when I stretched sewing fabric across it, even when I was fourteen. He's lecherous. And he's been waiting for his chance, don't you see?"

"Now, all men look," Papa said, "they can't help it, and I'm sure he never meant nothing by it but making sure you weren't about to tip over a lamp display or knock into the crockery."

"I won't do it," she said. "I'm supposed to have say so."

"You *will* do it. There's no choice."

"There has to be."

"Not this time!" He'd let his tone heighten, and Katie backed up a step. He regained his calm and turned his hands to her, palms up.

"Katie, be reasonable. Times are bad. We ain't had a boarder for half a year, and next winter's gonna be colder than the last. The twins can't lay quiet before the fireplace, it's too dangerous. Now, I can put in cast iron radiators and fuel them with a good coal-fired basement boiler, but I can't afford the initial installment of the ducts."

He looked at mother and spoke this bit at her, as if they'd rehearsed it together.

"Ezra Fletcher can give you comfort in his place up on the hill there. And he's promised me a job at his brother's sand quarry, washing, drying, and screening. It's a living, and it's done. Take me for my word, I wouldn't decide this unless I'd put my prayers to it."

"But my heart is saved for another."

"Who?"

"Adam Rothman."

Now Papa stood.

"I don't like him," he said. "His mother is mad, and his father is always off at the tavern. There's unhappiness in that household; I've walked past and heard the yelling. And they know nothing of the farming they've under-taken. The main house is falling apart, its chimney leaning, and the yard's overrun with rank weeds and pigs. It's no place for a girl."

"But I love him."

"Not anymore, you don't."

A knock came at the door then, and Katie went to it. A stiff blast of wind came in, and a tall, thin faced figure stood in the frame, bent over a bit, grey waistcoat, close-set eyes, small beard twisted to a point.

"Speak of the devil," Katie whispered. He removed his octagon shaped nose-pinch eye glasses and slid them carefully into his pocket.

"I wish to have a word with your father."

"Fine," she said, "but I wouldn't marry you even if you owned the Brooklyn Trolley Dodgers!"

She flounced to the stairs under the baleful glare of her parents, and Ezra Fletcher stepped forward. His eyes looked nervous, but his voice held steady.

"I must tell you what I have seen," he said quietly. "In private, with all due respect."

Mother took the baby away, and the two men had a whispered conversation before the cold fireplace. It intensified, almost turned to blows, and after the door slammed shut on Ezra Fletcher's exit, mother came in to see what was wrong.

"Bring my daughter to me," were Papa's words.

He'd said them straight through his teeth.

—

Adam Michael Rothman swore to himself that the second time would be slower, more meaningful, more for her pleasure if he could make himself last. He crossed the creek and retraced their steps from the night before, pine needles making soft melody beneath his boots, birches pressed close like lovers. He hoped he didn't have to wait for her, since she'd be so lovely on his approach if she'd arrived first, standing there in the high clearing, like a painting crafted in shadow and moon. There had been no ribbon left on the yard pump, their signal to abort, and he was not disappointed when he crested the rise.

She was there by the well, hands folded before her, black hair loose and flowing in the night breeze.

"Darling," he said, and he approached, and she held her hands out to him, and he didn't see the tears on her cheeks until it was too late, when the dark figures came from behind the trees at the edge of the clearing, her father stepping around the northwest corner of the demolished carriage house, club in one hand, burlap sack in the other.

"Get her out of here," he said softly, and just before Ezra Fletcher led her away down the path, Adam croaked out to her,

"No sign, my darling, no ribbon? But why?"

She put her knuckles to her trembling lips and looked down at the ground. Fletcher regarded him darkly and took Katie Claypool off into the shadows.

Adam didn't wait a moment longer. He sprung to the side suddenly and made to run off, but there were more of them than he'd first thought, and he was grabbed from behind and shoved over to the well. Someone clenched a fistful of his hair and pushed his face hard to the stone, breaking off a tooth that went half down his throat, cutting more and more inward each time he snuck a swallow, and through it all he only wished to be granted the moment he could cough it loose or choke it down. There was a rain of blows, and the yanking and ripping of his coat and shirt. Cold, gloved hands reached inside the slits in his back, and while a few backed off refusing to touch him, there were those who continued, muttering the name of "Holy Jesus" over and again.

They snapped the left wing off at the base of the humerus, and the right halfway up the ulna, the point of the second digit piercing one of them through the palm sending him shouting and cursing and shaking it like a snake was attached. For poor Adam, it was a thick swirl of pain and black and dark red, and there was an argument to end it quickly and a stronger argument that claimed murder was a sin before God, and if he bled out, he bled out, but they were to steer clear of the brain, the heart, and the jugular. One oily voice protested that they would be caught and tried, and the more guttural tone Adam recognized as that of Mr. Claypool said they had to make it look like ritual, like them zealots up in Coatesville did to them other Jews.

Adam wanted to choke out that his mother was from Ireland and didn't that count for something, and they turned him over. Mr. Claypool came into his vision on a slant with a pair of tin snips.

"It was of her own free will she gave you up," he said gently, "once I explained how aberrations like you can poison the mind."

There was nothing left between them but silence, so Claypool took a breath through his nose and bent to it, the others helping him intermittently, and by the latter half of the rough surgery, Adam Michael Rothman finally passed out. By the time they took his eyes, he lay dead.

They were tired and sweat-drenched and blood-covered, and halfway down the path to the birches, a hand fell on Claypool's shoulder.

"Did you check his pulse, John?"

He shoved the hand off and fought back a shiver.

"It's done."

"You sure?" They'd made a small ring now, blocking the way. John Claypool turned, pushed through them, and trudged back up to the clearing. And there lay scattered the results of their grisly work in the pale, cross-hatch spill of the moon: a farmer's sack coat rumpled next to two broken wings, base bones angled, jutted up like fractured Chinese architecture, dark feathers soaked and flattened, a litter of digits, one boot laying on its side, blood stained down the side of the well in half-dried streams following the rough contours of the mortar lines between the field stones.

And no corpse.

Adam Michael Rothman had vanished.

<hr />

April 2021

"And ever since then, these woods have been haunted."

"That's it?" Kyle said. Brandon had been doing his best straight scary face, and he still tried to hold the sincerity.

"Yes. And every twenty years or so, someone goes missing back here. Never any evidence left, just a witness or two that sees a figure dart between the trees."

Everyone kind of shrugged, and he poked the fire with the knobby stick he'd found down by a short ravine choked with elderberry and pricker bushes. A burst of sparks twirled up toward the sky which had gone all but dark between the pitch and cast of surrounding trees.

"But what happened to the father?" Melanie said.

"Yeah," Krista added, "and how about the perverted old store owner?" Robbie leaned forward and gave that crafty, goofy grin he was known for.

"I'll bet he broke a hip fucking her on their wedding night!" He rolled back in peals of laughter that the boys joined in with and the girls did their best to show they didn't appreciate.

"Pig," Valencia said. She adjusted the rubber band at the back of her braces, and tried to turn her marshmallow. It slid off the stick and hissed into the fire.

"He got them all," Brandon said, even though they all really knew it was over, the best part at least. Here, he was just making up shit as he went. "He killed Ezra Fletcher that following year when the old geezer went out to the privy to take a dump, and he got John Claypool when he went hunting for deer the next winter. All the body parts they cut off Adam Michael Rothman grew back on him bigger, thicker, tougher, more akin to his "bird" side. But even turned ninety-nine percent beast, he never went back after Katie Claypool for revenge."

"Why not," Melanie said.

Brandon shrugged. "It was a backward curse. They'd made a promise to love each other forever, remember?"

"That's lame," Robbie snorted.

"Shut up," two of the girls said simultaneously. Brandon dug in the fire for a moment, searching back for the creepier tone that had flavored most of his prior narration.

"But you can bank on the fact that he never forgot how he died, the torture, the disfigurement, the idea that he was bound by the dark magic of the wood to pass over the one who betrayed him."

"*Might* have betrayed him," Valencia interrupted. "The father could have grounded her making it so she never had the chance to put her spirit ribbon on the pump in the first place."

"They didn't have spirit ribbons back then," Robbie said.

"Whatever."

Brandon looked up, the reflection of the fire dancing in his eyes. "Doesn't matter what the truth really was. It mattered what Adam Michael Rothman *believed*. Fact is that Katie Claypool was exempt, Rothman didn't like it, and no one else was safe from there on in. No one. And she knew it when she got the general store, when she remarried, when all those long years made her old and bitter, twisted up in guilt every time someone new went M.I.A. She lived until 1975, always rocking on her porch, warning anyone who would listen about the betrayed, angry spirit lurking around up here in the woods."

"It's a good story," Ashley said. She stood up and brushed off her butt. Her shirt had ridden up a bit showing off the new dragon tattoo she'd gotten a few weeks ago, snaked there along her hip and the right side of her belly. The guys were all staring out the sides of their faces. She looked good at her middle, flat and hard, and she was a blonde.

"Be right back," she said. She had to "wee," and she wasn't going to do it too close to the campfire. Too easy for Brandon, or Dana, or especially Robbie to get it on a cell phone and post it on YouTube. They'd title it, "Squatter's Rights," or something that would really make Daddy proud. She side stepped down the short incline, and walked a few paces along the path, almost tripping and taking a header when she bumped her toe against an overgrown root raised there like some corroded old vein. She found a thick bush, made her way behind it, dropped her drawers, and delivered there in the shadows.

When she'd finished and pulled everything back together, she looked for a pile of leaves to hide the tissue under. Too dark. She got out her cell phone, aimed it at the forest floor, and hit the red button. The pale wash of light exposed dirt channeled and sloughed by past rains, twigs, patches of short weeds. She turned twice, and spread her view, but saw nothing but a grainy flash of bare ground and foliation, and then it went dark. She hit it again, and moved a bit south away from the path behind her, then a bit west, then a tad east; stands of intertwining elm, tufts of ragweed, snarls of thorn. There was a waist-high stone wall over run with vegetation, and the light went off once again.

Hell with this. She dropped the damp tissue there on the ground, and turned back the way she had come. She was glancing up in the general direction she thought would yield the glow of their fire up on the hill, but the afterimage kept her in a pale, temporary blindness.

286

She bumped into something. Hard.

"Ow!" she said, her voice deadened and close in the stillness around her. She felt at her forehead, already knotting with the bruise, and hit the button on her cell phone.

She had bumped into a birch tree, pressing close to its twin.

"No way," she whispered, turning the opposite direction, trying not to run in the mild state of panic that was rising in her. The light went off, and she hit it back on, and before her was the upper end of the creek and an old walking bridge, and Ashley let out a short scream and ran in the opposite direction, her thoughts a collection of jolts and starts that insisted the order and chronology and logistics were wrong, that according to the story she'd just heard, dead opposite the leaning birches was the floor of pine needles, then the lower part of the creek with the dark polished stones and the path beyond that led out of the forest, and she was climbing and moaning, and gaining footholds in nettles of roots, and she was lucky her cell phone didn't go tumbling off in the darkness.

She gained a crest of sorts, and she pressed on the light.

Before her was a flat square covered with briar and milkweed, and the petrified remains of a hitching post. The northwest corner of the carriage house had eroded and crumbled down to the height of about four feet, and the well still had ancient trails of blood-stains ghosted and shadowed down through the crevices.

Ashley about-faced immediately, and tore down the path as fast as she was able. She slowed when the light cut off, and she hit it back on again, chest heaving.

She was back at the well, two feet from it now. She was crying, moaning, and she looked at the phone so she could call her mother, and there was a red bar across the old fashioned rotary graphic claiming, "No Service."

There was a sound, hollow and echoed, coming from deep inside the well. Ashley backed off a step, and the cell light cut off, and the sound before her grew from within the bowels of the earth, and it was surfacing, and it was the furious sound of beating wings, and she hit the light button, and the stone structure erupted with a flood of barn swallows and sparrows, vomiting up into the air like hornets, and she fell back and struck her head upon the ground. Her last vision was one of inverted vertigo, the shapes above her fitting into the spaces between the branches and blotting out the night sky.

When she woke, she wondered how much of it was a dream, an illusion put upon her at the brink of consciousness. She blinked. She was lying down on what still felt like outdoor terrain. Dirt was in her hair, and above her was a perfect sort of darkness, like velvet. Her breathing was in her ears, and she wondered if there were actually enough barn swallows and sparrows to fill every nook and cranny of the forest canopy, and she pawed along the ground and found a small stone. She sat up slowly and then underhanded the projectile as hard as she could. It hit something up there, and plunked back down beside her.

She understood when the great eyes opened, straight above her, devil's blood orange, coal furnaces slanted like oil drops, and then there was movement to the east and the west, and at the farthest periphery of her vision she saw stars cut off by the gradated edge of a wingspan that measured fifty feet at the least on both sides. The wings lifted, made gargantuan tent-shapes at the carpel joints, and then thrust down with a massive whooping sound as the Falcon of Penn Wood knifed in toward its prey.

[This story first appeared in *Kaleidotrope Magazine,* Winter, 2012]

The Soldier

The first snow of the year never lasts. It usually starts with a few flakes dancing on the air like campfire ash, then graduates to a heavier pattern. I like when it thickens, makes the world into a snow globe.

I take the quilt from the bed and wrap it around myself, the pathetic old king with his robes trailing him across the floor. My breath makes mist on the window. When the display outside peters off, it will be bleak again, hard wind running through branches that bow in dumb servitude, the sky a defensive grayish blue, the clouds just bruises.

If only it would keep.

If only it would have intensified, swirled, buried the roadways, iced up the phone lines. If only that first December snow of 1978 could have been a storm instead of a tease.

I'd have been the first up for sure, bounding to the window facing the back yard.

Snow days meant extra cuddling time with Addy, two pots of coffee, watching the fuzzy RCA downstairs and getting the snow measurments at the airport, accident reports along the Schuylkill Expressway, all with the couch blankets pulled up to your chin and the dog with his snout across your lap. Safe and cozy. When you were a teacher, a snow day was a fun day, an "I don't have to run day," though the Bangles would preach it a few years later and trash what I had always thought a pure sort of paradigm for working Joe's on the front lines, not shitty little rich girls air guitaring what would have been best kept in Daddy's living room.

Snow days were times for watching stupid game shows, sipping Swiss Miss hot chocolate made extra syrupy, fluffy eggs and bacon and pumpkin pancakes, grilled cheese on seeded rye for lunch with tomato soup, marathon showers, Heinekens before noon.

Addy liked to screw on snow days. She was a short fireplug of a woman, strong thighs, awesome tits. When she let you do it from behind, she had a way of curving her back and turning you this wry look that drove you crazy with desire. She used to flip on Zeppelin 1, side 2, loud as shit when she knew you were going to bang her hard. She cried out those times, but not as loud as I did. She was a good girl. The kind that never bitched about money. Or laundry. Or the empty propane tank, or the bags of clothes you forgot to bring to Goodwill, or the old smelly rugs you rolled up and stuck in the garage because you never quite found time to make it to the dump. She looked good in a bathrobe, looked good cooking pepper steak in a wok. Made me love the world. Kiss the sky and all that.

Danny had moved down into the partly finished basement and swore it didn't smell even a little bit moldy. His old room became my "office" that Addy dolled up with an oak desk that had tons of drawers I didn't use, a leather chair, and a cherry wood mini bar with compartments that I most certainly did use. We put the eight-track in there, along with most of the pictures, some classic novels I swore I'd get around to reading someday, and all Danny's trophies.

Addy used to say that the kid moved down to the basement to exercise his independence, but I always thought it was the loud Zeppelin music.

I still walked down two flights of stairs every morning to give him a kiss, even though he was fourteen. Kissed him to wake him up, right on that hot part of his forehead with the little tan birthmark on the right side just below the hairline. I was also guilty of making that cone with my lips, putting it to his cheek and making "whub-whub" noises. Like Addy, he never bitched. I'd kiss him, give him the "whub-whub," and he'd squint, crinkle up his nose, and mutter, "Hi Dad," in that deep voice I was still getting used to.

On the morning that ruined us, I walked down the stairs and forgot to move around the creaks that might wake Addy unnecessarily. Chipster, our cocker spaniel, flopped his tail in the basket by the fridge, pushed up, stretched, and clicked over to me across the linoleum, cute as a button with the exception of that doggie gunk gathered under his eyes like the mascara of some weeping actress. I gave him a scratch behind the ears, opened the back door and put him on his lead.

The snow was letting up a bit. Probably a false alarm, but teaching shop in the inner city was far better than working the construction trades out in the elements. Still had vivid memories of that shit like it was yesterday. I shut the door and went down the basement.

Danny's "room" was a mess as usual. He had tried to make the place "his" with a black light, two lava lamps, and one of those spangly steel weeping willow desk lights from Spencer's that looked like vegetation from Mars. I thought I smelled incense. Had to talk to him about that.

"Time to wake up, dum-dum." I'd given him his man-kiss, and I ruffled his hair. Still blondish, all Addy's side, though it had darkened quite a bit since his baby years.

"Dan. *Danny!*"

I got a mumble this time, and a half roll away toward the wall. He'd put up new posters. Had them in the shadows so I hadn't noticed right away. Gloria Gaynor, John Travolta, and The Commodores. We'd *really* have to talk now. His Leo Sayer, Rod Stewart, and Gary Wright phase had been strange enough. I mean, all of our friends thought Addy and I were reckless in our seemingly endless hunger for new rock and roll, but I couldn't bother myself with my own generation's antiquated boardwalk, bee-bob, and show tunes slop. I loved music, loved it raw, and Addy was even worse with it. She's gone to catholic school way back when, yeah, plaid skirt and knee socks, and when the Beatles changed everything, she'd already tossed the tassel to the other side at Saint Joseph's. She spent much of her adult life making up for what she'd missed.

As for Danny, he always rolled his eyes at our fascination. I would say " Z.Z. Top, Aerosmith, Kiss!" and he would come back with "Kris

Kristofferson." Said he liked the lyrics. Me and Addy teased him about that one, and I even tried to talk sense to him, show him that music wasn't really about lyrics in the first place. Guitar, guitar, guitar, my man! But his undisputable, one-word answer always ended that noise.

"Girls."

Yeah. Disco sucked, but it was a tool for fourteen-year-old chick magnets. One of those Catch-22's that would never be solved.

"Danny. School."

"I don't wanna."

"Ok. Snuggle."

I laid down next to him, held him, said in his ear,

"You all right?"

"Yeah."

"You sure?"

"Yeah."

"Ok, breathe."

Both of us together then, in, out, then break, a ritual so ancient I didn't even recall when we first laughed about it. He sat up and chewed a hangnail.

He was really getting bigger. Even though his chest seemed narrow, it was developed, only in miniature, if you know what I mean. He was five foot five inches, but hadn't quite grown into that height yet if that makes any sense. A true man-child.

And gorgeous.

He certainly didn't get his looks from my side of the family, and sometimes we laughed and called him the postman's child, simply because he didn't quite favor Addy either except in the hair color category. He looked like a damned angel. His eyes were a bit almond shaped, and his features were simply portrait-worthy. Straight nose, soft lips, high cheekbones, sharp eyebrows. Almost feminine, though I'd never have told him that to his face. The girls loved him, and in turn most of his friends were female, sort of rare for a young teenager. The phone was constantly ringing, in fact, the closest thing to an ongoing fight in the house was Addy's constant frustration with the fact that the line was never free in case Barbara was giving a ring to go to the mall, or Gina was phoning over to change the time for their magazine and Tupperware club.

"You didn't hit off the tee last night." I jerked my head back toward the netting I'd hung from the exposed pipes by the water boiler. His twenty nine ounce Louisville Slugger and the tennis balls were by the black tee in the same places they'd been three nights running.

"I will tonight."

"Promise?"

"Yeah."

I paused so he'd look at me.

"Your back elbow's dropping."

"I know, Dad."

"If you don't fix it now, you're-"

"Gonna get burned by the high cheese, I know, Dad."

We both laughed and he let me run my fingers through his hair for another muff-up. He wasn't a straight "A" student in school, all B's and a few C's like in Spanish, but I was the last one to blame him for not finding himself seated quite flush into the "school thing" like a perfect little o-ring in an engine. He was sharp as a tack when it came to people. He had insight, a way about him that got folks talking about themselves, I'd seen it. We'd go to a pool party, and without being familiar at all with the terrain, he'd entertain discussions with thirty- year-old women about dieting, gender equality, and spiritual healing. I'd pick him up from school on a day he stayed late for homework club, and he'd be at the edge of the pick-up rotary, buried deep in a three way conversation with a girl that had flood pants, earth shoes, a relief map of forehead zits, and horned rim glasses, right alongside a leggy cheerleader with bows in her hair. Damned straight. He single handedly made them dead equals, which they were, but most fourteen-year-olds didn't see it that way is all that I'm saying. He had friends on the chess team and pals playing football, girlfriends who were shy and awkward and others wearing heavy foundation, fake eyelashes, and pants so tight they could have been spray painted. He was "Mr. Social," a bit book-dumb and a natural charmer; ladies and gentlemen, the next president of the United States.

"Dad," he said.

"Yeah?" I had already gotten up and turned to go.

"I don't think I'm gonna play ball this year. I'm tired of it."

"No you're not."

"Just kidding."

I turned to go again. This time I made it to the stairs, which needed carpeting or painting, I still hadn't decided.

"Dad."

"Yeah, big boy?"

He was staring at his hands.

"What if Bobby Fitz starts something?"

My neck went hot and I stalked back across the room.

"If he so much as touches you, Danny, look at me. He lays one single finger on you I want you to throw." I looked over my shoulder as if Addy had snuck down for a listen. I leaned in and my shadow covered him for a second.

"Now listen. That son of a bitch starts in, you finish it. You hit him square in the face and don't stop until he's down. You don't take shit. From anyone. Start with that kind of crap and it spreads around the school like brushfire. Next thing you know, you're everybody's pincushion, got it?"

"Yeah, Dad."

I took a deep breath and stood straight.

"You think he's gonna start in?"

He gave a short laugh.

"Crazy if he does."

"Why, Danny?"

"I'll kick his ass."

"Good boy."

Of course, we didn't tell Addy any of this, because she more believed in the fairytale answer to the shit that went on between boys, the go-to-the-principal-about-it answer that got the offender suspended and simultaneously cut a crack so deep in your street cred that you wouldn't recover until you hit your third year of college. Not the textbook response for a teacher, I know, but I was all too familiar with the reality in the foxhole. Did I preach this to my students? No. Did I have a problem with this contradiction? Not in the slightest.

And I'd never liked Bobby Fitz. Neither did Danny. Not really. The two of them had been hot and cold for years, same neighborhood, same classes, same little league. The kid lived with his mother at the end of our block in a rather dismal looking fieldstone flat top rancher with brambles growing all over the front walk and wild ivy on the picture window. I didn't know where the father was, but mom smoked Marlboros, wore bandanas and scarves, and talked in this rusty voice usually saved for New York cliché's in the theater world.

And plainly, Bobby Fitz was an asshole. We'd given him a shot, but he was the type that would be over the house for dinner and demand to Addy, "Put some ketchup on my burger." She'd give the rhetorical, "Excuse me?" and he'd reply, "K-E-T-CHUP," and roll his eyes. Then under his breath, "Ya deaf?" Addy and I would look at each other, wounded smiles of disbelief in our eyes, finally saying nothing, because I'd just been talking about spilling a beer trying to catch a fly ball at a Phillies game, and smack in the heart of the story I'd cursed a couple of times, bucking right up on the edge of propriety just to make Fitz feel like one of the boys. Now, it seemed like it was in the air that maybe I brought this on, keeping it all too loose or something.

One time when I was late because I had lagged back at school running a gentleman's etiquette club the mentor hadn't shown up for, she claimed Fitz had been over looking at baseball cards, playing some darts. Supposedly, he had burst into the kitchen and demanded a glass of water. Addy had gone to the tap, and he'd muttered behind her back,

"Cunt."

She'd called him on it and he'd had the brass balls to say,

"Well, can I say pussy? Snatch? Poontang?"

She'd asked him to leave, and he'd stood there, eyes drifting slightly in what Addy called "the crazy face."

"Pussy, pussy, pussy." Then he swiped over a bottle of cooking sherry before waltzing on out through the door. In retrospect, I should have been in his mother's living room that night, nipped it in the bud, but I sort of figured the apple didn't fall far from the tree and my words would fall on dead ears. I simply told Danny that this particular sixth grader was never to cross the threshold of my home again, and Danny quietly agreed. I didn't have much contact with the bastard throughout the next couple of years, and to tell the truth I sort of dismissed him. He was easy to dismiss. He was the kid in little league who would miss an easy pop-up and act like he got hurt diving for it, the type to egg people's windows even though Mischief night was long over, the type to steal shit from the K-Mart, smack girls, lie to himself. The last I'd seen, he was into the punk thing, studs, dirty leather, and "H-A-T-E" scrawled on both sets of knuckles in magic marker.

That, and fucking with people.

Danny had told me that Fitz was back with his name calling, at the bus stop and in a science lab the two shared, sneaking behind and whispering, "pussy," just loud enough for Danny to hear it in passing, sometimes adding, "Just like your mom likes to lick," for good measure.

I drove in to school that day with my teeth clenched. Gave me a headache. I wanted to *act,* to *solve this,* to walk into that junior high school when that rotten bastard least expected, catch him saying something, and bring him to the discipline room by his hair. I was no sixties reject, never a "sensitive man" by any stretch of the imagination, but I despised people who prayed on the good nature of others. They sucked the joy out of life and put everyone on edge. Made you twist yourself up in battle strategies and question yourself.

I turned down Belmont Avenue. The snow had stopped completely, and there were people waiting at the bus stop with their hats and gloves on. One was stamping his feet. Another spit on the cement. Winter without the benefits. A toss of dead leaves skipped by and did an idiot's jig in the police station parking lot to the left. I wondered why Danny had inherited this particular abuse from this particular boy, and quickly decided that no one would ever really know except them. Ever ask a fourteen year old about his day? You got a shrug. "What did you learn in school today?" *"Nothing."* "How do like your teachers this year?" The response: the classic jumble *"uhehuh,"* meaning in earthly terms, "I don't know."

Not that Danny was incommunicado all day, every day. He was just fourteen, that's all. We still watched television together, still made cheese bagels with extra butter on Saturdays, still went bowling every weekend and ate stale soft pretzels with extra mustard, our standard. But that was all stuff on the fringe by then. Kids were fast, changing friendships quicker than the seasons, keeping under your radar, it was a fact of life.

The only thing I could assume from my little corner of this thing was that the fall ball game a month and a half ago might have triggered this. I was surprised to see Fitz on the other team, actually. The boys had moved up to the big field, and I'd assumed he wouldn't be able to handle it. Besides, I thought I had heard he'd been banned from the league for throwing his bat in the dugout after a costly strike out a year before.

Anyway, he had been pitching for the other side, a real wild Injun, untucking his shirt in a sloppy flap in the back, kicking the mound dirt, spitting straight in the direction of the batter instead of back behind the rubber. Then when things started going south, he started in with the other crap we'd seen so often with him, bitching to the ump about the strike zone, snapping off the tosses back from the catcher, throwing his hat if one of his fielders missed a hard grounder. They relieved him in the third and re-entered him in the bottom of the seventh to pitch to Danny, two men on, all tied up, two outs. My boy whacked a fastball right over the center field fence. Almost hit the American flag. His team swarmed him at the plate.

But why on earth would Fitz take that personally? As soon as that thought ran through my head I realized how silly it sounded, but still, the bastard would have to have been from another planet to think that a fall-ball homer was anything significant when compared to the big picture. He'd been on Danny's team, The Renegades, when they were nine, and he'd been lined up across the diamond on enough of the opposing squads through the years to have known the drill by heart. Danny Taragna comes up to the plate, and the defending coach comes out of the dugout. Says to his players, *"For this guy...infielders get your heels on the grass...outfielders, back up...no, turn around and run...no, not a few feet, try thirty or forty."* Danny was the number one hitter in South Marple, possibly in South Eastern Pennsylvania. His hand-eye was literally awesome to behold, and except for an occasional lunging problem when he got too hungry seeing a strike right out of the hand, he was the toughest out any of us had ever seen.

So, what else could Fitz possibly expect? He was known for never practicing and trying to live off being a hot dog. On our side of things, I'd thrown Danny six thousand pitches a summer since that day at three and a half when he hit a wiffle ball back at my face so hard he knocked me down. I mean, Jesus, at four and a half, he was hitting tennis balls two hundred feet. We used to measure the distance, count it step by step out loud, side by side, heel to toe from the ball back to the plate. Each time the record was broken I'd lift him by the underarms and spin him. Want to see joy on a boy's face? Try it sometime.

I turned left on Montgomery, flipped on the radio, and found a Cars song, then The Talking Heads. Skinny ties and poor vocals, as if the latter was a conscious choice. Pure Bullshit. Turned it off. Maybe it was something else that had sparked bad blood between these two, a passing glance that rubbed Fitz the wrong way, a girl he liked that Danny cut in on, disco-boy versus the punker, whatever. Sometimes boys threw their shoulders back and socked each other around a bit to show who was boss. I only hoped they didn't have a scuffle and suddenly try to become best bosom buddies as it so often happened when dudes duked it out. Last thing I needed was to be fighting with Addy over whether we should have him over for dinner and remember to stick K-E-T-C-H-U-P on his fucking burger.

I got to school and had to push all this to the back of my mind. Someone had defaced the listening center with spray paint, and a neighborhood gang invaded the yard during senior recess. I was turned into an emergency security guard helping out with lock down, watching kids all day, monitoring the halls, supporting the staff in the lunch room.

By the time I got home, my head was absolutely pounding.

And my son's face had been destroyed.

—

"Hi Dad," he said. "I'm fine, so don't rag, all right?" He was sitting on the couch in the dark. I closed the front door and pushed off the Chipster, whose tail was wagging so hard her whole back end was swaying.

"Let me see you."

He stood, winced, looked at me straight. I gasped.

His face, his beautiful angelic face, was that of a monster. There was a sickly purple bruise high on his right cheek, merging into three others that puffed and blotched all the way to the jawline. The right side of his top lip was twice its original size. His left cheek was a hard yellow with two sets of angry red knuckle marks branded across it. His right eye had blood in it, blackened underneath in a wide swab, and the left was swollen shut completely. His forehead was cut in three places, and blood was crusted around both nostrils. My fists were shaking, but miraculously, my voice didn't follow suit.

"What's *his* face look like," I said quietly. Danny regressed, went from one foot to the other.

"I got him real good, Dad. I think I knocked out his tooth."

"That's it?"

He looked down.

"I hit him in the jaw. Lots of times. He had the better angle, he's taller."

"Where'd it happen?"

"Bus stop. Just an hour ago. Kept calling me a pussy, kept begging me to hit him. I threw the first punch when he called Ma a cunt-licker. I missed."

He looked up at me.

"He didn't."

I moved a step closer.

"How many times did you hit him, Danny?"

"I don't know."

"Think."

"I don't know!" His bloody eye was tearing now. "I tried, Dad, I tried to hit him and hit him, but he kept punching me, geez!" His nose was running, blood trails in it, and he wiped it ungracefully with the back of his hand. I reached out and grabbed it, a bit rough, and I turned it, looked at the knuckles. No marks. Baby smooth. Slowly, he took his hand back, and rubbed his side gingerly.

"Didn't I do like I was supposed to, Dad?"

My voice came through my teeth.

"Truck. Now."

—

I thought I was pissed when I tripped on a loose piece of flagstone along their darkened walkway, and more, when I hurt myself a bit hammering on their front door with my fist in the cold, but that was nothing compared to what raced through my head during the short visit inside. It all went by fast, in flashes, and I was honestly lucky I didn't kill someone.

She opened the door, I barged in, it smelled like cabbage and cigarettes, I said, "Look at his face," she said, "What's that to do with me?"

When Fitz came down he was wearing a ripped tee-shirt that said "Pink Floyd sucks," black jeans, and motorcycle boots. He looked big to me, at least a head taller than Danny, and his face was unmarked for all but a small cut at the corner of his bottom lip.

"Anything special happen at the bus stop today?" I said. He looked at Danny, smirked, and shrugged. I took a step toward him. He turned a shoulder slightly, but the smirk stayed.

"Just came home and did my math homework."

"You deny this?"

"Nothing to deny."

I turned.

"He do this to you, son?"

Danny tried his best to look away. The swelling had gotten worse, and the purple marbling had deepened.

"Yeah."

"Prove it."

That came from Mom. There were bird's-eye glasses hanging around her neck and they had dandruff on them. Gray hair pinned back, a wrinkled peacock lighting a cigarette.

"I'm going to report this," I said.

"I think you should."

On my way out, Fitz said after me,

"Better get him to the hospital."

Back in the car, I was thinking that we had to call the Newports, the Gosslingers, the Graystones, the Cohens, all who had kids that were assigned to that bus stop. Or maybe just the police, let them ask the questions, see if Fitz would smirk then. In the morning I'd go see Principal Wheeler, find out who Danny's counselor was, maybe set up some private therapy sessions so he could get his self-confidence back. I thought all those things, but didn't say them. Instead, I said,

"I thought you said you hit him, Danny. I had the impression there were even blows thrown, or at least close."

"I did," he said. "I thought...I don't know anymore."

We drove the rest of the way in silence. Addy came home a bit later with two bags of groceries. She saw Danny and dropped them on the floor. He cried hard. We raised our voices, and Chipster wouldn't stop barking. We told Danny to lie on the couch, and had him hold bags of frozen peas and cut corn to his face. Addy tried to get him up to go to the hospital, and I almost complied.

"No," Danny said.

"Not your choice," I returned. "And lay back down. You still have four minutes. Fifteen at a pop, it'll get that swelling down."

"It's cold."

"It's supposed to be cold."

"It hurts."

"Ain't supposed to feel pretty."

"I go to the hospital, I'll never be able to show my face at school again, Dad."

We never went. He was fine, just battered. Addy tossed up a last Hail Mary, claiming this was more about me than my son, and I wasn't hearing it. I made for the stairs, for my "office," where I was going to pour myself a shot of Jack D., maybe two or three, and brood about the unfairness of the world. Bullies were cowards, fakers, terrified of being exposed, and when you punched one in the nose he was supposed to move on to the next victim. Back in the day I stood up to around half the guys who bullied me in school, and never lost a pushy-pushy. I always felt I should have stood up to the rest of them too, always sort of kicking myself for not having a perfect record.

I was sickened by this family loss. I thought of my Danny, out on the corner of Boxwood Avenue after school in the bitter cold, swinging wild for the fences, for his father, with Bobby Fitz just raining down blows at will. How many times did he strike my son directly in the face? Were the sounds meaty or flat? Did Danny cover up at some point, curl in, and cry Uncle? Were there onlookers in a semi-circle egging this on? Did they follow Danny home in support or rally around their new thumper?

"Dad."

I was half up the stairs.

"Yeah."

"Stay."

I kept walking without turning around. He was better off with his mother, and I had to reevaluate things, come up with a way to work this into an emotional configuration that was somehow acceptable. I wanted to rationalize, but couldn't. I'd play nursemaid and Danny's big-ole teddy bear in the morning when I had some perspective.

I drank too much, and slept like a stone.

Next morning, I let the dog out and made my way into the basement. I thought about doing the "whub-whub," but I didn't want to aggravate a sensitive area on his face. I was feeling a little dizzy. I gave his shoulder a gentle shake, and he didn't respond. Tried it again, and got nothing. I turned him over, and the purples had turned to maroons and pale oranges. There was spittle at the corners of his swollen lips.

He was in a coma.

At 3:19 PM, at Bryn Mawr Hospital, tubes up his nose, and hands curled in, he passed quietly. The doctor said it was a result of massive blunt force trauma to the brain and a clotting issue, but it wasn't either of those things. He died of a broken heart, of shame, of not living up to his father's expectations. All day that day I held his hand, first hanging off the edge of the gurney, and then dangling off the side of the adjustable bed cranked to a forty-five-degree angle. He never squeezed back.

I'd killed him.

And all for nothing.

Now, I look outside the window and wonder like I do every year what would have happened if we'd been snowed in that day. I was never much for philosophizing, but I still can't help running the equation through my head, the possibility that somehow time and space worked in some rhythmic continuum, so that changing one little aspect of your life could yield alternate results. What if Danny never went to school that day? What if we shoveled the driveway together, made an igloo, played cards? What if Fitz suddenly put another kid in the crosshairs, or fell in love, or found God?

But that's all for nothing too.

My legs are constantly in pain, and the arthritis in my back flairs up more often than not. I live above the Gladstone drug store and eat canned food off a hot plate. As you might have guessed, I lost Addy after the trial, not Fitz's, ours. Lost my teaching gig two months later, mostly because I just couldn't handle being around kids anymore. Their laughter made me cry in the faculty bathroom and their meanness made me weep in the janitor's storage closet, or the audio-visual room, or right there out in the hallway. I went back to the trades, but drank away most of my money. By the time I was fifty I was swinging a sledge. By fifty-five it was a twelve ouncer for the oddball finish work, but by fifty-seven, any boss willing to have me wouldn't trust me with anything more than a spade shovel for ditches. I kept fucking up the measurements, losing time and money, making my co-workers mutter shit behind my back knowing I could hear it loud and clear, talk about your ironic, poetic justice.

I'm seventy-nine years old now, gray, bent over, broken. I keep waiting to die, and I just don't. I've thought of killing myself more times than you could imagine, but I have deferred time and again from being afraid of the pain. I also stand terrified that there is no God, no afterlife, no heaven or hell, just darkness. I am terrified that my Danny would be gone forever.

See he visits me. Once a year. On the first hint of snow.

He comes through the wall and walks the floorboards real as can be. I can see through him, but he's clear as day, fourteen years old, my gorgeous man-child, and he's smiling, always smiling.

He also refuses to notice me. I call out to him every year, tell him I love him dearly, get on my knees and beg his forgiveness, but he dismisses me, mouths animated conversations with phantoms, keeps his eyes focused above me. I've timed his visits. Always twenty-three minutes exactly, the length of time he laid there with bags of frozen vegetables on his face, crushed by the fact that his father wouldn't stay there to comfort him. Twenty three minutes of disgrace, capped off with the walk of shame down the stairs with the help of his mother. The last twenty-three minutes of his conscious life.

Addy was the best friend I ever had, but Danny was my soul-mate. I talked to him in his car seat like he was a grown man, told him about my plans. I let him sit in my lap and steer the truck in the graveyard, made him spaghetti with butter, stayed up past his bed time making scary shadow figures with the Rayovac, then going forehead to forehead, whispering our dreams to each other. When he was six, he told me he prayed on the North Star every night that he could be like me when he grew up, and when he was seven, he refused to sit on the sofa unless my arm was around him. At twelve, he hit a bases clearing double to win a game against Springfield in the interleague championship, and mid-ceremony, signaled me down from the bleachers, handed me his trophy on the third base line, and kissed my cheek in front of his team mates. He was a saint who drew people to him, like those thirty-year-old women who opened up to him at pool parties, like the ugly ducklings and the cheerleaders who let him love them equally.

I've got no books anymore, no television. Don't need them. There's enough pain and awareness in the air without them, especially with this he-man tradition of putting our sons through shit they aren't ready for. We do it because our fathers did it to us, and every father down the block might be doing it better. We train our young boys hard, we rehearse them, drill them, harden them up for the stage, the arena: the school yard, the ball field, the bus stop. Danny was a soldier serving his father's ghosts.

Now I am slave to his.

I see him. There is a portion of the wall where the brick was never covered nor finished, mortar popcorned and slathered, hardened by years, cracked and scabbed. My Danny bleeds out of this, takes shape, half transparent, but real as the world. I am on my knees before him, and he is looking past me, mouthing some secret or anecdote with a glint of mischief in his eye. He's imitating someone, making a face, but I don't get the joke. He's physicalizing a catch he made in center field, clearly narrating each slow motion step, but I can't peg the particular game.

I tell him I love him, and he doesn't hear me.

I tell him I'm sorry, and he looks away.

Something snaps in my head, and everything gets vivid. Me and Danny, we've switched places now, elder and child, and I've got to earn his favor. It's time to enter my own rite of passage, my moment of truth. I'm scared as hell, but it's all relative, isn't it? I raise the gun to my head and pray there won't be all that much pain. I pray there is a God. And right before I pull the trigger, I pray that my Danny might stand ready after all these long years to take this ugly, ugly duckling with him to glory and finally call things even and equal.

[This story first appeared in *The Turk's Head Review,* Winter 2011.]

The Legend of The One-Armed Brakeman

Bill Canadine was absent minded, not in a bad way, but one that often put him into annoying circumstances. Oh, he was *the man,* if you needed to contact an expert to manage things like government payment deadlines, penalty abatements, or liens and levies, but when he walked the dog in the morning he often forgot his keys. He made every one of Christopher's fifth grade chess tourneys and was punctual with his laptop every Friday night at 7:30 sharp to Zoom with Erin in her dorm room at Drexel, but he was terrible at keeping up with birthdays.

Here on the trail, he was dressed wrong. Katherine warned him about things like this, about being prepared and thinking ahead, but the details hadn't shaken out that way. To begin with, Bill was fifty-seven years old and had refused to sleep in a tent on the soccer field as most of the dads and sons were persuaded to do. He'd been penciled in for a room in Gibson Hall, but Erin couldn't stay there. They didn't want her on the soccer field either. A nineteen-year-old girl wasn't welcome at Camp Becket during Father's Weekend, in fact, no female was allowed on the grounds except for "Dad-Drop-Off" and the Sunday banquet.

The sign-in at the camp office had broiled into a scene. Bill refused to drive Erin four miles down to Pittsfield where it was smoothly suggested she stay in a hotel, and when the guy in the window tried to simply close the conversation, Bill Canadine had to work hard as hell keeping his voice smooth and subtle.

"Look," he said, taking off his glasses and rubbing them with a gray silk handkerchief. "I am an alumni. I started here at Becket when I was eleven years old, making my way through the Iroquois village, then Pioneer, Frontier, and Ranger. I was in your foreign exchange program that went to Japan, I was a C.I.T. when I was sixteen, and I've been faithfully donating a thousand dollars a year to this place, look it up."

The guy in the window had sandy-blonde hair, curling down to the shoulders in back. He had a long face with a silky-smooth jawline, and Bill could tell he thought himself one beautiful human being. The guy delicately folded his arms, and said,

"Sir. Women are not allowed on the grounds. It's a rule. Being an alumni, you should know this."

A line was forming, Bill could feel it. He turned to look back, and he was holding up maybe six people. The crossroad was packed with cars. The Frontier village grass was loaded too, moms saying goodbye, dads unpacking gear, boys trying to tug them away and show them *everything*. Across the way was the library with its rustic porch and rustic New England hand crafted wood rocking chairs, and beyond that the lake reflected the sun like brilliant slivers of currency. The guy right behind Bill had a walrus moustache and a mesh sailor's bucket hat with a string cord. He smiled amiably, but it felt like someone calling you "bub" or "chief." Erin was in the car, looking away, but this was what dads did. They stuck up for their own.

"Now look," he said, turning back, voice rising, "No. In my eyes, right here, pay attention. My son is not having a good summer. I called twice, and no one seemed able to handle his homesickness. I left two messages, one for his counselor and the other for the village director and got no response. None. Zippo, how's that?"

There was discomfort behind him now, electric interest, he could feel it, the dads in line jockeying to get a better position for a good listen. Good. Maybe a few of the moms were wandering over as well.

"Everyone here is good at giving sermons, teaching valuable life lessons like I see advertised in your pamphlets, but in the end it's just a bunch of talk. Hey! Don't look down and shake your head 'knowingly!' There are some basic responsibilities being neglected here. My son is homesick. I brought his sister. They're close. We drove for hours from Philadelphia to get here, and because I failed to read the fine print you're going to make my daughter stay in a hotel? I want to talk to the current director. Now. What's your name by the way? First and last, please, so there's no mistaking exactly who is standing in the window handling my concerns."

Bill didn't get rooms for himself and Erin in Gibson Hall, but he did get two tents. The agreement was that the three of them would camp out on the far side of the lake, in the clearing that had the rope swing, the same one Bill had loved jumping off as a boy. For tonight. Since that spot was such a popular daytime activity, they had to promise to be out of there by 8 AM. They'd figure out the rest tomorrow.

Bill hated hiking, but he was so steamed at having to argue his way into accommodations that stood lower on the totem pole than those he'd planned for, that he hadn't even thought to ask for a canoe. And he still had on what he'd driven up in, his favorite purple Ralph Loren silk & linen long sleeved dress shirt, Zanella trousers, and his black Salvatore Ferragamo's, complete with leather lining and soft soles for comfort.

Comfort, hell. By the time they'd gotten five hundred yards up the trail, his feet were killing him. A half mile into the woods, he had blisters.

When they'd gone down to the supply shack for their tents, backpacks, rain tarps and ground cloths, he'd realized they didn't have sleeping bags. The guy with the pony tail and designer sunglasses handed over bed rolls that looked like they'd been around since the Korean War, and that was when Bill smacked himself on the forehead, realizing that he'd forgotten to pack the travel bag with his shorts, Nikes, and tee-shirts. Yep, his boxers too, God damnit. He'd left the affair down in the basement by the dryer after doing a last-minute wash in their hurry to get out of there at 3:00 this morning, and he wasn't about to go shopping in Pittsfield, not now. Christopher wasn't allowed to exit the camp grounds, another of their nit-picky rules, and Bill wasn't leaving his side until Sunday, not for a minute.

So, he hit the trail in his office clothes, hell, he could replace his whole wardrobe next week if he wanted to, right? He'd take Katherine with him, take her out to brunch, have mimosas, make it a day.

They got to the clearing, and it was different from the way Bill recalled. Smaller. Lots of roots patterned in the soil, and the grass was worn in most places. Pine needles. The campfire area had ancient looking low-cut log benches on two sides and the pit had old charred wood in it, lots of ash. There was a gritty, blackened cooking grate there in the middle with spindly legs pushed in at four points, caved and bent down on one side.

Christopher had the smallest backpack and he wriggled it off, letting it fall to the ground. He had on a black tee-shirt, the type with a pocket, a baggy bathing suit with the strings out, and faded red Converse All Stars. Dark gray winter dress socks, his nice pair, usually saved for Bar Mitzvahs and weddings. He liked them because they were soft. Bill sighed. He hadn't been a natural "camp kid" either, but he'd learned to let loose, playing four square and tetherball and Capture the Flag. In his letters, Christopher described his Becket experience as sitting in the dark cabin by himself listening to other kids play outside.

"Don't suck your thumb," Bill said. Christopher took it out of his mouth with a "pop." Erin shimmied off her backpack, leaned it against a tree, and walked over to put her arm around her brother. He turned in toward her and she ran her fingers through his hair, bending to softly kiss his crown even though he was sweaty. What a blessing. Bill knew that girls could be tough on younger male siblings, hell, his big sister Regina used to slam doors in his face and punch him in the kidneys. But Erin was warm and understanding, gentle and tall like a willow. She had her hair short in the back with the front coming down over one eye, and while Bill had never been a fan of that particular style, she somehow made it seem humble.

"I brought cards, Chris," she said. "Help me set up the tents and we'll play Twenty-One."

"I want s'mores," he said.

"We don't have s'mores. They gave us hot dogs."

"Ketchup?" he said.

"I have a couple of mustard packs."

"You do?" said Bill. "From where?"

"Wendy's. I anticipated." She moved over to the backpack, flipped it around, and started opening the straps. "Hey," she said. "Let's get these tents pitched and jump off that rope swing!"

Bill walked over to the edge of the clearing where the platform was mounted. This had been his very favorite part of camp. He walked out onto the wooden planks and they creaked. The rope hadn't been left on the rusty hook screwed into the tree, and was hanging out over the lake fifteen feet out. There were old mossy ladder-like stairs fastened to the trunk where part of the embankment had been cut away, and bobbing down there in the gray current was an abandoned steel dinghy with rusted oar locks. Bill looked up across the lake and saw that it was about a half mile to the opposite bank, the water between shores reflecting the tree line. To the distant right was the camp, its buildings dotted along the landscape.

Bill put his hands on his hips. He could see dads and sons taking turns going down the slide at the edge of the dock, but couldn't make out their expressions. A few kayaks were out and two sailboats. He turned back left and put his hand up to his forehead to block the sun. There was more woodland, and about five hundred yards away, embedded in a rise of fern and high cattails was an old log cabin with a crumbling chimney. The planks creaked again, and Erin and Christopher joined him.

"It's beautiful," Erin said. Christopher shrugged.

"I don't like the lake."

"Why?"

"They make us do morning general swim and its cold."

She pointed down twenty feet to the right of the dinghy.

"Those lily pads are nice."

Christopher scrunched up his nose.

"There are frogs," he said.

"Hmm," she replied, and it seemed to close the subject between them. Bill smiled to himself.

"What's that?" he said, pointing a few hundred feet beyond the lily pads.

"A log," Christopher said.

"Thumb," Erin said, "You're too old for that." He popped it out and squinted up at her shyly.

"Yes," Bill continued. "It's a log, but what's it doing there? I mean, how did it get there? It doesn't make sense."

"Yeah!" Christopher said. "Why would a tree be growing in the middle of the lake?"

"Hmm," Bill said. It was a nifty log after all, now wasn't it? The thing was covered with fluttering ivy, jutting five feet out of the water in a rough elbow shape surrounded by pondweed and algae. Its upper end was jig sawed off to a ring of pointed slivers.

"Oh, I don't think it's growing," he said wisely. "I think it broke off in a storm."

"Neato!" said Christopher. "The whole top of the tree is underwater, balancing it. We're looking at it upside down! Shit and shinola!"

Bill smiled at him and then looked back out over the lake. It was a good conversation, the type Christopher enjoyed, no chiding, no teasing. Did it translate, however, as a good strategic base with camp-kids jacked up on store candy...busting balls, laughing at each other, making up clever yet insulting nicknames and such? Probably not. Christopher was a math nerd and looked forward to homework for God's sake. Erin was the lit major. She'd had friends growing up, a few. Quiet ones, most of them shy to a fault.

"C'mon," he said, "let's set up camp." He put his arms up like brackets and bobbed his weight making the planks creak again. "And hell if I'm jumping off this rickety old thing." He winked at Christopher and the boy smiled back, teeth gleaming. This was turning out to be a pretty damned good day after all.

The tents were functional, one made of canvas, the other some kind of blue polyethylene, and even though they were short two stakes, Erin made due with a couple of crochet hooks she had in her bag. Of course, there were no air mattresses, so Bill made a quick decision that Christopher could have the tent to himself, using both sleeping bags for cushioning. Bill would pull an all-nighter, stay up, look at the stars. He was an insomniac anyway, and there was no way he was going to spend the night with roots digging into his back.

They made hot dogs, ate them off sticks. The dude with the ponytail had provided them two filled canteens, a dented steel pitcher, and a packet of what he'd called "Bug Juice," a generic berry flavored powder mix that looked like it came from old military rations. Bill would have preferred Flounder Florentine and a perfect VO Manhattan straight up with a twist, but he wasn't complaining.

"So," Erin said, poking the fire with a long, crooked branch. "What are the kids like in your bunk?"

Christopher pouted, shook hair out of his face, and looked away.

"They're jerks," he said finally. There was a hitch in his voice and Bill wanted to shoot straight for the extreme, asking if they were pushing him around, but he contained it.

"Jerks, huh?" he said. Christopher shrugged again.

"How?" Erin said. "Are they taking your stuff?" Being insensitive?"

"No," he said, drawing out the long "o" and rolling his eyes up.

"Then what?"

"They're stupid."

"Stupid how?"

Christopher folded his arms with his shoulders hunched and his lips pursed, a move that looked babyish and melodramatic. Bill made a mental note to talk to him about mannerisms and body language at a more appropriate juncture.

"Everything is sports," Christopher said finally. "They get a kickball and throw it on the roof to catch it. They get tennis balls and throw them against the automat walls. They throw stuff in the dining room and argue about who's the fastest runner, all the time, I'm talking twenty-four seven."

"Don't they ever do anything else?" Bill said. "Don't you guys have siestas and cabin chats?"

"The cabin chats are lame."

"Why?" Erin said.

"Yeah," Bill tried. "When I went here, I looked forward to the nightly cabin chats. We all were in our bunks before bed time and the counselor put a candle in the middle of the floor. He organized a conversation. Seems it would be right up your alley."

Christopher reached down and picked up a couple of pebbles. He played with them for a second and tossed them into the fire.

"The first couple of nights were ok," he said. "Counselor Ralph tried to get us talking about our hobbies and the way we should appreciate each other's differences, but Henry Fagan kept hawking up and swallowing it, and everyone kept laughing, and then Billy Kumar and Branden Finnigan wouldn't stop gulping air and burping and licking their palms and putting them under their arms to chicken-wing fart sounds, so Ralph started telling ghost stories so they would shut up."

"Ghost stories?" Erin said. She was smiling. The fire made shadows pass in and out of the contours of her face. "Any good ones?"

"No," he said. "Just all the crappy old ones, like *The Monkey's Paw* and *The Legend of the Slither-Shifter*."

"Sounds fun," Erin said.

"Not," Christopher said. "Once those were used up, they went to the girly stuff, telling the *Bloody Mary* story and a bunch of scrambled up oldies from *Goosebumps*. Oh. And the one about Camp Becket, as if that's supposed to make it scarier or something."

"Which one about Becket?" Erin said.

"Uh," Bill cut in, "that would be *The One Armed-Brakeman* if I'm not mistaken."

"No," Erin said, "That's not about Becket."

"Is," he said, immediately regretting it, thinking Christopher was going to think he was mocking his fifth-grade speech patterns. But he didn't seem to notice, asking,

"You heard of *The Legend of the One-Armed Brakeman,* Dad?"

"Of course," he said. "It was told to us by our counselors every year, right here at this campfire spot. It's a Becket tradition."

"It's a feminist poem," Erin countered, smiling softly. "We read it last semester in my "American Folklore and Poetry" class. I did a paper on it and an oral presentation. I had to memorize the whole thing."

"No shit!" Christopher said.

"Shit and Shinola!" she returned, and they all chuckled softly. She stretched out her legs, crossed them at the ankles, and pointed her toes, one foot then the other. "But really, guys. It's a poem, legitimate, titled, *The True Legend of the One-Armed Brakeperson,* subtitled, *A Sentimental, Moral, Melodramatic Tragi-Comedy in Tetrameter Couplets,* by Tom Reed Junior. Note the word 'person,' not 'man.' Here you go, quote, 'In New York town, in 1910, One woman thus hood-winked the men, And won a job for all her pains, One working New York Central trains, She tucked her hair up in a hat, And bound her chest down extra flat, Said "Dang" instead of "goodness sakes," And joined the crew that manned the brakes.'

"Cool," Christopher mewed. "What happens next?"

"She works the trains for a while and finally decides to do it as a woman. She screeches the brakes when a boy is about to get hurt, and at first the men yell at her for the past masquerade. Then they see that when the cars crashed together, she lost her arm. They apologize."

"That's it?" Chris said. "And how exactly does she lose her arm?"

"Between the cars."

"Between, how?"

"Never specified."

"Does she haunt anyone?

Erin drew her knees in and folded her arms around them.

"The second half of the last long verse says, 'But if your way's to take a poke, At womankind, in tale or joke, Prepare yourselves – for one night soon, You may be moved to change your tune. For though she's loathe to slash and bind, The one-armed brake-person's inclined, To sit you down and lecture you, Until you for forgiveness sue.'"

Christopher stared.

"So, the horror-climax-out-tro part is that you get a lecture?"

"Horror stories don't always have to scare you."

"Says who?"

"Is yours any better?"

"No," both Bill and Christopher said simultaneously. They looked at each other, and Christopher put out his palm, as if to say, *"Please, go ahead Dad, you take this one."*

Bill cleared his throat.

"Well, if my memory serves me correctly, the backstory is that there's this guy who was the railway brakeman, working the levers down in Pittsfield. He saved a boy's life by pushing him out of the way of a train, but he lost his arm in the process." Bill pointed out toward the lake to the left. "That cabin in the reeds over there is where he lived, but it was in secret, in hiding, because he was ashamed of his deformity. The legend was that he waited for boys to camp right here in this clearing. Then when they fell asleep, he would mark one of them."

"Yeah," Christopher said. "With ash he kept in jars on the hearth mantle."

"Why not from the campfire here?" Erin said. "It would be more direct."

"Because the story is ridiculously stupid," Christopher said primly.

"Anyway," Bill continued, "if you got an ash mark on the back of your neck, you might wake up the next morning without an arm. You would look up and the freak would be standing over you, wearing a parka. Then he'd slide it off, and you would see your boy's arm sewn to his gash. Then you'd start screaming." They all looked at each other. Then into the fire. Erin sighed.

"Christopher's right," she said. "Both stories are flawed. Terribly."

"Yes," said Christopher. "Bad endings. And both have flagrant logical fallacies."

"Whoa!" Bill laughed. Erin reached over and muffed his hair. "Nice vocab!" Immediately, Christopher's face clouded over.

"My bunkmates don't like words like that. They're dumb, but the story's even dumber. The same way your poem makes the best part blurry, so does the Becket version. How does the train take off his arm? Wouldn't it just bump it? How did it happen exactly? And a little boy's arm sewed onto a big guy isn't scary. It's stupid. Cartoony. It's like cheating, same as throwing kick balls on the slanted roof, catching them, and calling it a sport."

"He's got a point," Bill said. "The story never scared me either, even when I heard it when I was a ten-year-old in Iroquois."

"Yes," Erin said. "The small arm wouldn't do the brakeman any good within the logic of the set-up either, because it wouldn't make him strong enough to continue the job that had been taken from him. And the visual is carnivalesque, odd, almost cutesy."

"Uh-huh," Christopher agreed. "Little things aren't scary. Take the *Leprechaun* movies and the ones with dolls: *Annabelle* and *Child's Play*. Some kids are weird about it, even freaked to the max, but to me it's not scary. It's…"

"Cartoony," Erin finished. "Cartoon-*ish*, actually. Are you sure that's all there is to it?"

"Pretty much," Bill said. She reached around to her back pocket and got out her cell phone. Christopher dug down in his sock and pulled out his.

"I thought cell phones weren't allowed," Bill said.

"I have my ways," Christopher muttered.

"Where have you been charging it? There's no electricity in the bunks."

"Bathrooms under the dining hall. Maintenance shed where they keep the trucks. Infirmary. Library. It's endless, Dad."

"Oh."

"Here you go," Erin said. "There's a movie."

"Really?" Bill said. "I haven't heard of it. And I'm all over Netflix. Amazon and Hulu too."

"Yep," she said. "Look."

She turned around the phone and there was a movie poster titled, *The One-Armed Brakeman,* with a graphic of two bloody hands reaching up.

"Can't be the same one," Christopher said. "There are two arms." He looked back in his phone and found the same site. "Oh wow."

"Hmm?" Erin said.

"It is the same one." He started thumbing the image down. "Listen to this. Quote – 'Directed by David Robert Mitchell, loosely based on the Camp Becket campfire story.' Geez-Louise! There's a cinematographer listed, editing, costumes, makeup and prosthetics, the works!"

"I don't know," Erin said, thumbing down herself, the images moving across her face. "It says it stars Naomi Watts."

"From *The Ring* and *King Kong?*" Bill said. Erin tapped some more, using both thumbs.

"Yes," she said. "But there's nothing on Wikipedia. And her filmography page on IMBd doesn't have it listed either."

"How updated is the site?" Bill said.

"2020. The latest is *The Burning Season,* in pre-production"

"Whether it's a real movie or not, it's the same dumb story," Christopher said.

Bill raised his eyebrows.

"How do you know?"

"There's a long synopsis on the fake movie page."

"You read it already?"

"Skimmed it. Same dumb stuff, but they drag it out like a murder investigation, making everyone sleep in the dining hall while the police guarding them get their throats slit. Typical."

Bill frowned.

"Becket would never let that movie be made. Bad press. Wrong message. Gotta be a fake."

"Yes," Erin said.

"Everything here is fake," Christopher said.

"Not everything," Bill said mystically.

"What do you mean?"

"There's a real tale. The true and final version."

"For real?"

"Oh, spill it, please," Erin said. Bill leaned forward, hands on the knees, elbows sticking out. Story telling posture.

"You see," he said, "the whole deal isn't about severed arms and a crumbling cabin with ash in the jar on the hearth mantle. That makes you focus on one guy, made purposefully childish and 'cartoony' to cover the real atrocity." He looked his kids meaningfully, first Erin, then Christopher. "Oh," he continued, "but the real deal did have everything to do with trains, beginning with the Baltimore and Ohio Railroad in 1828. Locomotives quickly became a national mania, and suddenly everyone was transporting goods by rail. Even a small town like Becket wanted in on the action, and they hurried to build The Berkshire Railroad in 1837 to export their lumber and quarry rocks."

He paused to look at his children. Erin was smiling and Christopher was riveted, mouth slightly ajar. The story was hanging together pretty well so far, but Bill didn't want to bank too much on the "history" of this thing, especially since he was stringing together facts that he was barely familiar with. Earlier this afternoon, he'd thumbed through a couple of pamphlets about Becket and the old train mania while he was waiting for Erin to buy a soda at a roadside historical center, and the only reason he was so relatively sure of the nearby towns he was about to name was that he liked old fashioned maps. The door pocket was stuffed with them, and when his daughter had been kind enough to drive the last leg of the trip, he'd been studying the area.

"The problem," he said, "was land and space, and since the Pittsfield Railroad was a competitor, the Berkshire Company was in a pickle. They couldn't lay their tracks in parallel down there because of zoning laws, and they couldn't go perpendicular because of the sewer systems connected through Dalton and Lebanon Springs. So...they had to build a rail line that circled right back through Becket Mountain."

"Here?" Christopher said. Bill looked down, drawing nonsense shapes into the dirt with his hot dog stick.

"Sort of here," he said. "Thing is, you're looking at the logistics of the camp all wrong. They established Camp Becket in 1903. In the 1800's when the rails went in, Becket was a small settlement. The area to the left of the docks back there with the bench pews that you guys call the Chapel by the Lake, used to be a small church. And Lake Rudd..." He pointed behind Christopher past the rope swing area. "Well, I don't know if you were aware, but the lake behind you is man-made."

Erin's eyes sparkled.

"Really," she said.

"Oh yes," Bill said. "Originally, it wasn't a lake at all."

"Do tell."

Bill grinned.

"It was a graveyard, biggest in Western Massachusetts."

"Whoa!" Christopher said, looking behind himself and turning back to the fire, wonder in his eyes. Bill clamped his teeth down to keep from laughing outright. This was good. About to get better. He tossed his stick into the fire, and sparks swirled up and twisted into the dark.

"Of course," he said, "the rail line had to go straight through the cemetery. And while it wasn't all that uncommon for politicians to make deals like this, there was in-fighting for months with the town council members and the state legislature, all about ethics and cost expenditures –"

"Holy Moly," Christopher cried. "You mean they had to dig up the bodies?"

"It's called 'exhuming,'" Erin said.

"Exhuming..." he repeated, letting it roll off the tongue.

"But that's not even the best part," Bill said.

Christopher made a face.

"I gotta take a wee, Dad. Hurry! Tell the best part!!"

"Right," he said. "The best part is that when they excavated the massive site right behind you, the workers noticed that some of the caskets had weird scratchings on the inside of the lids."

"Scratchings?" Erin said, the perfect sidekick.

"Fingernail marks," Bill said. "As if people had been buried alive and tried to claw their way out. Coroners also concluded that those in the coffins had torn at their own eyes and ripped clumps of their hair out, evidenced by gouges on the skulls and the inner rims of the sockets."

"Oh Dad," Erin said, sitting back, giving him a look. Ok. He had gone a bit too far, but this was turning into the improv campfire story of a lifetime. Christopher had his arms wrapped tight around his knees up by his chin, and it wasn't clear at this point whether it was from fear, amazement, or the need to go urinate.

"So," Bill went on, "they got out the records from the settlement's town center, now what you refer to as Gibson Hall, and they found that there was a cholera outbreak in 1805, similar to the Covid-19 virus that we endured a year ago spring, mass infections throughout Becket Town and all the surrounding areas, and a doctor of questionable competence and intention treated his patients with potato brandy and poppy water. Plainly, the combination caused patients to go comatose, heartbeats so faint you couldn't feel them by simply grabbing a wrist...breath so shallow it wouldn't even put mist on a glass."

"And they got buried alive," Christopher whispered.

"Buried alive," Bill said, with completion. But there had to be an out-tro, right? He let his voice go low and mysterious.

"And every Father's Weekend," he said, "the ghosts of the Becket dead rise from Lake Rudd to take a prisoner with them, down under the skin of the water, where your eyes will swell, you'll pull out your hair, and fight to take your very last breath."

There was a beautiful silence, but Christopher broke it by jumping up suddenly, and scampering over to the rope swing platform. Erin turned back to give a half-look.

"Chris!" she said. "Are you kidding me?"

Though his back was turned, it was clear what he was doing. Momentarily, there was that distinct sound of water on water, faint like an echo in a tube, and Christopher followed it up, saying "Ahhh!" Bill laughed.

"T's all right," he said. "I'll bet a test of that lake water for urine would yield amazing returns." Erin scrunched up her nose.

"Yes, boys will be boys, but it's disrespectful." She turned back toward her brother. "Disrespectful!" she called out.

"Don't care," he said, finishing up.

"It'll wake the dead in there!"

He walked back to the fire, looking sheepish.

"Better than going into the woods and doing it." He sat. "Dad...uhh... *Leprechaun* isn't in my hot-zone for horror. Neither is or *Annabelle* or *Child's Play*...but *The Blair Witch* is a different story, especially when it involves the woods at night and I'm thinking about it the right way. The wrong way. Whatever."

"Right!" Bill said, waving his finger up in the air. "A different story altogether, and not relevant to these Becket waters and woodland." He'd tried to sound "New Englandy" with that last part, but succeeded in merely coming off like a guy trying to do an accent and sounding snotty. No one laughed.

And Christopher wouldn't sleep in his tent. More of the *Blair Witch* thing, as he insisted that being trapped in there, not being able to see out, was going to make him too nervous. Instead of making Bill feel lousy, however, Erin agreed to move the sleeping bags out onto the rope platform. There was some disagreement as to which was the better positioning, since putting the woods at their back was similar to not seeing that the Blair Witch might be approaching, and having the lake to the rear made it so ghosts could rise up behind them.

The final solution was to put their heads near the edge so they could hear the ghosts moaning, and to face the tents so they could see someone coming. Bill stayed on the sitting log by the fire. Shit. He always fucked stuff up, going too far, yelling at counselors, challenging school administrators, forgetting his clothes in the laundry room, the camp rules, the sensitivity of his campfire audience. But the kid was so advanced with his critical thinking skills! Bill had just thought...

Thought nothing. He didn't think, didn't take into consideration the other most important part of a child's intellect. His maturity or lack thereof.

Something splashed.

Bill looked up. The fire had burned down to embers and the lake below the platform reflected gentle waverings behind his kids, sleeping there. Again, a splash, off to the right out there as if someone was throwing stones. A frog? Maybe. Bill pushed up and walked over to the platform. It creaked. Christopher was cocooned in his sleeping bag up to the chin, snoring softly. Erin opened one eye.

"You ok?" she said.

"Yeah," he whispered. "Go'sleep."

"K."

He looked out over the expanse of Lake Rudd. It was rippling gently, moonlight slanted in from the left, a soft mist coming off of the water. Directly across on the far shore the trees rose to a starless sky, and off right it darkened to shadows. Cicadas chirred in the woods. The dinghy below the platform made those soft metallic sucking sounds as the slight current lapped underneath it. Again, there was a splash, there to the right, and Bill got out his cell phone. He hit the button to brighten the stock pattern art. A flashlight would have been better, but it was buried somewhere in one of the backpacks.

The light of the phone didn't do much, but enough. It was the log jutting out of the water a few hundred feet past the lily pads. But it wasn't a log anymore. It was the silhouette of a man, hooded, with his tattered clothing fluttering in the shadows.

Of course, it was a sweatshirt, hung on the exposed tree trunk by its hood, the ivy quivering there at the periphery in the feathery breeze.

Bill's face started getting hot, the same way it had at the camp window. He was thinking about asshole bunk mates making fart noises with their palms stuck in their armpits, busting balls, calling his son names, and maybe the apples didn't fall too far, right? How easy would it have been to sneak out a canoe and hang that sweatshirt there? Had they been listening to the campfire story too? How many dads were involved?

Bill took off his shoes and rolled his socks into them. He cuffed up his pants and went to the edge, leaning down to take hold of the highest ladder rung just below the lip of the platform, uncomfortable from this position, teetering and inconvenient, but the crude wooden steps were fastened to the tree for the sole purpose of climbing up, not the converse. Careful. Careful. Half way down, he slipped on the mossy skin on one of the 2 x 4's, and he jerked down a level scraping his shin.

"Shit!" he said through his teeth.

"Y'all right?" Erin called from above.

"Yes," he said. His hands were slick with it; felt like cold grease.

"What are you doing?" she said sleepily.

He continued his way down and reached the bottom, where he stretched out his foot to bring the dinghy closer.

"I'm going to that stump in the water there," he hissed, sort of like a whisper, sort of like yelling.

"Why?"

"Someone left a sweatshirt on it to frighten us. I'm going to grab it. Bet it has a nametag in it. They haven't heard the last of me at the camp office, that's for sure."

"Oh, Dad…"

"Yeah," he said really to no one. He'd hooked the Dinghy with his toes and it was heavier than he'd anticipated. He didn't have a firm grip of the moist ladder steps anyway, so he did a "one-two-three" in his head before making the clumsy transfer.

There were wet smacking noises from underneath and he almost tipped it, doing arm-circles in the air, fighting for balance. There was cold water ponded in the bottom of the thing, filled with leaves that tickled his ankles like parasites. He sat down hard on the steel centre -thwart and the whole affair bumped and bobbed in the semi-darkness. He risked tipping the whole kit and caboodle again reaching out for the rope tie, but he unfastened it from the protruding nail in the platform support without capsizing.

No oars.

What the fuck. He started paddling by hand. It was a bitch to get it turned so the bow was aimed at the tree trunk out there, but once there he did a pretty good job keeping it straight, one side then the other. The problem was relative speed. It seemed he weighed the boat down too much and his paddling, while getting him fantastically wet up both sleeves of his favorite purple dress shirt, seemed only to move him in millimeters toward the dark figure there on the stump. At the quarter point, he was sweating hard enough to feel it dripping down the back of his neck. Half way there, his arms were burning. There was rustling in the trees to his right, small animals. An owl hooted. Somewhere a ways off a woodpecker knocked idiot-rhythms. Bill took a deep breath, picturing in his mind that he would paddle with a vengeance, to the breaking point, close the distance, mark time in an all-out campaign. He plunged his hand into the water and something touched him under the surface.

He yanked out and grabbed his hand to his chest as if he'd been burned. His eyes were wide and he was smiling brightly. That felt like fingers, a caress, stroking the inside of his palm. He shifted in the boat and snatched out his cell phone, hitting the button that lit up the screen.

When he swung it out over the side he saw something beneath the skin of the water, disappearing down into the murky depths. Bill could have sworn it had features, a mottled face with drifting hair partly ripped from the skull and its eyes swollen open. In front of him was a faint splash and he raised his cell toward it.

"Frogs?" he muttered stupidly.

The dark figure on the stump was dimly illuminated for a moment, but flashed off to darkness and after image when the cell light went off. Bill almost dropped it, feeling for the button, and something bumped the craft up toward the front.

"What?" Bill said hoarsely. He stared. It was dark but not that dark, and there was a wraithlike hand grabbing the gunwale. Bill hit the button and pinned his light on it. Nothing there. The boat waggled the other way, and Bill turned the light to the left. Before the device did its annoying auto shut-off, he saw the image of another hand, gripping hard, knuckles up with cracked, blackened fingernails.

Something from behind made the boat lurch upward in the front, and Bill turned back hard. There were knobby fingers clutching the top of the stern transom. The mist on the water had thickened to more than drifting threads, and there was movement back above the rope swing platform. Bill looked up and blinked. The mist there was forming a shape over the figures of his children in their sleeping bags, thick, like smoke hanging in the air after a building implosion, or more like clouds that looked like dragons and nursery rhyme unicorns if you eyed them up the right way. But this was no fairy tale.

The mist was forming into the shape of an apothecary's mortar and pestle. Then a lab beaker and a bottle with a big "X" on it. Cartoonish, of course, but having all the plotlines tie up in hideous perfection was the point, now wasn't it?

"Potato brandy and poppy water," Bill murmured flatly. The misty beaker tipped and appeared to pour fluid over Erin and Christopher, molding just above them in vaporous swirls.

Bill was about to shout hard enough to hurt himself, but the dinghy started rocking. There were dark hands clutching every part of the gunwale now, pulling on the boat one side then the other like an oil field pump jack gone haywire.

There was a sudden sound, and everything paused. It was coming from the darkness of the lake going back toward Camp Becket. Sounded like a train whistle, but forlorn, off kilter, a deep tilted echo.

The mist on the lake in front of Bill Canadine started forming an enormous pattern.

First was the rigid chasse with its gargantuan boiler mounted on the saddle beneath the smoke box, and the massive wheel sets on the sides, all rods and valve gears and cylinders, pistons working furiously, and then the mist gathered in front to blend into a configuration that rose up into the night, towering above the peripheral tree line, a colossal blast-pipe bursting up steam, and below it was humongous concave acetylene lamp blazing into the dark. Altogether, the monstrosity was bigger than three 747 air busses stacked on top of each other and it was coming on fast and boring down hard.

Bill jumped out of the boat, or rather he kicked off, pushing it forward toward the oncoming vision. He splashed back into the water, and it overwhelmed him, green and translucent with vegetation floating near the under-skin, and he pawed up and broke surface just in time to see the steel dingy get sucked under the pointed "cow catcher" grill ploughing through with its arrow-shaped frame and thick iron rail posts. Thirty feet back, the rowboat kicked out to the side, spun in the air, and landed with a smoky splash like junkyard scrap tin.

The train was almost upon him, starting to rise in the front as if starting on an uphill.

Aimed right for the kids.

Bill was treading water, sucking wind, wondering numbly where those deteriorated skeleton hands had gone, and something grabbed his ankle. Grip of iron.

Yet not; pure bone.

The cow-plough passed straight over Bill's head, undercarriage dripping, and in a last -ditch effort to stop the damned thing, he reached up and grabbed hold of the back-right edge of the grill. It was gritty from the railway, scalding-hot from the friction. There was the high -pitched smell of engine oil, whistling steam, and hard steel forced to brake upon steel.

The ghosts of Lake Rudd held fast to Bill Canadine's ankles and he held that front end grill frame with everything that he had.

—

Erin Canadine woke up in a stupor, morning sun streaming into her face. She didn't take drugs, but she pushed up on the platform, groggy and unsettled, thinking this must have been was what it was like to take Quaaludes or get hit in the head with a hammer. The back of her neck hurt. She rubbed at it, grimaced, and looked at her hand. There was a swath of black dirt there, and *God*, her neck was throbbing, almost as if she'd been burned.

She looked down at her brother. The hair above his collar had been singed away, and there was a mark on the nape of his neck, black soot in the ridges, almost as if he'd been branded with something that had road grit or rail dust caked on it.

She looked out over the edge of the platform and screamed.

Bobbing there in the current down by the ladder steps was a severed arm, long purple sleeve torn off at the shoulder and dead fingers curled-in and charred to the bone.

[This story appeared in S.T. Joshi's anthology, *Apostles of the Weird*, PS Publishing, 2020.]

The Boy in the Box

Isaac was the very last pick in the draft for the spring. He knew because the next day at breakfast his father said the embarrassing positioning was a good thing.

"How?" Isaac said. He wasn't looking at Dad. He was looking at the pulp in his juice glass, wondering who would ever call fruit-scum a winner.

"How?" Dad said.

"Yeah, how?"

"Well first off, call me 'Coach Dad,'" he said, pointing his fork. "Get used to it. The formality will help your frame of mind."

"Yes!" Esther cried out. "It'll help your bird-brain make a picture frame!" She was six. She was standing on her chair, leaning over her plate making swirlies out of her eggs and ketchup like she was getting ready to finger-paint.

"Don't play in your food," Mom said. She wasn't looking. She had her legs crossed over one corner of the chair and she was staring into her phone. She appeared to be very tired.

"I'm not playing, I'm cooking," Esther said. She poked her tongue out the side of her mouth and rubbed harder. Dad picked up his coffee cup, held it in both hands, and looked over the rim.

"I'm telling you," he said, "most often, the other coaches force you into picking your own kid higher than his actual value so you waste a first or second rounder."

Isaac's glance fell. A first or second rounder, ha-ha, he got it; the other coaches hadn't even bothered trying to work *that* angle. They all knew Isaac threw like a spaz. Eight times out of ten when he tried to catch a ball it bashed him in the face. He couldn't swing a bat to save his life, and grounders went between his legs like creek-water.

"Chin-up," Dad said. "I mean, look at me…"

Isaac raised his head, and his father winked back at him.

"I got two pitchers," he said. "Danny Winters and Connor McGonigle. Both can hit and Connor can catch and play third."

Isaac nodded numbly. He knew Danny Winters. He was tall. He didn't talk to other third graders who weren't popular. He could throw seventy miles an hour, he had a speed gun, he'd brought it in for show and tell. Connor McGonigle was a big boy with a ton of freckles and a nasty disposition. In gym class outside he pushed you down and mashed your face in the grass if you were on his team and you didn't win, even if it was kickball. If it was an indoor sport, he just punched you.

"Get happy," Dad said.

"Yeah, HAPPY!" Esther squealed. She almost fell off her chair but she recovered. She looked over at Isaac and shook her head accusingly. "You're never happy."

"Am so."

"Are not!"

"You're talking with your hands and spritzing," Mom said blandly, not looking up. Esther wiped her fingers on her shirt, paused, and adopted a quaint, haughty look.

"You never smile," she said. "You're the frowny face emoji."

"Well, you should be pumped," Dad said. "I worked it so I got six strong starters when most teams only have a couple of "A's" and a "B'" before the bottom drops out." He leaned in craftily. "I'll hide you in right field," he said. "I'm saying that you can chase down the balls, pick them up when they've stopped rolling, and then hustle them back in to the cut-off man who'll run out to meet you. You can handle that, right?"

Mom put her phone on the table and removed her reading glasses.

"You're being insensitive and condescending," she said.

Dad's Adam's apple moved up and down.

"Sorry," he said mechanically. "I should be more aware of people's feelings, even if they aren't those I might share."

Esther clasped her hands under her chin and gazed at her father adoringly. Mom looked back to her phone. Dad has said the magic words perfectly this time, and Isaac's face burned. He wasn't good at playing baseball, but he loved the game from a stats perspective. He could keep book. He could predict pitching changes and double switches when the Phillies played, and his ideas about putting on shifts were usually right on the money.

That's why he so well knew that six solid starters meant an airtight infield, while most of the kids on opposing teams would come up to the plate expecting meatballs to be served up to them like it had been in eight-year-old coach-pitch last year. Oh, they'd all have their moments in the sun, sure, but Dad's team was stacked. He'd be a hero. Altogether, you only had to put in the shitty kids three innings a game and give them each one at bat. Dad was an accountant. He was good at math. Good at rotating the garbage.

Isaac was to be the team clown.

Dad was thinking championship.

"Take Isaac out to the field and practice," Esther said. She'd gone to her knees on the chair and was spooning Mom's leftover oatmeal into the concoction.

"Leave my food alone," Mom said dryly.

"I'm making Slime."

"Take a shower and you can go to the field with your father and brother."

"Really?" Esther's face gleamed.

"No," Isaac said.

"Great idea," Dad said. Mom pushed up and started clearing the table with a look of satisfaction on her face; *God,* was Dad ever scoring points with her today!

"It's too cold," Isaac tried.

"No, it is *not*," Esther said. "It is a lovely, crisp autumn day." She nodded her head importantly and jumped off her chair to head for the bathroom. She wanted to be a meteorologist just like Karen Rogers on channel six when she grew up because the lady was *"funny, mommy-like, and totally girly."* It was ultimately annoying.

Esther turned in the archway.

"And when the ball's above your belly button, stop trying to catch it with your hand turned up like you're holding a bowl begging for soup. Windshield wiper, silly!"

She mimed the motion with wide eyes for emphasis, and then ran upstairs before her brother could kill her.

<hr />

"There's a boy in this box," Esther called over her shoulder. She was looking over the lip of the long brown contractor's chest that was chained to the foot of the backstop. Someone had left the lid open, and she had run up ahead of them through the playground, carrying the ball-bucket, really a big popcorn tin Dad had brought home from an office holiday party last year. She bent to pick the bucket back up off the ground, dodged through the cut-out in the fence, and began to prance across the infield toward second base, reaching in and tossing out hardballs as if they were mayflowers. Isaac prayed to God he didn't run into anyone he knew. Across the park there was a fall-ball game on the big field, but those kids looked like middle-schoolers.

"Son, see if there's any filler-dirt in the chest there. I think the mound is a bit muddy."

"Yes, Dad."

"Coach Dad."

"Ok…"

Isaac made his approach to the chest, and he got a slight chill up the back. A kid had died on this field last year, hit with a fastball right in the chest. Esther had heard the story like everyone else, and of course, she'd used the opportunity here to be dramatic, to *embellish*. She liked to *embellish*,

Isaac knew, because it was on his vocabulary test three Fridays ago. The definition fit her to a tee. She swore she saw stick-people living in the trees and a shadowy ghost-world in the reflections of puddles. Someone was burning leaves a block or so away, and Isaac hoped she didn't try and ruin that as well.

The contractor's chest was mud-brown with rust in the dents. In dim block letters, it said "JOBOX," on the front and Isaac wondered if they hadn't passed spelling class at the factory. Inside, there was no boy, of course. Amidst a scatter of empty water bottles and field maintenance stuff, there were two or three catcher's knee pads, all different sizes, all missing buckles. There were dirt-caked blue batting helmets, some with the inner foam totally picked out and a few weathered aluminum bats with the faded names - *DeMarini Voodoo*, *Easton Omen*, and *Ghost X Evolution*.

Really?

"Anything?" Dad said. He was gathering the balls and bonking them back into the tin.

"No, Coach Dad," Isaac said. "Closest thing is this old bag of line-chalk in the corner."

"We'll just have a catch then. Go stand in short center."

"Right."

Isaac was about to jog out to his position, but the breath caught in his throat. The bag of lime-stuff was torn open at the top. Moisture had gotten in and dried out, semi-hardening the powder, and there was a bite mark in it.

The Omen-Voodoo-Ghost-boy got hungry...

"Isaac!"

"Right, shit!"

He ran through the cut-out past his Dad, his face burning.

"Don't swear," Esther said, sounding superior. She was standing where the second base bag would be, making pictures in the dirt with her toe. Of course, she was. Even in short center, Isaac wouldn't be able to reach his Dad standing next to the pitcher's mound. He knew he was supposed to aim the glove-hand at his target holding the ball straight behind him, next drawing in glove-hand to chest and coming over the top in a circus-whip action.

But he could never make his body do the mechanics. "Wheels coming off" described his throwing motion…worse than Fifty Cent hurling the most horrendous first pitch in history back in 2014 before the Mets / Pirates game, heck, his sister didn't even need a darned glove! It was going to roll to her, and that's if Isaac was lucky enough to make it that far.

He passed her at second base.

"Weirdo," he said under his breath.

But she didn't respond with, *"Dork-o,"* her standard.

Instead she whispered,

"Make a wish…you can…the boy said so."

OMG, she was lame! But instead of his usual signoff completing the ritual, calling her a *"messed-up, mega-fart, monkey-faced-midget,"* he muttered,

"Just make me better at baseball, you freak."

He almost laughed outright, not sure if he'd been talking to his sister or the ghost she'd invented. Maybe crazy was contagious or something…

He got to his position and looked over across the park. Since there were no fences, he technically shared center with the big boys playing on the major league-sized field all the way over there by the Haverbrook Apartments. The scoreboard angled in deep right field foul territory said, "Home 4, Visitors 4, Outs 2, Inning 9," the last two represented with pieces of cardboard because youth baseball, even all-star, was only meant to go seven. The team in the yellow uniforms with black trim had the bases loaded, and clearly the team in dark purple and black had put in their closer, not a speed-baller, but a "nutter-butter," purposefully throwing slow-balls to screw everyone's timing. Isaac knew this, because the third base coach, a wide guy with sunglasses and his shirt hanging over the beltline of his long baggy shorts, was screaming at his batter to, *"Move up in the damned box! Let it come to your back elbow! Keep your weight on your back foot until it comes to the back part of the plate and stroke it flat and hard to right field, c'mon, win this battle!"*

Isaac squinted, trying to make out the nearest guy's number, but the center fielder for the purple team was at least a hundred and fifty feet from him, playing on the cut-out. An eight maybe…a three?

There was a hearty "pop" sound, like a sledge hammer whacked down on a train-rail. The kid up at the plate had gotten a hold of one, big time, and the ball broke the tree line, rocketing up into the sky. Normally, Isaac would stare up at a fly ball and get an immediate sense of backward vertigo, intense dizziness, always misjudging and flapping at it on the landing, but suddenly the angles and proportions made sense. Suddenly he realized that the purple-shirted out-fielder, all-star that he was, had made the tragic mistake of seeing it off the bat and running two eager steps in, when this baby was going to get extra legs up there in the stratosphere and land fifty feet farther behind him.

This was an absolute bomb to left center. At Citizens Bank Park, it would have reached Harry the K's behind section 144, and Isaac started running to the right as fast as he could. From the corner of his eye he saw both the left and center fielders running toward him, but they weren't even in the same zip code. Similar to the way he'd suddenly had a *real fielder's* feel for reading the apex of the ball rather than a bookworm's calculation, he suddenly under-stood the flight of the object in reference to the mechanics of his own body, and he tore to the spot, feet ripping like pistons.

It was coming down fast and hard on an angle, and Isaac leapt toward the estimated point of contact horizontally, full extension in the air, left hand outstretched in perfect backhand position.

The ball popped into the webbing of his glove, hard enough to bend his wrist back a bit, but he closed shut the leather, securing the catch. He landed on his forearms and stomach, sliding hard in the grass, feet crossed behind him in an "X" at the ankles. He'd always thought a move like this would hurt like all hell, but it felt good, like punching one of those socker-bopper-pop-me-up clown dolls.

He shot up to his feet.

Before him was a scene of mayhem. The two outfielders had stopped in their tracks and were looking at Isaac with their arms spread wide like, *"What the heck?"* Parents in the bleachers on both sides were shouting and pointing, some of them standing. The batter, a tall boy with a shock of wild red hair had pushed off his helmet to lolly-gag a victory lap, but now started running hard to second as if the ball was still live and in play. The fatso third base coach was going ballistic, screaming from his place in foul territory about automatic four-baggers and interference, and the umps looked like children lost at the mall.

Isaac felt a surge inside him of absolute swag, and he moved forward a few paces to build momentum for the massive bicycle kick. He stepped big with it, landed firm, reared back, and threw an absolute dart, almost no arc, clean over the shortstop who'd positioned himself for the cut, and straight in to the catcher, a perfect two-bouncer.

There was no collision at the plate. The batter was tagged out almost like an afterthought. Half the players, coaches and parents were still arguing with each other, and the other half were frozen in place, looking at Isaac as if they were watching Godzilla come around the corner of a building. One of the umps was barking something about an automatic double and that seemed to start to make the dust settle.

Someone was coming.

It was the coach of the purple team. He was wearing a long windbreaker, old gray sweat pants, and boat sneakers. He had a cigar in his fist. As he jogged closer, you could see he had a weathered face like a farmer with a pitchfork. Even closer, you saw he had hair in his ears.

"How old's your boy?" he said, limping now, stepping near, voice of sandpaper.

"Nine," Dad answered. He'd come up from behind and put his arm around Isaac's shoulder. The man stuck the cigar in the corner of his mouth, chewing on it for a second.

"Nine," he said finally. Well, that's good. We're an A.A.U. team based up in the Poconos and I can take anyone I want unless they've turned fourteen by September 23rd. No restrictions the other way backward."

"Poconos!" Dad said.

The man pushed the brim of his cap back.

"Don't worry," he said. "Most of the boys don't come to practice. We just travel to games. My second baseman is from Ohio. My right fielder hails

from Bluffton, South Carolina. Best in the country east of Patriot, Indiana."
He looked at Isaac, eyelids going to half-mast. "But none of 'em ever made
a catch like you just pulled out of your pocket. And that throw home was
almost four hundred feet, three fifty before the first bounce by my estimate.
On a damned clothesline, eighty-five miles an hour maybe, and I'm being
conservative."

He took out his cigar with his index finger wrapped tight around it.

"I ain't known for being conservative," he said. "I'm a risk taker. You a
risk taker, son?"

"I guess so."

"Make him a pitcher!" Esther cried. "I'll come to the games and wear
face paint and sparkles!"

"Hell," the man said. "Missy, you get your brother to work this kind of
magic, I'll set you up in a lean-to, make you a tee-shirt, and get you an air
horn."

Isaac and Dad were tight now. They sat next to each other at breakfast, and
Dad put his arm around his boy all the time, hugging him hard, talking
baseball. He muffed Isaac's hair and they smiled at each other like pirates.

The Pocono Stormcatchers were seven and one since Isaac had been
brought on to pitch and play center. He batted third and his average was
.798, a team record, unofficial because he hadn't been there the whole season, but official enough to make the toughest and most stoic boys on the
team line up to bump gloves with him before every game for good luck, even
Hunter McKutchen, the catcher from Blue Ridge, Georgia who chewed real
tobacco and didn't like anyone. Most of their games had been played in the
all-star complexes in Allentown, Pennsylvania, and their only loss had come
in a Maryland tourney, playing against The Pittsburgh Roadrunners in a
light rain.

It was 3 – 2 good-guys, last inning, last at-bat for the Roadrunners,
men on second and third, one out. Isaac was playing aggressive and close-in,

and the batter, their lanky third baseman, got all of a cutter that didn't cut enough, and sent it soaring over Isaac's head way out in deep center.

Isaac hauled ass and pulled one of his miracles, getting some of that "heel-kick speed" closing a ton of ground fast, and catching it over the shoulder, open-side on the dead-run, actually crashing into the fence where there was a sheet metal billboard advertising The Indian Lake Country Club. Both Roadrunners tagged, and Isaac spun around, stepped big, reared back, and threw home.

There was no way he was getting the guy from third, but the player on second, their little sub put in to be a jackrabbit, was all knees and elbows trying to make it. Isaac's throw home was epic, an absolute rope hurled straight for the catcher, no bounce, hissing through the air with rain-water spinning off it like something from the fourth of July.

The catch sounded like a gunshot and he should have had him, but Hunter got called for blocking the plate, new rule, total bullshit. Both benches cleared. Hunter socked someone in the jaw and they got banned from this tourney for life. It was a badge of honor. They were in it together like thieves.

At school, Isaac was popular. He ignored Danny Winters, and Connor McGonigle chose him first now in gym class. Isaac was a stud. No school the rest of the week, life was good. Tonight, the Cleveland cousins were coming in for Thanksgiving, staying the whole weekend. They were strange...nice and everything, but they were all total brainiacs. Usually, Isaac thought of them as a mild inconvenience, sort of boring. Now though, he was a bit surprised to find he was actually looking forward to their arrival. To brag for once, maybe...

"Isaac, grab the other side of this La-Z-Boy," Dad said. "We have to move it under the mantle."

"Why?"

"The cots are going to go here."

"I have to sleep in the living room?"

"Same as your sister."

"Yipee!" Esther called from the kitchen. She was baking with Mom.

"No, Dad, c'mon!"

"You'll love it. Like camping out."

"Can we toast marshmallows in the fireplace?" Esther's voice said.

"No fireplace," Mom replied. "Here, lick the spoon and stop making handprints."

"But the flour is fairy-dust!"

"Who gets my room?" Isaac said. The La-Z-Boy looked out of place under the flat screen, and it had left a weird bright colored rectangle on the carpet where the dust hadn't been able to get in and roost.

"Jill is in your room, son."

Isaac groaned. None of the possible answers would have pleased him, but cousin Jill was the worst. She was a spindly fifth grader with witchy black hair and big google-eyes. She smelled like milk.

"Can't it be Uncle Alan and Aunt Sandy?"

"They're adults. They get our room," Dad said. "Your mother and I get the guest room. Jill gets your room. Ricky and Steve will share Esther's room."

"That makes no sense, Dad. You have two boys in the smaller one."

"Well, Jill has asthma," Dad said, as if that settled it. He stood for a second with a lamp in his hand, looking undecided, and finally stuck it in the corner behind the CD tower they never used anymore. He looked at Isaac cleverly and rubbed his palms together. "Besides, they all agreed to come to your last fall ball game out in Kimberton tomorrow."

"Uncle Allen likes the football Thanksgiving-day."

Dad grinned, showing teeth.

"For you, son, he made an exception."

━━

"Let Isaac tell us about it," Uncle Alan said in his sly nasal voice. "And describe the strategic move you plan to do for us in tomorrow's game." Dad sat down, disappointed. He liked the spotlight. The cots were folded up and ready by the stairs. The adults were on the sofa and all the kids were on the floor except Esther who was in the mis-positioned La-Z-Boy, knees pressed into the cushion, elbows on the armrest.

"It's called a delayed-steal," Isaac said.

"Stand up and show them," Dad said.

"Yes," Esther said dreamily.

Isaac stood. Ricky the hippie had been working a Rubix Cube, but he stopped and cocked his head left. Steve sat with his hands folded in his lap like he was in synagogue, and Jill twirled a lock of her witchy hair.

"Yeah," Isaac said. "It's like...if you're on first, you take your lead, step-step-shuffle-shuffle, and hold there as the pitch goes in to the catcher. He might look over at you as if he's gonna throw down, but you wait until he tosses it back to the pitcher. When he does, the moment the ball leaves his hand, you take off for second."

"You have leads?" Ricky said. He was ten.

"Big boy rules," Isaac said, puffing out his chest a bit. Skinny Uncle Alan slowly crossed his legs the other way, twining them so intricately, the arch of his right shoe got tucked behind his left ankle. He was a lawyer.

"But Isaac," he said. "It seems to me you would be dead in their sights. And the throw from the pitcher to second is a short one."

"Yes," Isaac said. "You can't do it right off. You have to study the catcher. If he throws it back hard to the pitcher, you have to stay put. But even in A.A.U., they sometimes get sloppy. He throws a lolli-pop, you go. Now two guys have to make perfect catches, and the pitcher has to throw without time to plant."

Silence.

Then, the room applauded, Esther the loudest.

Isaac beamed. He liked being the star of the living room. He liked it a lot.

There was a noise. Off left. Disoriented, Isaac sat up, blanket balled in his fist under his chin. Scratchy, right, this wasn't his regular blanket with the Indy cars on it, but the itchy one from the cedar chest. It was creaky and wobbly under him, and he was in the living room on a cot in the dark.

Again, there was a sound, from the kitchen, something rustling like a racoon caught in a potato bag.

Isaac slipped his feet out over the edge and put them on the floor. The darkness made it seem as if there was a shelf right over his head and walls that were close in and menacing, but after a moment he noticed the little things keeping it real, like the tiny red light on the bottom corner of the flat screen and the vague outline of the recess behind the blinds covering the picture window by the front door.

Isaac reached for the flashlight under the cot. For a nasty second he thought for sure something under there was going to grab his wrist, but after a moment of fumbling, his hand closed around the Rayovac.

He straightened up and pressed the button. The cone of light shone across Esther's cot next to his. Empty.

From the kitchen again there was that sound, a distinct sort of shucking as if a cat had just jumped into a brown paper shopping bag, and Isaac aimed the light across the living room.

Caught in the bright beam, he saw a strange cloud of mist rolling out from the kitchen at floor-level, like a smoke machine at a rock concert. Isaac grinned with his teeth clenched. Of course. It was Esther playing with the flour bag, groping her hands in it and making palm prints on the big cutting board by the sink.

Isaac stood and made his way across the living room. The beam cut slants into the shadows and haze. He walked through to the kitchen and aimed the flashlight in to the corner by the dishwasher.

It wasn't Esther and it wasn't a bag of flour.

It was a boy in a filthy baseball uniform, bent over a bag of lime for the baselines. His head was buried in it, and sensing Isaac there, he pulled out and glanced back, his skeleton face covered with powder.

"I sucked at little league too," he hissed. "Got my moment in the sun, but afterward, it was like forever in there."

"Where?"

The ghost nodded his head as if to say, *You know...*"

"It's your turn," he said.

"For what?"

"It's your turn in the box."

Esther wasn't in the kitchen making handprints on the cutting board from a bag of flour in the middle of the night, but rather, she was making pictures in the dirt with her toe where second base would have been. Across the park there was a fall-ball game on the big field over there by the Haverbrook Apartments. The scoreboard angled in deep right field foul territory said, "Home 4, Visitors 4, Outs 2, Inning 9," the last two represented with pieces of cardboard.

Isaac jogged past his sister and said, *"Weirdo,"* under his breath.

"Dork-o," she said back.

"You're a messed up, mega-fart, monkey-faced midget."

There was a hearty "pop" sound, across the park, like a sledge hammer whacked down on a train-rail. The kid up at the plate had gotten a hold of one, big time, and the ball broke the tree line, rocketing up into the sky. Isaac was aware of the prior reality as much as the vividness of this one, and instead of the ball going off to the right, it shot up into the stratosphere, gaining legs, coming down toward him right where he stood.

Backward vertigo. He was looking downward from a great height, getting dizzy, watching the ball zoom straight for him at amazing speed. He put out his glove hand like he was begging for a bowl of soup instead of up like a windshield wiper, and he flapped at it, and watched it coming down straight for his forehead.

[This story appeared in Jason Henderson's *Castle of Horror* anthology, #2, November 2019.]

# AFTERWORD

Please know that I put this collection together because of the devastating Coronavirus. I am a Professor at The University of Delaware, Immaculata University, and Delaware County Community College. We went remote back in mid-March, and when grading was due, I was buried.

Most days; however, I was not.

And I've always hated crossword puzzles.

This is a time for battling sadness, anxiety, and claustrophobia. It is a time for empathy for our healthcare workers and all other essential personnel on the front lines of this growing calamity. Of course, by the time this collection hits print my Afterword here won't have as much meaning. It might even seem trivial, (or offered in bad taste), since we will all inevitably want to put this pandemic in the rearview, only stealing back the quickest of glances to assure ourselves that the memory will fade to a blur with nice rounded edges. Then we can rationalize everything and put it all in perspective.

For now, however, most of us are still committed to home quarantine and social distancing, and consequently, I feel sad, anxious, and claustrophobic. I know. I'm a writer, compulsive, usually the odd-one-out preferring isolation and quiet time, so what on earth is my problem? Well, trust me, I'd long considered trying to write my way out of this, if not for any other purpose than one of self-therapy, but considering the circumstances, the idea of coming up with new material was, and is, rather idiotic and somehow unimportant, even rude.

But I hate crossword puzzles. I don't know any card games besides Go Fish, and I knew early in the process of sheltering in place, that I wasn't going to laze around on the couch all day, watching Netflix and eating Bon Bons.

Then an idea came to me. Self-indulgent? Maybe. Unimportant? To others, quite possibly, but this was never a time just for gloom. It is a time for reflection, to call dear friends and family, to reminisce and get out the old photo albums.

For years, I have wanted to gather together my best short stories and give them all a good overhaul. The dream of course, would be to make a grand sort of collection (like this one) with a fresh, current feel. Many of the stories in the *Seven Deadly Pleasures* collection (released in 2009) were initially drafted back in the early 90s when I was still selling power tools. The *Voices* collection was created in the early 2010s when I moved away from public school teaching and first became an Adjunct Professor.

Case and point, I am a different person now. I write differently, I revise differently, I think differently. I also created a lot of new short fiction after *Seven Deadly* and *Voices,* and I have felt for some time that the best of them put together with the older tales, all rewritten, modernized, and streamlined, would create a nice mirror. Every one of my stories is a snapshot of the past for me, each fortified with rich personal backstory that the reader will never see. That is the sweet tragedy, and my dream is that a reader, maybe two or three, will mull over these snapshots and work them into the tapestry of their own intricate backstories. It's a win-win. We share something and keep a piece for ourselves. We endure social distancing without feeling so damned alone.

Talking turkey, it seems that this is the place in the Afterword where I might talk about structure. Still, I don't want to get too caught up in process. First off, it is a rabbit hole, and secondly, it plays like radio-static when shared. Patrons don't have to know exactly what went into a stew to enjoy it; in fact, going behind the scenes and seeing the chefs leaning in and sweating over the cast iron sauce pans might ruin the experience altogether.

So, for the sake of the stories you have just read that (hopefully) provided such a fragile illusion, I will be brief.

At first, I thought of doing a chronological order, yet then the *Seven Deadly* stories and those from *Voices* would have looked too much like they did in the original collections. I considered trying to do a "best to worst," and had to wonder then why I would even have a back half! The last thing I wanted was to give the impression I was using filler, so be assured please that every one of these stories you've read is my very best work; I have no favorites, and there aren't any misfires.

As you have observed, I decided to theme them.

The category-titles, *Girls, Psychos, Tools & Tech,* and *Martyrs & Sacrificial Lambs,* were not difficult to determine, each eerily fitting and evenly divided, almost like watching a Victoria Secret commercial with the sound off while blasting a Kiss song that seems to magically match up like a soundtrack. Seven of the seventeen stories in this collection are "new," and I hope that you enjoyed them.

This is my "photo album." Every story was reworked in order to match better the writer I have become instead of harkening back so much to the writer I was. Reflection is about pain, but it is also about growth and joy, about remembering and at the same time, moving forward.

Thank you for this read.

Thank you for being a part of this.

June 30ᵗʰ, 2020

PREVIOUS BOOKS

- *Seven Deadly Pleasures,* (Collection), Hippocampus Press, 2009

- *Alice Walks,* (Novel-Hard Cover), Centipede Press, 2013 (Paperback), Dark Renaissance Books, 2014, (Electronic Version) Cemetery Dance Publications, 2016

- *The Voices in Our Heads,* (Collection), Horrified Press, 2014

- *The Witch of the Wood,* (Novel), Hippocampus Press, 2015

- *Phantom Effect,* (Novel), Night Shade / Skyhorse Publications, 2016

- *The Sculptor* (Novel), Night Shade / Skyhorse Publications, 2021

Made in the USA
Monee, IL
09 November 2021

81338503R00204